CLAIRE McGREGOR

The MISSIONARY'S WIFE

First published by Kookaburra Hill Publishing, 2024

ISBNs:
pbk: 978-0-6489659-0-9
large print pbk: 978-0-6489659-1-6
hbk: 978-0-6489659-2-3
ebook: 978-0-6489659-3-0

A catalogue record for this book is available from the National Library of Australia

Cover images: Boungainvillea and watercolour, Adobe Stock; author image: Gray Tham.

Internal images: Map of New Hebrides, Trove; author image: Gray Tham; Day Spring, State Library of Victoria.

https://www.kookaburrahillpublishing.com.au

Kookaburra Hill Publishing Services recognises the traditional lands of the Wurundjeri People of the Kulin Nation on which we are based, and we pay our respects to their Elders, past and present.

Please note that this book deals with themes and issues that may cause upset. These themes include slavery, specifically the blackbirding trade in the South Pacific, as well as death of children and colonisation.

For Pete, Charlie & Alex

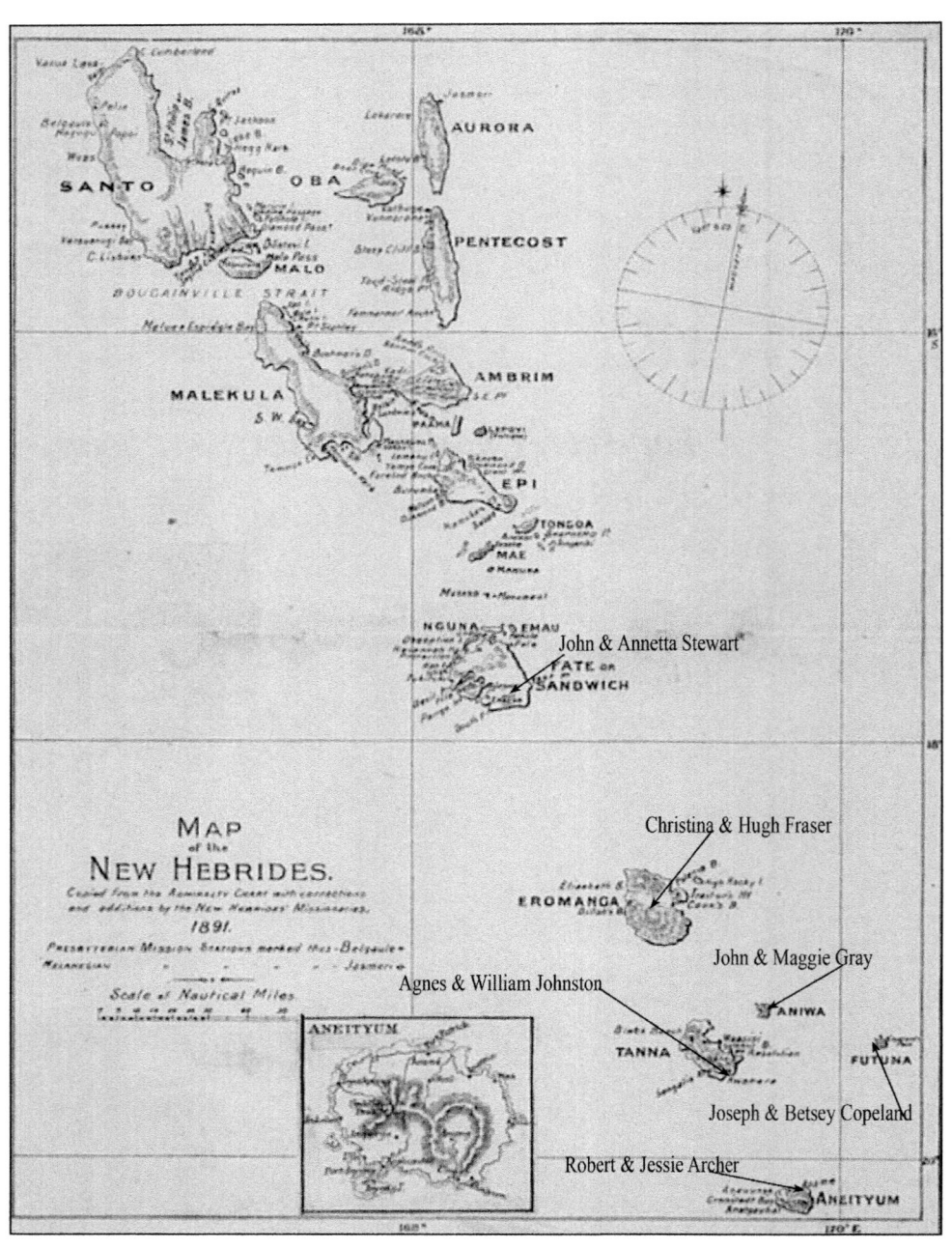

Source: S.T. Leigh & Co (1891). Map of the New Hebrides [Vanuatu]. s.n.], [S.l]. Trove.

Note: The New Hebrides became independent within the Commonwealth under the name of the Republic of Vanuatu on 30th July 1980.

Prologue

29ᵗʰ May 1871

Dear Sir

I take my pen in hand regarding the delicate matter we discussed recently at Salem Church. The reason for writing about this matter, rather than addressing you directly, is that I am fraught with angst in my answer to your question. The enormity of the prospect of taking Annetta with me to the New Hebrides, as my wife, leads to feelings of considerable concern.

I know you and Mrs Reid have deliberated this matter quite conclusively. I too believe Annetta would be safer going as a wife and not as a missionary alone, but I feel I must be honest and clear about the life that may await us. I feel I must caution you about these realities.

You would be consenting to Annetta voyaging to a heathen land and being subjected to the innumerable hardships and sufferings of missionary life. Many are the dangers of a tropical clime plagued by fever and ague, let alone the dangers of months at sea to even get there. She would be subjected to all kinds of want and distress with the possibility of persecution, malevolence and perhaps even a violent death at the hands of those we wish to save. The words fail in my mouth each time I attempt to utter them aloud. Yet I will not hide from you these truths.

Sir, can you consent to all of this, for the sake of perishing heathen souls, for the sake of Jehovah and the glory of God? For myself to have a helpmeet like Annetta would no doubt render my calling not just ten-fold more worthy, but ten-fold more successful too.

If the answer is yes, then I am writing to ask formally for your permission to marry Annetta. Such a joyful question under normal circumstances, yet to find oneself in the position of asking a gentleman and his wife to consent to giving up their daughter, with the prospect of never setting eyes on her fair face again in this world, still bears as a lead weight upon my heart.

I must ask for your attention in making your decision. I propose to leave Nova Scotia for the New Hebrides in October and would be wed on a date of convenience soon after my ordination in August.

I would suggest that this letter and the matter of our discussion remain between ourselves. Annetta and I have formed a happy acquaintance, and it is more than out of respect for yourselves that I am proposing marriage now. However, I do believe Annetta would rather know that the proposal came from me, and that you didn't request that I take her with me in the first instance.

Yours hopefully, humbly and respectfully,
John Alexander Stewart

PART I

Roll on, thou mighty ocean,
And as thy billows flow,
Bear messengers of mercy
To every land below.

Arise, ye gales, and waft them
Safe to the destined shore,
That man may sit in darkness,
And death's black shade no more.

O Thou eternal Ruler,
Who holdest in Thine arm
The tempests of the ocean,
Protect them from all harm.

Thy presence, Lord, be with them,
Wherever they may be;
Though far from us who love them,
Still let them be with Thee.

— James Edmeston

Chapter 1

HALIFAX, NOVA SCOTIA – 24TH OCTOBER 1871

I clench the handles of my worn leather bag as I look about me. John is shaking hands, being swallowed by the crowd, and only Tilly and Thomas are with me while I wait to board the vessel. The quay throngs. A fiddler plays – the mournful tune carried off by the biting autumn wind – while other huddles ring of laughter, children cry or cheers are raised. My whole self tingles.

"Many have desired to see those things which ye will see, and will *never* see them," Thomas says above the bustle, his eyes wide and bright. I let go the breath I had been holding and smile. *My brother the Reverend.* I try to take pride in his words, knowing he would dearly like to be in my position, but I am leaving for a far-off country, and for strange and untried surroundings. At this moment, fear is winning out in the conflict raging inside of me.

Thomas' face darkens as he leans close to catch my strained reply.

"I confess my heart and flesh feel much like shrinking from what may lie in store for me, Thomas." I widen my eyes against the sharp breeze then, to dissuade my tears. A shiver runs through me.

He takes me in his arms. "Do not turn away from your fears, Ann. God is the strength of your heart."

Perhaps I am weak of heart, too.

He pulls back, and I catch sight of Tilly's face. My dearest sister. We canna bear to release our eyes from one another. No words are left. I repress the sudden yearning to take her hand and run off to the lake, as we have always done, carefree and without a thought to anything more than us.

John startles me at my shoulder. "Are you ready, Annetta?" His voice is so strong, so sure.

His steady gaze makes me clutch tighter to my bag. "Aye, John." Then I steel myself and nod once, resolute. I breathe deeply and excitement rushes through me, finally, as I smile at Thomas and Tilly. Thomas raises a hand in farewell, while Tilly smiles through her tears and clings onto Thomas' arm.

My legs are shaky as we board the ship, but soon enough we are standing on deck looking down at the crowds on the quay. Before the lines are cast off, Reverend Dr Fraser Campbell gives out the hymn "Blest be the tie that binds". Dr Grant then commends us to God's loving care with what look to be a few earnest, heartfelt words, though I canna hear them. I have heard it all before, when I was the one on the quay waving off missionaries for a foreign field.

Oh, Ma, where are you? My tears threaten to fall again. In Ma's shoes, would I be able to stand in the crowds and watch my child be lost from view? I do not want her to struggle through it here. Saying goodbye from home, perhaps she could let herself think I was just popping out for a wee while, about to walk back through the door when the day is done.

"The will of God will never lead you where the grace of God canna keep you … I'm always with you too, dear Annetta." Her words from our farewell come back to me, and I grasp the locket at my throat. She had drawn back from our embrace then and looked at the tears on my cheeks before tucking an errant hair under my bonnet. She bit down on her trembling lip. "Come now! It's yer calling to go to the South Seas and be a shining light." She had widened her eyes and smiled as she squeezed my shoulders.

"I should stay, Ma, be here for you now. If I'd been there …"

I searched for her eyes, but she said, "Hush now, 'tis time to be away."

Pa had appeared as we walked to the gate. He lowered the milk pail and nodded once. "Now, lass, be sure and send a telegram when ye have arrived."

"Aye, Pa, I will." I put my arms about him suddenly and squeezed tight.

"Now, now, lass." His body was rigid. "If the Lord has asked for my daughter, I'll not keep her from Him."

I drew back and nodded, then turned to leave.

Thomas patted my leg after he had helped me up into the cart, and Tilly gave me a wry smile. "Well, what did ye expect?"

I had shaken my head and looked out to the fields – dry and ready to plough.

I sigh. It has taken so much to get to this day. Truro, Charlotte Town, St John's, Halifax – so many valedictory meetings and farewells. Though we were absent for Charlotte Town as a storm arose and the boats could not cross the straits. I remember the service at New Glasgow best; such a fine meeting and well attended. The Reverend Dr Roy, then in poor health, gave us words that have lingered: "You want good constitutions and health to carry on your work, courage, perseverance and, above all, the grace of God in your hearts, young men." *Somehow, I must be included in that too*, I had thought. I remind myself that I am a missionary too, in all but name. A missionary's wife.

Before those farewell meetings, we had our simple wedding. A supper and dance followed the service, as modest as Pa would allow. A fiddler played and I led the march for the first reel, while some drank whiskey, but not us, not missionaries. I put the hair ribbons Tilly made me into my travelling chest as a keepsake. It was a happy day.

But then after being at home for a week of wedding calls, which did not seem to be about congratulating us, rather for people to say their goodbyes as if at a wake, I almost could not bear to discuss it any longer. To answer all the same probing questions, which in truth I could not answer. How would we live? How would we survive amongst the *savages*? Some spoke heartily of their misgivings and said we would be adjourning for our longest rest before we even arrived. I know Tilly saw through my painted smile.

Our final farewell meeting was held at St Matthew's Church in Halifax just last night. The *Peruvian* should have been in already, but because of the fog the ship did not appear until twelve o'clock today.

I have played this moment often through my mind in the last few weeks. It is like a secret snow flurry inside of me each time I think of it being *us* sailing away. Nothing can have prepared me for it. I watch the farewells taking place about me to try to steady my mind, and I realise that times such as these soften the stern nature of man. They bring out some of our most honest feelings. Some are parting with no certainty of reunion in their mortal lives, but who of us that is, we know not. I clench my jaw, and my feet almost move unbidden back toward the gangway, back to the quay, my family … The thought blooms larger in my mind. *Go.*

Everything falls silent around me. I look to John at my side. He waves to his family and the church congregation gathered below us. His face is suffused in a wide, proud smile. How assured he looks. The Presbyterian Church of the Lower Provinces of British North America have prepared him well. Why, he has lived, studied and trained for this very moment, I realise. I canna say the same for me. Panic rises and my head feels heavy.

"How do you feel, my dear? Are you ready?"

I look askance at the lady who has startled me by touching my arm. I am unable to will words from my mouth and instead can only focus on the large teeth in her wide grin.

"Going to be helpmeet to your husband in his noble endeavour, why, you must be so proud. I hope ye are up to the task!" she continues.

Blood rushes to my face. "It is my endeavour too!"

The lady raises her eyebrows in surprise. John turns toward me at my side.

"Why, of course!" she replies. She is not grinning now.

"I'm sure Annetta will prove the finest help to me in the islands," John says in my stead.

I stoop down to retrieve my leather bag, hiding my clenched jaw. *This was a mistake.* I raise myself up. "I believe a missionary's wife to be a missionary too, in all but name," I say to her, resolved to leave now but trying to calm my voice. I grip the rail with my free hand. "I am not just a *helper*," I add.

John's face hardens.

I'll return when I'm ready, I think. *Be a missionary in my own right, just as I wanted.* Just as I am sure I am about to go, John clasps his hand down on mine, as if willing his strength into me. It feels to be keeping me solid on my feet, and I find I am grateful for it. I look into his eyes, and he holds my gaze. I let out a breath.

"Nothing so clears the vision and lifts up life as a decision to move forward in what you *know* to be the will of the Lord," he says then, his strong voice defying the emotion of the moment. I try to smile, though it trembles at its edges.

But I realise his words are not just for me or the woman who spoke to us. He turns to look at Hugh Fraser, on his other side. John's lifelong friend and fellow new missionary. Hugh nods and places a firm hand on John's shoulder. I catch sight of an elegant lady next to Hugh dressed in a loose, double-breasted Rob-Roy jacket and black hat with feathers that dance in the breeze. She looks excited as she smiles and waves to the crowds. She is beautiful, too, I note, and I do not feel up to an introduction yet.

The ship's horn saves me the bother, and I feel to be in a dream as we silently shake hands with those leaving the deck. Then, as the *Peruvian* judders from her moorings, my decision to be here, to do this, thumps me in my chest, snapping me to the present. Noise reverberates around me, heat courses around my body and my breath catches in my throat once more. I canna run now. I grip the rail hard and search the crowds for Thomas and Tilly. Their faces are fast disappearing from sight.

The final lines of the hymn resound in my ears. "When we asunder part, it gives us inward pain; but we shall still be joined in heart, and hope to meet again ..." I am glad then of the tears that blur the sight of the only home I have ever known receding from view. I stand until the grey-blue mountains are far in the distance, feeling the wind on my face and willing myself to remember it all.

Chapter 2

Under sail, 1871

My hands grip my skirts when the ship lurches and rolls in the great grey waves. I take to my cot and bury my face into the pillow. Perspiration builds on my brow, despite the cold, and my constant swallowing on a dry throat rises nausea within me. I am soon overcome. For what seems like many days that pass me by, I roll about in the cabin feeling sorry for myself. I am hardly even aware of John's presence, though I know he is suffering the same.

Hugh and his elegant wife, Christina, that is her name, come to check on us one morning and encourage us up to the deck for the breeze. "Trust me, I've done this before," Hugh says with a shake of his head.

John takes my hand and says, "Come, Annetta. It cannot possibly be worse than this!"

I struggle to even stand, but John hooks his arm under mine and helps me through the corridors. Hugh is right. Once up on deck the fresh sea breeze is as a salve to my cheeks, and I breathe it in hungrily.

"I have scarcely felt the ship moving," Christina announces as we stroll along the deck, "only I feel as if I'm sitting on a spring-bottomed chair!" We laugh, although I canna share her sentiment. She suggests to me a beautiful swan with her tall, slim figure, fair hair and complexion. As she smiles, I wonder if a fairer girl has ever entered the mission. She notices my hand at my locket and comments, "Your mama?"

"Aye," I reply. "My sister too."

"How precious," she says as I open it to show her.

"Do you have one?" I ask.

"Oh, I do not … My mother passed some time ago."

"Oh, sorry … I meant a locket." I feel my cheeks redden.

"I know." She giggles. "There are no pictures …" A wave of her hand finishes her sentence.

"Oh, well, at least she was spared the pain of parting then," I say, instantly regretting it. I look out to the sea.

Silence lingers before she says, "Oh! Time for potatoes."

"Yes, breakfast." Hugh laughs. "We're really quite sick of them already."

"I do *love* potatoes," I say, and as soon as the words are out of my mouth my stomach gurgles. I have not thought of food in days. We all laugh.

"Well, only another hundred-odd days to enjoy them," Hugh says, sarcasm lacing his words.

The rest of the journey to Liverpool is smooth, and I take to walking the *Peruvian* deck for an hour each day. I try to spot porpoises and stormy petrels, which skim the surface of the waves. John spends much time talking with Hugh, and I like the solitude.

At sundown, I often canna bear to go down to the cabin. Instead I marvel at the blinking stars above us and the reflected moon shimmering on the water below, so often obscured by fog at home. I have tried not to think of home too much, but the heart can be cruel when it is feeling deprived. I am stuck between places, where misgivings, worries and fears claw for my thoughts while I strive to push them down. The sea below me – almost black, so forbidding – seems to match my mood. I often steal looks at the picture in my locket. I knew leaving would be hard, but so hard? Tilly's picture is her, completely, in all her joyfulness, and a giggle will escape me, lifting my spirits.

We leave Liverpool on the *SS Great Britain* in mid-December, and my heart fills anew at the great distance there is now between us and home. The first night, a fearful storm whips up. I tremble in the dark confines of my cot with each sickening roll, praying to the Lord for strength. John holds me in his arms until I finally find sleep. Captain Gray is obliged to run to Holyhead for shelter, but by morning we are sailing along the Welsh coast. Great clouds loom above us, but the swell is steady and rolling.

We take our meals with Hugh and Christina, and despite their protestations, there are plenty of good things – roast beef, boiled cabbage, smoked ham, fresh eggs, pies, tarts and everything else good.

One evening at dinner, a few nights into the second journey, we discuss the islands we are going to. Hugh has asked each of us in turn, and now he turns to me. "What do you look forward to, Annetta?"

I pause my fork and look at him. "I'm not too sure, Hugh. Certainly the warmth … though I have to admit to being a little fearful of what awaits us." I nod before putting the ham into my mouth, not meeting John's eye.

"Oh, I completely agree," Christina replies. "Escaping the Canadian cold will be just marvellous. The mission houses look so pretty too, with their picket fences and coconut-leaf matting, roses and palm fronds, don't you think? Oh, and to have people cook for us, to be able to teach the dear children—"

"Are ye not worried?" I interrupt, louder than I intended.

"Why should I worry? Hugh won't allow any danger to befall us. I'm sure. Don't forget he has lived there already. John will keep you safe, Annetta. Leave all in his hands."

She pats my arm as she says this and looks at me in a knowing way, but I only think her a little ridiculous. It irks me to find that she is right though; I have found I am already glad to have not done this alone.

"Look," she says, in response to my frown, "yes, there will be privations, but think of the notoriety such a position can bring. How many will read our mission reports, and what good society we shall be in with the other missionary wives."

I smile. "I do look forward to meeting the missionary wives. And I look forward to writing about our experiences, as many have done. It's just such a journey, it has dampened my spirits, that's all. Pay me no mind." I smile at John too. He looks guarded but returns my smile.

"Do you think we'll ever make it home again?" I add.

Christina snorts with laughter. "Why, of course we shall. Whyever wouldn't we?"

Heat stings my cheeks and I swallow heavily. "Oh, you know, any one of *countless* reasons! Do ye not think you're being a little naïve, Christina?"

John squeezes my free hand. "Relax, dearest." His face is imploring me.

"Now, gentlemen," a voice booms out in a Scotch burr behind us, and my fork drops onto my plate as I startle. "I hope we shall have a pleasant voyage. Ye are the only clergymen on board, I understand, but as ye know, this is an English ship and I myself conduct Episcopal service on Sundays. However, at any other time and on any day ye arrange a service, if the weather is fit, I am ready to give ye every help. Perhaps you ladies might see to a Sunday school for the children?" Captain Gray raises his eyebrows in question.

"Oh, yes," Christina enthuses, "most certainly." She takes my hand and presses it with her own. Her grin and wide eyes are so childlike that I canna fail to soften, and I smile in agreement.

Hugh and John thank Captain Gray and set about planning Sunday services in turn. It will be good practice for them, I realise, and no doubt for me too.

I stand at the rail with the thoughts of our sixty-three-day journey on this ship running through my mind. My eyes are transfixed by the late-afternoon seascape. Captain Gray has assured us we shall dock at Williamstown tomorrow, just one day more than the record time to sail this journey to Melbourne. Perhaps he has been trying for the record as some days we have fairly raced along. "She is the greyhound of the seas!" he shouted from the deck one afternoon when we were under full sail.

My hand runs over my belly. It is not the sea that has brought more nausea in the past few weeks, and trepidation runs through me. What will I do without Ma when my time comes? I know John is worried for me and has tried to put me at ease. We have imagined the scene that awaits us and how the tropical sun will feel on our pale-white skins. It is an inviting picture we paint. We have laughed as he trials different voices and styles he can use to deliver his sermons. His services on board have been well received, apart from some rowdy elements, who are too taken up with liquor and gambling to appreciate our appeals.

One evening, when it was too hot even for the usual dancing parties, we arranged a lecture. The captain was chairman, and Hugh gave a short account of the islands we are going to. All were enthralled at his descriptions of the uncivilised peoples we will meet in the South Seas: savages, cannibals, warriors … These were the particulars people seemed to *want* to hear, perhaps so they could feel themselves so far above them. One man put an arm about the shoulder of his wife, who had gasped, shaken her head and covered her mouth with a handkerchief, as if she could catch *heathenism.* "Deplorable!" shouted some. I realised then what a play for a stage it was, but that I do not know the realities either.

I think back to that night, seven years ago now, when I saw the Father of the Mission himself – Dr Munro – speaking in Halifax. His earnest address had a thrilling effect upon me. "We must have missionaries," he said, "who will go and live among the natives, learn their language, teach them to read and show them what it is to live as Christians. Will not some of you who have done so well in giving your money, do infinitely better by giving yourselves some day?"

The charge in the air from the crowd was palpable as I looked about me. "If you come to be missionaries," Dr Munro continued, "you will find it uphill work indeed, to be sacrificing your whole life merely for the sake of those who cannot understand your motives, and who know not what it cost you to give up home and friends. You must trust in God and gird on your armour for the great work before you, in the assurance that He will bless you. Jesus regards every sigh, and whatever is done for Him will meet with a sweet reward even in this life, for He who has promised can never disappoint."

Can never disappoint, I thought as the crowd had cheered around me. I was in awe, even though his address was not intended for me at all. Surely there was no more noble way for me to spend my life too? To become one of these exalted people, looked up to and revered by so many. I had looked around me and recognised the same belief in the eyes of another who took inspiration from Dr Munro that night. It was a few more years before I met John formally, when Thomas introduced us as they studied together in Halifax, but I recognised him. Those glacial-blue eyes, clear and penetrating, that had watched Dr Munro with reverence and awe, had then turned to me.

I harboured a dream of becoming a missionary after that speech, to go perhaps to India as some women were beginning to do. But when Ma and Pa found out, they thought me foolhardy. Young, unmarried women did not go to the other ends of the Earth to be a missionary alone. I kept on though. I wouldna be quietened. My anger rose with their objections. I didna stop. *What good have ye ever done anybody?* Pa had shouted. That silenced me. To him, I did disappoint. They forbade my reckless talk in the house thereafter.

I swallow down on the memory as a movement to my right catches my eye. John is looking worse today from being in the confines of the cabin. He reaches me and takes my hand from the rail. A simple squeeze.

"Are ye well? I have to say you're looking awful, dearest."

John chuckles. "I should have followed your lead, Ann, and kept on deck."

"Aye ... next time!" We both laugh.

We fix our eyes to the horizon again. The endlessness makes me feel but a tiny speck on God's good Earth. But rising above it today is a sky so brilliant in its bands of reds, purples and blues with a corridor of gold where the sun has just dipped below the horizon.

"We speak of the realms of the blest ..." John murmurs.

"We speak of its pathway of gold," I finish, looking at the warm light radiating off of him. I feel blessed then, to be at his side. I smile.

The night John came to our house to ask for my hand in the presence of my family, he said he had already written to Pa, although Pa would not let me read John's letter. I didna need to; he spoke so confidently as he stood there by the hearth, his eyes sweeping the faces of my siblings in the room. He said how he wished me for his wife and to be helpmeet to him in the noblest enterprise of them all. He said he felt sure God would keep us safe in His loving embrace. He seemed to have no doubts at all. I realised then that I was being given the chance to do this after all – something I never thought would happen. If the Lord has made this happen, then I must do as Dr Munro instructed and gird on my armour.

John pats my hand and turns toward me. "How're you feeling?"

I smile and run my hand over my belly. "I shall be glad to be off this ship, John! But I'm excited now."

"One more night, Ann."

"Thank the Lord." I laugh.

But that night there is no sleep to be had. Cape Otway off Australia is sighted around midnight. All rush on deck, our thirst for dry land so soon to be quenched.

In the morning the coastline and lighthouse are a splendid sight. On reaching Cape Shank around seven o'clock, outside of Port Phillip Heads, the passengers cheer. So many goodbyes are rushed through as if we have already docked.

We pass a village on each side of the land and several lighthouses too before the deep-water pilot comes on board and tugs us in. The doctor comes on, passes inspection and we anchor in Hobson's Bay.

It is a fine sight with many ships, steamers and even men-of-war ships. We crane our necks, trying to spot the *Dayspring* – soon to be our next home on the voyage to the New Hebrides islands in the South Seas.

Chapter 3

The Dayspring

U pon landing, we escape the crowds and make for the Menzies Hotel by hansom cab. I am wide-eyed at the city on the way. Melbourne is most wonderful, it seems, for the time it has been in existence. The streets are wide, and there are some splendid-looking shops, most of them having shades before the doors advertising everything from a needle to an anchor, as the saying goes. There are plenty of theatres and low public houses too, their signs declaring "All drinks threepence".

It is said to have a changeable climate, where in the morning it will be bitterly cold, then in the middle of the day a hot wind will spring up, and at night a cold damp chill can set in. Our driver says they are much annoyed with dust storms, which comes in such clouds that business is often stopped.

We only have one night at the Menzies before heading to humbler lodgings, but it is a joy to have a steady, wide bed for the night. Well-rested, the next morning we return to Williamstown to visit the *Dayspring* properly. The smaller wooden houses of the town are like matchboxes, but the white painted ones are quite lovely. The town is being laid out in streets, but to me it looks as if everyone has just pitched their tent wherever they pleased.

It is wonderful to get on board the *Dayspring*. So many people on the quay stop to admire the little ship, and children wave to us as though we are celebrated folk. Standing on her deck, I recall being at her launch in Pictou some nine years ago, amidst the cheering crowd. We all felt that she belonged to us as so many people, children especially, had put in their mite for the building and fitting of her. The fact of calling her "the children's ship" endeared her to us all.

With some time spent sightseeing, visiting the Yarra River, public library, museum, botanical gardens and St Kilda, our time in Melbourne is joyful. The men are encouraged by the services and talks they give on our intended mission. But the easy existence must cease, and just a few weeks later, in mid-April, it is time to leave the dusty wide streets behind.

With a fresh fair wind, our square-sails alone being set, the *Dayspring* runs along the coast of Victoria as far as Cape Howe. There we strike out across the watery waste, and as the land recedes from view, I am glad to not have beloved faces to tear my heart from this time.

A shipboard routine is soon established, beginning with worship and breakfast. Mr Robert Archer, long-time missionary from the island of Aneityum, conducts divine service from the poop deck. With his wife, Jessie, they hold Bible classes and prayer meetings on different evenings during the week.

The roll in the Southern Ocean is more pronounced on a smaller ship, but after a few days I find my feet. Picking up the trade winds, the *Dayspring* fairly speeds along. I leave the deckhouse to stand as far forward as I can. The magnificent sails billow out above and behind me – white angels in flight. Wisps of hair fly out from my bonnet, tangling in their windswept dance, whilst others cling to my lips and cheeks, sticky with the salt-spray mist that finely showers me every now and then. On the *Peruvian* it was fear that made my knuckles white in their grip, but with the winds gusting on the *Dayspring*, it is exhilaration.

I clasp down on my bonnet as I turn to find John. He is sitting in the shade of the deckhouse, perusing an outdated *Argus*, catching up with the world from months ago. *The Slave Trade* pamphlet is held down by his heel, and its sight makes me frown. I do not want to think of it, and doubt it really concerns me anyhow, though I have caught whispers of what a curse it is in the islands. The whole idea when I try to look at it throws up so many questions. Not least of which is, why do the people leave their homes for Fiji or Queensland if they do not know why they are going, or what to? Those who are not taken forcibly, that is. Reading the details in the pamphlet has provided nothing but disquiet for me. I shudder to think what we will see of this situation for ourselves. I look to John. *Did he know of this trade when we left Nova Scotia?* It is hard to imagine he did not. Again, I feel little prepared.

Maybe he senses my gaze as he looks up then. His smile is warm from under his Panama hat, his face half in shadow. His crumpled grey jacket is open for the breeze and flaps against the deckhouse in a steady rhythm with the roll of the waves. I smile back.

George Campbell sits to one side by himself, clutching at his stomach and with a frown to his face, but still smoking his pipe and rocking on his heels to the ship's rhythm. From Geelong, George has proven a curious fellow. He is journeying for a year of adventure, he says, but he has also been tasked by Dr Mueller, the Australian Government Botanist, to collect botanical specimens from the different islands.

I turn back to the sea. I have my own nausea to worry about. I wish I could sit with Ma and talk about the changes happening within me. How will I face having a bairn so far from kin?

I sigh and turn my face to catch the sun on my cheek. I love the warmth of it, so far removed from the Nova Scotian cold I should be feeling in April. I wonder if the first robins have been sighted at home yet, heralding the coming of spring. I imagine Tilly sledding out with Pa as far as they can before trailing the edges of the river on foot, narrowed at its margins with ice, until they reach the glass-like lake.

We would squat low there as children, take our hands from our mittens and blow onto each other's fingers to warm them, hugging our shanks and skins about us. The slow crick-cracking of the thawing ice would split the still air. Neither of us cared to see Father bag his black ducks. We both felt simple peace from the beauty around us. The forlorn cry of a loon as dusk approached meant it was well beyond time to go home. Many times, Ma would have tried to find us, scolding Pa for our absence all day long when we could have been helping her at home. We were so caught up in ourselves, and I was a foolish girl. One day, Ma had fallen through the ice …

I sigh again as guilt washes over me. I know I still become lost to my daydreams, but I have that same peace here on the *Dayspring*. Riding the ocean waves, watching the schools of flying fish – flashes of silver leaping and soaring – and endless wave crests rolling up and over, spray showering the ship as she ploughs on her way. I find contentment from it.

The bell rings, summoning us to dinner. I wait for John to come over before we go down together. Dr Munro is in front of us, and we walk slowly to give him time. Excitement had whirled through me when I first saw him make his way on board in Melbourne, but each evening as he shuffles to the table, I wonder if this is even the same man we saw delivering that speech at Temperance Hall in Halifax. He is so stooped forward now. His right shoulder dips as he relies heavily on his cane. His once hard little knot of a frame looks so withered and fragile. Dr Munro was born in the same year as Pa, and how often Pa commented on it, but the difference in them is immense.

I sit and look down, realising that gracing our plates is the shark that caused such excitement yesterday afternoon. The crew had hooked it, and we had watched its black eyes scanning us before they had despatched it with a knife.

Once all are seated, Captain Braithwaite says, "Grace, please, if you will, Mr Archer." The captain is a well-built man with mutton-chop whiskers and a fiery temper, aimed usually at the crew, thankfully. This is his first passage as captain and he is much interested in his passengers, as we are too in our new missionary family.

Besides the human passengers, there are goats, sheep and fowls, a young calf, a small scruffy kitten and cockroaches. Right from the beginning of the voyage, unceasing war has raged between us and the cockroaches. We all agree the latter have the best of it.

"It's true man might annihilate a few by one stamp of his foot," George Campbell says, after we have begun eating, "but then the cockroaches assemble at night and retaliate by biting their adversary's toenails, flying against his face and running into his boots!"

"What cannot be cured ..." Jessie Archer replies, raising an eyebrow at him. "Of course, if this were *my* ship ..."

Captain Braithwaite clears his throat. "Yes, I believe you could indeed conduct the whole commissariat department of a man-of-war all by your lonesome, Mrs Archer. I, however, am but one man!" He turns his gaze to Hugh. "Has the *Dayspring* changed from your first voyage in her, Mr Fraser?"

"Still as many cockroaches!" Hugh replies. We laugh. A little older than

John, Hugh has a relaxed yet assured manner about him that puts you at ease.

"I remember the night before she sailed from Halifax," he says, wiping his napkin around his mouth, "a meeting was held in Prince's Street Church. One of the departing missionaries said he did not dread the work before him, the heathen, the terrors of the deep, but, he added, 'what I am afraid of is my own heart'. For me it was an adventure, but for these men it was much, much more."

"Aye, I remember James Gordon weeping that day you first sailed, Hugh," John says.

Hugh nods. "Weep ye not for the dead, neither bemoan him; but weep sore for him that goeth away; for he shall return no more, nor see his native country," he recites, as if he had heard it but yesterday.

"The weight of James' emotion as he said those words as we left the quay almost unnerved my own reason," Hugh continues. "It's never left me … but we got underway." He waves the heaviness off with a flick of his hand, smiling, aware he is putting us all in places in our minds we canna afford to dwell too long.

"On that voyage"—Hugh chuckles again—"we came across a ship and our captain hove-to and sent the chief officer to her. He found the strangers short of food and coals, so we supplied them. When he returned, he showed us a bunch of green bananas – the first tropical fruit I'd ever seen. 'Would you like to try one?' he said. 'Well, very much,' I replied. 'How is it eaten?' 'Oh, just take a good bite,' said he. 'No, no, don't bother taking the skin off, you won't get half the right flavour that way!'"

We laugh and Hugh says it was a long time before he was allowed to forget his first luscious fruit of the south.

"Bless yer heart! And you were already wed at this time?" Captain Braithwaite asks.

"No. I thought a missionary should first train for the foreign field, and second that he should have a wife." Hugh glances at Christina, then says, "While preparing myself in other ways, I had not left this duty undone."

Hugh rescues Christina's blushes as he continues, "A friend laughingly told me, when John and I were wooing our wives, of the man who prayed for guidance in the choice of a wife. 'O Lord,' he prayed, 'guide me in this matter and help me choose aright. I leave all in Thy hands and will be content with whomsoever Thou wilt point out to me. But, O Lord, let it be Betsy!'"

I catch Christina's eyes as everyone laughs.

Hugh says, "I fancy John and I were somewhat in the same state of mind, and, while professing we were leaving *this matter* in better hands than ours, were at the same time intent on having the women of our choice." Hugh reaches for Christina's hand. "And so, Miss Christina Dawson of Little Harbour, Pictou, became my wife." Pride reverberates in his words, and Christina beams at him.

"And one week later, Miss Annetta Reid of Middle Musquodoboit became mine," John says. My breath catches in my throat and I beseech him with my eyes to *stop talking now* before I look down to the lonely remains of shark on my plate.

"I know James Gordon has felt his solitude sorely," Hugh says, "and also the want of someone to charm the islanders with music, as the missionary's wife has often done. He even commissioned me to get a barrel organ for him when I visited Sydney. I found one capable of thirty tunes, would you believe." He chuckles before his brow knits. "His mode of work is eccentric and self-willed though and, when I was here at least, he didn't ingratiate himself well with the islanders."

"He is a difficult man to get to work in harness with the rest of us, just as his brother, George, was before him, before he was *murdered!*" Mr Archer replies. "But, after resigning his appointment with the Church of New South Wales, James is now alone out here in more ways than one ... He spares not himself in his missionary zeal; he is self-denying to an extreme, although his sermons can be so *aggressive—*"

"Not only that but he never laughs," Jessie interrupts. "Now, I am all for *temperance*, but I do believe he regards laughter as a *sin*."

She looks pointedly at me, and heat rises within me.

"Who murdered James' brother George?" asks Christina, her lips pinched thin.

"George and his wife, Ellen, were murdered by the islanders, my dear," Jessie replies.

"Hmm," Dr Munro clears his throat. "I believe the blame can squarely be laid at the feet of the slavers, actually." He looks over his glasses at Jessie.

"Nevertheless," Mr Archer says, "James resolved to go to Erromango and convert the murderers of his own brother …" Mr Archer, in his calm and reflective way, then says how it is better not to interfere by forbidding and denouncing abominations. How it is better to live quietly, observe carefully, learn the language and acquire knowledge, doing good as the opportunity presents. "Eventually, the people come to know the requirements of Christian living and give up without a grudge such things as smoking, dancing, feasting, drinking and beating their wives."

"But don't be too gentle either," Jessie says with a tut. "Sometimes you're too gentle, husband." She turns to him. "You make kind excuses for the natives, who allege indisposition or whatever else, when everyone knows it's downright laziness that is the matter with them."

I notice George Campbell nodding as if he is of the same mind, though I am sure he has not met any of the islanders himself.

No ill-feeling meets Jessie's scorn, and Mr Archer tips his head and smiles. "You can learn from my wife that although she doesn't encourage gossip, she is the first to know, through the women of the village, about anything that's wrong. Myself, I keep a list of every man, woman and child, and if something occurs, I send the elders to visit those involved without interfering directly … Anyway, you have made a wise choice, gentlemen. You need not think of working in the islands without a good wife. It makes your life much easier and thus enables you to do more work."

"She is more than that, *husband*, as you well know," Jessie's cutlery clatters on her plate, mirroring her exasperation. "The wife of a Christian missionary who performs her duties well occupies the highest and noblest position a woman can occupy in modern times." She surveys Christina and me in turn, and now pride rises within me as her eyes land on mine. "She, too, instructs and assists and directs and sustains the preachers of the word. She, too, labours in the Gospel of Christ. You will be asked to undertake duties unheard of for a woman from whence you have come, ladies, and you will need courage, resilience and, above all, faith." She holds my gaze but then smirks and tilts her head as if doubting I have what it takes. She still holds my gaze as she pops the last bite of shark into her mouth. "Waste not, want not." She smiles.

I let out a deep breath and try not to frown. My heart beats faster as I consider how to respond. I look to Christina, but she is occupied eating and appears not to have noticed. Perhaps I am reading too much into it. I look to John and his straight-lipped gaze makes me muster all my strength to just smile at Jessie in response. *I do not need her approval*, I tell myself. Perhaps she does not think me up to it, but I am here now!

Chapter 4

ANEITYUM

"Land-O!" I gasp and rush to the rail. My grip tightens as I press myself against the warm wood, as if being a few inches closer will enable me to see land quicker.

Seabirds circle overhead, pure white with longer tail feathers than those from home, their eyes as black as night in their white shrouds. Others have sharp black wings with a flash of scarlet at their throats. Their reflections shadow the water below us; the purest blue I have ever seen. My world reverberates in colour, so removed from the cold grey of the Atlantic of home. I want to paint a picture, to capture it somehow, but I canna tear my eyes from the sight of Aneityum. At first it is a grey haze, hardly distinguishable from a cloud on the horizon, but now developing into hills and trees in the shape of a great pyramid before us.

The ship slows and the wind eases, and at once the tropical heat smothers me. I realise my face has been too long in the sun and wind as my skin tightens around my lips as they spread into a wide smile. John takes my hand. He is grinning too and looks more self-assured than I can possibly feel. The thought of stepping foot on dry land makes my heart quicken, though from fear or plain relief I know not which. I scan the horizon in the direction the other passengers look. Will the islanders receive us or not? Friend or foe? Mistaken as traders or, worse, slavers?

I run my hand along the polished rail. We have all come to love this little ship, despite the assaults on our stomachs. We know that once in the islands she will be our only and enduring lifeline, both in getting out and in receiving news from home.

The crew turn out and fly about the deck, grasping and hauling ropes with all their might, shouting as they go. The sound of "Land-O!" has inspired them with new life. The *Dayspring* folds her white wings like a seabird preparing to settle itself. Now the white church and mission house are visible beyond the shore. Even the Archers, returning here after furlough, seem to marvel at the scene before us.

I become mesmerised by the waves that roll along, getting lighter and lighter as they mount the reef before breaking into spray. Coconut palms, with their feathery leaves waving, stand nodding their heads, giving a welcome all of their own. As we sail into Aneghowhat Harbour on the first day of May, over six months of journeying are finally coming to an end.

Almost as soon as we cast anchor, a small boat shoots out from one of the little islets.

"That'll be Mr Underwood," Jessie calls out. "A resident trader."

A burly-looking man in a string vest soon comes on board, and the Archers are first to meet him. After a minute or two, Jessie turns to us, and I gasp at sight of her grief-stricken face.

She looks down at the deck, then up to her husband and, finally, she says, "The savages of Erromango have killed James Gordon!" There is a tremble to her voice that sends a chill through me.

The stunned silence is broken only by the gentle lapping of the waves against the ship. My eyes go to John, and then Hugh; both have lost their friend. I do not wish to believe it is true and swallow at the fear that rises within me. I think back to our conversation at dinner a few nights past, and how we were to be meeting him at his station in just a few days.

Hugh goes below deck while the rest of us stand, wondering on the bloody details. Jessie breaks the tension by gathering her belongings.

Mr Archer says, "We shall regroup and discuss this tragedy anon. For now, we must see to our station." With that they make for the small boat to take them to Aname to the north. Just before they step off, Hugh comes up from below and slips a note into Mr Archer's hand before giving them a meek wave of farewell. I look to Christina, but her solemn face is turned toward the shore.

⌒⌇⌒

The small boat takes us near the beach, and then, one by one, we are carried ashore by two young islanders, who make a seat with their hands. I lower myself down and sit with my arms about their necks as they wade in. I wonder if they feel the tremble in my fingers on their hot, dark skins. I am ashamed of my fearfulness, and it is only on being lowered to the sand that I find I am once again holding my breath.

But what a delight to tread solid ground. I stand still, relishing it beneath me, though my head still feels to be in motion. Everything seems so strange around me. Fresh and vibrant tropical plants, slender coconut palms and majestic orange trees against the high mountains, with the noise and chatter of the people gathering around us, who exude their own exoticism. A smoky, warm spice fills the thick heat of the air.

I canna make a sound come forth from my lips. I blink back tears as the whole wealth of emotion rushes upon me that we are finally here.

A group of women have come down to meet us, each one dressed in a skirt made of a sort of grass, with a blouse or jacket on top. I notice at once their beautiful, sparkling black eyes. They are touching me then; hot hands all around me, prodding and poking. They feel my blossoming belly, exclaiming in delight and shaking my hands. I try to smile back, and then realise it is me pulling at my own pinching collar against the suffocating heat that has wrapped me in its thick veil. Sweat is beading on my top lip. I gasp, suddenly needing the sun off of me, and the people too, and fast, as if they were stinging insects.

Darkness creeps to the edge of my vision. I think I shall surely fall when John catches my arm and guides me up the beach toward the mission house. *Don't let go*, my mind screams as I look up to him, his eyes holding my gaze, reassuring.

"Relax, Ann, just take a breath," he says.

Soon enough a chair is brought forward, and I slide into it. I am truly wayworn, but I can breathe at last. A woman holds out a green coconut and nods to encourage me. I take it and put it to my lips. The liquid is so cool and pleasant to taste that I am instantly revived from it. Bananas are next; fat and yellow, larger and finer than anything I have seen before. "Taro, taro," she says with a nod, holding out a small piece to me. It is rather harder to get down, but I have more coconut water and nod in thanks.

The commotion of our arrival dies down, the missionaries begin rambling around the premises, and the villagers go about their business. I look around me at the mission house – built of stone and roofed with thatch – and the fine orange and lemon trees growing all around. A good deal of the fruit is ripe, and when Dr Munro is hot and thirsty again, he orders a feast of them. The pithy remains lie strewn on the ground before a young boy collects them into a woven basket. A garden is in front of the house, stretching down toward the shore, and at the back stands the kitchen and an enclosure for bananas and pineapples.

George Campbell takes the opportunity to explore around the harbour and start to amass his botanical collection. John is talking to the missionary men, so I wander to the beach too, where there is a slight breeze. The early afternoon sun is fierce, so on finding some shade, I sit on the sand and rest. I watch the seabirds stalking along as I try to collect my thoughts, feeling thankful for some peace. I am nauseous, but whether it is my babe within, the travelling, the heat, or the fear I have of the people, I can no longer tell. I just want to be alone.

My attention is taken by George, and giggles escape me as I watch him stuff this or that into his pockets. Then he looks pained – as though walking has become peculiar to him – and he hurriedly empties out his collection. As it drops to the sand, he rubs at his legs before stooping down to pick through the items once more; little crabs scuttling off across the beach.

John, Christina and Hugh stroll along the beach then, and when they get to me, John pulls me up. With Christina and I behind, Hugh and John amble along, talking together, heading to where there is a fine view of the island toward the mountains.

"Do you remember, Hugh? 'I'll see you out there!' That's what James said. That day I farewelled you in the *Dayspring*," John says.

Neither man can accept James Gordon is dead, I realise, not yet.

"There is a lesson in this for us, John. Dr Munro and Mr Archer have alluded to it too. You cannot ride roughshod over the natives' beliefs. A softer approach must be taken, and they must be employed to help us at every turn," Hugh replies.

The church bell tolls a little way off. Christina and I link arms as we turn back, half listening to the conversation of our men. When it is quiet, she confides, "I think I'm with child, too!" She squeezes my hand and widens her eyes at me. I am so pleased for her. She seems giddy in her joy, as much as if we were at home, neither of us considering then the hardships we may face.

I squeeze her hand back and smile. "I'm so delighted we'll have our bairns close together."

We walk up to the old stone church and go inside. Built by Dr Munro himself, it is a monument to his industry. But this is his mission station no more, and a Mr Murray is now to reside here as Dr Munro retires. The church is immense with low stone walls and a tightly thatched roof. It must be large enough to hold about eight hundred people, I should think. The floor is laid with a type of matting and on this the congregation are seated; men on one side, women and children on the other. The men wear Crimean shirts and pants, or shirts and the *lava-lava* – that being a sort of calico loincloth – and some have waistcoats. A few have even come out in full suits.

The women look fine in grass skirts with a calico shawl or cloak, and some sport plaited coal-scuttle bonnets. They wave fans with one hand and clasp a hymnbook with the other. None have anything on their feet, and few of the men anything on their heads.

We seat ourselves amongst them as the service begins. It is in the Aneityumese language, and, unable to follow, I let the lilting words waft over me as I realise that here they are clothed, they are at peace, they have given up their heathen customs and regularly attend church. They are a Christian community. It is everything and more we hope to achieve.

From their earnest looks, it seems these people do believe in the God they are professing to worship. My thoughts are soon put to flight when they start to sing. Although not entirely true to the tune, their fervour sends tingles shooting from my neck, raising the hair on my limbs. *What did James get so wrong?* I wonder.

Chapter 5

FUTUNA

After the service, Hugh takes us on a walk to see some plantations. We wend our way inland along a narrow path before coming upon several plots and huts nestling amidst the trees. Taro, bananas and sugarcane thrive.

"Every year, a man makes from one to four plantations according to the number of his wives and the age of his children," Hugh says. He continues on, seeming to relish his role as guide, but my attention is taken by two women who are sitting on the ground chatting. They pick up the rich black soil with their hands, rub it through their fingers and let it fall like dirty flour. It does not look to be work, just passing time. They laugh between themselves at their unexpected audience; their faces smiling and open. I smile back.

"In architecture at least," George says, sweeping his hand around, "they seem to have made little or no improvement since the days of heathenism. These huts look thoroughly miserable!" George often takes to rambling criticisms of whatever has perturbed him that day. His ample Roman nose leads his comments from one topic to another like a hen pecking at ripe corn.

We look at the simple frameworks of wood overlaid with plaited leaf, like narrow thatched roofs planted on the ground. They have no walls, are only about six-feet high in the centre and are entered by a hole at one end.

"I believe they find these places healthier than a house with walls," Hugh says. "Well, they clearly do as the chief here has put up a good specimen of a plastered house, yet few seem inclined to follow his example."

George merely raises his eyebrows.

We continue on the path under the shade of great breadfruit trees, and then into undergrowth so dense we canna see more than a few yards. Vines trail overhead. With the shadows of the trees it feels smothering with the cloying heat, despite the waning afternoon sun. I soon wish to be back at the beach with the breeze upon my face.

At last, we emerge upon the banks of a beautiful stream that ripples down in cascades until it opens out into a quiet deep pool at our feet. It looks refreshing, and proves so to George, who does not waste time plunging in. I long to do the same but do not think it would be the right thing to do. I should content myself with splashing my face and wrists, as Christina does, but then I canna resist unbuttoning my boots, hitching my skirts in my hands and soaking my feet too. I press my lips together to suppress a squeal of delight at the delicious coolness, then I glance up to find John looking at me open-mouthed. I do not need more chastisement than that and begin to pull my boots back on, while John turns away.

Oh pah! I think. *What of it!* But heat scorches my cheeks. Tilly's voice reverberates in my head, "Oh, Annetta!" Her exasperated face.

I take a deep breath and watch the birds, similar to swallows, that dip down for a cooling drink while butterflies abound. The bush is fragrant with jessamine. I breathe it in and feel to be in God's garden.

I raise myself to my feet as the ship's bell tolls in the distance. The next island awaits.

Before daylight the next morning we are close to the shore of Futuna. The small, table-topped mountain rises abruptly from the sea; its sides appearing bare and precipitous.

We round the island and heave-to opposite the mission house. There is no anchorage, so the *Dayspring* lies off and on while we make to go ashore. Islanders are rushing about and launching canoes. Several come toward us, paddled by lithe, strong arms, and in the foremost sits the missionary himself. Upon reaching the ship's side, Joseph Copeland, who looks to be a hairy bear of a man, calls out hellos before asking for news from the last few months, as though it were food to keep starvation at bay. He chatters on as Hugh and Christina climb into his boat.

John and I climb into another boat but, as we head for shore, we strike the reef and almost upend. I let out a cry and John reaches for my arm. "Here, Annetta!" We scramble into a canoe that has soon come alongside, wherein the Futunese men are almost naked. My heart pounds, and I just want to get ashore in one piece, so I cover my face and look to the wood beneath me. When I dare to look up, crowds await us, and I try to resist covering my face once more.

These are the first real *heathen* I have seen, and it is a shock after the Aneityumese. All the Futunese men have near-naked bodies, wearing just the "belt and wrapper", Hugh informs me it is called as we stand on the beach. It canna be called clothing and is scarcely a covering, though I do not look too closely. I fan my face as fast as my hand will permit. Some have painted bodies, others painted faces – a startling charcoal-black. The men have worked their hair into small cords with the ends in curls at the back of their heads. They carry spears, bows, clubs and muskets, and are fierce looking.

I look intently at the path I have to tread. Christina is at my side, her wide smile dimpling her cheeks. I raise myself taller and try to match her demeanour, but the people surround us. They hold out small pigs, fowls, vegetables, shells and bags in the hope of trade. I shrink back at the noise of it all.

The women wear short grass skirts, and many have bare bosoms. I look to John, but his face is impassive, although I notice George's holds an air of disgust. If John is at all worried what I think of the men, he does not show it, but I am discomforted by the women. He had known, of course, what to expect. I sigh.

"Bring everything you buy up to the house, or you'll never see it again," Mr Copeland calls out from in front of us. He is helping Dr Munro over the rocky ground as he is determined to visit each station before he retires.

George shouts out, "Me no buy, me no buy," and waves his hands in the air like a buffoon. After a little, the people move away from him. I hold onto John's arm and try to focus on the items presented to me in the throng. I notice the bags are fine and some of the shells too.

"Let us buy some!" I raise my voice above the chatter. John nods before bringing forth fishhooks to make our trade. Perhaps with this, George realises it does no harm to be interested and sets about buying as well. In exchange, he gives tobacco. Once this is known, he is blockaded – the crowd determined to get his tobacco at any price. "Toback, toback," they call.

"Good gracious!" John shouts as we watch one man shove toward George a little bony pig, another proffers a fowl, another a bunch of yams. George is tiring of it, so he sets his back against a tree and yells, "I will give you *no more*, I have none. You're foolish for wasting your time in such a manner."

Naturally, they do not understand him, so he turns his bag upside down and gives it a vigorous shake, whereupon the people trail off, grumbling and shaking their heads. But one elderly woman persists. In the end, George passes her a piece of red calico cloth, or turkey red, as they call it. No sooner does she get it than a man steps forward, snatches it away and ties it around his own head.

George makes his way to us. "Well, really, I am as much disgusted with the manners of these people as with their appearance! Can it be possible for any educated person to live among them and be happy?"

A laugh escapes me, and I cover my mouth as another threatens. "What do you think we are here to do, George?" My voice is loud. I turn away, not meeting John's eye or the reproach I will see there.

Trading over, the women are curious and proceed to prod Christina and I as before. They feel themselves at the same time, to see how far we are alike. "We are all sisters under God," I say, even though they canna understand me. "Your bones are in the same places as mine."

They chatter and laugh and the tortoiseshell rings in their ears make a dull clatter. On their examinations becoming too minute, we excuse ourselves and make our way toward the mission house.

The path up is steep, skirting the brow of the hill, before the home among the trees comes into sight. I am struck by what a lonely, buried-alive sort of life it must be for the Copelands, with their only means of communication being the *Dayspring* visiting but once or twice per year.

My heart flits at the realisation that this is soon what I will be facing.

Elizabeth Copeland is slight and pale with sunken cheeks. Before Jessie Archer left the *Dayspring* at Aneityum, she told us that Elizabeth lost her baby last year and has not been well since.

"Please, come and sit at our table," Elizabeth says as she leads us onto the verandah. The table is set with young pig, fowls, yams and green coconuts.

"You must have been cooking for days," Christina says.

"Was no bother," Elizabeth says with obvious pride. "You sit here, dear," she adds, pulling out a chair with a plump cushion for Christina.

Hugh makes our introductions to Mr Copeland as we seat ourselves, then lets him know the news about James Gordon.

"A dreadful business," Mr Copeland agrees.

"Have you had troubles yourself?" Hugh asks.

"Generally, we've been treated civilly," Elizabeth replies, her small eyes darting about, "and we're no longer troubled with crowds of them in the house, which was the greatest tax of our patience in the beginning. They've shown little desire to live with us as domestics though, and we can't say they've *spoiled* us with kindness." Her smile is thin. She is suddenly seized with a racking cough that makes me wince.

Joseph must be caring for her, and perhaps this accounts for the un-kempt appearance of him. He has the bushiest beard, which fans out from his bottom lip like an oversized shaving brush. His thick hair comes down low onto his forehead, smothering his close-set eyes.

"True, Betsey," Joseph says, "but at the end of our twelfth month they began to show more respect. For manual labour we have to pay them well …"

Elizabeth scoffs and says, "In bartering with them, we've found them greedy, selfish, hard to please and unreasonable." She lapses into a coughing fit and excuses herself from the room.

"It's true we've had our issues," Joseph speaks slowly, defeated. "They, er, seem to think that if they attend church on Sabbath then they may serve the devil all the other days of the week." He laughs but it holds no humour. "And if when they die they get a Christian burial, they think they'll go to heaven. They want very little religion really. Just enough to keep body and soul together." He nods, as if convincing himself.

"The labour trade is now taking many of the strong and able young men away," he continues with a shrug.

"Are they leaving voluntarily?" Hugh asks.

Dr Munro chuckles and shakes his head. We turn our attention to him as he says, "Well, some are taken by force, Mr Fraser, or are obtained by deceit practised on them by masters of labour vessels. Some are obliged to go by chiefs or relatives from whom they've been bought. Some go because they're defeated in war and are driven off their own lands. Some are returned labourers, who, finding their plantations destroyed, wives gone and so on, ship off again in disgust, as is their curious nature. A few accompany their chiefs when they go or are taken away, and some go from curiosity, or a desire to get muskets and other goods, despite not knowing how long they will even be gone."

Dr Munro frowns as he continues, "You see, the new Labourers Act says vessels must be licensed to procure labourers, but I'm afraid you'll find that it in no way deals with the force, fraud and injury committed against these people with which we as missionaries are coming into contact daily. It's plain coercion, trickery and kidnapping taking place, and it even has its own name now – that of 'blackbirding'."

"But what about the men's families, their wives?" I ask.

"Mrs Stewart," Dr Munro says softly, "helping the women and the widows left behind from these atrocities will be a vital task in your mission work." His face softens as he gives me a small smile.

I nod.

Hugh and John try to give the Copelands words of encouragement, though they appear too exhausted to wish to hear them. Betsey flicks her hand as if Hugh were a mosquito to be rid of when he suggests they go on furlough. Joseph has decided Betsey is too unwell to attend the annual meeting of Synod this year as well, so they will not be accompanying us after all. Yet they will also not consider travelling back to the colonies on the *Dayspring*.

"Come, let us show you the church," Joseph says eventually, looking thankful to finish the conversation.

Chapter 6

TANNA

After seeing the church, John takes my hand as we walk along a track on the brow of a hill. "What's troubling you, Ann, eh?" he asks, as lightly as if commenting on the weather, but I hear his concern.

I sigh. "It's a little overwhelming," I say, looking about me to see if we are alone. "Give me a little time … So far from kin, our bairn growing and with not knowing where we are to live, or how the islanders may receive us … There are so many unknowns, John. The labour trade … It's all so much to take in." I pause to look at his face before adding, "Did you know about the labour trade, slave trade business, whatever it is, before we left Nova Scotia?"

He nods, lost in thought. "I know we can do this, *together*," he says, by way of an answer, raising my hand and bringing it briefly to his lips.

"John! Did ye not think to inform me of all the troubles here? This is no ordinary mission from the sounds of it. I feel as if we're going onto a battlefield. Aboard the *Great Britain* you painted a very different picture of the life that awaits us. James has been *murdered* …" I shake my head, unsure of what I am trying to work out. "The Copelands, why do they not take respite? Elizabeth looks to be slowly dying here!"

John frowns. "She is not of a robust constitution, Ann. I'm sure we shall not have such troubles—"

"Why?" I cut in. "Why should we be any different?" I try to lower my voice.

John smiles again but it is forced, and he sighs. He stops and turns to me before whispering, "I believe in us, Ann … I need you to believe in me."

This pulls me short. "It's not that I don't believe in *you*, John. I just need you to not hide from me what truly awaits us."

"Believe and it shall be, eh," he says, raising his arms to his sides. "It's better to trust – let not your heart be troubled." He turns and walks on.

What a delightful platitude, I think, but I have never been one to not let my heart be troubled. His optimism infuriates me and answers nothing, but for the sake of my young marriage I decide to hold my tongue.

Beneath us the *Dayspring* lies mirrored on the azure water with the little boat wending to and fro. Seeing the flag of recoil hoisted, we continue to the landing to re-join her, and thankfully have a smoother crossing back to the ship.

The captain presses on toward Port Resolution, the principal harbour on the island of Tanna, while darkness falls. It is then that Yasur, the burning volcano, appears to us, as restless as the ocean. Every five minutes, sometimes more, the puff, puff, puffing like an old man's pipe begins before a burst of crimson fragments shower into the air. Thick clouds of smoke tinged with red roll up after them. Then the roar like thunder reaches our ears and seems to shake the very air around us.

"It's a splendid lighthouse, there's no mistaking it," George says at the rail, his voice in awe. We all gaze into the blackness, startling when the next vent bursts forth once more.

That night, before sleep, John tells me of the reports he has read of "dark" Tanna. How the islanders are ferocious and warlike, much broken up into small tribes who continually fight and eat one another. "Traders have supplied firearms to the people," he continues, "which has helped keep up the warfare and has supplemented their traditional weapons."

So, he is finally trying to prepare me a little better, I think.

After a restless sleep, we anchor at Port Resolution, named after Captain Cook's vessel almost one hundred years before. The traders' ramshackle settlements can be seen along the shore, and stores advertising liquor too. "When Thomas Neilson presented himself as the missionary, they threw the timber for his house back into the sea as quickly as it was put ashore," Dr Munro says with a chuckle followed by a cough as we stand at the rail.

We land the Neilsons' stores and sail on toward Black Beach. Next to me at the rail, George says, "Truly, 'distance lends enchantment to the view'! All looks extremely beautiful a little way off,"—he waves his hand, scanning the scene—"but the beauty vanishes when you set foot on shore. Broken shells and all sorts of rubbish are piled about … and, instead of sheep grazing, pigs are grunting in every direction, having apparently strayed from their sties, which are stuck here and all about, but which you soon find are the habitations not of the pigs but of the *people*!"

"Sheep? Really, George!" I reply and sigh.

"It may lack the touches of civilisation, Mr Campbell, but nature has swept a prodigal hand here, in my eyes, and I think it is quite beautiful," Dr Munro says.

George pinches his lips together and moves along the rail.

As we near Black Beach, we catch sight of some islanders waving. One jumps off from the rocks and swims toward us. He is met by the small boat, and when he comes on board, Dr Munro moves to greet him. The man says he has been trying to live a Christian life and lead others to Jesus. They seem eager to have a missionary here.

Dr Munro nods and promises to do his best to place a missionary with them, to which the man replies, "You no gammon now? Me want-im Missi, a'right!"

"Me no gammon," Dr Munro laughs back, adding, "only truth!"

John and Hugh decide to go ashore, but I decline to join them. Once there, they hold out their hands to the women on the beach, who scream and hide behind one another. They wear simple grass skirts around their middle and beads around their necks.

A few of them slowly come forward and take the strips of turkey red Hugh holds out to them. I feel sorry to have not gone then and want them to know we wish them no harm.

Could this be our station? I wonder. The muscular frames of the men are plain to see as they wear nothing but a belt and wrapper, and some have painted their faces the colour of black lead, laid on with a heavy hand, so the yellow of their eyes stands out even more. All carry a weapon.

In the fading light of dusk, the men make their way back on board. As the moon rises, singing, panpipes and wooden drumbeats fill the night air before we get under sail. Sleep eludes me in the close night as images of dark shapes fill my mind against the rhythm of drums and the rumbles and blasts from Yasur in the distance. I go up on deck and enjoy the breeze washing over me in the moonlight as we head on for Erromango. I canna help but think of the difference to the quiet Nova Scotian hamlets I have left behind.

I rub my stiff neck as I awake to a fine dawn. We are within a couple of miles of an island. Others make their way up from the cabins below, and, as the vessel turns for shore, a sail is observed. Through the glass she is reported to be a topsail schooner. They lower a boat, which comes swiftly alongside.

Captain Braithwaite greets the captain and two others from the vessel. We look down at them from the rail, although I notice Dr Munro scans their vessel rather than these men. I make my way over to him as we look out at the *Lyttona*. "About seventy islanders for Queensland," he surmises with a nod. The islanders look back at us as they line the ship's rail. Their captain is saying something about the boat of James Gordon and if we know of his murder.

Having received the latest news from us, he departs. As the distance grows between the vessels, Dr Munro says, "The more ignorant the natives are, the more money the traffic makes out of them. These captains try to stop the learning of the gospel because they know that if the heathen receives it, he'll no longer be as helpless or as easily imposed upon. So, they lead them in vice and speak against the missionaries." He shakes his head, turns and makes his way toward the captain, while John makes his way to me.

"Annetta, are you okay? You shouldn't be sleeping on deck in your condition."

"I'm fine, John. I prefer the breeze, ye know that." I take his arm and we make our way down to breakfast, with just enough time to eat before we cast anchor in Dillon's Bay on the northwest of Erromango.

We go up and find we are opposite a deep valley down which a river courses its way to the sea. The hills on either side are high and steep. Hugh points out where the first Mr Gordon – George – and his wife – Ellen – lived and were killed. He points to the beach next, where John Williams' blood mixed with James Harris' as they were clubbed to death in 1839 near the river, just where it joins the sea.

The house of the last missionary, James McNair, who died from a severe paroxysm two years ago, is a few hundred yards up the stream. Despite the sun's rays shining down the valley, lighting up one side and throwing the other into deep shadow, the hills seem dark and frowning, unwitting witnesses to so many scenes of horror.

I am reluctant to depart for shore, and I am not alone. "I've just read in George's book," John says to me, although all are listening, "when, more than a hundred years ago, a British ship hove-to off this island and sent a boat ashore. The natives, filled with astonishment, crowded down to the beach. They mixed cordially with the strange white beings at first but then began pulling up their boat and trying to run off with the oars. A quarrel arose and the arrows and spears of the natives flew until the loud report of the white men's muskets rang in their ears. Back on the vessel, Captain Cook sailed away after firing a heavy gun to frighten them further, and so the Erromangans were introduced to civilisation and its powers." He raises an eyebrow.

Dr Munro chuckles and says, "Indeed! And next were the sandalwood traders, who, finding Erromango rich in that precious wood, soon opened trading stations. Next to the slave trade, I believe no traffic has been so polluted with human blood as that of sandalwood. The vagabonds sacrificed the lives of many natives and destroyed many noble men who fell by the avenging natives' hands as a consequence. The sandalwooders hated George Gordon for exposing their atrocities. Who's to say they didn't rile up the natives against him? It's been done before, and, had the natives been fairly and kindly treated from the beginning, I'm sure we'd have had little or nothing to complain of them now."

"Although," George begins, pausing to raise his finger in the air, "even making every allowance for them, I cannot help fancying that a good broadside or two occasionally, such as Captain Cook inflicted, does help convince them that white men's lives are not to be sacrificed with impunity."

Dr Munro turns to George. "Our enterprise is one of mercy,

Mr Campbell, not of judgement. We forget our high office when we invoke the vengeance in our power on the people around us. We must draw them by cords of love and beware anything that will repel them." His voice has regular cadences, and, though of a melancholic tone, they are pleasing to the ear – gentle rhythms, no harsh edges, like waves on the shore.

"An appeal to physical force is far more likely to irritate than to soothe the passions of savage men," he finishes as we move for the ship's boat. Tension hangs in the air as we row over in silence.

Chapter 7

Erromango and Efaté

Once at the beach, Hugh leads the way, and we walk as a group toward the church. Several men, painted black, are lounging about the riverside as we walk up. I grip my skirts and avert my eyes. At the church, there are a group of people inside.

"It's the Christian party," Dr Munro enthuses. They are few in number. Dr Munro moves to greet a man who Hugh says is Soso, James Gordon's chief teacher, and who is conducting the service. The small group appear to be listening attentively.

"Despite all that could have disheartened them, they're clinging to their faith," John says, smiling. When Soso has greeted us all, he tells Dr Munro they have come here for safety as the heathen, after murdering James at the other station on the island, threatened to kill them also.

We move outside and gather under a banyan tree, whose tendrils overhang the spot where an old mission house once stood. Barricades are still visible, built in case of an attack on the place. Christina and I sit on an expansive bole and fan ourselves before the church members come and shake hands with us. Christina's eyes dart about and she is pale. Clearly neither of us are much taken with this place. I am again pulling at my collar, perspiration running in rivulets down my spine under my heavy dress. I reach for Christina's hand and smile at her. She nods but her smile is thin, and she pulls her hand away.

From this vantage point, I subtly observe the heathen. They all hold fierce-looking star-headed clubs. *Can lasting good come of us being here?* I wonder then.

An old woman comes forward and tries to tell Dr Munro of James' death, but she breaks down sobbing. "Ah, Missi, these people are heathen, heathen!"

Dr Munro speaks a few words to the Christian people around us, finishing with, "Are you able to hold fast to your faith?"

"*Kamfaneteme*", we are able, is the immediate reply. They sound resolute but their impassive faces give nothing away.

Dr Munro holds their hands in turn before holding up his hand in farewell. I am relieved to walk back to the shore. Some young boys walk with us, and John plays tag with two of them. *Is he really unperturbed by this place?* I wonder then how different my new husband and I truly are. Bathed in the shadowy light of the setting sun, we return to the ship.

The teacher, Soso, and his friend Yomot also come on board. Soso squats on deck and begins to tell the party what happened to Missi – as the missionaries are called – James Gordon that fateful day.

The summer had been unusually wet, bringing much sickness and death. "Missi was blamed by the heathen for the sickness," Soso says, explaining how a man named Nerimpow had lost two children. James gave medicine to them, and Nerimpow said it was the medicine that killed them. "He and another man came to James' house, watched for their chance and then struck James with a machete on the side of his head."

The evening is warm, but I wrap on a shawl then, needing the extra comfort as shivers course through me. John looks at me, and I force a wee smile.

Yomot speaks next. Dressed in just a loincloth, this strong man's dark, firm muscles catch the lamplight with every movement he makes.

"'Yomot, Yomot!' Soso called to me, '*oveteme utai Missi Gordon!* The people have killed Mr Gordon! Oh, what evil news was this to me! My Missi, who I loved, cut down *and by my own people*. My heart was heavy and for many days we wept for him. I was all the time restless, for right down in my heart was the longing for revenge. Was it wrong, Missi?" Yomot looks around the deck before fixing his gaze to Dr Munro. "What would *you* have done if your friend had been killed by lying men? How would *you* have felt if your brother had been slain by cruel hands, even though the murderer was of your own land? *Missi, I was just hungry for them …*"

"Where is James' body now?" Hugh's voice is hoarse.

"We buried him as best we can, but we cannot go there now. Port Narvin is not safe."

My mind swims. I gaze out to the ocean while Yomot talks on. I fix on the moon's reflection dancing on the ripples of the surface and try to calm my breathing. John squeezes my hand, reassuring, but I snatch it back. I had not wanted my concentration broken by him, bringing me back to this.

"I'm tired," I say and slip away to our cabin. I have heard enough. I do not want to believe that John was right, and maybe I shouldna know everything after all. But it feels to be the truth. My eyes fill and a sting rises at the back of my throat.

I spend another restless night, fitful and hot, dogged by vivid dreams, before wrapping on my shawl and going up to await the dawn on deck, enjoying the peaceful freshness. How can I come to terms with how these people live? I long then, more than ever before, for the comforts of home. My mind churns with how I could make this happen, what reasons I could give for needing to go back to Nova Scotia after all. My father's words echo in my mind. I guess he was right: I'll never be any good to anyone.

I awake with a fuzzy head and confused thoughts. I am scared to stay and scared to go. I dry my eyes and paint on resolve as the crew rouse the ship to life. They take Soso and Yomot back to shore, and we set sail early.

We pass by Pango before anchoring in Port Vila on the island of Efaté. In size, it looks about the same as Erromango and Tanna, but there appears more flat country than on the other islands, with the mountains in lofty ranges in the centre. My hand reaches for the locket under my collar while I silently describe it to Tilly. At least the beauty in nature is something to quieten my anxiety.

Almost as soon as the anchor bites the sand, canoes put off from Ifira Island. In minutes we are surrounded by a flotilla manned by crews of lithe-looking females. John comes and puts his arm around me as we stand at the rail, but I keep my focus on the islanders. Their canoes bang into the *Dayspring's* sides with no hint of reverence for our little ship. The women shriek and yell at the top of their voices as they scramble about and vie for the best positions. I gasp at their uninhibited nature.

Their hair is short, and they have no covering except a calico wrapper around their middle and ornaments. Their language is different again, but they seem, on first appearance, quite similar to the Futunese, with straighter hair and lighter skin.

They have come to barter, bringing shells mainly, and wanting in return a great variety of goods. I notice George spying one particularly pretty girl in a canoe. He calls out to her and holds up some beads and cloth, but she only shakes her head and shrieks "*Shooshah!*" at the top of her voice, shamelessly bold. George looks on, puzzled, ignoring her cries, trying to tempt her with other things. He is without success until he holds up a Jew's harp. Her eyes widen, she paddles over, grabs the Israelitish instrument with a smile of satisfaction, bundles the shells over to George as an exchange and paddles off in triumph.

Some of the women deftly clamber up the ship's sides and want beads, and it seems only the small blue ones will do. Others want knives while some go off with figs of black tobacco, which we pretend are for their brothers.

The men come out in their canoes next. They hang back, some distance away, until one of the crew calls out to them, "No worry! They not white men, they missionaries!" Christina suppresses a giggle next to me.

Feeling assured of our ship's purpose, the men proffer shells and calabashes, which they have made into water bottles. I want one or two and John agrees to buy them. We have two boxes to fill up with curios: one to give away to the villagers at our station, and the other for the congregations at home. On asking the man what he wants for them, he points over my head. I look to the sky, confused, before he tugs at my hat, shrugs and says, "*Olsaem blong wife, blong mi.*" I laugh and motion for him to wait there as I decide he shall have a hat, even if I have to give him my own. After changing it in the cabin, I come back and hand it to him. He grins, and I laugh again.

The trade goes on all morning. We are so packed on deck it is hard to find standing room, while the chatter is deafening. Some stand around the captain with pigs, fowls and taro. Others surround the missionaries, offering shells, mats, bags and whatever else. Some strut up and down in their new garments, to the admiration of all. I laugh as Hugh tries to stick someone's great awkward arms into the right holes of an outfit.

Christina and I move to the shade of the deckhouse. We watch George go off in a canoe with a man, no doubt engaging him as a guide, while we fan ourselves from the heat.

Christina sighs. "What a day! I just want to get there though, don't you? To have a home already."

I smile. "Oh, aye. Travelling is so tiresome, and I feel like we can't *begin* … Are ye still feeling okay about having done this?" I try to keep my voice even.

"Yes …" she says but canna seem to find the words to continue. "And you?" she says at last.

"Oh, I'm fine," I lie. "Well, feeling calmer each day," I say, already regretting my lack of truth. I take a deep breath. "Although," I begin, "the heathen at Erromango did perturb me somewhat." I look for her response, but her face is still turned toward the islands. "I'm trying to gain strength from Jessie Archer," I continue. "She seems so *capable*."

"She's a lot to live up to," Christina agrees, rolling her eyes. "Look, Annetta, the last thing we want is to be one of *those wives* blamed for the ruination of a mission through lack of courage and strength. Goodness, there could be nothing worse." She looks back to the water.

My heart sinks. I decide then I can say nothing about my longing to go home. "Aye, I am of the same mind," I say instead, "and I just hope that with time, and knowing where our home shall be, we will settle and make the best of all we have, eh." This last part is the truth, at least.

"Goodness, absolutely! Just don't give me Tanna or Erromango," she says behind her fan.

I giggle, relieved at her candour. "I don't think we'll have much of a say, I'm afraid."

She shrugs. "We'll see."

We return our gazes to the buffeting waves and notice George returning. Christina rolls her eyes again before we realise that he is in some difficulty. The wind has risen and soon water is rippling over the sides into his canoe.

The islander with him starts baling water, while George takes the paddle, but it is of no use. The man at the pumps flails his arms in disgust before jumping overboard, while George just sits there as it fills to the waterline. One of the flotilla is returning from our vessel, and the women paddle to the rescue. George rewards them with wet tobacco as he flops into their canoe, to their delight.

Once on board, he wrings his shirt and shows us a few damp sketches of the village huts. Captain Braithwaite calls out, "Mr Campbell, I'm visiting Iririki for yams if you'd care to accompany me?" At which George grabs his book back and hurries off once more.

They manage to get a good supply and George reports, "They're fine, strong men, but have the name of being great rascals according to the captain. A good many have been away to Fiji or Queensland and are said to be none the better for it!"

Early next morning we start on foot for Erakor. The captain suggests Christina and I stay behind, afraid we will be tired out, but we have already decided to go, knowing this is another station in need of a new missionary. Christina just laughs at his remonstrations. "When a woman says she will, she will," she trills. Then, when he is puffed out on the walk, we do our best to look as fresh as when we started. We are already becoming quite adept at showing only what we wish people to see.

After the walk, we are met by canoes and paddled across the lagoon to Erakor itself – a tiny islet just off the main island of Efaté. Erakor reminds me of the shark caught on our journey – thin at the tail and extending out to a wide head at the top, facing the open ocean. The lagoon is a clear, pale green. A bed of many-hued corals lies down in its depths, where small fish dart in and out. With the soft ripple of the canoe as it glides along to the island ahead – with its sparkling sandy beach, the background of coconut palms and the greenery – I have seen nothing prettier.

The old mission house looks neat from a distance, and I know at once Christina is setting her heart on this being her new home. It appears to be a healthy spot with the breezes off the open ocean, and a fine garden sits in front. I, too, canna help envisioning myself here, but I realise Christina is quite determined to have the station of her choice. *Will I stand in her way?* I wonder.

The people come to greet us and pull the canoes up. The men wear a loincloth or a broad belt of matting, while the women's dress consists of two aprons. All wear bracelets – small rings ground out of shells, neatly strung in black and white rows. The men have adorned their necks with boars' tusks and around their arms too. The women's hair is close-cropped. Many older ones have figures tattooed into their chests; leaves in the most intricate patterns that are not at all displeasing to the eye.

"They're ugly, with such large noses," George mutters.

"*You* are hardly one to comment, Mr Campbell," I say. His face pulls up sharp. John loops his arm through mine as he tries to lead me away, but I *tut* and shake him off. I do not meet his eyes as I go to look at the multitude of croton plants.

An Aneityumese teacher, Tupatai, is disappointed Dr Munro has not accompanied us today, but tells us how Dr Munro left him here to look after the stations and encourage the people. "Please tell Father my work is good," he says, as we make our farewells.

Back on board, we sail around to Havannah Harbour. Several traders' establishments are here, and the ship takes on supplies. It is copra harvesting time and the air is smoky and sweet with drying coconuts. We only stay a day, but long enough for the men to decide it also affords a good opening for a station.

Our travels continue for a further two weeks until, sailing from Santo, we commence the return voyage, and begin to feel the force of the trade wind. It was pleasant as long as it went with us, but it has not decided to turn around and blow us back again, so we have some days of weary beating and tossing about.

On the 24th of May, the captain and George resolve that her gracious Majesty should not be forgotten. Rummaging out some revolvers, they adjourn to the forecastle and fire a triple salute in honour of the day. The rest of us rush up in alarm, imagining we are being attacked.

Later, we deck the vessel with flags, the national anthem is performed with hearty voices, accompanied by Hugh on a shaky accordion, and we pray to God to bless Queen Victoria and her reign.

My heart feels heavy then as I think of home, and how to us this occasion signalled summer was beginning and we were truly through the long, dark months of cold. I think of the quilting we always do in the quiet of winter that Tilly would be finishing now. Our centre of all comfort was the hearth around which we gathered – Pa stirring the logs, sending a stream of sparks up the chimney, revealing the black bake kettle, its lid covered with glowing embers. Ma busy at her knitting, helping Tilly with her sewing. Thomas and my sisters reading in the firelight chapters from the Bible in turn. I picture myself back with them.

On our last night on board, George plays his guitar and sings. It turns out he is quite accomplished at it, and he seems quite invigorated since our encounter at Ifira.

The evening is still, the sea like glass, the reflected moon laying a corridor of silver from us to it. The soft lilting music and our little band of missionaries, so far from kindred and country, about to separate for their lonely homes and not knowing what trials await us.

Chapter 8

ANAMÉ

A day's sail brings the white houses and thin smoky spirals of the Archers' house at Anamé into sight. Mr Archer, wearing his familiar Panama hat, waves a green umbrella from the shore. In lee of the coral reef, we drop anchor. On landing, we are met by a crowd of islanders – neatly dressed women and men, and healthy, happy-looking children, who tug at our hands in welcome.

The station has a romantic appearance with the palms and bananas, the whitewashed house with the brown thatched roof, neat reed fences, large mimosas overhanging the sea and the most magnificent orange trees loaded with green and yellow fruit.

"They are more than twenty years old, and each bears several thousand oranges per year," Mr Archer explains to our awe-struck expressions. After showing us over the grounds, we sit in the shade of an orange tree and drink the golden liquid.

Jessie welcomes me and Christina into her home and shows us our rooms. We will stay here while the missionaries go on to the annual missionary meeting – the Synod.

"I hope all goes well, eh," I say to John when it is time for them to go off to the *Dayspring* next morning.

"Take the chance to rest, Ann." He squeezes my hand.

Next to us, Christina turns to Mr Archer and says, "Be sure and don't settle us on Tanna or Erromango!" knowing he has authority in these matters. She laughs, while Mr Archer shoots Hugh a look.

I wish I had the bravery to say something similar, though even I feel it a rather imprudent thing to say, even in her light-hearted manner. John has made it clear he is trusting in God that we will go where He needs us most.

Along with the question as to a change of headquarters for the *Dayspring*, the decision of who is to take up which post is the most important matter to be decided.

We wave them off, and I take Christina's hand as we wend our way back to the house.

"Come along, girls," Jessie calls over her shoulder.

We cradle our pregnant bellies and grimace at each other.

Over the next week, our spell with Jessie gives us a good insight into running a home in the tropics, although I grumble at rising at four each morning. The Archers have no bairns and everything about them is neatness and order. They seem to lack little from the comforts of home, but there is an emptiness in the air that Jessie endeavours to fill with chatter, or, rather, instruction.

She explains, with at times man-like authority, what jobs we will need to find young boys and girls to fill. She has trained the local girls well in helping with her house, and the chores are shared equally among them. There is no hurry, no bustle, no fuss, just clockwork routine. I take comfort in seeing that though we may have to tend to more roles in our situation, it is not to say we should do them alone.

One evening, we have retired to our bedrooms, and I am writing a letter to Ma when a mysterious shaking begins. I hold onto the bed frame as it grows worse. I cry out as objects begin falling from a shelf as the floor sways and changes shape beneath me. I hold my breath. When it abates, Jessie calls out, "If you're frightened, come into my room."

I breathe out and move toward the door, but Christina calls out, "Oh! I'm not at all frightened, thank you."

I gasp. I canna muster the courage to say otherwise and lie awake trembling for what seems like hours. I find a disturbed sleep, jolting awake every so often until daylight, though there are only a few smaller trembles. I hide under the covers when the dawn light penetrates the room and, thankfully, I am left be.

I am late to breakfast, but the earthquake is still the topic of conversation.

"You handled yourself bravely, dear," Jessie says. I look up and Christina tilts her head and smiles in thanks.

"And what kind of night did you pass, Annetta?" Her smirk tells me she knows full well. I say nothing.

When Jessie goes to fetch more goat milk, I grasp Christina's arm. "Please sleep in my room tonight!"

"Oh, certainly!" she replies. To my look of relief, she adds, "Don't mention it. I shall be only too pleased," before whispering, "I'd been wondering how I was to pass another night alone."

Just as we finish breakfast, a young boy brings Jessie a letter.

"Ah, from Mr Archer. It's been sent overland. This often happens if there's news to report from Synod," Jessie says. "Now, where are my glasses?"

Christina delicately motions to Jessie's neck and smiles. "Oh yes, of course." Jessie chuckles. "Now, let me see ..."

As we stand behind Jessie, I take hold of Christina's hand behind our backs. Jessie scans the writing, moving the paper in and away to focus on the words. "Well, that's settled then. It's been decided that *Sydney* shall be the *Dayspring*'s port henceforth, instead of Melbourne."

I expel a rush of air despite myself. This is not what we wanted to know.

"So, as we know ..." Jessie pauses, "Mr Murray is already in charge of Dr Munro's former station of Aneghowhat on Aneityum. It has therefore been decided that a Mr MacDonald, who is soon to arrive, should open the new field of Havannah Harbour on Efaté. Mr Stewart shall take up the work on Erakor and Pango on Efaté. And Mr Fraser is to go to Dillon's Bay on Erromango," she finishes with delight. "So, Mr MacDonald is the only one sent to open a new station then. All others are going to those that have been occupied before ..." Jessie goes on, but Christina and I are no longer listening.

Christina drops my hand and moves quickly toward her room. A muffled sob escapes her the moment she closes the door behind her.

"Well, really!" Jessie rises and says, "Whatever is this matter?" She is across the space to the door before I can intercept. "Whatever is the trouble, child?" she calls out. I stand uselessly, picking at the skin around my nails. Christina opens the door a crack and says, "Forgive me, Jessie, but I do *not* want to go to Erromango." Her jaw is clenched.

"Why? You could not have a better place. There is a nice river, and you'll be able to have a boat and keep cattle."

This picture brings to my mind the blood of missionaries flowing down that picturesque river and bleeding into the sea. Christina clearly has no thoughts for boats or cattle either. "Erromango is the last place I want to go … Please, excuse me." Her face is strained as she closes the door once more.

I see little of Christina the rest of that day, despite trying to steal away from Jessie to check on her. I will talk with John, I decide; there must be something we can do.

Chapter 9

Tanna

A few days later, we know the *Dayspring* has returned when wild shouts of *Sail-oh!* ring out around the station. We rush to the shore as the small boat comes off. Our bags are packed, ready, and we hardly give a backward glance as some of the crew row us to the ship. As we board, John takes me in a quick embrace. "Are you well, Ann?"

"Aye, John, and better now! It felt like so long." Relief floods through me that we are reunited, and he is well. "How did it go?"

"Good and bad, Ann," he says, drawing me to one side. "I'm sad to say Dr Munro was unable to attend the closing meetings as a sudden stroke quite disabled him." John turns as Dr Munro is being helped up from below deck. His right side looks stiff, as if no longer made of soft flesh. He is helped to a seat in the shade.

"Can anything be done?"

John shrugs. "We have to hope he can make it back to the colonies and get help there, eh."

John turns back to me. "Erakor and Pango, Ann, are you pleased?" He takes my hands in his and smiles as he leans toward me.

I look around for Hugh and Christina. They are deep in conversation, and a frown inhabits Christina's brow. "Oh, very much … but why are the Frasers going to Erromango?"

He gives me a puzzled look.

"Is it safe, John? Really? I was thinking that—"

"There will be trials at any station, Annetta, and really, it is not for you to question the decisions of Synod. Hugh has no objections … He feels it is God's will."

I know he sees my frown, but he simply turns and calls out to the captain about us getting underway.

God's will or foolhardiness? I wonder, biting down on my tongue as he puts his back to me. Have the actions of the Erromangans not been enough? Surely, we should leave the place alone, at least for a little time. Aye, Tilly, I am naïve. I sigh. I know at once that the wives are here at the bidding of the men, their helpmeets, but fellow missionaries? In all but name, I realise. We knew there were dangers in becoming missionaries, but surely going to Erromango is inviting, or *heaping*, danger upon danger.

In front of our husbands, Christina has resumed her stoicism and wears a thin smile. *Perhaps she has resigned herself that Erromango is to be her new home*, I think. I search her face, but she seems to avoid my gaze.

For now, John and I are to go to Tanna to stay with the missionaries there, the Johnstons, as my time of confinement fast approaches. The sail is quick and when it is time to depart, Christina and I clasp hands. She is subdued and we resolve not to say goodbye, only wishing each other luck. We promise to pray for each other and write at every opportunity until our next meeting.

As I stand on the shore and watch the dear ship with her precious cargo sail away, I can only give a cheerless wave.

William and Agnes Johnstons' station is close to the beach. Agnes comes to my side as I raise my face to the cooling trade winds. She smiles and says, in her gentle Scotch lilt, "The only disadvantage of these breezes is that no flowers can be grown around the house, and the front windows can never be kept clean on account of the spray showers flying up from these breakers." Her arm sweeps across the bay in front of us.

The breakers are spectacular. There is nothing to stop them until they roll in upon the pebbly black beach. The spindrift, white as snow, flies up into the air like the ashes of the volcano, dazzling in the glare of the tropical sun. "The time at which they appear the greatest is not during a gale, as ye might imagine, dearie, but immediately after it. During a gale, why, the waves come rushing on and dash themselves blindly upon the rocks in too confused a way to rise into breakers. But when the fierceness of the storm and the angry lashing of the waves is over – when there is nothing left but the great rolling swell – then ye'll see the breakers in perfection." She smiles, satisfied.

"Ye need to rest before your time is here, Annetta. I hope ye'll make yerself at home and look upon this time to renew yer vigour after all the journeying ye've done. Childbirth has been a difficult time for so many of the missionary wives," her voice quietens before she turns to face me and, smiling again, says, "but ye are young and vigorous, and I am sure, in God's good care, ye shall be just fine."

I smile in thanks. "I confess I never expected my own dear mama to not be here for me when this time came." I try to sound as bright as possible, but this has become my enduring thought.

"Well, I helped my mother in her times more than once, dearie, and despite no bairns of my own, I hope to bring ye as much comfort as I can muster in the absence of yer own kin." She pats my arm, and we turn to walk up the beach.

Five white steps lead onto the verandah, and we are welcomed into the little whitewashed home enclosed by a neat reed fence. A low reed railing painted deep green skirts the verandah, and the doors and windows match. Inside, the main room is open up to the rigging. Against one wall stands a large mirror. "Fer the use of the natives," Agnes remarks. "That and the coloured pictures amuse them greatly. Do ye have a harmonium, Annetta?" Agnes runs her hand down the backboard of hers and then back along the faded white keys.

"I do … I just hope it's withstood the rigours of the journey."

"The natives are just fascinated with them. It's a good way to encourage them to come to you … when ye want them to, mind."

Agnes shows us to our room at the front of the house. It looks freshly whitewashed and has a light-green trim and window frame. The floor is laid with coconut matting and a mosquito canopy hangs over the bedframe. A vanity stands against one wall and an ottoman sits under the window with a vase of pale-pink hibiscus on top. I stoop down to smell them. The breakers can be seen rolling onto the beach below, and in the days that follow I know the seascape will become my study. I can see along the beach for a great distance, and the island of Futuna rises directly to the east. I look at the bed and wonder whether childbirth here, with just Agnes, will be straightforward at all. But Ma's voice pipes into my mind, "There's nothing that worry can do about it now."

I make my way downstairs. Two tables have been pushed together to make a nice large one in the main room. We sit down to a well-cooked dinner of fowl broth, yams and native cabbage, tea rich with goat milk, bananas and more.

The Johnstons arrived a few years ago but tell us they have made little ground with the heathen. Tomorrow is the Sabbath, and John is to accompany William itinerating in a heathen village.

"I wish fer us to accompany them too, Annetta," Agnes says over dinner, "if ye're up to it? Only, a heathen high chief is dying there, and we must be there fer the women of the village, fer what they're purposing to do."

Her raised eyebrow spikes my curiosity.

Numerous outbuildings are dotted around the mission house: storeroom, duckhouse, goathouse and others. Past this a stream flows, its banks adorned with creepers and ferns. Before breakfast, John and I sit by the stream and talk over what our first tasks will be once we arrive at Pango and Erakor. It is nice to talk without feelings of anxiety, without worrying about our own station yet – we can suspend our fate.

We have not talked again of the Frasers. I presume John thinks the matter resolved. My mind often wanders to what is happening with Christina on Erromango though. I pray for her often, but with little to write about yet, and not knowing what will happen when my time of childbirth comes, I want to wait and write once I have some proper news to tell.

We set off after breakfast and the walk inland to the heathen village is none too arduous.

As Agnes and I make our way along the worn path, she talks of living at Pollock Road in Glasgow, where she was much involved with Christian work – tract distribution, reading scriptures, teaching at the Sabbath school and the like. "I was the eldest and a good many domestic duties also fell to me." She shrugs, as if it were no consequence.

A thorough Scotch woman, Agnes has a plain, round face. Her dark, wavy hair is swept back into a tight bun, no wisps out of place. She has a beautiful Christ-like character though and seems kind as well as devoted.

"We were somewhat anxious when we arrived here," she continues, "that we'd be assigned to Erakor, as Mr Morrison was retiring at the time from poor health."

"You *didna* wish to be on Erakor?" *What do I have to worry about?* I wonder.

"Don't misunderstand me, Annetta … much ground has been gained there, I'm sure ye'll like it, but we were looking forward to settling on Tanna, despite its chequered past. Kwamera here was considered a very promising opening. Certainly, the people gave us a hearty welcome …"

William laughs from the path in front of us. "That was before we realised the calico, knives and other things we brought were more highly prized than our teaching," he says drily.

"Indeed." Agnes smiles back at me.

"Efaté is a resort of traders and white settlers though, and the stations have especial difficulties on that account," William says.

"Oh aye, mind you, they're *all* rogues, wherever they may be!" Agnes says. "There is a new trader here, an American, who's given himself out as a medical doctor and professes to cure all. Only, ye must pay the piper! He won't prescribe unless ye lay down a guinea, or its equivalent – a large porker … a pig, dearie," she says to my frown.

"He *treated* a wee child here who was all covered in sores. Well, he cleared away the sores, 'tis true, but by means of *mercury*, leaving the poor wee one without eyebrows or eyelashes and scarcely a hair on his head. In that state they brought him to us.

"We saw at once he was dying and told the mother we could do nothing for him. She pleaded with us to try, and so we gave a little medicine, and two or three days after we gave a second dose. Ye can imagine our feelings when we heard of his death next morning." Agnes shakes her head and looks down at the ground. We all pause in the shade of a tree to catch our breath as she continues, "We were afraid they'd blame his death to us, and we didna know what they would do to the trader either, so we tried to defend him too.

"Sometime after, we visited the sorrowing mother and she said she'd suffered much from the heathen around. They reproached her with having caused the death of her own child through *our* medicine, and that the trader had told them so. We gave him the benefit of the doubt, but to be honest they seem ever-ready to harm our cause … Yet, despite it all, I have come to find that I do *live* for Tanna," she says simply, "and, if needs be, I will die fer it."

I can but admire her resolve. This question seems straightforward to her.

"Indeed, traders and labour vessels are a trial wherever you may be," William agrees. "Backsliding from the Christian path is often a quick course in the company of traders. Don't expect too much when you first settle at your station, Mr Stewart. The journey is long, and much patience is called for."

John raises his eyebrows and nods, then says, "I'm sure we'll be just fine."

I let out a breath and shake my head at the ground, as though it is the heat that perturbs me.

We step out into a clearing. Some adults run off into the bushes at our approach, but their children are curious and friendly. Their little limbs are like spindly twigs attached to their bodies with a bulbous belly protruding at the front. Many are dirty, all are naked but are having great escapades running around, left to their own devices.

John, Agnes and William go to sit with the people in their meeting ground while I look on, unsure what to do. William begins beckoning the people with his hands, but many men are twining their hair and take no notice. Agnes rises and waves to me to follow her to a hut. Three women are sitting outside. "The chief's old mother and his two wives," Agnes says. She speaks in Tannese, motioning at the hut. They smile and nod, then laugh together behind their hands. Their pandanus-leaf skirts are their only covering, and the fruits of time and childbirth are evident upon their bodies.

It is dark and musty inside the hut. The earthen floor is hard and bare, worn smooth with time. Baskets, mats and bones hang from the ceiling, and we have to crouch low. Once our eyes adjust, we make out the shape of a man lying down. His laboured breathing is enhanced by the closeness of the space.

His head is raised from the ground by a piece of wood; his "pillow". He is quite filthy. Agnes at once stoops and takes his hand in hers, holding it to her, which takes me aback.

She begins praying in Tannese in a low voice. As she speaks, I notice the chief's eyes lift to heaven. Then, looking at Agnes, he says, "Jesu!" with great feeling. He is unable to speak more. After a few more moments she beckons me to leave the hut with her. She explains how she was asking the Lord to have mercy on him, even at the eleventh hour. She spoke to him of our sinful hearts and of Jesus the Saviour, of the perishing nature of all earthly things and that bright home on high for all who trust in Jesus.

We find John and William have finished too, so we begin the walk back. I ask Agnes about the last part, where the chief nodded, as if in agreement.

"I asked him to be buried as a Christian, Annetta. I asked that no muskets, no kava, no sacred stones be put into his grave, that he wear a simple garment, and that, above all, no lives be taken."

"Lives?"

"It's not been done here fer some time … to my knowledge," she says, "but I've been told they mean to strangle the old mother and his two wives on the death of this chief. It's an old custom. In Aneityum, their wedding ring used to be a cord placed about the neck of the bride, so that when her husband died it would be twisted tight until all life escaped her. It was often carried out by her own son, would ye believe."

My hands cradle my pregnant belly and I wince. "Here on Tanna, though, two men enter the hut while the woman sleeps, and, fixing two pieces of wood on the ground on either side of her neck, squeeze them together until she's dead."

"Are their lives not worth anything without the husband?"

"Well, 'tis true that no one would be there to provide for them … Careful, dearie,"—she takes my arm to help me over the gnarly tree roots—"but in the case of a high chief, it's more of an indignity to him, and a degradation to her, if she marries a man of lower rank. Also, when they die, they say their spirits go to another world, called Ipai, which just means very far off. There they live as on Earth, they dig and plant, give and are given in marriage … So, the wives are going to keep their husbands company in the afterlife."

Chapter 10

TANNA

One night, two weeks later, I awake with a start, my hands clutching at my throat. But the cord is only in my nightmare. The pain, in any case, is not at my throat but deep in my back and at the top of my belly; a hand squeezing and crushing, making it hard to catch my breath. I reach out for John and, realising the situation, he goes for Agnes.

I am scared but Agnes is calm as she encourages me to get up and walk about the room. "It'll help the position and ease the duration, dearie." She rubs my back before shooing John away from the doorway. She closes the door and says, "My mother never abided lying down. I've sent a lass fer the local midwife; she'll be here presently."

Everything happens in such a rush, which is the least of what I am expecting. I have witnessed Ma give birth after birth and each, although slightly shorter than the last, has still been such a drawn-out ordeal. I didna know an alternative was possible. Agnes and the midwife never leave my side, and it is to my utter joy and relief that my dear wee daughter, Mary, named for my youngest sister, arrives on 2nd July 1872. Nothing but the lack of my own kin blemishes this perfect time for me. Overcome with it all, I cry not to have Tilly or dear Ma near, to show them my perfect wee girl.

The emotion and fear of the last few months have wound into a tight knot that has now found its release and spirals out of me. John is worried but Agnes assures him everything is fine; there is nothing wrong with a *guid greet!* Mary is a bonny, strong girl, so they are not tears of sorrow. But I miss the tenderness of Ma's nature and can picture her cradling Mary with love in her eyes.

In quiet moments, I stare at Mary's sleeping face and try to see their likenesses in her. I want to write every detail, to give them a picture as clear as the blue sky outside, but, in truth, I canna see anything of them in her. She is her father's daughter. She has his narrow jaw and almond-shaped eyes. John's own eyes have become a reflection of love.

William informs their small congregation of our news but forbids them from visiting me. All but two elderly women abide by his words. They creep in one morning and seize my hand, sympathy writ on their faces, whispering in Tannese.

Agnes appears in the doorway and laughs as she translates, "They want ye to forget this day!"

I frown, but she only laughs again.

"Ye are sure to have many sons before ye die, they're saying, and, we have all had to bear the same disappointment; we canna always have sons." Agnes draws herself up then and makes it clear to them their sympathy is wasted.

I laugh and show the women the fat dimpled face and wee toes of my bairn and how loved she is by me.

"The only consolation is that it's us missionary wives who become a home for the unwanted girl children," Agnes says as we watch them leave, more comforted than when they arrived.

I have been lost in a fog these last few weeks as when the *Dayspring* arrives one morning, carrying mail and readying to take us to our new home, it takes a lot to ready my mind to leaving the comfort of the Johnstons' house.

George Campbell and Dr Munro are on board and, while we pack, George comes ashore, intent on visiting the volcano before we leave. By night we have often been shaken by Yasur's fiery show to the north of us. "One theory," George says to no one in particular, "is that the interior of the Earth is a liquid mass of molten matter, and volcanoes are the outlets for the gases generated by this heat. It's a very uncomfortable theory indeed, don't you think? And one which should *not* be encouraged …" He shakes his head with his nose held high.

As he babbles on, I find myself more interested in what Captain Braithwaite has brought, and that is the mail. Guilt sweeps through me at sight of Christina's handwriting. I have been so taken up with myself these last weeks, and I tear open the letter to read her news.

Dearest Annetta,

I do not know when you shall receive this, or what our fate may be when you do, but I trust you are well. As I have not heard otherwise, that thought alone helps bring me comfort. I long to hear how you are faring and whether you have news yet from your confinement. I'm sure that news is already on its way to me. I'm often standing at the shore looking for our white-winged angel, although Hugh assures me the Dayspring won't be here for some time yet.

My own "time of trouble", as Hugh insists on calling it, is not far off now, and I confess to feeling terrified. I'm trying not to show this to Hugh, of course, but I shall be entirely without female comfort except for the native teacher and midwife here, and that is where my terror lies. As yet, we don't understand one another at all. I wanted to prove myself strong enough to do this alone. What a stubborn fool I am.

After the Dayspring left, the Christian party and teachers made us most welcome, but all the same I fear we are a responsibility to them now, given the fate of our predecessors. For weeks the Christian natives have watched the house day and night lest the heathen attack. They don't want our blood on their hands, but on one day, I'm afraid to say, they almost had it.

Hugh had decided to erect a new house nearer the shore. The old mission house being unhealthy, and, to my mind, too full of old associations. I wanted to start anew, and Hugh felt that too. He was at the end of the house making a towel-rack and I was sitting inside sewing, our teacher's child Sampat at my feet.

Two middle-aged men, both naked, each carrying an iron bar about two-feet long appeared on the scene, laid the bars down at the door and came right into the house. I didn't know who they were, but I gave the salutation, and then Hugh came in. They made no reply. I asked then, "Who are you? Are you from Cook's Bay?" and to that they answered, "Yes."

The Cook's Bay people are our only friends, and so we felt safe, but in a moment I noticed little Sampat looking frightened and crouching behind my chair. I said, "Come, Sampat, why don't you shake hands with your friends?" But the girl wouldn't move. I spoke to the men, and, thinking they had come to inspect our house, began to show them some pictures. They seemed to take no interest in anything, so Hugh began his work again at the open door.

One man slipped out and, getting his iron bar, went and stood beside Hugh, while his friend also lifted his bar from the ground. Not suspecting anything we went on talking to them. How silly that sounds now as I write it down. Just then, Netai and Novolu came rushing along and pushed their way into the room, both very much excited. Novolu turned and stormed at Hugh in Aneityumese, "Who are these men, Missi? Why do you allow them in your house?" To which he replied, "These are friends from Cook's Bay." Then Netai, his voice trembling, said, "No, Missi, he no Cook's Bay man; he bad man, Unepang man."

The strangers, thank the Lord, at once slipped out and slunk away, one in his haste dropping the bar. We have not seen them again. Netai was terribly upset. He'd got warning from someone that these men were in our house, and he had run at once to our help.

There could be no doubting their intention was to brain us both, for the people of Unepang are the sworn enemies of the Christian party. Since Yomot killed the young chief in revenge for James' death, there has been a deadly feud. The very name "Unepang" being enough to strike terror into the hearts of our people.

I do not recount the ordeal to make you worry, dearest, but because it simply weighs upon my heart and mind that these people would have no compunction to harm me, and while I am of such a delicate nature. To have stared into the eyes of a man who wished to murder me ... I am not sleeping soundly any longer. I feel a great distrust of those around me now and so vulnerable. Who is my friend? Who is my foe? I was easily and thoroughly deceived. It has been a bitter pill. That I have given up my life and family to travel to this island to help these people at once seems the worst decision I have ever made.

I'm sorry to sound so aggrieved. I know you'll have worries of your own but know that I am thinking of you and long to be able to sit and collect our thoughts as we did on the Dayspring.

Affectionately yours,

Christina

Tingles creep down my neck at my lack of care for my friend. Our trunks are being taken to the ship, so I scrabble in my leather bag for some writing paper. I scribble out our news, but when I read it back, it sounds weak and uncertain. Why would she want to know how easy it has been for me so far? I try again but the words will not come, and I canna get her letter from my mind.

John calls to me that it is time to go. I scoop up Mary from her crib and we make our way on board after a hastier than planned farewell to the Johnstons. Our thanks for their kindness and care canna be expressed in any adequate terms, but I trust I will see them again soon.

George has returned from his volcano adventure and proudly shows off some smooth black obsidian for his collection. I approach Dr Munro while the others are preoccupied, including John.

"Dr Munro, it is good to see you looking a little recovered." I swallow and press on, "I am sorely worried for the Frasers on Erromango. Can you please request Captain Braithwaite to visit them just once more before the last journey south to Australia? To assure them of the loving sympathy of us all, and to make sure they're sustaining in their strength?" It is all I can think of to say.

He studies me a moment and then nods and smiles.

"Oh, thank you, thank you. I am so relieved." I smile and touch his hand lightly. I go below deck to pen another letter to Christina, hoping it will be less trite this time, as the trial of arriving at our own island approaches.

Chapter 11

PANGO

We sail to the narrow peninsula of Pango on the island of Efaté, where we will take up Mr Cosh's former abode. I had hoped we would move straight to Erakor as I was so taken with the island on our first visit, but I am assured that this house is in less state of disrepair.

I am eager enough to step out of the *Dayspring* into the little boat that is to take us ashore, finally to our new home, but there is no missionary to welcome us here. As we row over, dark faces peer out at us from among the trees. There is no flicker of a smile of welcome on any one of them. I begin to tremble with a sort of dread, clutching too tightly, I am sure, at the little bundle in my arms.

I focus on the light-blue waves sparkling in the sun as they chase each other along the beach. Not a blemish mars the sky. I try to hum a tune, to keep up at least a cheerful appearance, but the sound dissolves in my throat. All I hear are the oars scraping in the rowlocks with each successive, slow pull, while my heart pounds in my chest.

As we near the beach, a large group is gathering. There are women and children too, and that at least is a good sign. As we step onto the shore, the crowd takes a step back. Finally, two people come forward. The woman, in a pretty buff jacket and straw hat, takes my arm at once, cooing over Mary. She motions to guide me over the rocky sand. Her face is beaming, and she looks so gentle. John introduces her as the teacher's wife, Kakita. What a rush of relief her presence gives me. How could I have forgotten Tupatai and his wife are here? I breathe deeply, begin to walk with a firmer tread and at last a smile finds my lips.

We make our way to the little church and house, set back in the undergrowth. Kakita motions for me to sit on a box while our possessions are carried up. A large group of villagers turn out to stare at us, and some take to helping. *Just fancy me*, I think through gritted teeth. I am perched on a box like a queen while John is at the boat landing receiving our boxes and getting them sent up to the house. In truth, I would prefer some task too, to shake off so many eyes, but Mary is in my arms. John thinks it prudent for me to keep a lookout to prevent any of our belongings disappearing.

The heat from the vegetation is already cloying at my skin and the hotness hits the back of my throat when I breathe. There is not much air here in the undergrowth, and I crane my head up, as if there must be a sliver of air thwarting me, just out of reach. Kakita comes forward with a leaf and begins to fan me. I am thankful, but I am not comfortable with her doing that. I smile at her and reach out, as if I would like to take the leaf. She hands it to me with a smile.

I fan myself and watch for welcome from the other women, who are fast gathering around me. I smile and that is all it takes. They come forward to shake hands and all wear bright smiles. I put the leaf down so I can shake their hands properly. They paw at Mary and exclaim their delight at her tiny pink fingers, but she is starting to mewl. I know she needs nursing. I look around but there is no suitable, private place.

I take a shawl out of my leather bag and drape it over my shoulder, while sweat runs from my temple to my chin. I am almost faint from the heat, but I canna bring myself to simply open my dress and nurse Mary with no covering. Some of the women around me are bare-bosomed, but there are men here too, and it is not just the thought of arranging myself in front of them that worries me. It is appearing inexperienced. I have not found it easy to nurse Mary at all. Agnes was such a help, but she is not here now. I do not want them to think me incapable. Their children seem as if extensions of themselves. *Oh, to have dear Ma here!*

I stand and pace awhile, patting Mary, hoping she will go back to sleep. I smile at the women, unsure of what to do. A woman motions with her hand for me to sit with them, but instead I turn away. I take myself into the old mission house, where I find an upturned box to sit on. I wince in pain but once I finally have Mary nursing, I sit watching the dust motes dance in the shaft of sunlight from the open window. I wonder what the women think of me now; rude, standoffish perhaps. I bite down on the sting of tears and wipe my shawl around my face.

The *Dayspring* leaves late that afternoon. We finally know how it feels to be alone, new missionaries at their new station, while experienced hands sail away. But it has none of the desolation I am expecting. John looks at me and smiles, and I smile too. It is just us, this is our station now, and we want to begin. He takes my hand and gives it a squeeze as we watch the ship's sails filling with wind.

We head back to the house, where Mary sleeps under some netting in a wicker crib. Four Aneityumese have remained to help us set up. "Time to eat," I say, gesturing to them. They look keen, and we have plenty of provisions, but nothing unpacked to cook with. I pass around a barrel of biscuits, and, thanks to Agnes' kind forethought, cooked salt-beef and bread. She has packed us a basket of eggs sufficient to last some time and a sponge cake too. Kakita comes back with a huge roasted yam, and we all profess our thanks to her.

Tupatai takes off his hat, asks a blessing, and we all proceed with gusto, having eaten nothing since morning. Boxes make do as tables and chairs, and the Aneityumese squat on the ground. It may not be the way people commence their households at home, but I smile at its novelty.

"Tupatai, how is it going here?" John asks slowly, in English.

"We stay along Erakor by and by, Missi, 'tis better there." He explains that the Christian population is about fifty at both places. A heathen population is inland, though diminishing in numbers. They have been friendly but still against the Gospel of Christ.

"Missi Cosh met the bush chief, Marik Tikaikow. He be plenty friendly and ask stop again," Tupatai says.

"That is welcome news! We must go there as soon as we are settled then," John replies. But Tupatai also says the labour vessels have brought havoc in the last few years, with a great many of the young, strong men having been taken or recruited for Fiji and Queensland. It seems the schooner *Lulu* arrived recently from New Zealand, taking twenty-seven men from Efaté alone, the captain paying bribes to the chiefs to acquire them.

Tupatai and Kakita are from Aneityum, so they too have given up home and friends to come here for Christ's sake. These teachers are the true pioneers of this mission. Tupatai tells us he has instructed the islanders in divine things, conducted worship and taught them by example. Mr Cosh translated the *Book of Genesis* and the *Gospel of John* in his time here, and a primer has been prepared of scripture history, too, so at least he has had those to work from.

After our meal, the teachers leave us and we stand in the house, which is more of a shell to be fair, and decide to screen off one end with matting to make a snug bedroom. The other end, where our boxes are piled up, we cover with bedding for now. There is simply no space or enough furniture to unpack it all into, and besides, we need the middle space as sitting room and sleeping spot for the Aneityumese. We start unpacking but, in the thick of things, darkness falls. We can only make our way to our beds, having forgotten to put out lamps while we could still see to find them.

I awake many times in the night, and not just for Mary. The lapping of waves at the beach is comforting enough, but the slightest sounds from around the house have me on edge. The Aneityumese sleep well, going by their murmurs and snores. Outside, a multitude of scratching, chirrups, gecko calls, rooster cries and flapping wings disturb the still air. I hear drums in the distance too, another village I suppose, a feast perhaps. My imagination spikes and runs away with me. It is so close in the bedroom, and I am suffocating once more. *Have faith*, I scold myself, gripping the bedspread in my fists as I calm my breathing and say a silent prayer.

The next I know, the morning light is streaming in, and John is singing a hymn of praise from the church next door. A few voices attempt to join him. How sweet it sounds after my tumultuous night.

Our little band of Aneityumese are a great help, and I think the heathen will hardly attempt any harm while they are with us. Kakita keeps close by and helps me with the unpacking, and with Mary. She has two children of her own and another on the way. When she saw me feeding Mary for the first time, she made a swift and gentle adjustment to her position that brought me instant relief.

John goes away for hours at a time with Tupatai to get to know the area and the people. He seems to take for granted from the first that they are all his dear friends, though most do show a great deal of friendliness, although perhaps more than I am able to return just yet.

News soon spreads of our arrival, and day after day heathen travel from inland to see us. I have hardly arranged the furniture before people come in and lounge about on everything, peering over my shoulder, scrutinising the contents of drawers, although not trusting themselves to touch the letters and books therein. They sit on the chairs, the table, the bed, the windowsills. It unnerves me if I am alone with Mary. I often scoop her up and stand near the door, rocking her, watching their movements, painting a smile on my face. The groups seem different every time and some are fierce-looking warriors.

At first the men all carry axes or muskets into the house, and I do not know what to say. Though when I explain to Tupatai how I feel about it, he talks to them, and they agree to leave them at the door. Some bring us yams as presents but maybe it is not the right time of year because they are as dry as sticks. The hall mirror is an endless source of fascination and the groups huddle around it. Often, they beg the loan of a pair of scissors and a hand mirror to sit under the trees, where they prink and preen, trimming their beards.

Tortoiseshell rings hang in their ears until the lobes are lengthened some inches. Some have figs of tobacco protruding through these holes as well as a pipe, and calico often fills up the space in the other. Ingenious little carrying spaces, you could say. Shells, beads and whales' teeth are strung around their necks and arms. The weight, I imagine, quite burdensome from their quantity.

When I am more used to their presence, I notice how some keep one foot near the door if it is their first time in the house. It is a relief to realise we are not so different after all. We show them how to shake hands, as it is much preferred to the prodding. When Tupatai asks them to shake hands with me though, often they are too nervous. At first some place a leaf on their own hands, so that ours might not touch them, and it softens me toward them.

Soon enough they shake hands on every meeting and say, "*Fakecari.*" Welcome. Sometimes the chief, Poma – who has welcomed us warmly – explains what they say: "Very good you live here." And one said, "I am just wondering at her goodness." This makes me blush.

Little boys and girls, who seem few in number, begin to come with coconuts, and I barter with them in return. Some of the women seem frail and worn but others are plump and open-faced, and far less given to personal foppery than the men. The women come daily with things to sell, and in this way a friendly feeling soon grows between us. In fact, I soon relax around the women.

We are a ramshackle setup to begin with. The house is smaller than I had imagined, and many boxes remain unpacked. The sandy soil outside brings a film of dust onto everything in no time. If it is not the heathen marching in, then hard-shelled, spiky crabs do so, and in the dead of night too, scuttling along the edges of the walls, rousing me from my still fitful sleep.

After a few weeks, we are already making gains. One day when a man, looking toward John, said to his friend, "*Taha neigo?*" John concluded he was asking his name. John pointed toward them and repeated the words, and they at once gave him their names. From then on, he has collected as many names for people and things as he can, writing them down with notes as to their use. We discuss his findings in the evenings after dinner so that I can learn them too.

Some are shy about giving away their language, so John bribes them for words with biscuits. They have names for every tree and plant and even for many of the stars. A little band of them vie to be the ones to accompany John, and soon his ease with them has allayed most of my fears.

With our spirits buoyed, John plans a trip to look over Port Vila, before making his way inland to meet with the prominent chief, Marik Tikaikow, or the "grey Tikaikow" as some call him. He tells me his plans while we take tea on the verandah one afternoon. I assure him that I am strong enough to join him, feeling excitement at the thought.

He shakes his head. "I think you should remain, eh."

"John, I'll not let ye go alone!"

He sighs as he deliberates whether to pursue the matter or not.

"We can bring the teachers to help too," I say.

Eventually, he smiles. "I should like you to come." He reaches across and strokes Mary's cheek as she lies in my lap. I catch his hand and hold onto it for a moment longer, thanking him with my eyes.

Chapter 12

EFATÉ

We walk to Port Vila early the next morning.

"It's the *Carl*," a voice calls out from behind us as we stand at the shore looking over a ship at anchor.

We turn to find a man leaning against a post. A black retriever sits at his feet, panting, while the man wipes his brow with a grubby-looking handkerchief.

John walks over and introduces us.

"Captain McLeod, resident trader," comes the reply.

"What's their purpose?" John asks with a nod toward the ship.

"Land and men, it would appear," Captain McLeod replies. "A few crewmen have come over to trade. I've heard them recruiting while they're at it, tempting the boys to ship off with 'em. They talk about finding land for a plantation too, so I've shown them over the island. I shall be glad to have more civilised neighbours for a change," he says, hitching up his shorts, "should they set up here. Although,"—he laughs—"some of the crew appear to be the scum of Fiji! And what's your purpose then, Mr Stewart?"

I would have thought that obvious, but John is friendly as he tells of our establishing a mission at the villages of Eratap, Pango and Erakor.

"Well, good luck to you. You'll need it!" McLeod chuckles again. His eyes disappear into his florid cheeks as he does so. I look away.

We excuse ourselves and walk along the shore, looking at the other small establishments. They are ramshackle and hold little of interest, so Tupatai suggests we turn inland and press on into Efaté's interior.

Tikaikow's village is Imitang and is said to be the worst place for cannibalism on the island. He is said to have thirty wives by some, and one hundred and twenty by others. He keeps a bodyguard of men to shoot anyone seen speaking to any of them, so jealous is he, Tupatai regales. "Those who are shot are cooked and eaten," he says. "His own wives and children, if they offend him, are killed and eaten!"

John glances at me with a smirk. I shrug, hoping it is a tall tale too.

Kakita has also accompanied us, to help me with Mary, and another man clears the path with a machete. Many times, I stumble over great roots and logs that splay like eagles' claws into our path. I am weak from the heat of the close jungle, but I try to keep my face impassive, thinking of Christina's demeanour. My thoughts are consumed by what we are going to find at the end of this trek.

We stop at a cool stream for a drink. I am mesmerised by the profusion of butterflies all around us as condensation drips from the ferns. Birds sing in the trees. *God will protect us*, I think.

We continue on, but it is hard to see the sky in places. The shadows confuse my sight. Sounds thrum from the jungle, but I know not what makes them. All at once the man with the machete raises his hand and we all stop.

"What's the problem?" John calls out. I am thankful for the rest, and I can see Kakita is tired too. We smile at each other and look about us for a place to rest, but just as we are about to sit, cries reverberate from the jungle around us.

I gasp and search the trees, turning in circles. I blink and realise there are faces there, and spears.

"John!" I call out.

"It is okay, keep calm, please," calls Tupatai.

I reach to take Mary from Kakita and grasp Kakita's hand when she passes her over. John comes to stand with us.

Warriors with spears emerge all around us. They begin talking to Tupatai and the man with the machete. It is hard to tell from their tone whether there is friendship in their speech. They could be talking about the weather. They could be filled with anger.

Tupatai motions to us. The warriors raise their eyebrows and eye us with suspicion, still talking to Tupatai, questioning him.

It is as if time stands still. I look to John, wondering what we should do. Mary starts to cry, awoken by the stop in motion and my pounding heart, no doubt. The warriors all turn to face me.

I try to shush her, but I am too anxious. Her cries grow louder. I swallow hard and do all I can think to do to the warriors around us – I smile. Then I shrug and say, exasperated, "Babies!"

The men smile back and raise their eyebrows at me, knowing. Some laugh. Some come closer and peer into Mary's shawls and talk animatedly to each other, smiling and showing unabashed affection on their faces.

"Hello," John says at last, raising his hand.

Each warrior raises their hand in hello too, and relief sweeps over us.

"It is okay, we follow them," Tupatai says at last.

The warriors still surround us, but we move off along the track, coming up a valley. We cross a broad plain covered with thick brush, and at last emerge on the edge of a village. Imitang.

Women and children dart to their huts while the men come out to their *malel¸* or meeting place. The warriors move into the space and squat down, not bothered about our presence any longer. We hold up our hands in hello to the other people gathering. I resist the urge to wipe my brow or look out behind me. My heart beats wildly once more, but I keep my eyes open and smile at the people before us. Clothing is conspicuous by its absence, I notice.

A tall, plump fellow eventually comes forward, clapping his hands before laughing jubilantly. His grey woolly hair flops about as he claps.

John steps forward, his hand outstretched. Marik Tikaikow, I presume it is, frowns and looks at it for a few moments before taking John's hand and shaking it vigorously. Without letting go with one hand, his other hand begins squeezing John's arm at the top, down to his wrist and then over his midriff and continuing down one of his legs. I gasp, despite my resolve, and anxiety arises that I am to expect the same. "Annetta, dear, it is okay," John says to reassure me.

Marik turns to me and laughs. "*Yufala e no fraet,* Annetta-dear! *Mifala e no save kaekae yufala!*"

My eyes widen but then Kakita whispers next to me, "Don't be frightened, Annetta-dear! We're not going to eat you!"

A nervous laugh escapes me as Marik continues and Kakita translates, "Your teachers are here, we not kill them. You come here, if we wanted kill you, we would have killed you long before."

I let out a long breath. He is indeed an imposing man – tall and broad – and his voice has a resonance that compels to be obeyed. But I realise it is easy to do as he asks – I am not afraid.

John says, "We are here to teach the word of God … and we will help you in any way we can."

Marik nods and motions for us to sit. Another man brings out roasted yams and a soft pudding, but only a couple of women make an appearance. Marik nods as John speaks more, but he does not touch the food. "Chiefs don't eat of a meal cooked on the same fire as for others," Kakita whispers to me. I am so grateful she is with me.

Marik's eyes are yellowed and bloodshot, with age and kava drinking, I suppose, but they hold a mischievous spark. His skin is scarred and lined, but strong muscles lie beneath and flex in the sunlight. He says, in all seriousness, "*Mifala e fraet long skul.*"

Kakita whispers as he continues, "We are frightened of school. Suppose we come to school, get sick and die."

"A life in darkness is a fate worse than death, Marik." John lays his hands on the ground in front of himself. "'All manner of sin shall be forgiven, for him that cometh unto me, I will in no wise cast out,' thus sayeth the Lord."

As they talk, Marik seems to admire our kindness and says our message is good, but they seem to think the worship only fit for women. It requires them to wear clothes and that, of course, is not manly. Anything mean, weak or cowardly is called womanly, I am learning. I realise how much I owe to the gospel for having elevated us from that state in which heathenism places every woman.

Finally, Marik says, "How can we give up the *kastom* of our fathers?"

I look to John. *Well, how can they?* I wonder too. We seem to be asking so much.

John speaks more of the one true God, and by and by Marik agrees that those who wish to come to worship can do so, in peace. John asks that he visit too, but at this, Marik's face just reads *perhaps*.

"For now, we can but pray that light shines into his darkened understanding," John says, buoyed by the encounter. "I knew it would go better with all of us there," he adds.

We set off back to Pango in the last light of day, with a hearty farewell from the grey Tikaikow.

On our walk back, my thoughts turn to our *uota*, chief, and how differently these tribes live, yet they are not far from each other. Although a heathen and with two wives, Poma has shown us the greatest kindness since our arrival. He urged the people to accept a missionary, though we know it has angered some.

Poma wears the insignia of rank with blue tattoos on his chest and arms – whorls of leaf patterns, intricately drawn. Anything good the chiefs do not want the people to possess is *tabu* – sacred for their use alone. One of these for Poma is a good fishing spot. It is his great delight to go at night and catch flying fish, lured by a lantern. He brings them to the cookhouse silver and wet in the morning, giving Simetone, our new cook, strict instructions to dress them for our breakfast. It always brings a smile to my lips when I spy a wickerwork fish trap at the door. Poma's eyes glisten with delight as he sees us enjoy them, for he is our unfailing guest every morning and evening. He so enjoys a cup of tea and the soft bread I make for him, too.

The sky is black as we arrive back in the village after our trek, and all is quiet. Poma's hut looks deserted but small fires flicker around other huts. Voices are hushed, but I think little of it as I am so wayworn. My mind is to Mary and getting her settled into her crib and getting off my feet. I thank Kakita for her help today before rushing into the mission house and taking off my bonnet.

I sigh in relief that all appears as we left it. John enters the house behind me, and some others follow, clamouring for his attention. Why they canna let him have a moment's peace after the long day I do not know.

As I emerge from the sleeping area, I notice Kakita is back and her face is strained. She comes over to me and reaches for my hand, worry knitting her brow.

"What's wrong? Has something happened?" I whisper.

"Yes, Missi. Come, you must speak with John." I try to control my rush of thoughts as Kakita leads me outside. Already, half the village appear to be standing around John. Voices are raised and some of the women are crying. I catch John's eyes and his face is pale.

Poma is standing next to John and wipes his hand down his face. He turns to his people and motions for them to calm.

"The ship, Missi, at Vila, came in today and drag men on board," Poma says, his face set in anger.

"The one you traded with?" asks John.

Poma nods. "Men come to the village unasked. Talk went round they are thieves, come to take men away. We fire rocks, arrows."

"We take our canoes," another man steps forward and says, "follow boat back to ship." He waves his arm in the direction of the sea.

I think of the men we saw at Port Vila from that vessel Captain McLeod was talking about. The *Carl*, was it? What did he call them? *The scum of Fiji*.

The man continues talking in an Efaté dialect, so Tupatai translates for us. "The white men rounded and shot at them," he says. "The white men plucked the people out of the water … like fish."

We can scarcely believe it. This has happened and we were away. The first time these people could have used our help, and we were not there for them.

"My son, Missi, my son … they take Taniela, my son …" Poma is distraught, and I realise the young chief is among the number stolen.

"We will write at once to the Consul in Fiji, Mr March, as well as to the Premier of Queensland to ask for their return, Poma," John says, placing his hand on Poma's shoulder.

"Simetone, help me make some tea," I say, but many of the villagers are already filing away. I feel helpless, and they realise there is not much we can do either.

Damn those slavers! My anger spikes.

Once we are back inside, John says he must attend to some things before he retires. I lie down on the bed as he paces about, knowing he is doing little but fret.

PART II

Sail oh!
Far, far upon the sea
Looking out for blacks are we
We've got a decent cargo in the hold.

If a hurricane don't blow
We'll soon back in Queensland show
With a good lot of kanakas to be sold.

— "The Recruiting Song"

About our Consul in Fiji
Was held a consultation
His conduct as all agree
A grievance worth narration.

As of his just authority
He oversteps the borders
What joy t'will be when Mr March
Receives his marching orders.

— *Fiji Times*, December 10, 1872

Chapter 13

PANGO

Iwake early but do not rise until first light for fear of waking Mary. I bundle up some of yesterday's bread and walk to Poma's hut. He is sitting, staring at the ground, quite still. His two wives, Terokia and Sopi, are sweeping the ground with a brush of sticks and collecting pots while fowls scratch in the sand and dust around them.

They smile and shake my hand, but I am unsure to go to Poma in case I am disturbing him. Then his gap-toothed smile is welcome enough when he turns and sees me. He hastily lays down a banana leaf when he sees I am going to sit. He grasps my hands before I even have a chance to speak, and he looks into my eyes with such an intense sadness that I catch my breath.

"Me not good man, Missi," he says then in English. I begin to shake my head, but he goes on, "I have done bad things. Your God is not happy." He shakes his head.

"Because of your son?"

Poma scratches a rough line in the earth with a twig while he thinks. Then says, "Men came in ships and wanted our men. We wanted trade, we wanted muskets and toback. They gave us these if we let our men go in the ships. They say they be gone three yams, so we thought we see them again. They were young, without wives. I took the muskets and toback, Missi, and they take our men." Poma lowers his eyes to the bare ground.

"From what we've learned, Poma, all vessels carry a trade box with which to … compensate the chiefs for the people who go away. Did the men want to go?"

"Some yes, some no. I made it clear if they did not it would be worse for them. It is for this I am punished. They took my boy, Missi. I did *not* sell him. I would not have let him go. He was my sister's son. That in our *kastom* is closer to me than my own son. He was to be chief soon as I am not long for this life. They stole him. Taniela has a wife, two sons … Your God, he is punishing me."

I do not know what to say. I think of Agnes. I take a breath and reach for Poma's hand. "God loves you, Poma. The people who took your son are to blame for this, not you. God will show us the way … We are writing to the Consul in Fiji today and will do everything we can to bring Taniela home."

Poma nods, claps my hands with his own and smiles through his tears.

"Poma, will you let your wives and daughter, Lameka, come to the house to learn to sew?"

He nods and says, "Taniela's wife, Kawiwi, she come too?"

"Of course." I smile.

At the end of our first five weeks, the cry of "Sail-oh!" rouses us into a flurry of excitement. We soon spy the *Dayspring*, come to pay us her farewell visit for the season. It will bear away our voluntary helpers back to Aneityum, as well as Dr Munro to Melbourne. He is carried ashore with George to see how we are settling in. It is such a joy to have their company, any company, even George's, that I confess to wanting to protract their visit as much as possible. I talk more than is necessary, or indeed wanted, I am sure.

We sit on the verandah while Simetone roasts a fowl for our dinner. George entertains us with descriptions of the other islands they visited. He tells of the fiery volcano at Ambrym and the islanders there. "They are a strongly made people," he says, emboldened by his attentive audience, "oh, but you should have seen the natives on Maré! They go away outside of a sunken reef, upon which the waves are rolling and breaking in fine style, and then mount upon the crest of an advancing wave on a plank of wood. They career along on top of it, then hurl over into the boiling water. It looks rather dangerous work, but they seem to enjoy the sport amazingly." He stands and attempts to impersonate their actions. I laugh and envisage the islanders show a great deal more grace at it.

"The Maré men are famous swimmers," Dr Munro agrees. "And you'll be pleased to hear we found the Frasers well on Erromango, Mrs Stewart—"

"Mr Fraser remarked that the population appears to have diminished quite considerably since he was last in the islands though," George cuts in before I can respond, though I sigh in relief.

"The islands of this group were at one time thickly populated," Dr Munro says, "but the natives are now *greatly* diminished, yes. Sadly, it is mostly through our means … Disease, unscrupulous traders, muskets with which they hasten their own demise … and now they're being carried off in their droves by slavers."

"But there have been many instances of ships' crews being killed by the natives too, have there not?" George says, while Dr Munro labours to get his breath back.

"Indeed, Mr Campbell … it is their custom to meet an eye for an eye, blood for blood no matter whether it is revenged on the correct person or not. Soon after some teachers were murdered once, a sickness took about one hundred and fifty lives." Dr Munro explains how it spread to the mainland and struck down great numbers, including Pomare – Poma's father – who had remained faithful through all the ups and downs and died a Christian.

"When Mr Cosh came here, the heathen were still talking about a sickness as a judgement upon the people who killed and ate the teachers. Thus, light and shadow have pursued each other, the light brightening for a moment but upon the whole the shadows deepening … It was the continual loss of teachers that convinced me we must train New Hebridean converts to take the good news to their own people."

Dr Munro looks down with a heavier weight of sadness on him than I have yet seen. *Will I be this dejected if we are here that long?* It is not a question I can even begin to contemplate, or want to. His weight of despondency falls upon me too.

"Look, the longer I live amongst them," George says with a somewhat annoyed expression, his fingers rubbing over his black obsidian, "the more I know of their character and ways. I am now beginning to see how unjust it is to class all the people of one island under the same category, or to brand all of them with a bad name for the evil actions of a few."

These words seem a revelation from George, and we all savour them in silence as the waves lap at the shore.

"They are assaulted at their home, Mr Campbell, or they are dragged away from it to be assaulted elsewhere," Dr Munro finally says, his voice ringing with the hopelessness of it all, but he is determined to go on.

"There are no persons who can explain the terms of a contract to them. The people speak at least twenty different languages. No white man – with the exception of the missionaries – can speak any one of them. They have no words to express years, wages and so forth. They cannot form the slightest conception of what three years' steady labour under plantation laws even means," his voice wavers with emotion.

"They sometimes arrive home with literally nothing save, perhaps, a few shillings' worth of goods as the fruit of their three or four or even five years' toil. Some come back broken down in health, while some never come back at all but die on the plantations. They're not of a robust constitution, and are unaccustomed to steady labour, so it tells on them severely, however well they may be treated. While those who're treated as no better than slaves cannot be expected to return stronger and healthier men than when they left."

"And yet they still go," John says at last.

"You're here to educate them, Mr Stewart. Let us hope you can help stem the flow!"

I gaze out to the ocean.

"We seem particularly in want of young, strong men here," John says at last. "From what we've seen, so much more than normal has fallen to the womenfolk, already so overburdened with their day-to-day chores. Only the young and old are left, it seems."

"Particularly the old, in fact," I say.

"Infanticide has long prevailed here, Mrs Stewart. The women are woefully overburdened and often cannot cope with more children when they come. The *King Oscar* anchored a few years ago and lured away nearly all the young men of Erakor from under Mr Cosh's nose. Those on whom he'd expended a great deal of strength and hope. It was a severe blow to his work and a source of great discouragement. He felt the impact in ways that could never have been predicted …" Dr Munro lapses into coughing once more and his voice trails off.

"Missionaries make a great sacrifice here, Mrs Stewart, of that I am certain," George says. "The work is to them one of toil and great discomfort, not to speak of danger, and so those who sneer at missionaries, ascribing to them motives of personal gain or whatever, are very much in the wrong, I believe. They're perhaps influenced by a bitter prejudice against everything Christian and philanthropic."

Late that evening, George uncovers my old harmonium and brings music out of it, to the delight of us all. The following morning, he leaves us some fine drawings of island scenery to decorate our new home. He will reproduce the rest in a volume of his tour, to be published on his return. But for now, he will go to Ifira, where he has been given permission to make a settlement.

Dr Munro's last act before he is carried back on board the *Dayspring* is to sit under a spreading banyan tree and hold the hands of an aged blind man, whom he calls David. He was baptised by Dr Munro some time before Mr Cosh came and appears such a happy and contented fellow. "Who can tell the value of each jewel that adorns the Saviour's crown?" he says, after farewelling his friend.

After our own farewells to the Aneityumese helpers, the captain and crew, Dr Munro and George, we stand on the reef and watch the little vessel as she rises and falls on the vast sea beyond the surf, carrying our letters to reassure all that we are safe, as well as our earnest letters for Consul March in Fiji.

As we wave goodbye, it feels like staring into the distance of time we will now be alone, and emotion surges in me that I have tried to subdue. The feelings of desolation are like a breaking wave about to overwhelm me, and my legs falter. John's steady, firm grip is around my waist, although his face shows tight, pinched lips. He feels it too.

Chapter 14

ERAKOR

On January 6th, the wind rises all afternoon and the aneroid falls. "John, it's too early, surely? Agnes said to put battens on the roof from the 12th."

"Try not to worry, Ann. It's just wind at this stage."

We retire for the night, but the wind rises higher until the roar outside is like distant thunder, while the waves pound the beach. I clutch at John's arm in the darkness, and he closes his hand over mine. By midnight the whole house is shaking, the thatch lifting and creaking with each new gust. I am trembling, sure it is to come crashing down on our heads at any moment.

"Get Mary, Ann. Let's secure the house any way we can, eh."

My heart races as I fling back the quilt. I scoop up Mary and awkwardly take down pictures and place things in boxes and drawers with my free arm, throwing a blanket over my seam tray and sewing machine, while John secures windows and doors. Finally, we just throw things under the tables and bed, thinking it should afford them some protection, as time feels to be running out.

The walls bow and shake before the thatch begins tearing away up at the ridge pole, the rain soaking down on us in an instant. I cry out and John reaches for my hand. We scoop up blankets and head into the torment. We crouch together, expecting to be dealt a blow by something flying past in the black as objects whoosh around our ears. We make for the church, knowing it to be a sturdier structure.

Spray, cold and blinding, dashes into our faces as we move, the rain in torrents. In the short distance before we get inside, we are drenched. We fall in at the door and find the teachers and some villagers huddled together. They smile and beckon us over, so we crouch with them, shivering and gasping for breath.

We keep lighting the small lamp each time it is extinguished by the wind, despite its sheltered corner. I take comfort in the shadowy gaze of my little girl, rudely awoken but somehow unperturbed lying in my arms. John puts his arm around us, and I rest my head on his shoulder. He holds me tighter when shivers tremble through me anew.

The walls shake in the fierce wind until daylight. Snatches of sleep are grasped but not held onto for long. As soon as we think it safe, we emerge into a gloomy morning, sticky in our clothes from the damp blankets, and with wild grey clouds overhead. The wind has spent its fury, but the sea is still loppy, and everything seems cold.

The mission house has lost its roof though some of the walls have held. Fences lie flattened all around. Coconut trees, ripped from the sandy ground as if from butter, lie strewn at queer angles atop each other, or snapped in two like twigs, their precious baubles tossed about. Hardly a green leaf can be seen; the salt spray and wind has browned and scorched everything, as though in fire.

Everything in the house is soaked and covered inches thick with thatch and dirt. I am glad then that not all had been unpacked. The windows are smashed where branches have been hurled against them, and there is no clear space on the floor even to sit and take stock. I do not know where to begin. The villagers, too, stand about and talk quietly in wonder at the thorough desolation.

After looking upward for strength, I hand Mary to Utevo – a young girl who has taken to following me about over the last few weeks – and set to getting the main room cleared before righting what little furniture remains. John sets the people to tasks and says to Simetone that we will not mind for breakfast but that if he can only manage to milk the goats – if he can find them – that will be sufficient.

The cookhouse door is blockaded with debris and not a bit of dry wood can be seen, but Simetone shakes his head and says, "No worry." Soon enough he appears with the coffee pot steaming. How we are all comforted by that simple gesture.

A few days later, whistles ring out from the shore. Charlie, a local man recently returned from working at a whalers', has rowed over now the seas have calmed. John and Poma gasp as he starts talking to them, though he talks too quickly for me to keep up. I catch the word *Dayspring*, and sure enough John turns and says, "She went on the reef at Aneityum in the hurricane."

"No!" I cry. Our white-winged angel. It is a relief when Charlie says no one was harmed, but what will happen without our little ship, our lifeline to the wider world? Not only that, but she was returning to the islands, bringing us supplies, so we know this will affect the months ahead.

I worry for Christina and know she will be for me. I write many letters now, feeling sure another ship will service us soon, but entrusting our letters to traders when we can. Often, they pass with news as they go about the islands.

We soon hear that the wreck of the *Dayspring* has been sold to a French slaving company. They have cut a passage through the reef and floated her again in the bay, elated, no doubt, at the prospect of employing her in the bloodstained kanaka traffic. Our souls sink. Many islanders will trust themselves to the *Dayspring* and revenge could be taken on the missionaries when the deception is found out. Day and night we pray for a different outcome as we think of the intended degradation of our noble little ship.

After the storm, the season is hot and wet. Sharp showers descend, and then the sun pours down his rays as steamily as before. I am becoming convinced that Pango is not a healthy place to be. In the heat it is suffocating, and I am enclosed and cut off. I am forever looking for signs of fever in Mary, petrified she will become ill.

John shares my disquiet. We resolve not to rebuild here but move to Erakor and erect a new house there instead. Being surrounded by water, yet still sheltered, Erakor enjoys cooling breezes and fine views. We have building supplies left to us, and Mr Morrison's old mission house to make use of, so John quickly plans it out once we have righted what remains here.

John seems to shrug the difficulties off and, being lithe and nimble, works effortlessly through the heat. He mobilises the able-bodied and oversees the building of the new house. Poma has instructed the people to help us, and they raise no objection, at least that we can see. But I feel to be in a time that does not exist. The women go to their plantations of a morning, John is busy building … I do not know what my place is other than to take care of his and Mary's needs. I am attempting to learn the language, but I am finding it hard.

The old house at Erakor was patched up before we moved some things in, but there is little point trying to make it a home while I wait for the new one to be ready. Naively, I imagined myself working away as a teacher and taking sewing classes and all the rest, but it simply canna happen straightaway.

Many days I spend in the shade on the ocean side of the island, watching the foaming breakers. I cool Mary in the heat, and drink in the beautiful seascape around me, before wandering along the rocky shore, seeking out curious shells. I know I become lost to my daydreams once more, and I know I should find more to help with.

Birds are not numerous, but I study those I can see. Two kinds of pigeon – one with bronze wings – some shore birds and a kind of thrush are the usual ones. But also this small bird with a crimson head and curved bill, which sucks the honey from the flowers and trills cheerfully in the trees. That is my favourite. Such a happy, ceaseless song. It reminds me of Tilly. I think much of my dear sister at home.

At sundown the flying foxes abound. These strange creatures, a delicacy to some, come over from neighbouring islands in flocks to feed on plants. They make such a screeching cacophony you would think murder was afoot, before they roost like ripe fruit pods dangling from the guano-streaked casuarina trees.

Sometimes I lie on the boat landing and stare into the dreamy depths of the clear-green lagoon, at the shimmering fish or the bright corals within, or at the multitude of blue and yellow starfish. It brings to mind George quoting from his Milne Edwards book. *Animals organised for a sedentary mode of life, having no locomotive organs …* I imagine George pushing his spectacles onto his copious nose as he speaks. I even miss his ungainly demeanour. I am surprised he has not been to visit us yet as Ifira is not far away.

Other times, I watch sea snakes gliding over the rocks – bright bands of silver and black – as they dip and wind under and over, round and through. Or the puffed-up sea slugs that lie semi-torpid on the sandy bottom. The sea is so flat and glass-like here, almost as if it were a lid, keeping everything secret beneath.

Some days I wade into the cooling freshness, where no one can see, feeling the water rise up my legs with each new step, biting my lip at the exhilaration of it. It is delicious.

The sand around the trees is dotted with holes, and I try to spot the crabs scuttling out and in again and show them to Mary, who smiles and flaps her pale little arms. My sweet, fair-haired angel is such a consolation to me when I long for company. The women always stroke her face as they chatter on, but I know not what they are saying. Kakita and Tupatai have stayed on at Pango to rebuild there, and I miss Kakita's quiet company too.

I can walk around Erakor in under an hour on the winding coral paths amongst the trees, or on the beach at a slower pace. Sometimes, canoes just offshore catch my eye, and boys leap into the surf from the poles on their sides. They laugh and yell in delight, the sun sparkling off their wet skin, while one of them sits baling out the water. It seems a happy, carefree life.

The winds are strong today, and I sit and watch the grandeur of the "green breakers and the wind-tossed foam," recalling Jean Ingelow's poetry that Ma loves. I think of them at home together before the slanting rays of the sun warn me to escape the miasma of the dusk air. The sun sets opposite our Erakor home. I know I will never tire of watching it dip into the ocean. The sky is so often an outpouring of radiance then mellowed light; every shade reflected from the liquid depths of the Pacific.

Hunger, tiredness, missing family – these things bring out a different, true side to people, I decide. I am not suffering hunger, at least, but sleep eludes me still, and I miss home terribly. I want to go home, and I realise fully, for the first time, that I cannot. I chide myself for my self-pity but cry anyway, then paint on resolve for John's eyes.

I begin to rise from the sand, as the itch from the sand fleas is driving me to despair, when a cry rings out.

Chapter 15

ERAKOR

"Sail-oh!"

I scan the seascape.

Soon, a small boat is wending its way to the boat landing. A mail sack is passed to Marifatu, who has become John's right-hand man. Before the man rows away, they talk for a little. I make my way to John before Marifatu comes over and relays the news that the French slavers, after anchoring the *Dayspring* in the bay, went ashore to celebrate their good fortune. They drank and feasted but the wind arose, their prize dragged her anchor, and at daybreak she was seen again on the reef. This time her back was broken in two, forever unfit for service, either fair or foul. We are elated and distraught all at once, knowing we will never see her again, but at least she will not become part of the slave trade either.

Once Mary is settled after dinner, I devour the letters from home and am comforted to find all is well. John receives news that Dr Munro, after arriving in Melbourne in November, went to his eternal rest in Geelong on December 15th. What a great loss to the mission. My heart sinks, knowing I will not receive his wise counsel again. At least peace has come to him at last. We learn, too, of David Livingstone in Africa having gone to his eternal rest. To him his calling was no sacrifice – he was simply paying back a debt to God. "Shame upon us missionaries if we're outdone by slave traders!" His words hold a whole new meaning for us now.

We receive news from Christina and Hugh, and learn they are rebuilding, too, and it seems Christina is in the same lonely state of mind as myself, although she has suffered frequently from fever. But somehow the letters are out of order, and heat prickles the back of my neck as I canna resolve my confusion. I gather all the letters, my hands shaking, and put them in date order to start again, in the hope I have not really read what I think I just have. But no, I am not wrong. The last is a missive from Hugh.

Dear John and Annetta

It has fallen to me to write to you of our latest sorrow, and I shall do so without further ado.

With the damp place in which we've been living, dear Christina has suffered much from fever and was getting weaker every day. As her time of trouble was drawing on, I feared she would never get over it.

She became so much worse one night that I roused the men to go in the boat for Mr and Mrs Allen, the traders. They arrived and Mrs Allen was most kind and attentive. It was a great comfort to have her with us, but Christina got no better.

On the 18th our child was born — already with Jesus. For hours, Christina's life trembled in the balance. It was not until the next day there seemed any improvement. The Allens had gone home, but the natives were sympathetic; they could not have been more so.

On account of the heathen, it was not safe for us to go to the graveyard by day, so I awaited nightfall, when Soso and I crossed the river in a canoe. In the darkness I buried our little girl in a tiny grave, just at the feet of the martyred Gordons.

Christina has begun slowly to improve. How thankful I am that my dear wife has been spared. We didn't expect it. Soso gathered the natives, and they were praying for her. When she began to improve, I went in among them and said, "Why, Soso; Mrs Fraser is better!" "Of course, Missi," he said, "have we not asked God to make her well?"

He seemed surprised at my want of faith, and it has been a lesson to me.

I shall end this missive here. Our hearts cannot delve more fully into this now, but with the Lord's help we shall recover day by day and see the light anew. Sadly, I confess I have brought this upon my dear wife. Not because she came with me to the New Hebrides, but because it was I who requested taking up James' post here to Mr Archer as soon as we heard of his death. There has surely been more anxiety and weight of worry here than it was possible for Christina to bear.

Your friends,

Hugh and Christina

I lie on my bed and weep. I do not know how Christina will sustain any more difficulties. My anger rises at Hugh, too, remembering the note he passed Mr Archer. I wonder again what, for my friend, I can do.

A little later, John seeks me out and strokes his finger across my tear-stained cheek.

"Anything I can do, eh?" He tips his head in question.

I pass him the letter. "Did you know?" I ask when he reaches the end. He recoils his head, knowing I will not like his answer.

"There was no dissuading him from his course, Ann."

"Did you try?"

"No … Hugh felt compelled to be on Erromango. Always liked a challenge that one!" He smiles.

"Don't make light of it, John. Would you have discussed it with me, if it were you?" I look into his eyes.

"I would hope you'd support me wherever I felt it God's will to go. You've come this far. Does the final island really make that much difference?"

"To some … I *have* supported you, have I not? It's the concealment, John, the deception, if you like. He should have discussed it with her. He knew she didna want to be there."

"Oh, come on … Look, I shall always discuss such issues with you, my dearest. All right?" He squeezes my hand, but I just give him a nod. We will see.

I write loving letters to Christina that I hope will raise her strength, while John hurries on with the new house. I have made Mr Morrison's old house as comfortable as I can in the meantime, and have brought over the cook, Simetone, from Pango too. He is doing a good job of learning how we like things. He only agreed to come after hearing he would not be obliged to marry one of the girls. He seemed relieved when John told him we did not come here to make matches. We will leave that for them to look after.

Simetone has long, straggly hair that I worry over with regard to fla-vouring the cooking, but do not think it polite to suggest he cut it off. John does not wish them to be forced either. "These things will be given up when their hearts are changed," he says.

I intimate to Simetone that we could at least tie it back, to which he nods and smiles his crooked grin. He has only been with us a few days before others come and ask that they might be allowed to do something for the Missi too. There are many tasks to be done: chopping wood, black-leading the stove, looking after livestock, and so on.

By the middle of April, the three-roomed, weather-boarded house, including a wide verandah, is finished as far as can be done just then. The roof takes an enormous amount of thatching. The leaf is tied on a reed about four-feet long, forming neat fringes. The men come in a band, each carrying a load on their shoulders, sometimes from miles away.

They sing and shout with the lead man blowing a conch shell. Others, though, hang around and pick up nails with their toes, passing them to their hands before making off, a picture of innocence. Soon someone is posted to keep watch.

The house is a model of simplicity and comfort and looks out to the seascape beyond. A fine coral walk winds down to a gate and reed fences like light basketwork enclose the property. We plant bananas inside the fence line; their great broad leaves stirring with the slightest breeze. Behind the house is the cookhouse, bathhouse and other storerooms.

Altogether, I think mine a lovely and inviting home. Most importantly, it feels healthy. I do not believe I shall ever appreciate a house as I do this one, having seen the labour it cost. We lay the floors with fresh coconut matting and all is clean and neat. I relish not keeping a pine floor white with scrubbing sand too — always my most detested task at home. Poma's daughter, Lameka, as well as Utevo, the young girl who is so good with Mary, have come to live with us and help as well.

By careful imitation of their sounds, John can understand the people well by the time the housebuilding is done. But the number of different languages perplexes us. If people visit from villages further afield, it is hard to hear similarities in their tongue. This will be a challenge.

The building of our own home reinvigorates me. It is our true beginning; we have our footing. I resolve to not get lost in myself so much anymore. I have a job to do. I suggest to John that we hold a housewarming for the village to get to know the people better, and he readily agrees. Word spreads and islanders from all areas gather when the day arrives. George makes the trek over from Ifira too, though I am taken up with tasks and leave him to John to catch up with.

I help Simetone cook great pots of rice and make tea, while Lameka and Utevo hand it around. I am more relaxed with the men now, who all wish to look through the *great suma* as they call the new house. Tupatai says they enjoy new properties because the fleas have not moved in yet.

After the food, everyone is lounging around, so I bring out the harmonium. I am nervous as I sit to the keys and take a deep breath to steady myself. I soon relax at their enthralled faces — mouths and eyes wide open at the sound. If I stop, someone steps up and says, "Missi, make him bokis (box) sing! Plenty man come hear you make-im bokis sing!" I can only laugh.

At the end of the evening, most people have dispersed, so I clear away dishes and pots. My back is aching. I know Mary will be ready for nursing soon, so I decide most of what is left can wait until morning. Mary is asleep so I do not light a lamp in the bedroom as I begin unpinning my hair.

A shifting sound startles me from under the window, and it is too loud to be a crab. I turn and hold my breath as I scan the shadows, realising a form is lying on the floor.

"Who's there?" I say sternly.

The form turns over and it is a man. His eyes open and he blinks at me a few times before raising himself. He is tall, and I step backwards, putting my hand to my locket.

"Oh, what are you doing in here? I don't have anything for you. Get out!" I do not hide my agitation or fear.

His face turns angry. "What for you look me?" He raises his hand as if to shoo me off. "I no st-eal! You plenty lie." He comes toward me, and I back up.

I gasp as he comes closer.

"I no st-eal," he says again.

I feel for the door handle behind me and open it just as John is entering. "Ann?"

"This man was in here. He startled me!"

"Oh … It is okay, Kalumtak. No problem," John says, seeing the anger on Kalumtak's face. They talk for a few minutes before John nods and says, "Sorry."

After he has left, John says, "He wanted to sleep in the house, Ann, that's all. He meant no harm. He was angry that your first thought is that he would harm you or steal something. Try not to be so quick to anger, *please*."

"John! I was in fear. I'm alone in here with Mary. I didna know his purpose. Think of Christina …"

He frowns and turns to leave the room again.

I clench my fists. *Am I really being unreasonable?* I wonder. My anger boils at not being heard, again.

Chapter 16

ERAKOR

The air is cool between us for the next few days, though I am sure John has not given the matter further thought. It is easy for him to say to control my anger. He gave no thought to *my* situation. I am ruminating on the matter a few evenings later, while enjoying the quiet starlight from the verandah. I rock Mary in my arms when I give a passing glance down to the sea. The vision of a great ship rises before my eyes.

I turn away and back again and there in the dim light really does loom a large schooner in full sail, close to shore and framed by the trees. I recover myself and shout, "Sail-oh!", startling Mary. I laugh and rain kisses to her forehead as the whole place is ablaze with voices in a twinkling.

John rushes onto the verandah. Utevo and Lemeka tumble out behind him, worried it is the French. It might be an English gunboat, and I worry that they have landed with no one to receive them. John grabs his clerical suit and dashes out the front gate, putting it on as he goes.

I put Mary in her crib. I have only just got the drawing room lit and the antimacassars arranged when Lameka rushes in to announce that Missi is bringing in "great chiefs as tall as trees". I go to the cookhouse to light the stove and, when I return, the hallway is filling with villagers eager to know if it is a man-o'-war ship. I am as eager to know as they, and pace the hallway, waiting for John to come out and tell us who they are.

I look down at the print I am wearing. It is clean but a bit old-fashioned and hardly the thing for Her Majesty's representatives. I sigh as impatience gets the better of me, and, with a last smooth of my dress, I enter the drawing room with a smile. Inside, two men, with nothing on but dirty old nether garments and threadbare woollen shirts stand next to John. Lameka, who I instructed to follow with the salver and cake-basket, is close behind me. I turn and usher her out again as subtly as I can before coming back into the room.

The men are asking John to sign a notice for them. He looks it over, then says, "You want me to sign that the labourers have voluntarily engaged with your ship with a full understanding of the nature and conditions of their agreements? Don't you have a government representative on board to do this?"

"He's, er, unwell at present," the larger of the two men replies.

"Well, where did you enlist these people?"

"Havannah Harbour," the other blurts out, and a look of reproach follows from his friend.

"Then you asked Reverend MacDonald to sign this?"

"Er, we couldn't locate the Reverend gentleman."

"You mean he would *not*! I'll not be party to anything akin to slavery or the slave trade either," John says.

The larger man's face turns sour before he turns to the islanders in the room. "What you want stay here for? Plenty muskets, tobacco long Queensland, my friends."

"Get out of this house," John says, his voice raised but even. But the men are already going, chuckling as they walk out.

Once everyone has filed out, I look to John. He shakes his head in disbelief.

In the morning, determination is written on John's face. I feel the same. The ships appear to be increasing in number. We must establish regular school and sewing classes. We must occupy the people's minds at home.

At first, attendance at school is irregular and for weeks no more than three or four will come at a time. One day, when John opens a book and reads aloud, some seem to shrink back from him. I realise they are suspicious of the book.

Poma's younger son, Samuel, then grabs the book. "Missi, make it speak to me," he says in awe, turning it over and back as though the words should tumble out in a formed speech.

"You don't know how to read yet, how to make it speak to you, but I will teach you. Then it will speak to you as it does to me, Samuel," John replies.

The younger boys are harder to cajole. Some show an interest, but then we find their parents have forbidden them from coming, so progress is slow. Most valued is a fishing line. This proves a useful lure in tempting them to learn, although it can work against us as often some ask payment when taught a lesson and then are surprised when we decline to give it.

Sometimes a party come in and say, "We want to go to school and church, but we have no *su gori*." We give each a shirt and *kalu*, loincloth. Soon the same lot turn up again, naked save their sheaths, no *su gori*, but would like to get some to attend church and school. It takes a while to realise how we are being taken in.

I am getting disheartened when one day Poma's first wife, Terokia, comes to look at the house. John whispers to me, "Annetta, the younger ones look up to her. If you can get her enlisted, others will be sure to follow."

I put it to Terokia, but she laughs at a half-blind old woman like her learning anything. Then John approaches her with some eyeglasses. She puts them on and gasps and smiles. She then comes regularly.

We start lessons with letters and writing on slate. Everything but numbers can be done in their dialect, for they have no numbers. They use the fingers on one hand for five, "my hand", and then "my two hands", then their toes and beyond this is "many", "a great many", and so on. We have to introduce English numerals. I grin when one evening I find Utevo under the table, counting up her neighbour's toes when she has run out of her own.

Utevo has beautiful large eyes that glisten with mischievousness, and there is no telling what she is thinking or planning. She covers her tidy white teeth with the back of her hand when she giggles, which is often. She enjoys a joke and often laughs so hard she has to work it off by rolling on the ground. But this has taken months. In the beginning, she followed me about but dropped her gaze when I tried to engage her. Her eyes then were dark pools that I wondered how deep the sadness flowed in before the child re-emerged. Since living with us, she has become enchanted with Mary.

Utevo has straight hair, a mark of the Polynesians. People say she is a *meta busa*, orphan. Over time she tells me her grandmother raised her. When she was born her mother left her in the bush because her father had shipped off to Queensland, but her grandmother rescued her. She is perhaps twelve now. One day we were on the ocean side of the beach, dipping Mary's toes into the shallows and collecting shells. Utevo said, "My grandmother, she was picking up shells on the beach, and never returned, ever." We can only presume she was stolen.

Utevo has become so affectionate now that on my return from anywhere she runs to meet me and throws her arms around my waist in a tight squeeze. I believe she loves Mary as her own sister too.

Soon we hold school daily for the adults and then one for the children too. We give a prize when one masters a given task – clasp knives for the boys and beads for the girls. They become "man school" and "man bush", Christians and heathens. As they are so fond of pictures, we spend many an hour explaining them, realising we can get a good deal of our message into them without seeming to preach.

"Have you any pictures of the houses in heaven?" someone often asks. And when told that God was the creator of all things, Poma said, "If He had only not made sharks!" Sharks are the enemies of the fishing folk here.

The next time we hear the cry of a ship, everyone is at once calling and shouting out, laughing and singing aloud. I run to see if John knows, and of course he does. We are more on guard now, but I cross my fingers that they are welcome visitors. We stand at the shore looking out at a big, lead-coloured barquentine lying becalmed but at least pointing in the right direction.

Those in the habit of getting daily deliveries of letters and papers can have no idea of the excitement the arrival of ships causes us, after the lapse of three or four months without news of any kind. The most mundane newspaper is read from beginning to end, advertisements and all. I realise Ma was right: it is only being deprived of certain things for a time that I can properly appreciate them.

"It's far too big to be a mission ship. It's probably a labour ship, Ann."

Somehow, I know that is not the case. After the *Dayspring* was wrecked, it has been months without word.

"No. You'll find that I'm right," I sing out, before hurrying to make preparations.

I organise Lameka to get blankets and bedding. I talk to Simetone about roasting a fowl and preparing vegetables, adding, "Be sure and pluck the fowl *after* you've killed it this time!"

Simetone rolls his eyes at me, reflecting my own habit, but I look at him pointedly, trying not to laugh. He shrugs as if to say, *that's how it's done here*, but I look at him again and he nods. Some *kastoms* I will not abide.

I begin making scones when John walks in. "For returned labourers?"

"No, for missionaries!"

He looks at me with a smirk. "Whoever it is won't be here for a while, you know that, don't you?"

"I just want to be ready!" I rush about putting water on for tea and making ourselves presentable.

The vessel's sails are spread in anticipation, and a vivid sunset takes place behind her. It is not until later in the evening that the rowlocks are scraping, and a voice calls out, "Good evening, Mr Stewart." It is Captain Braithwaite, and we rush out to meet him. In a moment he springs onto the shore, followed by a friend of John and Hugh's from Dalhousie College, and the latest missionary recruit, a Mr Annand. What a feeling of delight sociable company can bring.

A torchlight procession brings them up to the house and we pester for news. The captain says the ship is the *Paragon*, a three-masted schooner chartered by the church for four months to do the mission work and bring down our stores. This is especially good news as on board is our own small boat, as well as building supplies.

Our boat is landed, and I know John's mind is whirring to the building of a boathouse. "We shall call it the *Chance*," he says, after a favourite harbour at home.

We sit and converse and entertain, offering our guests a restful bed. They accept, glad to be free of the cockroaches for a night, although it is long into the night before any of us retire. Captain Braithwaite asks if we are joining him to sail to Synod this year. Despite our recent progress, and our wish to not leave so soon, I canna forego the opportunity to see Christina and our fellow missionaries, and answer, "Aye!"

Chapter 17

ANIWA

We sit far into the next day sailing toward Erromango. I sit in the shade, devouring letters, while the crew work around me. I read news of Tilly's engagement. *Mrs Matilda Kaulback*. It rolls off my tongue. How proud I am, and how happy she seems. My happiness only tarnished by the realisation that I will not be there to see her wed, renewing the weight of homesickness.

In sight of shore, I move to the rail. Christina and Hugh get into the small boat to be rowed over to the *Paragon*. Relief floods through me that they appear well, and my grip loosens from the rail as I breathe deeper.

I take Christina in an embrace as soon as she climbs aboard. Her cheek is pink and hot against my own.

"Goodness, I'm always so glad to get out of the little punt," she says, smoothing down her full skirts and giving me a small smile. She is in emerald silk today, always so fine next to me in my cotton prints. She bears the weather with more elegance than I, too, and I canna bring myself to be so outfitted, even if I would want to be.

Hugh and John shake hands and move off to the ship's rail to wave farewell to Yomot, Hugh's loyal friend, who is calling out farewells from the shore.

Christina draws out her elegant ivory-boned fan, and I say, "Come." Taking her hand, I lead her to the shade of the deckhouse where Utevo cradles Mary.

Again, the crew pull ropes for all their worth, and I, too, wish us to be moving again, to feel the breeze once more. I did not remember my fan. As soon as we sit, Christina says, "How's Mary?" while looking at her with a smile. Utevo looks to me, and I nod and take Mary from her before lowering her into Christina's arms. My throat constricts as I watch Christina's face move through sadness and joy to love and pain.

"She's well," I start, "but how are you? Are you … recovered?" I grit my teeth. I had not wanted to bring this up so soon, but I canna delay after seeing her sorrow.

We are silent for a time before Christina passes Mary to me and frowns. "A westerly sea came up in the thunderstorm last month. A young woman had a narrow escape from drowning …" She pinches her lips together then sighs as she looks out to the ocean. "The people are behaving strangely once more." Her eyes dart back to mine then away again. "I cannot pinpoint exactly what they're doing wrong, but they're showing little sympathy after the giant waves smashed some of our property. They're shying away. After the baby …" She stops then.

"Do you worry they'll try to throw off the worship?"

She nods sharply, twice.

I take her hand in mine. "It's true for us too that the people indulge little in what we'd call sentiment, dearest, and when we look for something of the kind we seem to be met by hard faces. One Sabbath," I continue, hoping I can lighten her mood, "John tried to reproduce a sermon he'd heard Robert Archer give in Melbourne on the text, 'He saved others, Himself He cannot save'. John explained the wonderful love of God in giving Himself as ransom for us. When he asked the villagers why He stood the jeers and taunts of wicked men, the agony of the cross, and didn't come down and save Himself, Simetone, our cook, piped up, 'Why Missi, because He was nailed!'"

Christina's smile is thin. She sighs again, laying her fan in her lap and drawing the sides of it together. Her fingers smooth over each successive crease. "I'm afraid it has come to more than that." She looks at me then, hope lost in her eyes.

I hold back my flyaway hair that has escaped my bonnet as the *Paragon* gets underway.

"The heathen made another stand against us," she says at last. "They planned to ask Hugh for teachers until every district had one. Then, at a given time, all were to be massacred." She shakes her head at the recollection. "But one of them apparently said, 'What is the good of that? Missi will just place more teachers.' Another was said to reply, 'Kill him, for he is the *noatnin*, the root, of it all, and the *nesekil*, snake, who is working against us. Many missionaries have been killed here, and if we kill him the white people will not dare send another.'" Her lip quivers before she laughs. "They don't know the missionaries!"

I wait until she is ready to go on.

"In the confusion of hearing the news so suddenly, the alarm was raised that our enemies were even then coming down the valley. Of course, all was excitement and dismay in a moment. When Yomot came in, he said, 'They are always talking of coming … now let them come.' I turned to him saying, 'Yomot, do you think they would have the heart to touch us?' and with one of his expressive gestures he said, 'Mrs Fraser, they will have to cut this body of mine in pieces ere ever they get near you.' Dear, brave Yomot!" Christina smiles but a tear escapes and slides down her now-pale cheek. "I was still recovering at this point and simply wouldn't have had the strength to flee."

I pass her a handkerchief.

"Before morning the house was surrounded by armed men, ready in our defence. Then a great party of people came down the track on Mount Gordon. Our foes had arrived … But soon they realised the plot was out, and a number skirted the mountain and went on to Sufu to the north. The leader of the plot, a determined old heathen, died suddenly after this. It was probably his heart but, of course, the people – both his friends and Hugh's – said it was a judgement on him for his sins.

"Hugh said a loving Father had us in His tender keeping and allowed no evil to befall us … Now, at least, the heathen seem ashamed of their conduct and are being friendly once more. The alarm stirred up our Christians to greater energy too, both in caring for us and showing some sentiment for us and our work.

"But you know, Annetta, Hugh has been *lionised* in the press at home for having *such courage* as to tackle Erromango. Did he do it for the honour? That's what I ask myself." Christina quietens as she looks around. John and

Hugh are standing with Captain Braithwaite at the rail, talking amiably.

"Among the letters brought by the *Paragon* was one from the church disapproving of us going to Erromango, but, withal, assuring us of their sympathy and prayers. But it's been so incredibly hard. I can't say we feel like we've made any gains at all. We have to take things slowly, and I'm only just getting used to who is who around me … I feel so wanting in friendly company … and my child …" Her voice cracks and she does not go on.

Christina is on an emotional edge that she could slip either side of from one word to the next. My heart aches for her. I sigh as we cast our eyes to the horizon. I grasp her hand tighter then, not knowing how to ease her burdens.

After picking up Agnes and William Johnston, we are within a mile or two of Aniwa; a small, low-lying coral island. There is little beach and no outlying reef to break the force of the waves, so that the sea comes rushing in, as if to overwhelm the land, and bursts into white foam upon its jagged edges.

"There's Maggie!" says Hugh with a chuckle as we stand at the rail.

Mrs Gray, I presume it is, is rushing down through the palms, waving her arms. The Grays are somewhat infamous in these islands, having been here for some time and having overcome many trials. I am excited to meet them as they were on furlough at the time of our arrival.

We make our way over in the small boat as Maggie calls out in breezy Scotch, "Hello, hello."

Introductions are hurried through as we make our way up the broad, winding path. Tall palms are on either side of us, the long leaves almost meeting above us.

Christina and I are charmed with Maggie's garden, which seems to lift Christina's mood, though I know she has drawn a veil over her feelings once more. The flowering shrubs, both English and native, are in profusion. With the neat white picket fence it looks most fetching. Maggie stoops to pinch the head off a withered rose, and I realise by the way she scoops her arm under her belly that she is with child, though her dress gives little away. My eyes dart to Christina. She returns my look with a raised eyebrow.

"What a fine situation," John enthuses, looking around.

"Isn't it, Mr Stewart! Although we didn't think so at first, I have to say. When we arrived and asked for land, the people were most insistent that *this* was to be the site, even though it was covered in mounds."

"Oh?" says John.

Maggie's eyes widen and she looks at all of us, as if only just realising we have not met her before.

"Oh, Maggie!" Agnes says with a shake of her head before she walks on alone to the house.

"Well, on clearing the land," Maggie says to the rest of us, "we discovered heaps and heaps of bones and ashes. It turns out it was the site of their *cannibal feasts*," she lowers her voice for effect as she says this, but mouthing the words clearly, her eyes still wide, while gauging John's reaction.

He is about to respond when Maggie continues, "None would eat from the fruit trees and none but their sacred men were allowed to touch the bones. All expected the missionary and his *frail* wife to soon be struck dead from the *malign* influences of the departed spirits." Maggie laughs.

"Mr Gray even said to the chief, 'How do these bones come to be here?' The little man simply shrugged and, with a perfectly serious face, said, 'Ah, we are not Tanna-men! We don't eat the *bones* too!'" Maggie shrieks with laughter then, quite taking us aback.

John shakes his head a little, as if ridding a fly, and then gives an exasperated sigh and dabs at his forehead with a handkerchief as Maggie strides off toward the house.

Maggie shows us to the verandah where her husband, John Gray, sits waiting. He is a kindly looking older gentleman with a long white beard. Quite senior to Maggie, I think, and quite frail. The bushy, snowy hair atop his head reminds me of my own Scotch grandfather. His strong accent as he greets us adds to my recollections, and I feel quite tender toward him from the first.

We gather around a happy tea-table, set as if from an upmarket tearoom in Halifax. I wonder how many hours Maggie has spent at it. She clasps her hands together as if to hold in her obvious pride at the job she has done, while taking in our expressions.

She can hold it in no longer. "I am trying my very best to make it the prettiest and most inviting home I know. As refined and civilised as our limited resources will permit. We must not let ourselves *down* because we are amongst savages, but, rather, try to lift them up to our Christian level in all things," Maggie says.

Then, looking at me, she adds, "I don't see why missionary wives think they must live and dress in the most primitive way. Some think they must set examples of great gravity and solemnity else they be talked about! We should do our lifework all the better for having a home in harmony with one's tastes."

Christina smiles and says, "Oh, yes!"

But I canna help thinking Maggie is criticising my attire. My cotton print may be primitive, but in this climate, "What's wrong—"

John clears his throat, cutting me off, and says, "I remember it used to be a favourite subject of discussion at debating societies … whether the state of savagism or civilisation was the happier. Diocletian, who both ruled men and planted cabbages, said that, of the two occupations, he preferred the latter. So, I daresay the life of a South Sea Islander, with its freedom from care and responsibility, is happier than that of many an envied and busy member of a highly civilised community." He raises his eyebrows at me.

I look away and catch Agnes' eye too. She shakes her head a little as if to say, *pay it no mind*. I shrug, pretending the conversation and this woman are not bothering me at all, though I pick at the skin around my nails in my lap to quash my anger at John too.

Hugh nods as he raises his napkin. "I have little doubt it's happier than the life of those who lurk in the background of our great cities, enduring want and cold and entirely forgotten by the majority of their more favoured fellow-countrymen. I—"

"I, too, have often thought what a fine thing it would be to pull some of those *poor, miserable, starving* wretches from the slums of London and transfer them to these fair islands, with their warm airs and abundant fruits," Maggie interrupts.

"Well," she continues, "it is the most exquisite treat to have discourse with kindred spirits in our own tongue after jabbering so many months to the darkies. And to get all the news from the civilised world, that's for sure!" She claps her hands as if signalling the conversation is now finished. We each lower our eyes to our tea.

Maggie's long dark hair is plaited tightly on the top of her head, with no hair on the wrong side of parting. It gives her a somewhat pinched look. Often the conversation is punctuated by her laughter rising in a scale before the final note hangs high in the air as she throws her head back and up, no hair moving a twitch.

Her exuberance is overwhelming, and I am rather relieved when tea is finished. I motion to Christina that we could go for a walk, but, as I begin to rise, Maggie gains attention with a wave of her hand. "Now, gentlemen," she says. "I must get to know these tenderfoots. Go about your business, please." The men stand and leave without a word, while Christina and I sink back down.

Chapter 18

ANIWA

I take a deep breath and try to relax. I watch Maggie's children, Minn and Frank, dart through the palms chasing the ship's cat, which they have brought ashore. Utevo is playing with them, having left Mary sleeping in a crib next to me, and so I canna use her as a reason to excuse myself from the table either.

"Now, *tenderfoots*," Maggie says again, eyeing Christina and me, "how are you coping with the lack of *clothing* on the natives around you? It is a shock to the system, is it not?" Her name for newcomers makes me feel like a child. Why we have to discuss this again perturbs me as well. It was a shock to begin with, but is it really such an issue? Maggie does not appear to be waiting for an answer, at least.

"Do you know, in the beginning, the trial I found hardest to bear was that which befell me on Sabbaths," she says, settling herself further into her chair. "The first of these days presented a *ludicrous* scene in the way of dress, and it was only by a most desperate effort that I managed to keep a straight face while watching them come in to church. One man, I remember, came prancing in, looking delighted with himself in a snow-white vest ... and absolutely nothing else!"

At this, Maggie shrieks with laughter, and receives a slight reproving glance from Agnes. I wince as Maggie continues, "Another came stalking in majestically with a woman's skirt pinned around his throat, and the tips of his fingers appearing at the bottom of it!" Christina giggles as Maggie wiggles her fingers at her. "And a third had a bag done up so as to represent a hat, which he took off with quite the air of a gentleman as he entered the door. One man had on a nice wee jacket I'd presented to his *wife*; and, indeed, everyone who wore anything at all did so in the *absurdist* of fashion." Some Aniwan people are in the garden, and I cast my eyes around, wondering how much they can hear or understand.

"The women weren't quite as grotesque as the men,"—she has not finished yet—"though for a long time they preferred putting on a dress as they would a shawl, with the sleeves crossing in front. They've made such a *slow* advance in this respect since we arrived, although nearly all wear clothing now, thank goodness. I had to fight for *three years* to have Mr Gray insist worshippers be decently covered." She wags her finger now.

"He was satisfied if there were worshippers at all, but I insisted we have a right to Christian privileges, including the right to worship in the Lord's sanctuary without having practically naked people stuck in front of us. They do so like to run around naked, don't they! Really, it's quite sickening to see so many of them coming about with nothing but paint stuck all about their bodies. But in the heathen state, of course, they're positively ashamed at the idea of wearing anything as we would be at the idea of proposing to go *naked*."

A loud sigh escapes me, and I wince as I realise all eyes have turned to me. I glance up and Maggie is looking at me in question. "But it must be so liberating, too, Maggie, don't you think? Not to mention the heat. I'd probably go naked if I could get away with it!" I laugh, alone. "Aye, I was shocked at first," I continue, "but I've come to see that something is lost from the islanders donning clothes as we do, their way of being, their way of standing even."

Agnes nods a little, but Maggie raises her chin as she looks at me. "Some men haven't even donned nether garments, Annetta, as they say they're *frightened* of them. This is a land of strange superstition! You will learn."

I glance away and Tilly comes to mind, and how, as a child, she would loudly say "la la la la la" over the top of someone talking if she did not like what they were saying. I laugh at the memory, despite myself, and Maggie gives me a severe look before leaning back and crossing her arms.

"Well, this is exciting," she says with a wry smile.

My cheeks pink as I look down. "Surely the clothing is not of so much importance as the change of heart?" I say at last, looking her in the eye.

She looks about to argue but, instead, softens and holds her arms out toward Mary in her crib, who is still sleeping peacefully. I hesitate but then scoop her up and pass her over. Mary startles whenever Maggie's voice rises high or another laugh exudes from her, and then begins to cry. Minn, only four, comes over and peers into Mary's scrunched-up face and up at her mother before saying, "I want you to have another baby, Mama."

"Even when they cry?" Maggie says with a laugh. A fleeting streak of pain crosses her face then before she speaks, quietly, as she looks at Minn, "With the Lord's blessing, we shall have many more, my dear. Run along now."

She clears her throat. "When the hurricane struck, I lost my newborn baby, Lena, to fever. A darling child, a darling child," she says, her eyes settling on Mary.

I realise then that behind Maggie's loud, laughing voice lies a deep sadness — you can catch it at the edge of her thin mouth at the end of her smiles — though she hides it well. I canna help but soften toward her then as Minn skips off.

After a few minutes' silence — the first all day — Maggie turns and says, "We wondered at her beauty, you know, when no one dreamt of her being taken, as she seemed the strongest of them all. We even bantered each other about her very wee mouth, which seemed buried in her fat cheeks. Everything seemed to go so nicely …" She pauses and sighs, gazing out to the mountains. I place my hand over Christina's under the table, to find it trembling.

"When she died," Maggie continues, "I thought not then of my own loss, but felt as if I'd let my child go away alone, out into the dark, where I couldna follow …" Agnes comes forward then, passes Mary back to me and wraps Maggie in her arms. Christina dabs at her eyes, and I squeeze her hand once more.

Synod time passes swiftly, though I am yearning to get back to the peace of Erakor. I spend many hours with Christina, working on embroideries that we plan to send home to Nova Scotia. She has divulged that she thinks she is with child again. It is only months since she lost her wee girl. Although I am pleased for her news, I wish trepidation was not the first feeling to course through me.

After two weeks, and the men's final meeting, we gather at the dining table one last time. The mood is not light as the missionaries have just learned of the passing of the Pacific Islands Protection Act, what they call The Kidnapping Act, since the Queen's speech.

"So, what we have ended up with is *not* abolition, but *regulation*," Mr Gray says bitterly as he carves slices from the fowl. "Yet to regulate a labour system such as this is to sanction and promote its continued existence and growth, is it not?" He raises the knife into the air and orchestrates his words with it. "All it's done is *condone* the labour traffic to continue, just to go about it in a better way, just so they can't call it slavery! I believe we must educate the people to the best of our ability in forewarning them of what awaits them before they decide to leave." Maggie gently reaches up and lowers his arm and smiles, whereupon he takes his seat.

"But that's supposing we get the opportunity," William Johnston says. "It must be brought to light the *deceptions* that are practised. Why, a man from one island will be shipped as agent on board a vessel and, going to a neighbouring island, invites the men to come with him and visit his *friends*, thus dispensing with the need of an interpreter altogether. Not suspecting anything, they go on board and the vessel sails off. These practices are, I'm afraid, more common than is imagined."

"We can only protect them when faced with it though," Hugh says. "It isn't, after all, our mission to stop the traffic wherever it occurs … We cannot put a stop to free, voluntary migration. Although recently a small vessel arrived from Noumea and two men deserted from her in the night. They said they'd been working for years and had received no payment at all. The next day the captain came on shore and the men refused to go back with him. He didn't press them to do so, but only perhaps because they'd come to me."

In the pause I see an opportunity. "Our chief's son, Taniela, was stolen away on a ship just after our arrival," I say, picking at the skin around my nails under the table as everyone looks at me. "He's asked us to help find him, but I feel so helpless in what we can do. We've written to the Consul, of course. The chief said the ship's crew shot at the men in their canoes and dragged them on board. Then they heard that cannon was dropped onto canoes to smash them at other islands, where the men were then plucked from the sea. Could this be true?"

"That sounds to me like the *Carl*," Mr Johnston says, tapping his finger to his lips.

"Aye, that was it!" I nod.

"What with the wreck of the *Dayspring*, news has been so delayed, but from what I recall, those were the tactics used by that slaver … I remember the name of the ship because after you left us to take up your station, Annetta, a Mrs Bell and Mrs Grut and her daughter sought refuge with us. The *Carl* had stranded them on Tanna with their husbands, but sadly in an area where warfare was taking place between some tribes. Mr Bell, an invalid, and Mr Grut were killed and apparently eaten by the tribes, I'm loathe to report—"

"A most dreadful business," Agnes agrees. "We were lucky to get the women and child on a trader's ship back to Melbourne."

Mr Johnston goes on to explain how the crew of the *Carl* cruised the islands and dropped cannon and pig-iron onto the canoes at their sides. They dragged the men on board, bloody and bruised, and threw them into the hold. Then, when the islanders fought back – for they had captured fierce warriors from Bougainville and Buka – the ship's crew massacred some sixty or seventy in cold blood, firing down into the hold with their muskets.

"After they'd disposed of their bloody cargo overboard, and cleaned up the ship, they were intercepted by Commander Markham on the *Rosario*. But even he's admitted he won't charge a vessel with slaving unless he *catches* them in the act. You see, charges have ended up being levelled at captains before if, or well *when*, it seems to be, the case fails in court. And this boat was now freshly whitewashed. No complaint was heard of the natives still on board."

My mind is reeling as to what we will tell Poma.

"The atrocities on the *Carl* came to light because after they'd landed in Fiji, the vessel set off again in search of more labour. Apparently, this voyage was more 'by the book', but the owner, a Dr Murray I think it was, turned madder by the day – he was a drunkard by all accounts – and he threw himself overboard!"

"Good gracious," I say. "What became of the islanders then, do ye know?"

"Well, just a moment, you see, Dr Murray was rescued. On getting back to Levuka, he was invited to stay in the house of the British Consul, Edward March, whom you have written to. Murray was there apparently *seized with remorse*, broke down and divulged the atrocities that had occurred on the first voyage. Dr Murray swore an affidavit stating that some of the crew were the murderers, and a court-martial took place. A couple of men were implicated, who have since had the death sentence passed against them … Meanwhile, Edward March granted Queen's Immunity to Dr Murray for turning in the evidence."

"And what of Murray, then, was he innocent?" John asks.

"Well, I'm afraid it came to light he was anything but – he'd framed the two men – but by that time, thanks to Queen's Immunity, he couldn't be touched. He's probably shipped off back to England or Ireland, I'm afraid." Mr Johnston turns to me. "The chances of finding your chief's son alive are, well, remote to say the least. I also imagine Mr March will be trying to forget the name of that ship ever existed."

"One thing we do know," Mr Gray says, "is that if the trade goes on much longer, the whole of the young and able-bodied will be carried off, and the islands will be left barren and desolate."

Chapter 19

ERAKOR

It is a relief to make sail and arrive back at Erakor a few days later. As we are about to leave the *Dayspring*, I take Christina in an embrace and say, "Do you know what Agnes and Maggie do, dearest?" And, not waiting for her answer, say, "They send each other a 'monthly thought' ... We don't have to call it that"—I wave my hand flippantly—"but I'd love for us to do the same." I smile.

"We can share our thoughts on different subjects, or on a specific text, or just any subject and the Lord's helping of us, but it could be *for our eyes only*. We aren't encouraged to write home about our trials and wants, are we? Hugh and John's reports have to be cheery too, to endear people to our cause, so they're not going to tell the half of it. Honestly, Christina, I don't think it wise to confide all my worries in John in any case. My Ma's words have oft wrung in my mind: *A contented heart is one of the best gifts you can give your husband.*" I raise my eyebrows at her. "Sometimes she said it through clenched teeth, but she always meant it." We giggle. "Besides, John and Hugh have worries of their own."

"It's a lovely idea, Annetta." She smiles.

I squeeze her hand again. "Let's begin next month then."

"Yes." She nods.

She waves as we get into the small boat.

We turn to face the island and my heart sinks as Poma is coming down to meet us at the boat landing. I have been resolute to John that I should be the one to talk to him about Taniela, though I worry for the task.

After we are landed and everything has been taken up to the house, I ask Poma to walk with me. I tell him honestly of what I know and the story as it was told to me. Although I caution him that Taniela may not be alive, I say that we must not give up hope. I will write once more to Consul March, who was so duped by the captain of the ship that stole Taniela. Poma looks downcast and simply nods.

Later, as I rock Mary in my arms on the verandah, I think about these people, at their taking up of the Christian worship, of clothing. I know that I will never laugh at them. Maggie is wrong. The dark colour of their skin softens the effect of wearing little. There is a look of free independence and dignity about them as they walk so erectly, one after the other, for they never walk abreast. The athletic torsos of the men are lost in the levelling outfit of a Crimean shirt, and I realise what an equaliser dress is. It feels out of place here.

I confess to feelings of envy, too, and in the heat of the day I can only dream of throwing off my tight blouse with its pinching neck and hitching up my heavy skirts to feel the liberation of a cooling breeze across my limbs. Although, I *have* rashly taken to going barefoot most of the time.

I wonder if Maggie has ever really gotten to know any of the people they live amongst. I think of Poma, who has brought us several presents since we arrived, such as pigs and fowls, and how he is really one of nature's gentlemen. He is never rude to us and does not laugh at our attempts at their language. In fact, he talks quietly and gently to everyone, except when someone has broken the Missi's word, as he puts it, and then he will dig his great toe into the coarse sand and send it flying around him like hailstones, while he pours a torrent of abuse on the guilty party.

John comes out and seats himself next to me. He holds his arms out for Mary, but I shake my head. "She's just gone off," I whisper. He nods and we look out to the seascape.

"I'm going to start itinerating more on Efaté, where the population is larger."

I nod. "I'll accompany you. Are there others who can go about in turn too? What about George Campbell?"

He frowns. "George is far from a minister, and I can manage, Ann. You and Mary can come when you're able though."

We both know Mary is a useful ally when itinerating. The people crowd around her, touching her fine blonde curls and she endures it all generously. It endears them to us and us to them. Family is such a strong part of the message we are bringing, and it seems natural to present ourselves together.

John thinks it will be easier to talk to them while they are yam planting, so often we sit and observe their labours and, when ready, they come and sit with us. The languages are still the difficulty. Tupatai helps in a measure, and we try the sandalwood English too – a peculiar broken English where you sprinkle in expressions such as, "plenty", "what name", "along", and "which way". With this we make ourselves understood. Some knowing returned labourer will nod and say, "Break agreement along Satan. Sign along Jesus."

Often, local chiefs talk to John of loved ones who have disappeared. Usually, it is young men they speak of. We are cautious of telling them they have been stolen by the white men in the man-stealing, catch-catch or snatch-snatch ships, as they call them, but that may well be the truth of it.

In time, we return to their villages when the green tender shoots of the yams appear, and the people are making trellis supports for the vines. The plantations now are a pretty sight indeed, and they are used to our quiet presence by then.

Sometimes when John visits villages further afield, he finds they are at such odds with each other that if a man from one district comes, it is sufficient to keep the rest away. Poma will say, "Oh! You leave-im bush-man, he all right. You teach-im salt-water man." But despite the rumour of wars, some seem more willing to worship than to fight. These people become John's very purpose, believing them to be the key to opening the hearts of the rest.

The feasting and dancing season is drawing near. John thinks that if he can get them working together, it might draw them in a friendly way and prevent the wickedness we have been warned will prevail.

One afternoon, John gathers the people in the *malel*, lays plans before them, stands and says, "I wish for all the people of Erakor, Pango and the surrounding villages to build a house for Jehovah. It will be a *nasuma fatu*, house of stone, and I wish every man to help cut and bring stone to put it up, and every woman to plait coconut leaves for the roof. It will be a great work and take many days to finish. You will receive no payment, for this house is to belong to all the men and women, not to the Missi. I will work with you and give all the nails or other things I can provide that you cannot."

There is to be one other difference – our church is to have seats, just like pews. Seats for all. John has fashioned a design where each is made of one piece of wood.

He leaves the plans with the villagers, and they brain several pigs over the subject, as is their *kastom*, eating and talking for hours.

While they deliberate, John wrings his hands and paces the verandah, wondering if he is asking too much. He is trying not to keep looking over. Eventually, they call out to him, and he stumbles in his haste to get over to them.

Poma stands and speaks. I know the answer from John's jubilant face, so I smile and return inside.

When John comes in, he takes me in his arms and does a little jig, sending me into fits of giggles. It is a delight to see him so buoyed. "A date has been set for commencement," he says.

We are making gains and can only pray that what happened to Taniela will not happen again.

The church building begins in earnest. Food is brought in the morning and the women cook it in the *malel*, where the children frolic unsupervised while the men work. Sometimes there is a roar of laughter as a woman pitches a coconut shell at a man who is slyly running off with a choice morsel. The atmosphere is uplifting. Poma oversees all. He is an intelligent old man and often regrets to John that his arms are too weak to help in building or anything of that sort.

When carrying the heavy loads, the men give uproarious yells. It seems as natural for them as for the *Dayspring* sailors when pulling ropes. As if saving the best for last, the loudest yells are when they bring the pillars to support the roof. The noise waxes louder until thirty or forty men appear with an enormous tree on their shoulders. They shout as they pass the house – some looking out the corner of their eyes, their bodies drenched in perspiration, to know if they are seen. I make sure I am at the door to cheer them on. They give a triumphant shout as they lay a pillar down at the church.

At the end of a day's work, the people gather at the cookhouse to enjoy a kettle of tea – something they have become rather fond of – and they will smack their lips if I bring out fresh bread or scones too. Preaching is all very well, but they also have stomachs to be satisfied.

At sundown the men assemble at the kava house, each bringing a bit of the precious plant. It struck me as grotesque at first as I watched each man dip in his dish, take his draught with a loud gulp, and then lay about on the ground. It causes them to spit for the first hour after drinking it, too, but at least it has a soothing, stupefying effect, rather than exciting them, as Newfoundland screech excites my countrymen, and for that we are thankful.

John has to do a great deal of the manual labour, for there are no shops and no skilled workmen. He often laments there are no straight edges either, as the people resolutely round them all off. Instead of walking about in a black suit and white tie, he is always working hard, in his shirt sleeves, having to be everywhere at once. Being light of foot, it has never suited him to be encased in a pulpit anyhow.

He makes a raised platform for himself, with a seat at the harmonium opposite for me. There are eight windows, but really I do not know the height of it, only it seems so grand. The ground is laid with fine white coral. The people sit, gingerly at first, on the wooden pews built to John's design – the women on one side and the men on the other.

After just five Sabbaths, we again assemble in a new building. The roof is thatched, and the framework finished until more lime can be made to plaster it.

How proud the people are, and we are no less so. I decide that few churches could have been opened with such intense feelings of hope. On the first service, all sing with such reverence that it is hard to focus my eyes on the harmonium keys.

John asks if someone will engage in prayer, and Blind David rises to his feet. After turning to face the congregation, he raises his hands and recites the Lord's prayer: *"Teniman o nag ku ba tok ... "* he begins, and I understand him. I do not think I have ever heard it mean more. I can finally see God's hand in the work we are doing here, and this is what I came here for ... *"Ke tu kai tu mou tu. Amen."*

We sing "Nearer, my God, to Thee" before it is time for John's sermon. He undertakes it completely in the dialect. How adeptly he has learned the language. As he finishes there are nods from some but a look of impassivity from others.

As everyone files out, John catches Marifatu's arm. When not tending goats, Marifatu has become his shadow.

"Did you understand what I was saying?" John asks him.

"No," Marifatu says, looking down at his great toe wiggling in the sand.

"I spoke your language, did I not?"

"Yes ... but I don't know what the words mean."

John thinks for a moment. "You know that God made the world, and that we are all sinners in it?"

"No, I don't know."

"You know that Christ came down from heaven and lived on Earth?"

"Did he live in a house like yours?" Marifatu raises his eyebrows in interest.

John smiles and pats his shoulder. "We shall learn, Marifatu." John is not deterred and is just thankful to have accomplished the building before the feasting begins.

Chapter 20

ERAKOR

"So many are arriving!" I say as I clear away the breakfast things. John is standing at the window looking out. He nods.

"Let's hope the church building has helped ensure the feasting will be on a friendlier footing."

It has become a daily occurrence to see people on their way to the big *in tamate*, like a ceilidh to us, I suppose. Poma has said it is the new yam feast, and a man is guilty of sin if he eats the new yams before the chief has made a feast to Supwe, who they believe is the creator of all things.

The men, daubed in paint, have no clothing on but their sheaths, but the women are covered in grass skirts. Their faces are painted, though not with rouge. Their cheeks are black, their noses and sometimes their foreheads a startling red. I have seen them oiling each other's skin and daubing the dry paint on with their thumbs. Flowers and leaves are in profusion about their bodies. With children strapped on their backs and great bundles of sticks on their heads, the women are in front of the march.

The men, carrying clubs and sacred stones, are in the rear, with long, waving plumes fixed in the top of their hair. Shells, beads and everything fancy is stuck all about them.

Blind David does not seem to be partaking in the heathen rituals, but many of the churchgoers have resumed their *kastom*. John seems to be taking it calmly. He has retreated a little, and I think that best, too, to give the people space.

Pigs are killed by the dozen and there is an excess of a cake or pudding of mashed taro and banana. After this the women appear, and dancing commences to the music of wooden drums and monotonous chants. We stay up late that night, watching from the verandah. Had I seen it when we first arrived, I would have struggled to stay five minutes.

The men give a ferocious yell, rushing around in a circle before stopping just as swiftly. Others strike their sticks on the wooden drums – hollowed out from trees ten-feet long. The chanters keep time with them perfectly. They beat the ground with their feet too, every now and again yelling and rushing around as before.

As the night wears on, the men gesticulate wildly, their bodies contorting, their eyes wide with excitement. The firelight shows their lithe bodies, shining gold from their hot, glistening skin. They seem to be working higher into a frenzy, and my own pulse quickens with their quickening beats, although every foot still comes down at the same moment and every hand meets the other with wonderful precision. Tension permeates the air about us. It is mesmerising and, somehow, I feel connected to everything around me.

The music seems to be a living, breathing thing that sweeps you up and holds you in its grip until it feels a part of you. I am quite overcome by it, so I focus on the dancers and breathe deeply. I am struck with how modest it is compared to some dances at home – in that the men and women never touch. Would these people be shocked to discover that Europeans press against one another? This seems *savage*, yes, though peaceful revelry. It seems to have a purpose and looks to be telling a story too. We simply do not understand it.

Despite this, the mission has always regarded these feasts as harmful. We know not what occurs after we retire, but I sleep fitfully as visions of writhing bodies glowing in the firelight permeate my dreams.

Some villagers come the next morning to ask John if he is angry – if it will break the worship. He thinks it best not to interfere with their old habits until he has taught them more. I am pleased at his gentle nature then, not riding roughshod over their traditions, not expecting everything be given up at once, not being over-zealous in his manner. I hope it will always be the way.

But soon the results to their health are of grave concern, from getting overheated and then chilled, I suppose. Many are wrapped in blankets for days and then sickness ensues.

A few mornings later, Poma rushes to the verandah where I am sewing with the women. He stoops and takes my hand, saying, "Come, come." His agitation is clear. I hasten to his hut where his second wife, Sopi, is lying on a mat. A little flickering fire lights up the sorrowful faces of those around her. Her breathing is laboured. Her body is besmeared with powdered charcoal and her hair has been cut as short as possible. John calls out, "What's happened?" as he arrives behind me. He *tuts*, I presume admonishing the heathen *kastom* when Sopi has professed herself for the Lord. I warn him with my eyes not to say anything. I find I do not mind that they have done what feels right in their grief.

The breeze is low and there is nothing to break the solemn stillness but the quiet sobs of her family, and stillness from her daughter, Lameka. We sing Sopi's favourite hymn, but with difficulty get through it, for our voices are not steady. She is such a kind and affectionate woman. She always sits before my seat on Sabbath and is the first to turn and shake hands with me.

"Do you love your Saviour, Sopi?" John asks.

She nods. Mary is crying in Utevo's arms a little way off, and when I must go to her, I take Sopi's hand in mine. She presses it again and again, and then with great effort brings her other hand around to close upon mine. It feels like deep affection, and it humbles me greatly.

"Who are you trusting to help you in the hour of death?" I ask.

"Jesu," she says at once. I am glad, for her, for her faith.

I take Mary home. An hour later I know Sopi's spirit has passed away as the wild death-wailing begins. Having heard it before, this time it sounds more sincere than affected, and there is more the next day as Sopi is buried.

Poma looks desolate. "Missi, there is a great void here," he says after the funeral. Instead of laying his hand upon his heart, he claps his stomach, saying he has no food and could we give him some tea?

But it is only the next day that we come to fear for his health, too, as he takes to his bed. A sickness is taking hold, influenza it seems. The brother of the chief at Pango takes ill and dies, followed by some from our congregation. Threats are made to the teachers, Tupatai and Kakita, and we take them into our house. It seems some of the heathen blame the Christians for the disease, though we do not know why. A little later, a man is shot dead and left in the bush.

Samuel, Poma's son, comes to us and says, "The heathen say he broke *tabu*, he gave up his sacred stones and became Christian. The *atemates*, spirits, are not happy." Many villagers kill pigs to appease the ancestors and stem the deaths.

I worry on this as we go about our days. Surely their feasting, revelry and mingling together is to blame, but the labour ships often bring sickness with them, and many have been arriving at Havannah Harbour and Port Vila.

We go among the people and administer all we can. I have soon exhausted my supply of Hunter's Cough Mixture on the wee ones who are keeping their parents up at night, and our quinine goes like snow off a dyke. If they are not cured by two or three doses, they go to the sacred man, who cuts over the painful part to "let the pain out". Their sacred men are said to breed disease as well as cure it though and are paid readily by their patients for both – the one set that they may cure, and the other that they may not kill.

Some of our new Christians make offerings to the sacred men too, but, of course, people still die. Each time the death-wail sounds it sends shivers through me. The long, drawn-out wail swells up from a group of mourners before ebbing into soft, melodious strains, so well expressing sorrow, but such a mournful dirge. When the real mourners stop, an old white-headed and blacked professional will croon on. They besmear their bodies with soot from a pot in our cookhouse as a sign of mourning.

In the severe cases of vomiting blood, John uses laudanum or English paregoric elixir, along with the blessing of God. Some rally but still look at us with suspicion. The missionaries are also sacred men, in the people's eyes, so the natural thought is that if they can cure, they can also cause disease. Thankfully, Mary only suffers slightly and so my energies go into helping the people. But I fear for our safety as it is proclaimed that all who take the gospel are sure to die.

"Our attendance must not waver, Ann," John says.

We go daily to help those who will let us, including Poma, whose grief at Sopi's passing has thoroughly weakened him. My heart feels like to break over him, as surely as his has over Sopi.

The villagers are in despair, and someone calls in a sacred man to *koros* Poma. We do not see what he does, but Lameka says he will say an incantation and breathe upon him.

But Poma is sinking. I sit with him as he lies in his hut. He sleeps fitfully between bouts of shivering. That afternoon he holds onto my hand and says, "Taniela, Taniela. Find out, Missi." I know he does not believe Taniela was killed aboard the slave ship. I assure him I have written to all the powers in the colonies and Fiji, and that my letters have gone unanswered.

"I will not give up hope," I say, but I canna give the poor man the answers he so longs for. I am ashamed of the white men who have given this sentence to him. I quote the words of David and say, "I shall go to him, but he shall not return to me." I explain the idea that he will meet Taniela in heaven, and it seems to soothe his sorrow, at least.

That turns out to be his last effort, and he soon falls asleep. John and I are bereft; we have lost our faithful friend, our first true friend here.

Next morning, the villagers, led by Samuel, come to us for something black to wear rather than besmearing their faces. I am taken aback at the turnaround in their *kastom*. "The people have recognised what Poma would have wanted," John says. "You remember what he said in church recently, Ann? 'Plenty white man savvy Jesus along head,' he said. 'That no good. We must believe Jesus along heart, we must trust Him, and take Him for our Master.'" He sighs, triumphant as I find some black alpaca coats and vests from the mission box and hand them around.

The church members follow Poma's remains to the portion of ground we have set apart as a cemetery. Under the shade of coconut palms, Poma is laid to rest. Lameka, subdued but stoic, lays plaited coconut-palm fronds in the bottom of the grave before the body is lain on top. John reads some scripture before Samuel lays more palm leaves and a withered leaf on top, thus mingling the green with the sere – spring with autumn, life with death. The family fill in the earth with their hands before treading it down.

There we stand, missionaries from a far distant land, mingling our tears with the Christian islanders of Erakor, letting them fall over one who only a few years before was a heathen, and whom we now mourn as a brother and an Apostle amongst his people. It brings us together once more, more determined to fight the scourge in these islands than ever.

Chapter 21

ERAKOR

I sit at the escritoire late one April evening, cool rain thrumming down outside. I look through a "monthly thought" Christina has written and am elated to hear she has given birth to a baby girl. She says Agnes was kindness itself and has mothered both her and little Mabel. She was glad to have respite from Erromango, and I am glad they decided not to go it alone again. Christina lets on that Hugh does not question her wishes any longer. *What she had to go through to achieve that!* I think. Mr Johnston baptised the baby in March and then they returned to Erromango.

I feel sure the baby will help endear the people to them and hope for a brighter future now. In my reply, I confide that I, too, am with child again and how glad I am to not be on ship this time. I feel more robust than I did when Mary was born.

Mary is nearing two and is adored by all. The islanders flick their hands down at her, an upside-down wave, and she will toddle over and play with whomever beckons. Utevo kindles mischief in her, chasing fowls and patting people on their head while at rest. Mary has started speaking two languages at once and gabbles and chatters, chatters and chatters, just like Tilly. She loves to shadow John on his wanderings, calling, "Pa, Pa," quite without end. My heart fills at the patience he has for her. All the villagers have taken to calling him "Pa" now too.

I stretch my fingers out, aching from writing, before I read a letter from Agnes. She remarks that Maggie has returned from Sydney, having established Minn and Frank at school there. It is the done thing, "for the best", everyone says. I recall Maggie instructing Christina and me that, "Children in the New Hebrides learn immoral words and deceitful ways!" But it must have been a great trial to lose baby Lena and now part from her other children too. I think of Mary and dismiss the thought of school. I will not think about such trials yet.

I wonder at travelling to Agnes' again at my time of confinement. A notorious rogue of a trader was murdered there by the islanders recently, and I wonder whether Tanna is a safe place to be, but do I wish to be alone instead?

I turn as John places his hands on my shoulders. I know from his sigh that something is wrong.

He hands me a telegram. "I have this for you. I've wanted to wait for a good time, but … there is no *good* time."

I look up to him with a frown. I open the telegram with a heaviness settling in my stomach.

My dear mama has died.

It happened back in January, and all this time I have known nothing of it. I am so removed. I do not think it is real, in fact. Shaking my head, I take myself to bed.

After a fitful sleep, I open my eyes with the shock that I have lost my mother. When my breathing calms, I rise and try not to wake Mary as I slip out of the room. Lameka is already up and turns to me as I enter the cookhouse. John must have warned them as her face is solemn. She looks down at her feet. I manage a small smile.

"Missi," she says with a whisper, "was it the mother who gave you birth?"

Mother has such a wide meaning here. I can only nod as the sting grips the back of my throat.

"Please listen out for Mary," I manage to say.

Lameka nods before I slip out. I steal off to the edge of the shore, just before the island rounds back onto the windward side. It is a place I canna easily be seen and can quietly reflect. I sink my toes into the loose sand and become lost to my thoughts, taking comfort in the constancy of the waves. They break at one end and roll along the shore, each waiting its turn to end its journey at the beach. My thoughts tumble and fall in the same way. I should not have left her. I should not have agreed, but then I always thought of myself. Was I really no use to her? I was just a child. I know Pa was angry, but he was right. If I was not so taken up with myself, she would not have fallen through the ice searching for me. I canna get back the time we have lost. I canna make it right.

She is at peace now at least. Free from the pain that drained her for so many years. This is my only consolation. How I long for the particulars of her last days. So much is unknown and unable to be communicated in a simple telegram, no doubt in letters on their way from Tilly and Pa. I canna quite accept she is now with the Lord, to whom her whole soul was devoted. She was always so sure of his unwavering protection.

After a little, the school bell tolls, but I canna face it. I know I must get back for Mary, so I rise, but once back I avoid everyone and lie down on my bed. I run my hand over the quilt of blues that Ma made for me with such love and time. She forgave me, I have to hope.

John must have told the people I am busy as, thankfully, I am left in peace. Utevo is entertaining Mary, and I can hear their giggles and shrieks outside.

The days roll together, and I find I canna rise myself to anything. My belly is growing, and I am so tired. It does not occur to others to wash dishes so long as there are clean ones to be had. They have gone through the whole stock, leaving all to be cleaned, until I take command again. I wonder at my skills at training the house-help, but at this point I do not much care. Yet all have been kind in many ways and are not bringing me their worries or questions as much as they usually would.

One evening, while sitting writing letters, John tells Mary he is writing to her grandmamma. "You have only one grandmamma now," I say, before I can stop myself. I had not known how distance would make it so much harder to bear. I envy my family all together, surely better able to take comfort from one another.

John sees it all plainly on my face. "Although we're shut out from the world and the sympathy of family, yet we can, perhaps to a greater extent than at home, enjoy the sympathy of the Man of Sorrows, do you think?" he says.

I know what he is encouraging, and as always, I do turn to the Bible for comfort. Perhaps it is He who sends the toothache to distract me from my heart's emotions, and it sort of works. I sit and oversee John baking the bread, which only I have been doing, thrice weekly, while I put a compress to my face. It is John's first attempt at such a thing, and he goes about it most awkwardly. I resolve to show Simetone instead.

That June we have unpleasant and relentless weather. It is hard on the people – they go to their plantations wet or dry. Day after day it rains with but short intermissions, sometimes in torrents, and there is no sign of it ceasing. It does not take much to dampen my spirits still further. The days seem long, and I am so big now, and tired. My housework becomes more overseeing than doing as the months draw on. The women all assure me I will have a boy this time. I do not understand their hopes, but I do not berate them either.

I am still working on the embroidered sampler for Tilly's wedding, though she wed many months ago now. I imagine how Ma and my sisters would have helped her prepare, putting flowers in her hair, orange blossoms, perhaps. But Ma will not accompany Tilly to the sewing circle anymore. It was always a precious time together. I try to sew my love into those stitches.

We decide to forego the annual meeting. I canna bear the thought of another sea voyage. I am thankful John is not comfortable leaving me alone. Then I find out Christina will be staying at home and Hugh will attend the meeting. I know I should have her courage; she seems to have such hardihood.

The *Paragon* delivers supplies on its way through. We stand at the shore as they are unloaded, then from behind us a whistle pierces the air. We both turn and see it is Captain McLeod, the cotton plantation owner from Port Vila. He appears to be coming over in high dudgeon, waving his walking stick about and whistling to his dogs with a stern frown to his face. I sigh and clench John's arm as we make our way back to the house.

McLeod's black retriever is at his side now, while two smaller dogs *yap*,

yap, yap. McLeod is a tall, powerfully built man. A Nova Scotian by birth, he has been trading in the islands sixteen years now and is well-known to all. John has had a few dealings with him since our first introduction when we saw that cursed ship, the *Carl*. John encourages our villagers to trade with him as, generally, he appears level-headed. He assures us he does not trade much liquor to the islanders. "They're not sufficiently civilised for that!" was his response to John's questioning.

McLeod comes to rest with one foot on the verandah step. He leans on his globe-headed walking stick and wipes the sweat from his brow with some turkey red. I notice his usual florid face, his eyes sinking into his cheeks, and realise he appears to be flagging under the weight of his epaulets.

"I'm havin' problems with runaways, Mr Stewart! And others threatening to make me sick." He spits into the dirt, and my hands clench together. "Have you had a group of youths come into Erakor?"

John shakes his head and says, "We've not. Should you find them, I appeal to you to resolve the matter in as civilised a manner as possible, Captain." Then adds, "Perhaps you should consent to pay them a little more? We've often heard complaint that they're paid poorly. We all know of the falling price of cotton around the world." John looks at Captain McLeod with his eyebrows raised in question.

"Me, pay more?" He looks incredulous at this. "I'll pay them with a stick!"

My eyes widen, and I clench my teeth before breathing out slowly. I look up to the swaying palms to calm myself. John squeezes my hand, always doing so to stop me picking at the skin around my nails, and I pull it away. It feels like a warning almost, to control myself. He looks at me then and holds me with his eyes before I look away. I resign myself to not speaking up.

McLeod pats his retriever, and it seems his anger is abating. "I visited Ifira a few days back while looking for my runaways. I must say I noticed Mr Campbell has made himself right at home amongst the natives, Reverend." He smirks and winks at John, and we glance at one another. "Yes, right at home," he says again, gazing at John. His insinuation of George is clear, but this is the first I have heard of it.

John shakes his head and says, "Well, no doubt your runaways were not there!"

McLeod laughs. "No, indeed they were not. I've visited some of the inland tribes looking for them there too, though I know to proceed with caution with them. Once, when Captain Proctor and I were on Tanna, we found a party of natives around a fire where they'd been broiling human flesh ... Most scarpered quick-smart at our approach, let me tell you," he says, smiling, leaning heavily on his walking stick once more, "except one old gourmand who was gnawing on the palm of a hand. I've often been told it's the choicest of morsels!"

"I doubt you'd find such practices prevailing on Efaté," John says, his voice prickling.

"Oh! You can be sure, Reverend, they may deny it ... but they all do it *on the quiet*," he whispers before laughing out loud.

I swallow heavily, despite myself.

Chapter 22

ERAKOR

John never wishes to be drawn on this debate, and instead says, "What will you do should the cotton prices continue to tumble?" Some planters have turned to maize and the number of traders has dwindled. There is talk that the French at New Caledonia have their eye on Port Vila close by, which could afford shelter to their vessels during hurricane season. But they also have their eye on Efaté as a whole, as they are in want of plantations for taro and yam.

McLeod pulls out a chair next to John and sits down, slouching back and huffing. I raise an eyebrow. "Us old traders – Yankee or English – we'll all give a cheer if the French flag goes up … Not that I love 'em too much, you understand, but I believe they'd be fairer to us, and trading would be easier." He whistles to bring his retriever to heel. She bounds up the steps and lies down at his feet, her dark eyes looking upward, expectantly, at me. "The High Commissioner and Commodore Wilson have persecuted every white man in the Pacific, so the French could be a relief!"

To us, the islanders have made it clear what they think of the "oui-ouis", as they call the French. They are deemed more brutal than the British, and the desire has oft been expressed that the Queen should, "Send a big-fellow ship to fight the oui-ouis!" Those who have been to both Queensland and New Caledonia always say, "No good man-a-oui-oui," and some even surmise that as it was "Captainey Cook" who found the islands "long time back" and he "belong-a English" so only the English have the right to be here anyway!

"Oh, I have to say, I don't think you traders have too hard a time of it … Can you tell us honestly that you don't treat the natives how you wish, simply through worry of prosecution from a man-o'-war?" John says.

This isn't the day to cross my husband, I think with glee.

Captain McLeod tips his head in deliberation as John continues, "Have gunboats made inquiry with you into your conduct, Captain McLeod?"

"Look, I know to what you're referring. And, aye, I did chain two of my workers, leg to leg, as given to running away as they were …"

"For several days, yes?"

"Aye. But if they ain't given to running, I've no need to treat them thus, now do I! And yes, a gunboat was informed but they made no inquiry, 'tis true. But when their time's up, I don't just stick 'em on the first passing schooner, as some traders might, hoping they get to the right islands if the captain's agreed to and *if the wind is fair* … I make sure they're landed at the right place meself, and they're paid, fed and housed while they're with me. What more could they want?"

Captain McLeod calls his small dogs over. I hope it means he is leaving. Sure enough, he begins to rise. Then he turns and says, "I say, do you think these people will go to heaven? Well, I wouldn't like to be there with 'em, that's all. They stink too bad for me."

"Now look here—" I rise myself then, clenching my fists at my side, my blood boiling, but John grips my arm. I look at him, angry he should try to prevent me once more.

He, too, is clenching his jaw, but in a measured voice says, "The *savage* does not see the good of slaving and toiling for the advantage of a man who loathes him … and feeds and houses him as a bullock or horse is fed and housed, Captain McLeod. Perhaps you'd be wise to remember that? Good day to you!" And with that he reaches for the door and pulls me into the house, pulling the door shut behind us.

I am shaking with anger, not just at Captain McLeod, but also at John, for always silencing me. "You may have spoken more eloquently than I was about to, John, but does that mean I canna be heard?" I say loudly. He draws me into a tight embrace. *Is this an apology?* I wonder in surprise. In my anger

I try to push him away. Then I realise his chest is jiggling up and down. He is laughing! Before I know it, I gasp and burst into laughter too, so thoroughly has he disarmed me.

We know Captain McLeod is not the worst of them, but to us the law is wholly on the traders' side. Who can prove a plantation owner has not murdered one of his labourers? He may be the only European there. The talk amongst our villagers is of runaways having been murdered. Not McLeod's as such, but it would no doubt prove a temptation to a penniless trader whose only means of keeping his head above water is the sacrificing of islanders so as not to pay them. Later, when we press Simetone for information, he says that talk is that these runaways were taken away, or shipped voluntarily, we know not which, in a Queensland vessel.

"They are flying from ills they know to others they know not," John remarks. "I must get out to the inland tribes more, Ann, more than ever … I must get to Ifira too, to check on Mr Campbell." He raises an eyebrow, and I nod.

With John away so much, I am kept busy from six in the morning until four or five in the afternoon, when I am quite wearied. Most evenings, after six, I see no more of the people and I relish the time with my wee girl, though it is not often quiet as she is tired too. We look at simple pictures, or, if I have something to finish on the sewing machine, I distract her with an offcut to play with, and she shrouds herself in cloth.

On Sabbaths I rise at half-past six and have breakfast before dressing for church, just as if we were at home. Sometimes I daydream that everyone is with me as it used to be: Ma, Pa, Tilly, Thomas … and I even talk to them all in my mind about our day ahead and what we will do next.

Tupatai will ring the Sabbath bell at nine and we go to church, already crammed with people. Some are out of heathenism, others still in it, but friendly. Some, still not knowing one letter from another, open their books and hold them, often upside down, during the entire service, which Tupatai takes in John's absence.

But we do not always worship in the church. Sometimes in the evening, Samuel or Kalumtak – Poma's brother – collect the people under the large, spreading banyan in the wide *malel*. It reminds me of the Tyrolese hymn, "Come to the sunset tree" and this service, above all others, I love. The quiet hour, the gorgeous sunsets reflecting everything in mellowed light, and the murmur of the waves makes the whole scene enchanting enough to forget my loneliness. We often sit and sing all our hymns over and over until all is dark, nothing heard but the soft rustle of the leaves and what Longfellow called "the symphony of the ocean". Such a feeling of contentment will wash over me then.

The worshippers call themselves the "people of light" now, while the heathen remain the "people of darkness". We teach a singular message: life out of darkness, liberty out of tyranny, and life out of death.

I take what little respite I can by the ocean with Mary. One afternoon I bring a can of peaches for us to share as she loves them *almost* as much as I do. I confess, our stores of canned peaches have reduced rapidly in the last few months as my belly has grown. With Mary's back turned, I smile to myself and lift my head up, put the can to my lips and wait for the last drips of sweetness to dribble into my mouth.

My thoughts of our losses and isolation still turn and whirl like the sea amongst the rocks, but they are calmer now. I shake my head as if that will settle them more, before voices from around the point, just offshore, reach my ears. My skin prickles.

Mary is occupied making a line of coconut shells, so I rise and peek through the undergrowth. A man in a small boat is gesturing to a youth on the shore. "Where you go work?" he calls out to him.

The youth smiles and shrugs his shoulders. Another white man, standing on the shore, comes to his aid with the word, "Bundaberg".

The lad takes his cue and says, "Bund-a-berg".

"How long you go work?" This from the man in the boat. I presume he is a government agent as he appears to be scribbling the answers in the jotter laid out on his lap, while the boat rocks side to side.

"Three year," replies the man on shore – the recruiter, I presume he is – into the lad's ear, who repeats it parrot-like.

"How much you get one year?"

"Six pounds," the recruiter says, quietly, and the recruit says, "Sixy pounee."

"What you work along?"

"Soogar cain," he says, echoing the recruiter to the best of his ability, and then the recruiter hands him tobacco and a pipe. Other youths come forward and are coached in this way. I guess they know that if they fail to answer correctly, they will fail to get their tobacco.

The recruiter then says to a woman, who stands back from the men, "You won't do as we say because you listen to the missionary. If you come with us, we'll give you plenty calico, but if you stay with the missionary, what will he give you?"

I clench the skirt of my dress in my fists as I begin to push my way through the bushes.

"No, I cannot."

"You believe what the missionary tells you?"

"You do not?" she asks, raising her chin at the man.

I stop, curious now.

"No," he says as he makes his way to the waiting boat and climbs in. "Once we believed, but they took too much of our money, so we don't like missionaries anymore. Listen to the missionary and you'll be poor, without anything, but do as we say, and you'll be rich!"

I move through the bushes then and emerge onto the beach. The villagers scatter. The men do not even look embarrassed – the recruiter sniggers – but they turn, quick-smart, sit down in their boat and start to pull away. "Be off with you!" I shout, simply for my own satisfaction, clenching my dress tighter.

I remain at the shore looking out to make sure they do not try to come in again. Mary, having heard my shout, has toddled to my side and looks up at me. I run my hand over her curls. "It's okay, dearest."

When John gets back to the house later that evening, he writes these circumstances down for Daniel MacDonald, the missionary at Havannah Harbour. He is writing another report to enlighten minds in the colonies about what is taking place here. We have heard the slavers are desirous of obtaining women now because men are more content at the plantations when they have their wives with them. But if it is too difficult to procure their own wives, they seem to think any might do. These men and women are simply chattels, as if dogs or pigs. I am failing too, as I remember Dr Munro's task of me in these islands was to help protect the women.

I pace about the study, airing my thoughts to John. "What use was the government agent at all? The prevailing air around them has always been one of seediness, and I realise little has changed … John, I canna manage all of this whilst you're not here. I canna prevent it!" I let out an exasperated sigh. "Our bairn is almost here! Think of the toll you're taking on your own health, too. You're working yourself to the ground, covering such large distances by yourself. You're now quite thin and gaunt, John! We canna help these people at all if you yourself are with Jesus."

A chasm is widening between us over his gruelling schedule as he pushes himself on relentlessly. Our family time has been taken away too. "I feel large and tired and rather useless right now." I sigh.

John nods and seems to shrink in defeat. "I'll engage four teachers, Ann, to go about in turns." He looks resigned.

I nod and give a weak smile, though I am relieved. But John's face is cold. *Is he angry at himself, or also at me?*

"John?" my voice appeals.

"I trusted you to be running the mission in my absence, that's all. Isn't that what you always wanted?"

I gasp. "That's not fair!"

PART III

Still the Syren singeth
Mid the happy isles,
Luring men to ruin
With her wicked wiles.

Leave your laughing children,
Leave your loving wives,
Little will it cost you,
Little but – your lives.

— Sydney *Punch*, 19th September 1868

But ah! what wish can prosper, or what prayer,
For merchants rich in cargoes of despair,
Who drive a loathsome traffic, gauge, and span,
And buy the muscles and the bones of man!
The tender ties of father, husband, friend,
All bonds of nature in that moment end;
And each endures, while yet he draws his breath,
A stroke as fatal as the scythe of Death.

— William Cowper

Chapter 23

ERAKOR

January arrives and with it my time of confinement. This time I have decided to go it alone and not make the journey to Agnes'. I do not wish to press upon Captain McLeod for a boat to assist us. Lameka brings in the *mitimauri* at my request when my pains begin, and the midwife lays her hands on my swollen belly. I look at her kind eyes shrouded in rumpled lines as she begins chattering to Lameka. I find it hard to follow what she is saying, but she appears so calm and just shakes her head at my worried face.

She asks for a vessel of water to be brought in, as well as a young coconut. She takes the water up in her hands and blows on it, rippling the surface as it trickles through her wizened fingers as she intones an incantation over it. Lameka whispers that it is the ceremony of *na koroen* and she is *koroing* the water. I only catch snatches of her words, but it sounds to be: "Nature, nature that puts out! It shall for whom put out? It shall for Missi put out; it shall for Pa put out the little child, that it come down and be upon the ground. It is a good *koro*." After *koroing* the coconut milk in the same way, she passes some of it to me to drink. It is as fresh and delicious as ever, though does not taste different.

Somehow the peaceful atmosphere with these women eases my fears. As I breathe, the *mitimauri* gently rubs the milk and water over my belly. It runs down and around to the small of my back, sending tingles shooting through me as it does so, before dripping down to the sheet below. "To soften the skin," Lameka murmurs as she holds my hand.

The *mitimauri* breathes on my belly too, while I breathe deeply in turn. When finished, she squeezes my hand and gives a reassuring nod, then sits back on a stool. I decide I will not recount the *kastom* we have gone through to John.

Lameka stays with me while Utevo tends to Mary. As the night continues, the *mitimauri* returns to my side and rubs my belly again, with a bearing or pressing down motion. The pain builds and builds but, finally, in the small hours, it is with joy that I welcome my child, a son. I look down at his ruddy face. "Arthur," I say through my tears.

The *mitimauri* cuts the tie between us with sharp bamboo. I press her hand in thanks. Even if much of what happened was driven by superstition and a magical belief, I found comfort in her presence and her care for me.

I awake from rest to find John stroking Arthur's face in his bassinet. John's gaze is contemplative. "Isn't it a happy occasion, Pa?" I ask, teasing.

"Of course!" He frowns then looks back to Arthur. He comes over and kisses my cheek. "Rest," he whispers.

Utevo looks in as soon as John has gone. She claps her hands and squeals as she looks down upon Arthur. He is as gold-dust in her eyes, and I know she will become his faithful and loving nurse.

"Bring him to me, please, Utevo." She looks scared as she gingerly picks him up and holds him out before placing him on my chest as he mewls. "He is a stout little fellow," I say, to encourage her. He takes to feeding with gusto. He is so fair, with sparse hair as white as snow and eyes the same almond shape as John's.

A storm blows through in March, with heavy floods at the streams and rivers. It brewed for days, and when the seabirds flew to land for shelter, we feared it would prove disastrous. It was the sea I dreaded most, but thankfully it did not rise before us. The sudden drop in temperature catches us unawares, and all are taken with colds. I return to my bed and nurse Arthur with constancy, though he develops a cough too.

Despite this, the birth of our little chief has caused rejoicing in the village. Some watch by the house on the chance of getting a look at him. When I take Arthur onto the verandah, every movement of his little hands brings smiles and laughs – for is he not a man baby? Mary is none too sure at having less attention but is playing the attentive big sister. She will bat away fingers if, in her opinion, they prod her brother just a little too much. Samuel says he is their own white chief.

Utevo tiptoes about the room when Arthur sleeps, or sits down beside him, fanning him from the flies and heat. She keeps a strict guard on the door, letting no one enter but John and Lameka, though only as a great favour and only now and then. I giggle when she shushes them and instructs them to speak in hushed whispers.

A few Sabbaths later, I am back on my feet and able to attend church. I watch, one eyebrow raised, as Utevo reaches down and brushes her fingertips along one edge of the coconut matting on the floor. Her eyes widen a little as her hand comes to rest before her forefinger and thumb grasp at an object obscured from my sight. I already know what it is, and I shake my head a little, imploring her, but she is not watching me. Mary sits next to Utevo, swinging her legs under the pew. Thankfully, her eyes are to Pa.

Utevo straightens then and a look of innocent passivity settles on her features. I try to keep my lips in a pensive line too, but I struggle. In a swift movement Utevo hurls the little pebble across to the men's side of the church, where it strikes Kalumtak square on his cheek.

Utevo lowers her head and covers her giggle with the back of her hand as Kalumtak starts from his slumber. His bare feet shoot out in front of him, and a grunt escapes him before his eyes dart to the sides as he realises his surroundings. Samuel, to his right, looks to him in alarm. Kalumtak looks sheepish, takes a deep breath and straightens up in his pew, before looking up to see whether John has noticed.

I bite down on my smile as I look to John too, but his eyes are cast upward. His hands are upturned as he comes to the end of his sermon on The Plant of Renown, illustrated with the trees and fruits of this island. Patches of sweat are already showing through his tired grey jacket, though it is always a devil to wrestle off of him long enough for Lameka to scrub it.

It is time for a hymn, and I am glad of the distraction as I place my hands on the harmonium keys to begin the introduction. We are working our way through Sankey's latest collection, and "Tell it out among the nations" is the new favourite of us all.

The pandanus-leaf fans make a soft *slap, slap, slap* as the women lay them on the floor before they rise to their feet. I look over the women's attire – mostly simple cotton prints with a calico shawl or cloak, some plaited coal-scuttle bonnets, though many are in grass skirts. I hope a box will arrive from Halifax soon to replenish our calico supplies. Everyone raises their hymnals, and we begin. As they start to sing, their usual gusto sends a thrill through me, and my smile widens. It is an uninhibited fervour that knocks at my heart; a willingness to try.

At the close of the hymn, John rocks on his heels as he asks, "Who would like to say a prayer today?" His smile is broad as he scans the faces of his flock. Kalumtak clears his throat and raises his hand. He looks around for any competitor. This is his favourite part of the day. John bids him forward, though I know he would like an alternative for a change.

Kalumtak stands before the congregation and raises his chin slightly as he begins in his usual vein. He tells his brethren they are like pigs, dogs and serpents. I mentally make a note to talk to him about being more polite, though he is an elder and surely knows far more than John and I ever will about what really goes on in this village.

I turn back to the harmonium and let out a long warm breath through narrowed lips as Kalumtak wades on. He asks the people how long they mean to continue their black-hearted conduct. In his pauses, he surveys the congregation while the gentle swishing of the leaf fans disturbs the repressed air. The sun is rising higher.

Kalumtak has picked up the piousness of a Southern preacher, I decide, just as the church door bursts open, startling us all. Kalumtak tuts at the interruption to his oratory, his hands still held aloft, but all eyes turn to Noai, our goat-herder. He stands panting in the doorway with his little brother, both darting wide-eyed looks all around.

"Sail-oh! Sail-oh-wi!" Noai says, looking to John. There is a tremor to his voice as he hops from one foot to the other.

John and I exchange glances but then he simply nods, excuses Kalumtak from his prayer-giving, and asks Blind David to come forward to recite the Lord's prayer. I steal myself for an audible groan from the congregation, but they are subdued, though even I am puzzled at how John can carry on.

John helps David to the front and then turns him to the congregation.

David begins with reverence, and when it comes to the last line the congregation recite with him with gusto. They are already rising when John gives the signal, and everybody rushes outside.

The children run to the shore ahead of us and wave handkerchiefs, leaves or whatever comes to hand in unconcealed delight toward the ship casting its anchor. Following behind, I wring my hands, hoping it is the new *Dayspring* arrived early, bringing our stores and news from the wider world before taking us on to Synod. A thrill of anticipation thrums through me as my own pace quickens.

I reach the shoreline and look out to the reef, shielding my eyes from the sun as the sea sparkles in front of me. John puts his hand on my shoulder, startling me a little, and I return his smile before we both look out to the ship once more.

"Who do you think she is?" I strain my eyes.

"She doesn't look like a man-o'-war … and it's not the new *Dayspring*." He sounds despondent.

I sigh. "A labour ship, ye think? On a Sabbath?"

Soon the ship's small boat is leaving its side. An islander is at the oars while three others cradle their arms over cedar boxes and lean into them to keep them steady in the waves. One more person sits in the prow, his strong arms in a gaping shirt hold on to the boat's ledge as they head in for the landing.

"Returnees!" I say, shaking my head. So few return.

Some of the villagers make their way to the landing and call out as the boat comes in, but we remain in our place. I wiggle the sand through my toes and breathe deeply to unclench my jaw. The men and their boxes are soon landed while the people look on. Then the man in the prow stands up and holds aloft some turkey red in one hand and a musket in the other, calling out to the people.

"What the devil …" John says, "he's actually recruiting too!"

We walk toward the boat landing then, and already two villagers have climbed into the small boat. They cast their eyes downward as we approach, and the boat attempts to pull back from the landing in haste.

John strides the last few yards and calls out, "I am amazed at you, openly profaning the Lord's day."

"I don't like it neither, but I'm under authority and must obey," the man says, folding the turkey red before shrugging. His face is set.

"Well," John says, "it's sad to see you, of whom we expect better things, trading in goods and men on a Sabbath."

The man laughs. "The Sabbath is clearly lucky for I've got two!"

John shakes his head. "Perhaps, but I question if you'll gain much by your luck. You shall one day have to answer for this work."

At that the man turns himself around in the boat, faces the open ocean and does not look round again.

Chapter 24

Erakor

We turn to the shore as a woman starts crying behind us. She reaches her arms toward the small boat. We realise it must be her husband who has gone in it, and she is crying for his return. Some start calling out to launch a canoe and take her off to him, but they are too late. The small boat never slows, the recruiter never lifts his eyes and soon they have re-joined the ship, where they will fast slip out to sea.

The woman sinks down into the sand on her knees, burying her face in her hands, sobbing. A little girl crouches next to her, her arm resting on her mother's back while her dark eyes look out to the horizon. I look around and Lameka's eyes meet mine. She nods to me and moves over to the woman, sinking down next to her and talking quietly. The other villagers around us move off, while a few remain, in expectation of trade with the returnees, I suppose.

I unclench my fists then and turn to look at the returnees too. The three men seem transfixed, unsure of their surroundings, and I wonder whether the unscrupulous captain has left them at the wrong island. It would not be a first.

John turns and sighs to calm himself. "Hello, hello," he says, his arms outstretched. "This is Erakor. Is this your home?"

The men look to one another and slowly nod.

"How long have you been away?" I ask, pulling wisps of frizzed hair back from where they are sticking to my forehead. I should have picked up my hat.

One of the men steps forward and places his hands on his hips over the dirty loincloth he wears. His thin torso is bare and his wiry muscles flex in his arms and chest. They may leave Queensland in civilian clothes, but they soon put them aside on the boat journey home.

"*Taem blong bifo,*" he says slowly and with finality, his eyes narrowed by the frown inhabiting his brow. *The time that belonged to before.*

Perspiration prickles on my top lip, and I open my mouth to blow upward. It brings little relief. I am uneasy, too, and my hand runs over the locket at my throat. The man's eyes follow my movements.

His cheeks have little nicks in them that have grown over into thick scars. His hair is long, straggly and dirty – twisted strands like pieces of rope. Only a few yellowed teeth appear to remain in his mouth as he adopts a sloppy grin, but his voice is angry, matching his frown.

John nods and eyes me with a look of caution. "I am Reverend John Stewart," he says then. "This is my wife, Annetta. We are the missionaries here at Erakor."

The other two men raise their eyebrows in hello before beginning to manoeuvre their boxes from the ramp. The awkward size of them belies the little of substance they contain, but once slid onto the sand the men begin prising the lids free. The third man is eyeing us still and a flutter alights in my chest under the weight of his stare.

I turn back to the other men in the hopes of distracting him. They have succeeded in removing some items of clothing, work boots, two or three machetes, an old musket, calico, a Jew's-harp and a few other worthless things as the sum of their few years' toil in the colonies, which they place on the sand around them.

The remaining villagers come forward then. The gun will sell, the machetes and knives too, though for a lot less than what they paid for them, but no one will want the boots. *What need do islanders have for boots such as those in a tropical clime such as this?* I think.

Behind me, John is attempting to engage the third man in conversation, but he seems hesitant to respond.

Finally, the man says, "Who ask you stop here?"

"Chief Poma gave us permission to be here," John replies in a reassuring tone. "What is your name?"

The man replies, and I spin toward him and gasp. "What did you say?" I ask.

"My name Taniela," he repeats.

"I thought that's what you said." I am in disbelief. "Poma's *son*, Taniela?" I want to be sure. Perhaps I am too eager in my speech as he looks doubtful as to whether he should answer, and then … he nods. He looks so much older than his years can make him. We do not even recognise him.

I clap my hands together and laugh. John is smiling too. "Welcome back, Taniela," he says then, reaching forward and clasping Taniela's right hand in both of his. Taniela flinches at the touch and his face is wary.

"After all this time! Come," I say, "let us take you to your family."

I see the realisation cross John's face that Taniela will not know that his father, Poma, is dead.

We walk with Taniela to the hut where Samuel now lives. Kalumtak, his uncle, catches sight of Taniela and rushes over too. We don't need to say anything, and really it does not feel to be our place.

We raise our hands and wave to the small group before I take John's arm. We walk back to the house, lost to our thoughts, while Taniela remains with his family. It is for them now to welcome back the person we all thought dead, for them to tell him all that has come to pass in the time he has been away. Although it is too late, I am elated that Poma did not give up hope.

When I climb the few steps onto the verandah, three women are already seated in a line near the far side of the house. I smile to them and say, "I'll just get my seams."

They smile, nod and hold up their own sewing before continuing with their chatter.

When Arthur was born, I missed the women's sweet voices singing while we sewed of a morning, as they did not carry on without me. Now I am stronger, it is good to be back among them. It is such a peaceful, relaxing time as I have not had to teach so much as their proficiency has grown, and we just enjoy the company of one another. Or I simply listen to their contented chatter, supplying in some small degree the want of a local newspaper, what I understand of it anyway.

When I return to the verandah, more women have seated themselves next to the other few, and laughter and chatter rises from them all, making me smile. Some have brought their babes and will sew and nurse in turn, while some older ones sit in their new spectacles and are already concentrating on their stitches. Mary likes to sit with us and practise sewing too. Utevo and I will bring the cradle outside where she rocks Arthur, so that she can join in the singing.

I am always struck by what a contrast it is to the rather proper sewing circle Ma took us to in Middle Musquodoboit, although that embodied the congenial company of women too. I could not have foreseen what delightful work it would be, teaching the women here. My heart is so drawn to them. I shall always feel grateful for their warmth when I first landed amongst them, timid and fearful at being the only white woman on these shores.

In the beginning I longed to talk freely with them, but the language was slow work with me. It still is, but the sewing brings time to practise, and although I must make some awful blunders, they have the good heart not to laugh at me. I can make myself understood enough by now.

They are talking of the woman left behind this morning. They call her a *malib* now, a widow. She is not known to me as she has not attended church before. John and I worry for the widows in each village though, and I encourage the other women to bring them, particularly, to the sewing classes. I ask the widows to bring old garments, too, so they may see how useful their learning to sew can be now they must support themselves.

As I seat myself next to Lameka, she looks up and smiles. She is wearing a string of fine blue beads around her neck that look lovely on her, and I tell her so. We are working on cutting and pinning girdles of calico for trousers. They are given to the boys when they renounce heathenism and attend our classes and church. We are also working on garments for baby girls. Something Jessie Archer said is that if I show great love to the newborn girls – dress them, kiss them, praise their clear, bright eyes – and speak kindly to the mother, asking her to bring the baby back often, I can improve the chances that the girl will survive.

Lameka and the other women are helping me with the sewing tasks, and I am grateful for it; my fingers are constantly blistered. But I have to ask her if she should be elsewhere, now that her brother has returned.

"No, no Missi, it is fine, I have seen him," she replies, "but he only talks of finding the traders." She looks down as she purses her lips.

"I see. It will be an adjustment for him, I think, to be back."

"Yes, I think so." She nods.

She hides her worry as usual and moves the talk to other things with the women around us. I think of Kawiwi, who is not here today. After we had spoken to Poma of the unlikelihood of Taniela's return, he decided Kawiwi was now a widow and could marry his son, Samuel. John asked them to marry in church. I let Kawiwi choose what she liked from the latest box from Greenhill – a nice blue jacket and a white hat trimmed with tulle – if only to tempt her companions to follow her example and have a Christian marriage.

She was brought to me in tears with nerves but after she saw herself in the hall mirror, she seemed to think she had indulged sentiment long enough. Drying her tears, she looked out from under her long eyelashes with admiration, showing her bright, wide smile that could light up any dark.

Now that she is married to Samuel, I wonder what will happen. They are raising Taniela's children as well as their own. Samuel has thrown himself deep into the work of the mission, assuming the role of chief too. Poma's brother, Kalumtak, is helping Samuel and they have the respect of the village.

Apprehension jolts through me then, but the women's chatter brings me back to myself. They still talk of the widows in the villages. I keep hearing *saibirien* and *ba aulien*. These words are not familiar to me, and I ask Lameka their meaning.

She shrugs and says, in her forthright way, "For some woman who wishes *saibirien* she eats the plant of *saibirien* – to kill her baby inside. And when a woman does not wish to have more children, she eats the plant of *ba aulien*."

It is a few moments before I respond, "Women are procuring these?"

"Yes, Missi," she replies with a shrug. "Often the widow does this when her husband is no more."

The image of the woman left crying on the beach this morning springs back to my mind. If infanticide was prevalent in heathenism, I realise, it appears it is abortion that is procured in the Christian villages. My baby dresses are coming too late. My mind moves unbidden to "After the darkest hour", and I start singing softly. The song moves like ripples through us until we are all singing together, though the apprehension does not leave me.

Chapter 25

ERROMANGO

Later, while discussing food stores with Simetone, something like the tops of three small triangles appear above the trees at Pango point. "Look! What is that?" I say, straightening up with my hands pressing into the knot at the small of my back.

His reply is a wild shout of, "Sail-oh! Sail-oh-wi!" He grins at me and, sure enough, in another minute the new *Dayspring* comes into full sight. Anxiety sweeps through me on the tide of relief. The months without her accumulate into an agony of suspense, from the time her sails are discovered until we have opened the letters and found all is well, or not.

I dig my nails into my palm to pull myself together and fly to start preparations but find not a soul around. All have rushed along the shore to see for themselves.

I call out for John and find him in the study with Kalumtak, and both stand as I come into the room. "Are you ready? She's here! Hello, Kalumtak," I add, regaining my breath.

"Excellent, dearest." John laughs. "I'll be there presently."

"Is everything okay?" I ask, hoping for a short answer.

"Yes. Kalumtak was just informing me that Taniela has gone to Port Vila to seek work with the traders and, in his words, to get grog."

"I see." I nod, not knowing what else to say. This is not unusual for returnees. "Lameka has instructions for the housekeeping in our absence," I say.

"Good, well, let's make haste. We can't keep Captain Braithwaite waiting!"

Kalumtak laughs and clasps John's hand, tipping his hat to me before heading out ahead of us.

We wait at the shore with a packed trunk, and I wince as my shoes pinch my toes. John may not disapprove of me going barefoot when we are on our island alone anymore, but he would positively have a Christian fit if I attempted to go elsewhere without them.

We are rowed over to the *Dayspring* in the small boat, and Captain Braithwaite is his usual blustery self as he welcomes us on board. "Bless yer heart, ye look like another woman, Mrs Stewart!" I know what he is meaning as I did get rather gaunt after the tidings of Ma's death, despite being with child. It seemed as if I could not get over the shock. The thought engulfed me like a great blackness: my dear mother was gone, and I was not there for her. It was a crippling realisation that my life could never return to how it was before.

I shrug the comment off and stand on deck looking back to the shore, then wave to the children who are seeing us off. Travel on this *Dayspring* is not pleasant at all, and many have had cause to complain, so I know it is best to keep in the open air rather than go below. A private minute was even passed last Synod calling the attention of the captain to the fact the "pantry is in a filthy state, smoking and shaving take place in the cook's galley, the toilet is not ventilated, and the mattresses are never aired. Cockroaches, grubs and sections of various insects have repeatedly been found in the bread, porridge, soup, rice, butter, sugar and tea."

John passes a fat mail packet to me, and I smile in delight. After our hellos to George Campbell and the MacDonalds from Havannah Harbour, Mary takes a newspaper to scribble on and sits next to me in the shade of the deckhouse. I settle Arthur on my lap before breaking the seal on the mail packet. I cross my fingers for the news I will find therein. The first is blessed news – Tilly has had a little chief of her own. I wonder how similar they might be, and even, optimistically, what close friends these little cousins could be one day. She writes me all the news of wee Henry, and I decide I will make a new embroidery for her. There is not much other news of note, and I am relieved.

Mary is using a pencil to colour in words and tracing letter shapes, so I turn my face to the breeze, trying to close out all sounds but my own breath as the sun's warmth flushes my cheeks. Seabirds circle above me before I close my eyes and breathe in the fresh sea air. Arthur has drifted off to sleep in my arms and it is a beautiful day for a sail. I am looking forward to seeing our missionary family this year.

We head south to pick up William and Agnes Johnston, Robert and Jessie Archer, and, finally, John and Maggie Gray before turning north with a fine breeze in our sails to Erromango, where Christina and Hugh are hosting the Synod. I hope I might get advice from the other mothers as to what I can try for Arthur's lingering cough, though he seems much improved for the constant air, so I relax about him. I am especially excited at the prospect of seeing Christina. Our correspondence has waned of late.

Agnes joins me and we catch up on her news, only to find they have endured their most trying twelve months so far. At one point she had to seek the protection of the heathen against her own countryman – a notorious captain came drunk to her home while William was away. They had guarded her well and drove the wretch back to his boat, but still the heathen will not come into church.

"Many a time my spirit fails me." She shakes her head. "When I think of the days and years we've spent here, the thousands in Glasgow and elsewhere that are praying fer us and yet"—she sighs—"the natives' bones are still *very* dry. About a month ago a young woman, who was coming forth to Christ, died, leaving a helpless infant. Her death has been a sore blow to me … and it has taken many away from attending church. We are like a ship ready, waiting for wind, Annetta, every sail is set. *But what if there is no wind?*" Her voice is hoarse then as she looks into my eyes. She has never looked so despondent.

We are quiet for a time as she dabs at her eyes with the hem of her apron, and I keep my hand on hers. Eventually, she smiles, stands and moves to the ship's rail where she watches the sea.

Finally, Erromango's mountains loom their hoary heads out of the surrounding blue, and dense, rugged vegetation meets our eyes. We arrive just as dusk is falling and Christina's house is set in a blaze of lamps, giving us a cheery welcome. Christina stands at the shore waving.

As we walk toward the mission house, Maggie wrings her hands as she asks after Mabel.

"She is quite well, thank you, Maggie," replies Christina.

"Oh, and Mrs MacDonald, how are the children?"

Christina turns in surprise, and we all look to Daniel and Lizzie, wondering what we do not know.

"Well, we had a rather anxious time with little Alexander in Melbourne," Daniel says, "he had an attack of inflammation on the lungs. He has not been well since ..."

"Oh?" I say. "I would dearly love to know what—"

"Did you see *our* children, Mr MacDonald?" Maggie cuts in, her voice rising above us all, quivering in its tension.

"Oh yes!" he says. "We met them all at Mrs Beattie's before we left, looking so well and happy."

Maggie sinks at the knees before throwing her head back in relief. The toll of having her children in the colonies is all too evident. I realise this question will soon present itself to us with regard to Mary. How has this come about so soon?

Later, I ask Lizzie to look at Arthur. She thinks it is the same ailment that her Alexander was suffering. She does not have much advice, only to keep him in healthy air and away from dank places where miasma resides. Arthur's cough seems to have reduced already, and I am gladsome to have come away.

"Today, we are to have a day of sports!" Christina announces at breakfast.

"Oh, what fun!" Maggie says, with more than a touch of sarcasm. I giggle but am relieved that with a small baby I shall be exempt from most of the frivolity.

"Count me out," replies Jessie, though with a gentle smile. The few years I have known her have softened her nature a little, although she is still for total abstinence and temperance at every turn. On our first evening here, Mr Archer announced that he is retiring the mission field, and he and Jessie will leave for Scotland next year. She has suffered much from fever and ague.

Frequently during the day, we find her at rest, but she often attempts to pretend she was not asleep at all. She admits to Maggie that, "The influences of the subtle malaria are weighing me down like a nightmare, depriving me of sleep." We are tender toward her then, like to our own grandmamma, but she does not take kindly to that! The climate here really can be our most formidable adversary.

Bunting is hung from two coconut palms and a fine, wide grassy road is made for a course. There are running flat races, walking races, sack races and jumps, in which most compete, including the villagers.

I sit to one side in the shade, nursing Arthur with Mary close by. Maggie joins me as she declares herself far too nauseous in the heat to partake in the games. She is in her usual form and keeps some amused, even if I cringe at most everything she says. She is a raconteur, John tells me, and likes her stories to be controversial.

I think she does it more for the hilarity than through actual cruelty, so somehow it is passed over. This time she is recounting how an old man died at their station whom they called "the missing link". She says, "It's convenient to have a pet name for some of our best-known natives – that we may talk of them without arousing their suspicions …"

Maggie continues, but I ignore her and watch the races. Christina comes over and flops down on the grass. "Oh, goodness, I cannot take anymore." She laughs.

It is so good to see her happy once more. She is beaming and radiant, clearly enjoying having company to entertain. She looks aged though – her brow lined in a permanent frown – and I am not surprised given the constant anxiety about her safety as well as being with child once more.

In the days that follow, the men conduct their day meetings in the old grass church and in the evenings in the mission house. We have readings from some new works from the *Dayspring's* library, from *Rudder Grange* to Shakespeare's plays and Byron's Hebrew Melodies. Cockroaches and other insects make such terrible ravages in our home libraries, and with the moist heat loosening the cloth covers too, we are always crying out for new reading material. Croquet has also been the order of the day. Then walking and music and getting photographed, of course. We finished one day with a magic lantern exhibition and a concert for the villagers.

We ladies retire often to the verandah to sew and discuss and pretend not to listen should raised voices come from the church or study. Although, the only jarring words come from John toward George Campbell. I do not catch the words, just his tone, and I wonder whether something has gone awry at Ifira. John never told me there were any problems when he visited George after Captain McLeod made his insinuations. The ladies look to me. I shrug and shake my head, wondering what I do not know.

In the evenings over dinner the talk is also of the annexation issue. Some say that if France annexes the New Hebrides, she will send recidivists by the thousand from their penal colony at Noumea. "Our work will be finished," John says in consternation. "We've fought the heathen powers of evil, but to be frank, the civilised article would be too much for us!" The missionaries have sent petitions in earnest, begging to be annexed to Britain, but we have heard nothing more of them.

The children delight in being together and make quite a group, keeping the house lively. We get them out as much as we can, and nearly every afternoon they have rides on old Bessie, Hugh's horse, which they look upon as a super treat. They are many chattering tongues as, in their excitement, they lapse into the native tongue of their home islands. Some, Maggie for instance, strive hard to keep their children from learning the languages, "for the sake of their morals", but I do not feel the same with Mary, and she so loves playing with the children from the village and Utevo.

Despite the competition, Arthur makes himself heard, and having such a lusty boy is quite a surprise for me. I endeavour to retain my patience at times. *The days are long, but the years are short*, Ma used to say. He is now a stout baby, all creases and folds. I know his cough is troubling him, and I worry his lungs were somehow damaged from that first cold, but his strong spirit helps allay my fears. I turn my back on the looks of reproach from Maggie at how unbothered I am to have his cries reverberating off the walls. Still, I prefer those looks to the ones of pity. Many have lost children here.

Chapter 26

ERAKOR

"Only one more night, Ann," John puts a consoling arm about my shoulders. His wiry beard grazes my cheek as he kisses my forehead. We sit at the end of the bed in the quiet of our room.

"I know, dearest, and I am being uncharitable, I know that, but she does grate on my nerves so!"

John laughs, takes my hands in his and gently unclenches my fists before kissing the backs of my hands. I roll my eyes and smile, cupping his chin before I push him away playfully. I rise and seat myself at the vanity to brush my hair. The men's meetings have finished at last, and we are all in a state of anticipation waiting for the return of the *Dayspring*.

"You canna honestly tell me you're not longing to get home too?" I raise my eyebrows at his reflection in the mirror.

"Certainly, I do not deny it." He stands behind me and then his face turns to a frown.

"What is it?"

"Oh, probably nothing. I'm a little concerned about the village, that's all. I hope everything's going well and no labour ships have come in. And Taniela …" He shrugs.

"I'm sure he'll settle, in time, once he gets his strength back. Lameka was certainly shocked at his appearance. She remembers him as such a strong young man."

"It tells on them severely, that's for sure. And we don't know what happened to him there either." He squeezes my shoulder and smiles, as if saying he is not worried for an answer. I return his smile and finish pinning up my hair.

"Is there an issue with George, John?"

He tips his head and pauses before shrugging. "His time here is almost up, I think. He should return to Australia to be fully ordained or decide what his next moves are."

Well, that wasn't an answer, I think, but I do not press the matter. We make our way down to meet the others.

When assembled, we walk to the new Martyrs' Memorial Church. The beautiful wooden building has been presented to the Erromangans by friends in Sydney in memory of the five missionaries murdered on the island. Hugh and Christina want to officially open it as we are all here. It is said to seat two hundred, but with the one hundred and fifty who have turned out for the day it is already uncomfortably full.

"Such a band of clean, well-dressed natives!" Maggie gushes.

Christina smiles with pride. The devout appearance of the people seems more pleasing to some than the church itself. As we amble around after the service, admiring the structure, she tells me and the other ladies present, "When the church was opened a few weeks ago, we announced that all who wished to attend must come well-clad. The men in shirts and trousers, the women and girls in light print dresses, and boys are allowed to come in a *netoitingi*, loincloth. We said we would help them in this as much as possible, and they've taken it up enthusiastically."

Christina smiles and smooths down her skirts before clasping her hands in front of her. "Their attire the first Sunday was startling, though, to say the least," she says, wide-eyed, looking at Maggie. "Every man had on some kind of coat or shirt, and trousers of all colours, shapes and sizes were not forgotten. Sadly, Umas, Tangkau and others were rather *shocked* at the appearance of their wives, 'They look far too slim,' they cried, and decided they could not *possibly* be allowed to appear in society with so little on them!" She laughs.

"Indeed, Yomot and Atnelo came in perplexity to me, asking, 'What do you think, Missi? Perhaps they'd better put on a few of their own skirts?'

Well, I explained I'd never intended the women to leave off *all* their native skirts, but only a few of them, so they might appear less like balloons than usual. And so the rest of us might have room to turn around in the church! Anyway, after a little they seemed to understand matters better and took the affair more calmly. We told them we don't *insist* on their wives forsaking their skirts for European clothes, just as we don't *insist* on their coming to church in the first place. But, as they want to come, we feel sure they will respect our wishes and come into God's house in the very *best* attire they can get. Since then, there's been no more trouble." She smiles, drawing out and opening her fan as she does so.

I am shocked that she sounds just like Maggie.

"Are you all right, dearest?" Christina lays her free hand on my arm. I realise the other ladies have gone quiet, and I must be standing open-mouthed. "You look rather perturbed."

I close my mouth and shake my head, easing my frown. "Ah, I was just thinking ... sorry, to be so distracted," I whisper, mustering a thin smile. Erromango may be an anomaly in the number of skirts the women wear, but it only seems to bother me that this path of clothing has been decided upon that has led to the throwing loose of their own moral society. These husbands are aggrieved at their now *scantily clad* wives. It does not sit well with me, but I bite my tongue.

All at once I feel I do not know her. Is it all just about fitting in? Appearances? I worry at confiding as much to Christina of my innermost feelings as I have – on our mission and our influence here – which I do not feel she must understand, or agree with. *Have I been blind to her true thoughts?* I wonder. *Or is this just for show?*

I excuse myself and pretend to be looking at the plants as I wander off. I tremble with disappointment and sadness, knowing I do not fit in with this society. When the other women have moved off, I look around me. At least the lack of skirts does not detract from the beautifully straight figures of the Erromangan women, even if it comes from the heavy loads they balance. A child on her back, a load of yams on her head, a bundle of sticks above that and a bamboo filled with water over her shoulder too. The men, too, may look trim in their clothes, but they still keep their loose matches, or whatever else, safe up top in their thatches, and a pipe snug in their earlobes.

"Annetta?"

"Aye, John." I look in the direction of his voice.

He strides over through the palms, a beaming smile to his face, which quickly fades. "Are you okay?"

"I'm fine. Please tell me it's time to leave."

"It is! Come."

I sigh in relief as we walk back to the house, where I see the *Dayspring* at the shore.

Once we reach Efaté, John and I say our farewells on the deck. We make our way to the small boat, which will row us to where Marifatu is waiting in our boat. He smiles and waves as we make our way toward him.

He rows us up the lagoon to Erakor, and it is as dreamy a journey as ever. We are surrounded by tropical foliage, while the clear, pale-green water ripples as the canoe glides along to the island ahead. Mary rests her head on the boat's side and stares over the edge into the depths below. John and Marifatu talk quietly behind me while I trail my fingers through the top inch of glass-like water. I am lost in the steady rhythm of the oars pulling back and forth, interspersed by a young boy baling out water with coconut shells. Somehow, we have never been able to make the *Chance* watertight.

A thin, smoky spiral rises from the house as the boat landing at Erakor comes into sight. It is a relief after what feels like so many weeks away, despite it only being two, and calls are raised before some people run down to the landing. I smile and wave as Utevo rushes down and waves both her arms at us in unconcealed delight. She wades into the sea and cries out with glee at Arthur's face peeking out from his shawls. As I climb onto the boards, she puts her arms about me and Arthur in a tight squeeze.

Mary is pulling at Utevo's dress, so Utevo scoops her up, though she is more than a handful, and then waddles toward the house. I laugh as we reach the house and see Utevo has spelled out "Welcome" in shells in front of our gate. I pass her Arthur and she sits on the verandah step and gazes down at him.

Lameka stands on the verandah, proud and poised. Inside, everything is in perfect order; even the pins I left on my dressing table have been carefully rolled in paper. Delicate white roses stand in Ma's porcelain vase, which brings a thump to my chest.

Kalumtak and Samuel soon arrive and they, too, seem relieved at our return, more so than expected, to be honest, or is, indeed, usual.

We stand in the hallway, and I notice that they are shifting their weight from one foot to the other and darting anxious looks to one another. I look to John, but he is relaying some of the news from Synod as he takes out some documents from his case and appears not to notice their unease. I take off my bonnet and lay a hand on John's arm. He raises his eyebrows at me in question.

"Perhaps we can hear what's been happening in our absence just now, John, eh?"

He looks confused but then catches my meaning. "Of course, of course," he says, turning to the men. "How is everything?"

"It is Taniela—" Kalumtak begins at once.

"He is away," interrupts Samuel, "mostly staying with the traders at Port Vila. They give him work and he takes liquor in return." He looks embarrassed to talk of his brother thus.

John tips his head in question. This is, after all, common enough.

"He has lost control and become a menace," Kalumtak says at last, shaking his head. His words hang heavy in the air. "His rants are about the colonies, but on finding Poma dead and Kawiwi remarried ..." He does not go on. We move into John's study, and I ask Lameka to bring in some tea for us all. Her jaw is clenched, I realise, and a prickling anxiety starts to rise within me.

Samuel says Taniela was calm to begin with, although straightaway believed himself to be chief, and had quickly married a local girl, named Basiva. "He claimed her and paid her family for her, but he's already mistreated her – beating her and going off for days at a time, wandering the villages, inciting war and distrust before going off for grog once more." He casts his eyes downward.

"Most are wise to his nonsense and stay out of his way," Kalumtak says, as if to reassure us a little, "but they do not know when he will reappear, and so are in dread."

"Taniela has threatened revenge on Kawiwi for marrying me"—Samuel defiantly prods his own chest—"so I have taken her and the children to a distant village." He runs his hand down his face and sighs, losing his bravado.

"You're really worried what he'll do?" John asks.

Samuel nods. "He believes he is chief now our father is dead," he says again. He bats away a fly as he talks. "He thinks this means he can do what he wants. He has attacked people and burned their houses. He breaks the seventh commandment on every hand."

Samuel has always shown us the finest Christian spirit. His quiet attentiveness, readiness to learn and gentle demeanour have endeared him to us all. He is taller than Poma was, who had the stoop of age and bow to his legs.

Now, he waves his arm again but this time in frustration. I have not seen him this worked up before. He is always so calm that this change in him is unnerving me. I wonder if John is feeling this, too, or if this is not new to him. If he knows him better.

Kalumtak goes on to say how Taniela, despite marrying Basiva, has also dogged the footsteps of a young girl who is the daughter of our teachers at Eratap. Her name is Ohai, and she is a sweet little thing – small and always singing. "He's tried to seduce her several times, but she told him she is a worshipping person and cannot do that great wickedness. At this Taniela ran for his club and struck her two vicious blows on the side of her head, and then ran off, leaving her for dead!"

I gasp. All at once I realise the depth of their concern.

"Some people came by and ran for the teachers, who brought her home, where she lies now in a bad state."

"I must go to her," I say at once, rising. John frowns and motions his hands downward as if to calm me.

"I am angry," Samuel is emphatic, "and I will not rest until I drive the wretch out of this place, even though he may be my brother."

Despite the finality and anger of his words, this would be a devastating consequence. "I'm going to ask for your patience and that you direct Taniela to me when he returns," John says, to my relief. "Please, Samuel, let me see what I can do," he adds.

Samuel nods. "But you must beware too, Pa ..." He looks up at John, who has started to pace the room. "Taniela believes the white people must pay for all that has been inflicted on him."

John stops pacing and clenches his jaw before nodding.

The men leave and we pack a bag and make our way to Eratap. The teachers are aggrieved, although Ohai will recover. We give her some laudanum for the pain and re-dress her wounds.

Thankfully, there is no sign of Taniela on the tracks.

Chapter 27

ERAKOR

I awake to the sounds of the church bell tolling for the beginning of school. It is a universal sound, and many times over the years I have awoken imagining myself in Nova Scotia. The warmth on my face brings me swiftly to the present, no matter how I try to extend the dream. This can sometimes lead to a melancholy day.

I must not delay though as already people are walking past on their way to the schoolroom.

Utevo is waiting outside the front door for me, humming a tune, and takes my hand as we walk to the schoolroom. As we enter, I notice our numbers are down again. This is unusual when we have returned from Synod. Often the supplies of fishhooks are depleted, and many come to lessons to procure more. It almost feels as though we are starting again as only some six people are seated. I know at once it is the tension in the village that must account for this.

Utevo counts the heads in the room before seating herself and clapping, twice, which is usually *my* signal that lessons are about to begin. I open my eyes wide at her in question but she only giggles. I roll my eyes. I canna be cross at her.

The students are writing their letters on slate with chalk, while I walk around and give them guidance. Then the door opens, and four youths stand at the entrance. All eyes turn to them, and heat rises to my cheeks and my heart quickens. Taniela is amongst them, and he looks stony faced.

179

"We want to go to school and church, but we have no *su gori*," says one, while the others nod; one laughs.

"Come, I'll give you each a shirt and *kalu*," I reply.

The men hold up their new clothes as I hand them out. They laugh and chatter before heading back out the door. Clearly, they do not mean to begin today.

I am relaying the story to John over breakfast a little later when loud voices ring out from the *malel*.

After a little, shouting ensues. "Time to sift this matter to the bottom," John says, raising his eyebrows at me before standing up. I scramble to my feet; he is not going alone. We walk over and find Taniela surrounded by villagers.

"He was seen at Eratap, calling out that the people of Erakor are going to shoot them on the morrow," Kalumtak says. "After, he walked here and told our villagers the same thing about the people of Eratap." Kalumtak eyes Taniela with disdain.

John looks at the aggrieved faces but before he can speak, Taniela throws his head back and laughs. "I go to hell, I no care. I want to lukim blood run!" His eyes are reddened, bilious, but wide and staring. Never have I seen such a crazed-looking man, and so unlike how he appeared just a short while before in the schoolroom. He seems bent upon *nafakal*, war, as though burning houses has become tame work.

There is no denial of what he has done, and he seems to think himself invincible. "Englishmen come big ship, plenty talk, do nothing; he no good fight." He laughs again, crossing his arms over his chest. "If you no fight, why else you carry muskets?" He gestures then to the people around him. They all talk at once, saying it is only him who has reintroduced this carrying of muskets by threatening all with his own. "If you no fight, then come out for the worship," he challenges, pointing to those who have not yet attended our church.

Sweat glistens on his brow and he is getting more excited by the minute. The people are agitated too, so John suggests they engage in prayer and then get on home. Kalumtak at once waves his hands, with a majesty only he can assume, before he says, "Thus saith the Lord, 'Take heed for your life's sake and bear no burden on the Sabbath day. Cast thy burden on the Lord and he shall sustain thee'." Adding reverently, "My word is ended."

I smile to myself, and we begin to disperse. Taniela tries to coax the people together again, insisting everybody convert on the spot. But we have momentum as a group and his audience is lost. This religious tack throws me, and John is just as perplexed. We know not what Taniela's motives are.

Over the next few days, Taniela accosts people about coming to church and learning about "Him big-fellow master". He preaches any biblical words he can muster. Everyone's nerves are strained. One day he stands in the *malel* and presents a pig to the very men he has tried to incite to war but holding his musket toward them at the same time.

It looks like it can only end one way. John stands from where we have been eyeing the situation from the verandah.

Before he can intervene, Samuel steps forward. "The people will understand us better if we burn our muskets and show we will not fight, Taniela. Here goes mine!" Samuel snaps his old musket and flings it into the coals of a fire.

Taniela looks to his brother with suspicion but wonder. Finally, he follows suit, with a grand flourish. This meets with intense relief from all of us.

While he professes for the worship we can at least feel in less fear of our lives. Samuel visits Eratap and smooths the way with the chief there. They are set for Taniela being dealt with but agree for Samuel and John to handle things for now.

I resume my sewing on the verandah in the afternoon, blowing on my blistered fingers to cool them. Despite the lack of attendance at school, the villagers are more clamorous for clothing after we have been away. Lameka and I have disposed of one hundred girdles of calico, and have cut, pinned and sewn twenty women's dresses. I think about how well they have done while we were away though, replacing parts of the thatch, whitewashing the walls and scrubbing the floors. Outside stands a new goathouse, and I know to thank Kalumtak for that – he is our master-builder – and a new fence sits to the west of the house.

"John!" A shout startles me from the left. I know immediately who has made it, and tension ripples through me. John is outside somewhere too, and as I look for him, he comes around the corner of the house and stands before Taniela. I hold my breath. Without a word, Taniela holds out a little pig. John's face relaxes as he accepts the gift. Taniela does not look John in the eye though, and will not shake his hand, so I know this is a big effort for him. I shake my head, knowing this sorry saga is no doubt not over yet.

John says, "Come!" and leads Taniela to a storehouse where he gives him several yards of rope in return. Taniela turns and leaves, again without a word.

John comes to where I sit and wipes his brow. "Now is the time for me to seek him out, Ann … If I talk to him and listen to him, maybe he can keep a hold of this lucid state of mind, and I can help him find peace."

"My presence could help, John. I'd like to come too."

"I shall have Kalumtak or Samuel with me. I think it'd be best for you to stay here."

I look up to him with a frown. "I really think I should, John!" I sigh and tilt my head a little, with a gentle smile. "Family, remember? And what harm can it do?"

He nods and stretches his hand toward me. I take it and we head out to find Kalumtak to help us.

Chapter 28

ERAKOR

Taniela is at his hut, squatting by a fire outside and whittling a stick. Basiva is in the doorway but at our approach he motions with his head for her to go inside. I attempt to wave at her before she goes in, but she does not meet my eyes. I see she is with child though. Surely it is too soon to be Taniela's, so I wonder on her story too.

Taniela looks up to us and shrugs. It is no invitation but then it is not dismissal either.

"Taniela," John begins, as he squats down on his heels, "can we sit awhile?"

I look about me before deciding on a tree stump to sit on, while Kalumtak squats next to John.

Taniela remains silent so John presses on. "Do you remember your life here, before you went away?"

Taniela nods. "Some times, some things." He shrugs again. *"Taem blong bifo,"* he says again.

"Can you tell us what happened?" John asks gently.

At first Taniela shakes his head and frowns, but at John's silence he shrugs again. "Me brought there and worked and worked." He looks upward and shakes his head. "So tired," he says.

"Fiji?" John asks.

Taniela nods. "Two moons were up, I ran away. I frighten me die there, me no want-im stop there. I cut grass, go home, me cry, cry every night."

He seems to relax a little then and goes on to say how when he first arrived, before he was even put to work, he had to cut down trees to make his own hut, with a floor of dirt and a box for a table.

He speaks slowly, staring, not at any particular thing, just lost it seems to an inner story playing out inside himself.

"Us *boys*, the overseer say, 'too careless for machine'. We have hoe, mattock, axe, digging bar ... shovel, fork, stone hammer, cane knife ..." He counts these out on his fingers. "Do cutting, clearing, planting, weeding, loading, on and on, on and on. Then back to hut for rice, potato ... day on day on day ... So many *boys* die ... new ones in, they first to die. Each time I ran, white man overseer chain me up to other fella, put-im whip on me ... 'boy you cut cane', 'boy you work', he say ... work, always work ... He push, push 'til one day he take-im me pipe. I shout, 'Me kill-im you', me take-im spade, want hit-im overseer ..." He looks to John then, who meets his gaze.

"But no hit him, no kill him." He shakes his head. "If only white men let-im me say goodbye to my children, I would not have felt it so, so much," he says then. The weight of sadness is clear on his whole person – it pushes his head down, his shoulders, his eyes. In the end he says he learned not to run.

Something in him snaps then. Perhaps it is a memory too far. He spits into the dust, curses, then leaps to his feet before striding around us in a circle. I focus on John as my heart beats wildly in my chest. Kalumtak is first on his feet, and he makes placating sounds and motions calm with his hands. Taniela sighs and throws his head back before sinking back down to his heels. We all relax a little as he regains his composure and appears to calm. He puts his hand over his clenched eyes.

After a little, he begins to talk of how he and the other kanakas had nothing better to do with their little pay than drink the hell-fire liquor supplied by the French. When someone did kill the overseer one drunken night, he was implicated and put in gaol. There he felt to be going madder by the day, not eating the gruel and just wishing to die, trapped as he was in the close confines.

But death would not come. He was eventually transported to Queensland, where he worked in the cane fields once more. Here, he joined bands of kanakas who frequented the roadside sly-grog dealers on their way to the sing-sings, where drinking, gambling, swearing and fighting abounded. Then came the ritual of the white men with whips and dogs chasing them out of town at nightfall. "Worse were the snipe-shooters," he says, "who came out, hunting, just to kill us. When men die, they were planted along Fairymead, buried in the cane fields. Fertiliser."

My throat is dry and tight, and I swallow heavily. I look to John; his jaw is tight too.

"A lot of 'em die of broken heart." Taniela shakes his head again. "If one got sick and he no better in half a day, they give-im half bottle of castor oil. If they ran, police go out with black trackers to round them up again. But the Abos, they fright of us too." He laughs. "Plenty be frighten of men from Malekula. They always fighting, drinking, making big trouble and killing Chinaman. They kill plenty Chinaman. They reckon-im good kai-kai, *plenty sweet!*" He convulses with laughter then, shocking me, and I cover my mouth to stifle my gasp.

In the newspapers I read after Taniela disappeared, I remember that some islanders of Malekula had attacked the crew of the *Carl* and had been kidnapped as their reward. They were most likely incited by revenge for the *Syren* had only just before stolen twenty-one people from the island and fastened them down in the hold.

Taniela gets up then, clenches his fists and strides into his hut. He moves a board across the doorway behind him. The talk is over. John rises and calls out to him, encouraging him to read the Bible and to try to move forward with his life. That God will help him. Silence is the reply, and so we walk home together.

"Don't preach at him, John," I say quietly when Kalumtak has left us. The sun has almost dipped, and we stop at the verandah to enjoy the last of the golden glow. The dusk sounds vibrate the air about us, and the fruit bats are beginning their evening escapades. "He needs to see love in us, do you not think? Just love." I turn to look at him.

"I am working through love." John's voice belies his hurt.

"I know that." I smile and reach for his hand. "I just mean that … maybe the words of God won't hold their true meaning for him whilst he is coming to terms with all that's happened. He doesna know of God's love and protection like we do. I think it'll be a long journey for him, and first must come simple love." I know, at least, that when Jesus said to love people, He was telling us the right thing to do.

John nods, lost in thought.

A few evenings later we are in the schoolroom, near the end of lessons. As the printing of the *Acts of the Apostles* has been finished, John presents our best readers with copies. They are pleased to get them for they have been reading for a long time in Matthew. Taniela is present, but on not receiving a book he rises from his chair with such force that it scrapes and topples behind him. No one makes a sound as he eyes us all before picking up his hat and stalking off outside. It is only a few moments before Basiva's cries come from the direction of their hut.

Those in the schoolroom implore us not to go, but I shake my head. John and I rush toward the sounds.

"Taniela," John calls sharply, "come out and talk to me, my friend."

The silence is interminable. All I can hear is my blood rushing in my ears above the cicadas whirring in the trees.

"Taniela!" John shouts again.

Taniela runs out from his house then and stops an inch from John's face. His own face is set into a sneer. John inhales sharply, as I do too, but he stands his ground. Taniela turns just as swiftly and runs off into the darkness.

I am shaking, but, somehow, John has not shown his fear. I call out, "Basiva ... Basiva." Eventually, she appears in the doorway. She shakes her head and will not come out and simply motions with her hand that we should leave. We nod, defeated, and turn back for the schoolroom, where we adjourn the lessons. We attempt to read when we get back to the house, but it is obvious from our mutual sighs that neither of us is taking anything in.

I look up to John and am about to suggest we retire to bed before a tremendous crackling and roar makes us rush to the window. Taniela's house and all that is in it is one mass of flame. We rush outside and find Basiva wailing and clutching at her head. Taniela stands on, arms folded across his chest. I gasp then and reach for John's arm as I think Taniela is going to strike her. He raises his arm up and brings it down, but instead he tears the jacket from her back and flings it into the flames too.

"Taniela's intentions are clearly not to convert at all," John says in a hoarse voice. Though he has tried to hide it, Taniela's true mood has bubbled to the fore once more. "Come!" John says.

"Quick," we call to the boys and girls. "Fetch buckets of sand." We half expect to lose our outhouses as only two fences are between these and his house, but the wind carries everything onto bare ground the other way. The fire is soon under control, though their hut has been ruined.

In the chaos no one knows where Taniela has gone, though Kalumtak says his musket has been stolen. I give Basiva a spare jacket and implore her to stay with us, but she is too fearful to cross Taniela more. I give her a blanket to sleep in instead. She shakes my hand and says she will take shelter close by. Kalumtak and Samuel decide they will keep watch over our house, but we all know no sleep will be had by anyone this night.

It seems to me then that Taniela is like a youth who has run away from his parents and has become so entangled in his new ways as not to be able to get out of them again. We have heard of this. These men lead unsettled lives, oscillating between civilisation and savagery, falling between two stools and often perishing because of it. *Will that be Taniela's fate too?* I wonder.

"The woman absconded to live with another?" John asks. It is our monthly members' meeting the next day. These are held for John to appoint work and change it from one to another, so that tasks do not always devolve upon a few, and cases of sickness or wickedness can be reported.

Kalumtak nods. "Yes, John. Her husband wants to go away, so ..."

"I see ... If there are no other matters?"

The door opens and Taniela walks in, with the greatest boldness. He is in a clean shirt and sits down as if nothing has happened.

We eye each other around the table as no one speaks. John nods and raises his eyebrows. "Then you are free to go," he adds.

I remain but John shakes his head as if to say he wishes me to leave too. Everyone files out as John starts giving Taniela a thorough talking to behind us. As I pull the door to, he is telling Taniela he is suspended until he proves his foolish behaviour is behind him. I remain at the door but do not hear Taniela speak or move. I peer around the door again. Taniela's shoulders slump a little, though his face is impassive. This saddens me. John has not taken heed of anything I have said. But I also know the people have to see him dealing with it in a way that shows Taniela his actions are unacceptable.

That Taniela has become unhinged, no one who sees and hears him can doubt, but still, he seems sane enough at times. I pray he can hold onto these periods for longer as time passes.

"The white men spoiled my head, Pa. I know not what I do," he whispers then, in his defence. I feel a thump of sadness for him, and I come back into the room. I sit down next to him and take his hand, without looking to John. "My head burns hot, and I am *driven*. That man, that Dr Murray, he bad man, bad, bad man." I realise he is finally speaking of the captain and his kidnapping on the *Carl*.

"Us kanakas, we rascals, but that man, he just bad inside … They shoot so many … island after island, they throw down cannon, smash canoe, drag men on board. Oh, that stinking hold. Blood, piss, shit, sick …" Taniela retches then at the memory.

John lays his hand on his shoulder, but Taniela twists away, snatches his hand from me and spins, growling at John as he spits out, "Why am I alive?" His face is in a snarl. "Why I have to live with this my whole life?"

We sit in silence while he breathes and calms a little. Finally, he tells us how the ship's crew captured men from island after island before taking many from Bougainville and Buka, but they were fierce warriors. He describes how the nerves of even the quietest captives in the hold were frayed as the hours had rolled on. The swaying ship – where they could not see what was happening, when they could not see what was coming, when they did not know where they were going, when they were longing for their families, when they felt so sick, tired and thirsty, when they longed for their island homes – had become their prison.

Fear had grown. In the Bougainvilleans this turned into the need to fight and escape. Fear overcame rational thought. Fear even overcame self-preservation. Some started pushing the quieter ones, saying they needed to fight to become free. Pushing became shoving; anger a ticking bomb.

"Tok! Tok!" Taniela had shouted. Stop! Stop! But the noise had reached a crescendo and nobody in that dank place, as far as he knew, understood him, even if they could hear him. His only friend had been injured and thrown overboard upon first being captured.

Cross-pieces had been lain on the hatchways above them like gratings and were barring their escape. The Bougainvilleans broke down the poles from the sleeping places and attacked the hatchways with them. Others rubbed coconut shells together to try to ignite fire. The white men shouted at them from above to quieten, but still the fracas went on below. And then the firing began. The white men's muskets pointed down through the gratings into the dark hold below.

Taniela had tried to crawl through the mass of fighting, wounded men, trying to make his way to those cowering in fear, unwilling to fight. But they were being let out and up onto the deck ahead of him. He saw little in the dull shafts of moonlight and the blinding flashes of musket fire. Dazed, he fell down again. Crawling on his knees, he looked up to find the hatch closed again. Behind him the warriors continued fighting under the main hatch, trying to break it down while shots rang out from above once more.

A hand had grabbed his arm; a Malaitan man. He pulled Taniela and with two others they got to the fore-galley hatch. A white man let them through, and they scrambled up before slumping, trembling on the deck where other peaceable islanders were huddled.

"All night they shoot," Taniela speaks quietly now, tears rolling from his wide eyes. "But it was not enough. That man, Murray, he make holes in the bulkhead. He push through his revolver. *Bang, bang, bang.* Firing at the men in the hold. Firing blind. And ya know what?" Taniela looks to John. "He sang. He sang a *happy song* while he shoot. That song … me never forget-im that song." He whispers slowly, *"Hurrah! Hurrah! We bring the Jubilee! Hurrah! Hurrah! The flag that makes you free! So we sang the chorus, from Atlanta to the sea, while we were marching through Georgia."*

Shivers spread over my limbs as he recites. I rub the back of my neck with my hand; it is clammy and hot.

Taniela says then how the next day Murray ordered a few of them into the hold with ropes to fix around the bodies of those too wounded to come up by themselves. I shake my head as I realise then how it is little wonder he could not abide being tied up in the colonies. They had to bind the hands of the wounded or bind them leg to leg if their arms were useless, and then haul them onto the deck.

"We not understand then the words the white man say, but now I know, now I learned – 'Pick 'em up and throw 'em overboard,' he say. He start with one boy, maybe he twelve. He put-im on the rail, squatting, like a bird, blood oozing from him arm. Then he push-im over ... They push 'em all over ..." Taniela's voice is hoarse.

Then it had been time to bring up the dead.

Taniela says he had been ordered into the hold once more.

He looks up to John then with unconcealed hatred. I swallow and feel the blood drain from my face. "Murray, he say a *prayer* then, ya know, he pray a lot, always preaching, big Christian man, just like *you*. This one I remember, he say, 'Let *me* not be ashamed, O Lord, for I have called upon thee: let the *wicked* be ashamed and let them be *silent* in the grave.' He meaning *we* are the wicked, not *him*."

I draw in breath sharply as Taniela leaps up, growling through his teeth once more. He rushes for the door and runs out.

John hangs his head and sighs.

When Taniela is "driven" like this, when he does break out, it is like he is possessed. Other people's fear simply emboldens him. John seems able to rise to the trouble and stay calm, but my nerves are at their frayed ends.

Chapter 29

Erakor

When Taniela reappears, he moves Basiva into an empty hut while theirs is rebuilt; the occupants having fled in fear. He does not allow her out or anyone to go near, which most obey, as frightened as they are. But not me, though for her sake I go as stealthily with food as I can. I have found some hardihood. Then one night, when he goes out in a canoe with some boys for a night's fishing by torchlight, Basiva's round face beams at the door at having an hour or two without him.

Kalumtak told us earlier that the *natamole tabu*, sacred man, has been summoned. John's face belied how he was not best pleased at this, but he did not raise an objection either, believing it would come to nought anyway, I suppose. The *natamole tabu* has been to the grave of Poma and presented an offering, beseeching his spirit to destroy Taniela for his wickedness. Such a man's fate is said to be evil – his canoe drifts or founders and he drowns, or he falls from a tree and is killed. So, when Lameka puts a plate of supper in front of Basiva, she leans in and adds, "I hope his canoe turns bottom up and he gets eaten by a shark!"

At this Basiva puts a hand over her mouth to stifle her giggles, and I canna help but do the same. But then unearthly yells from the shore make us all gasp, and she cries out, "Taniela!"

Basiva flies home in terror, while John and I take to locking up all the doors and windows. I realise then he is keeping us in hourly dread. But it turns out to be a hoax. The boys' canoe has indeed turned bottom up, but they can swim like corks and are in no danger; they are just whooping and hollering whilst splashing about.

The next morning at breakfast, voices are heard at the front door. Lameka soon comes in and says Taniela wants to sharpen his axe at the grindstone.

John puts down his fork before going to the front door, while I stand in the hallway, wringing my hands. John shakes his head. "No, Taniela, you'll learn to put your axe to better use first."

"What do you mean, Pa?" Taniela shouts.

John hesitates before saying, "I just mean that I want you to give up your bad conduct."

"My bad conduct! What have I done?"

"Do you not *know*, Taniela?"

At this Taniela turns and strides away, calling over his shoulder, "I let you know who you talking to."

John's shoulders slump and he cusses under his breath. He turns to me then, "I wanted to resolve the situation, Ann, not escalate it!"

I am about to speak but he shakes his head, turns and goes out of the door, setting off in the direction Taniela has taken.

"John!" I call out in alarm, but he does not look back.

I pace the hallway, unable to slow my breathing. My eyes flick to the clock at least a dozen times as I will time to move forward. At least then I will have good reason to pursue him and rush him in for church.

The wait seems never-ending, and at last I decide I can wait no longer. I set out in the direction they have gone. The inland paths snake and twist. After a little, I feel sure I should have come upon John by now, but there is no sign – only the breeze in the palms and the children playing in the shallows at the shore reach my ears. I force myself to breathe as my eyes search the vegetation.

"Annetta!"

I spin. John is coming toward me. I rush forward but then stop short at sight of his pale face.

I clasp my hand to his arm as I lead him back to the house. "I was pursuing Taniela when I heard a rush of feet from behind. I knew instantly who was at my back. I turned and Taniela was aiming a musket at me. Then, almost in the same breath, the barrel was pointed high in the air and four strong arms grappled with him. Two men were also following him!" John had been saved.

"The time for talking is done!" I say as I clench my jaw.

"I want to consult the village about what to do," he says.

But once inside the house it only seems a matter of moments before Taniela is outside once more, flourishing his musket. He bounds up the verandah steps and tries the door. I cry out in fright. With no luck he attempts the window but, thankfully, Lameka has them fastened. How he has escaped the others we canna fathom.

Lameka and Utevo rush into the dining room with Mary. All are in great fear. John pulls Mary to him while I grab a hand each from Lameka and Utevo. I am thankful Arthur is sleeping and hope he will remain so. Wild shouts ensue from outside, and we all look to the window. The news must be spreading like wildfire, and soon people are running from all over.

Kalumtak is amongst them, and he stops and orders Taniela from the premises. This only makes Taniela wilder, and he yells like a demon, but a group surges forward and seizes him. We know they will take him to the *malel* and bind him hand and foot with ropes, as is their way. It is a terrible noise and scuffle, for Taniela seems possessed with the strength of ten men, and I find I am gritting my teeth against the uproar.

My anger and fright subside as I regain my breath, though I am still shaking. Then a rush of sadness overwhelms me. John and I look to each other in disappointment and disbelief.

"Come," says John. We make our way to the *malel*.

Perhaps Taniela sees the sadness on my face as he calls to me, "Missi, Missi, help me."

He is trying to get up sympathy by changing his voice to a whine about what he sees as the injustice of it all. Basiva, gentle Basiva, walks up to him then, and before the crowd says in a loud voice, "Look at the marks on me and say if you deserve to be tied or not!"

Some church members say they fear that some of the wilder young fellows will come to Taniela's aid, but when Kalumtak makes it known he tried to attack Pa, their fears are allayed. "No one will lift a finger in his defence," Kalumtak proclaims.

But now what to do with him? There is nothing like a prison, asylum or secure place on all the island. Awaiting a ship to take him to the colonies is suggested, but we canna inflict that upon him. The native method, when any person becomes insane, is to first hold him fast and discharge a musket close to his ear. If the shock does not bring him back to his senses, they tie him up for two days or so. And, finally, if that does not restore him, they shoot him dead.

I look around and catch John looking at me with an expression I canna quite recognise. My brow knits as I try to decipher it – acquiescence, perhaps, determination or resignation, maybe. Then he walks over and sits himself in front of Taniela on the ground. "You may shoot or murder me," he says in a loud but appealing voice, "but I am your best friend, I love you, and I am not afraid to die. You will only send me sooner to my Jehovah God, whom I love and serve, and to my dear Saviour, Jesus Christ, who died for me and for you, and who sent me here to tell you all His love. If you will only love and serve Him and give up your bad conduct, you will be happy, Taniela."

John carries on in this way, and I am proud of him for showing the love in him, but still, it is preaching.

It is impossible to tell from Taniela's impassive face whether any penetration is made. John then instructs the men closest to Taniela to release him. I nod at John in agreement when he searches my face. It looks to be torture how Taniela is bound, and after what he has told us of his past, we canna do this to him. John then takes my arm, and we walk back to the house, but I bring Basiva with my free hand too.

Kalumtak tells us later that, once released, Taniela got a little boy to tell him where they had hidden his musket. He was then seen divested of clothing, adorned in paint and with musket shouldered. John's outpouring of love has not worked.

As the sun sinks, Lameka calls out for John from the verandah. There is fear in her voice, and we rush to her. We find a *tabu* has been planted at our house, signifying that we are ordered to leave the island.

John bounds down the verandah steps, pulls the bundle of reeds from the ground and throws them into the bushes, quoting loudly, "I shalt not be afraid of the terror by night; nor the arrow that flieth by day …"

He appears unbothered by Taniela's latest threat, but I can tell from the stiffness in his shoulders and the tightness of his lips that he is rattled. Kalumtak places guards over our premises, and we bundle a few articles by the door to snatch and run should the house be set on fire. I think of my bairns. *What if something happens to us or them?*

The slightest sounds from around the house have me on edge through the night. I sigh at the loud snores from the guards outside our door. I toss and turn and feel to be suffocating. Three times through the night we are startled at a raised alarm from the village.

Finally, we snatch sleep and awake to a cool and fresh dawn. I am befuddled in mind and despondent in heart, but still hopeful that the Sabbath will be a better day.

Basiva has decided that she prefers going to church with us as the safest plan. We wait until all are ready and emerge from the house together. Straightaway, Taniela runs from a concealed place and launches a large stone at her head, shouting that it is the price of her speech the day before. He laughs wildly and is gone. Thankfully, it merely grazes her brow, but she is trembling as if a palm frond in the breeze.

The service is tense and stilted, as though we have forgotten what to do, and the people beg John to be short. Everyone has one eye to the doors and windows. It is a stifling, hot morning, so we have one service in church, and, instead of school, a prayer meeting in the *malel*. John tries to reassure everyone and says, "The Lord Jesus stands between us and those who may wish to do us harm. Remember the words, 'Fear not, I am with thee. I will not fail thee. Be strong and of a good courage.'"

When praying, Kalumtak, in his majestic way, says, in a loud whisper, "You can shut your eyes, Pa, but I am *not* going to shut mine!"

Taniela, meanwhile, is now reclining against Samuel's hut, arms folded, eyeing us intently. Samuel is there and appears to be guarding against him approaching us. We have not seen so much of Samuel in the past days, and I realise then what a cut to his pride this situation is. He will barely meet our eyes. As I glance over, they appear to be in heated discussion.

At the close of the meeting, Taniela moves forward. We look to Samuel, who nods his head in reassurance. Taniela has a changed look, it must be said, and appears humbled. He calls to Basiva then, his face beseeching and sorrowful, his palms held out in supplication.

She looks to me for guidance. I canna tell her not to go to him, although I want to, but I at least whisper to not trust him. Taniela sees the unease on my face but keeps shaking his head. "I no hurt her," he says, over and over.

She goes to him, and I know at once I will sit up praying half the night for that helpless girl, who is being killed inch by painful inch.

Chapter 30

Erakor

All is calm for a few nights, and how quickly we are lulled by it. Then, around three in the morning, I am roused by Lameka.

"Oh no, what's happened?" I cry out.

"No, no, Basiva, her baby is come," Lameka replies.

"Oh!"

"I'm worried at your going, Ann," John says, his voice thick with sleep.

"You know I'll not think to leave her with just Taniela, John." I dress and then ask Lameka to boil some water, gather up some towels and take a lamp. Utevo says she will help too.

I am so grateful when we arrive and find Taniela has allowed the *miti-mauri* near. I shake her hand. Basiva is already well-progressed, and the midwife looks calm and unworried. She is thankful for the towels, cooing and smoothing them under her hands and across her face. I do not object when she lays one carefully in her wicker basket.

The night is long, but a baby boy arrives safely late the next morning. Taniela, outside the hut, raises a loud, deep cry. My eyes widen in terror as I look to Lameka.

She laughs a little and says, "No worry, Missi, it is a cry given by a man for a male child born."

"Thank God," I say, laughing too.

"That is the very thing I said, Missi, for you know, it might have been a *girl!*"

"No ... I, oh never mind." I frown.

"The cry is for the wish that when he grows up, he will be a man indeed," she adds.

"I see." I am relieved indeed and take advantage of his happiness – as it is only through Taniela that I can reach Basiva – and go outside to praise him for his son. I ask him if Lameka can light a fire now, to which he nods. His grin is broad and genuine now, and I am relieved at the sight of it.

Kastom says that no man goes near a house in which a woman is being delivered lest he contract the "uncleanness", but if Taniela cares for this, his paranoia at leaving Basiva alone wins out and he does not leave her at all.

I come back in a few minutes with a fresh kettle and a bassinet. Basiva is lying in the hut by a bright fire with the lamp lit beside her. Smiling at Taniela and congratulating him again on his son, I return home.

Taniela has to find and cook food for Basiva now as women remain in their house for thirty days after childbirth. Because he has to come to me for some supplies, he has no choice but to be civil.

As the days wear on, and peace and calm resumes, my anxiety wanes. I realise I had not been as frightened and anxious since we arrived in the islands. I remember again that day with wee Mary in my arms as we were rowed ashore for the first time. I try to take comfort from all I have learned since then, and the hardihood I have found.

On the thirtieth day, Lameka and I walk over and watch with others as Taniela takes his babe out of their hut and lays him in a dish of saltwater. He waves his arms over the babe while Basiva is away bathing in the sea. He is performing *seliad* for his child. My heart is full at the pride on his face.

The next morning though, alone in their hut, something happens, something snaps. We know not what the trigger is, but that gruff, loud voice yells out across the still air once more.

I shut my eyes, praying that I am wrong again and it is a normal cry, but I canna deceive myself. My stomach lurches in dread as I rush to find John in his study.

He is not there, and that only makes my heart beat quicker. I go outside and Taniela is in an excited state. He has thrown off his clothing and has stuck on paint. I recognise the blue from the balls in our washhouse. He holds his musket and is yelling that he is going to shoot someone ere the day is through.

"Mama," Mary cries out from behind me. I go to her and usher her inside with me. John comes inside close behind me and says, "Get locked up, windows and doors, Ann."

"What's happened, John?"

"I don't know," he says as he picks up his medical bag.

Voices cry out in alarm outside, and then a scream rings out from the direction of Taniela's hut. I fly to the window in despair. John drops the bag and rushes past me out of the door, "Do not hinder me, Ann. I cannot listen to that poor girl being killed."

I look back to the window and there is Marifatu, so I bang on the pane. When he looks up, I shout, "Go with John!" pointing wildly in the direction John has gone. *How fortuitous it should be Marifatu*, I think, for how often is he John's right-hand man! He nods and starts running to catch up to John. They meet Basiva staggering from her house, blood streaming from the back of her head. John catches her as she falls, and Marifatu takes up her baby.

I am about to go out when Mary clings to my leg and cries, "*I ga tok, I ga tok*, Mama," "let it stop, let it stop."

"*Be kasua*, Mary!" I say gently. "Be strong! Keep up your heart."

She cries, her teeth chattering.

John reappears and snatches up his medical bag once more. "We've carried her to the *malel*. Stay here. I'll bind her wounds and try to revive her," he reassures me.

"Here, take some fresh coverings," I say as I manoeuvre to the linen pile, Mary still clinging to my skirts. "I'll bring some food in a little while … Where is Taniela?"

"He reappeared, but I gave him a look that made him back off into the bush in quick style!" John says before letting out a deep breath.

"Be careful, dearest." I run my hand down John's arm after I hand him a blanket, scared at him going back.

He nods and is gone.

Later, Taniela saunters past the house in a clean shirt and looking like it is any other day. My jaw drops as he walks right onto the mission premises. Then he starts helping a group of men who are carrying some planks of wood that John has asked them to bring. John shakes his head and waves him off the premises, whereupon Taniela just shrugs and walks away.

We set up for afternoon school, even though we know Taniela is outside somewhere. I catch sight of him grinning from ear to ear and chatting with the passers-by as if nothing has happened. We are dumbfounded that after we have come here at such sacrifice to health and family ties, to devote our whole life to this work, it should be so retarded by one individual. Only four have the courage to come to school and we could as well be teaching fifty.

Basiva leans against the schoolroom wall, too weak to do anything but cradle her babe, but at least feeling safer here with John than any place else. At the close of the lesson, John tells the people in the room that Basiva must not be left at her husband's mercy any longer.

"But Pa," one man pipes up, "it is his own wife."

"It's not acceptable for a man to use his wife as his own peculiar property, to be abused as he likes," John says. Then adds, "Listen to me. Woman was made of man's rib, not of man's head to rule, nor of the feet to trample, but from the side to be man's equal, from under man's arm and therefore to be protected, and near his heart and thus loved. You must take Basiva to one of the distant villages, and, if needs be, protect her with your muskets. It would never do for me to use arms. My work is to teach; yours to protect each other."

We make our way home, but their faces perturb me. I know they feel the force of John's words, but I can also see there is no heart in their agreement. They will not look each other in the eye, and each then backs out of it one after another, leaving Basiva behind. She is too shy to ask protection from any of them.

When we hear she is left with only one friend, we both feel it our duty to shelter her, regardless of consequences. John runs out to fetch her in, only to find she has fled with her little one to hide for the night in a plantation.

Despite her plight, she is mindful of us and sends a messenger to warn that Taniela will be sure to burn our house tonight if he can.

I stand clutching a verandah post, looking at the retreating back of the messenger. The post is keeping me stable. I turn my face upward as I realise it is beginning to rain. Such torrents can fall in the tropics – fat, hard rain, the like of which you feel could split you deftly into a million shards. And certainly enough to extinguish all flame. I smile.

I send Marifatu with coverings and tea for Basiva by a little-used path, asking him to pretend they are for someone else should Taniela meet him. I watch him going on the task while the rain thrums and bounces off the edges of the thatched roofs, glistening at it catches some sunlight somewhere on its upward spring. I look for the rainbow that must be there, but it is nowhere to be seen.

The rain keeps up, and we awake to a cool morning, our house unscathed. Basiva's friend returns, whispering to me that two men have taken her to Imitang, and that Taniela has no idea of her whereabouts, supposing her to be with us. I am so relieved, even when Taniela comes around and becomes enraged at not finding her by the afternoon. He stalks off to go in search, armed with club and killing stone. He then frightens Blind David, whose face he cruelly yells into as he leaves the village.

But Taniela's wrath grows the longer he canna find her, and, returning empty handed, he tells Kalumtak, in a voice thick with anger, that he is now going to Imitang to kill Basiva if he finds her there.

Marifatu flies through the bush to warn of Taniela's approach. John and I go to the study, sink to our knees and commit Basiva to God. I realise then that I do not know what I would do without Him to turn to in these troublesome times.

We sit on the verandah after, deliberating the situation, our interference in the issue and course of action. We feel powerless, and helpless. We canna sit by while this man, seemingly insane, murders an innocent girl, or others, but it is the islanders' issue. We are not here to settle their disputes as it could lead to all sorts of consequences for us, and for them.

Calling in a man-o'-war could set many against us. In fact, we have realised the gunboats tend to increase problems instead of solving them. They prevent the people from complaining in their own way, and they will not complain in ours until it is too late.

"But we do know Taniela is keen to go to Tanna and get *supplies* from there," John says as we deliberate. "If we can get him on a boat leaving Port Vila, perhaps we can help Basiva get away too, maybe to Christina's care on Erromango?"

I nod. "It feels devious to be hatching this plan, but then the whole village needs a resolution."

"I'll talk with Captain McLeod," he says. He sees me grimace. "Well, what choice do we have?"

I shrug and shake my head.

The evening is so still after the rains. The air clicks around us with the night sounds – cicadas, frogs and the two-toned gecko with their little padded feet, such a favourite of Mary's. She can imitate their sound so cleverly. But then the sounds are cut with the piteous cry of an infant.

We rise to our feet, turning to locate the sound. Kalumtak is running toward us. He reaches the verandah and places one foot on the step, leaning down on his thigh to catch his breath before he says, "Taniela dragged Basiva out of the house in Imitang. Others pulled him off her, but he rushed back at her. He tore the baby from her, rushing home with it, knowing she will follow …"

Chapter 31

Erakor

It is near dawn when voices are heard outside. By the baby's cries ceasing we know Basiva has come. A little later I raise myself out of bed, stand tall, determined, but John will not let me go alone, and I will not let him go alone. We dress and take each other's hand to go together. I ask Simetone to pack a plentiful breakfast in a basket, and that is our excuse for intruding on the couple's privacy.

I shiver in the half-light, though I feel the Lord is with us, and I am almost relieved when we find their hut deserted. John calls aloud for Basiva several times, and at last she comes out from an enclosure opposite. She is trembling with pain and weakness, her face dirtied, skin missing from her jawline and a round swelling blooming over one eye. Her baby, thank goodness, seems content in her arms. We make to go over to her, but she looks alarmed and says, "No, you must not, Pa."

We do not know where Taniela is, so we speak where we stand, telling her our house is open to her, night or day, whenever she needs shelter. She nods and takes some of the food from me but rushes to eat it while we are there.

Kalumtak and Samuel wander over and join us at the fence, and I relax. They have come to ask what is to be done. It seems we canna delay a decision any longer. Tying only makes Taniela worse; confining and shooting are the only alternatives, according to Kalumtak.

"To confine him is impossible." John sighs before running his hand down his face as if to shake off the enormity of his thoughts. "Are we to shoot him?" He looks to me, though I know he is not really asking that question. "I'll not hear of it!" he adds. "I'm going to appeal to Captain McLeod to give Taniela passage to Tanna as soon as possible."

"Is there no medicine to cure his madness, Pa?" Samuel asks. Whatever their sacred man has tried has come to nought, but we know of nothing and there are no medical missionaries to consult. John asks them to talk with Taniela once more, to try to warn him of what could happen. They look to each other and give a half-hearted nod.

The moment they leave I go to sit on the other side of the fence to Basiva. It seems incredible to me that this poor girl, who so longs for relief, should survive so much ill usage, for I canna describe the cruelty – the refinement of cruelty – with which he has treated her.

We know that women sometimes commit suicide to escape the cruelty of their husbands, and it is something I have counselled the women of the village about when the subject has arisen. Although, when I pointed out that it was wrong to leap over cliffs to take one's life, Lameka had piped up, "Yes, it is better to drown yourself."

I fear Basiva will sink under her trials, but her spirit is humbling. "However difficult it might be to believe it, Basiva," I whisper through the fence as I pass her a damp towel, "God is caring for you every moment and will not let you have one more trial than you can bear." She takes the towel and starts dabbing at the dirt on her cheeks. *I hope that to be true*, I think as a sliver of doubt enters my mind. I want to see God's hand here, helping these people, but I am struggling to. I sigh as I look into her bruised eyes. "It will relieve you to take your sorrows to Him."

"Oh, I know it, Missi. My whole words now are prayer. I tell Him everything. I know that it is all right even if Taniela should kill me, for he cannot harm me beyond the grave."

"Not a single night passes that we aren't praying for you." I clasp her hand that is wrapped around a post.

"These prayers have been answered,"—she smiles through her tears—"for he has had the wish to kill me and burn your house, and he could have done both had not God stopped it."

❦

Kalumtak and Samuel report that Taniela would not let them near him to talk. Taniela soon turns his attention to the other villagers, stealing ammunition and plundering plantations, shooting all the pigs in his way. Many people come to Samuel with their complaints. Taniela brings Basiva part of the spoils when she is back in their hut, but now she seems to have the spirit of half-a-dozen – though I worry it is resignation – and she refuses to touch one morsel.

When next she is out, Taniela has gone. She runs over and begs of me a dose of poison. She thinks the stuff we kill the rats with should do. "He is too wicked to live, Missi. I have such a chance through the night when he is sleeping," she whispers, her eyes wide at the enormity of her suggestion. "I have a great wish to take his life, but I am afraid God will not like it." She looks away, then wipes her eyes.

I nod. "Just a little longer, Basiva. Pa is asking about the boat to Tanna. We're all eager to see it happen." I squeeze her hand.

John continues in his duties, though we stop school since the numbers have dwindled to one or two, and instead give out some scripture to those who wish to study it. We receive reports that Taniela is back at Port Vila working for a trader, but we do not know how long this will last.

The next morning an entourage of five or six men arrive at the house saying they are from Marik Tikaikow's tribe at Imitang. He wants to visit us and *aspiou* the house. We say he is welcome to see all of our property.

Only minutes later, Marik strides up to the house. He is his jubilant self and greets us warmly, shaking hands with less hesitation than before. "Come, we will give you the grand tour," John says with a chuckle.

He is curious about all of our belongings, and particularly at John's skeleton timepiece. He watches the inner workings with fascination as John explains how the hands and figures track the course of the sun. He gives John such a look of disbelief that we decide he should just look for himself after that.

Marik declares that we have a great house. He seems perplexed at the space and wonders where is north, south, east and west. Simetone prepares us dinner and we sit in the dining room long into the evening.

As Marik and his people get up to leave, he rises, turns to John and raises his hand, signalling silence to his people. All his exuberance is at once replaced with a deadly seriousness. He says, "What for you open-im window, open-im door when you got-im light inside? Plenty heathen man all around, John. He shoot you too easy! ... Taniela shoot you too easy."

It is a heathen trick to get people to show a light so they can shoot them. John looks thoughtful and nods. "Thank you for your advice, Marik. You are welcome any time. Our door will always be open to you, just as it is to anyone who needs us. Our light is always on."

Despite leaving me a bodyguard, John is not so careful of himself. I know Marifatu is at his side, but that only allays my fears a little.

"The Lord is my helper, and I will not fear what man shall do unto me," he calls out, much too joyfully in my opinion, when I ask him where he is going one morning with worry no doubt writ upon my face. The villagers are thoughtful about him though and will not let him take turns in watching our house at night.

They again beg John to arm himself, but he is adamant he will not. "A missionary's trust is in the arm of the Lord," he repeats. He and Tupatai are the only ones who will not carry a weapon or give in to Taniela when it is right to stay firm, and they are the only two he has the slightest fear of. But soon enough, glimpses of Taniela are seen as he prowls about our premises again, day and night.

The villagers take to whistling to signal his departure or return. When he does set off it is a relief to throw windows and doors open for air, though another whistle will have us scrambling to secure everything quick-smart in what seems like no time at all. Poor Mary gets white to the lips when the whistles sound, for all have learned their rise and shrill, and she has begun to cry, "I frighten Taniela!" I am pleased Arthur is too young to know what is going on.

The only time I am thankful for Taniela's return is when I do not know where John is. Otherwise, my mind believes Taniela is tracking his footsteps or murdering him in the bush. Then one afternoon, from our front verandah, John goes off to make some repairs to the *Chance*, with Marifatu and Noai a little in front. Taniela appears at John's back on the path – axe in hand. I struggle to focus from the verandah and hold my breath to steady my vision. When John stoops to examine a bush or fern or some such, Taniela seems to stoop too, a few metres behind, stalking.

Visions of the murdered James Gordon with a machete languishing in his head rise to my mind. My heart pounds in my chest, sweat prickles on my top lip and I mumble, "no, no, no," under my breath. I know John and the boys are on their guard, but a blow could so easily be struck.

I call out for Tupatai, who is translating a hymn at John's desk in the study. If he thinks there is real danger, we can go to John. He looks anxious as he comes over and takes in the scene, but John has moved off a little by now and we canna see Taniela. Tupatai smiles and goes back to his work. I try to follow suit, forcing myself to breathe deeply and pick up the seams I had been sewing. But my gaze flicks back and back again, to the place I saw them last.

Chapter 32

ERAKOR

The following Tuesday morning, as Utevo and I are sorting through picture books on the verandah, Basiva passes the fence, looks around then motions to me. I go to her, and she says, "When will the boat be leaving, Missi?" Her brow knits in desperation.

"Captain McLeod assured John it would sail on Friday, so only three more days." I clutch her hand and squeeze it in excitement.

She jumps up and clasps her hands, saying, "My heart sings, for he is sure to go!"

Taniela's last days are spent pulling up the people's bananas and sugarcane. He takes our boys' fishhooks and knives and walks off with blankets from the verandah.

On the Thursday morning, we have just finished breakfast and John is going to his study when the church bell is furiously rung a full hour before time. I look out and the villagers are staring at each other in question. Some hurry forward thinking they are late. The usual bellringer raises his hands, wondering why his work has been taken away from him.

It is Taniela. The more they beg of him to leave off, the quicker he rings the bell, until John runs out and shouts, "Stop!"

Taniela is wide-eyed and sneering. In an instant he lets go of the bell rope, picks up and raises his club high into the air, and runs at John.

Before a sound even passes my lips, he brings the club down in a wide arc. I close my eyes. A wild cry of, "*Uana!*" rings out. "Look out!"

Time stands still. I canna bare to will my eyes open again, but when I do John is falling, and Marifatu is falling with him. Taniela screams out before running off into the bushes; those around too stunned to move or give chase. The hairs prickle all over my body and then sobs escape lips, but whose, or mine, I know not.

My legs are leaden as I run to John. Each crunch of sand moves slowly beneath my feet. When at last I reach him, I sink down, trembling, and cradle his head in my arms. Blood streams from the angry gash on his forehead.

"Marifatu took the blow, Missi," Samuel says close to me as he tries to revive him too, but he is out cold. Blood springs brightly through his thick woolly hair, glistening scarlet droplets against the black.

"Carry them to the house," comes from my mouth, although it does not sound like me.

Kalumtak motions to some men to help, and they carry John and Marifatu into the house and lay them on couches. Some of the women are crying behind us as we leave the *malel*, but I canna give reassurance to them.

Once inside, I grasp the small bottle of smelling salts from John's medical bag and crouch low to his couch. John moves his head to the side, but he does not open his eyes. I try Marifatu, but there is no response from him. Lameka and I set about cleaning and dressing their wounds, while I ask the villagers to leave the house for now. We will send word when we can, but I canna have so many bodies to manoeuvre around. My head is buzzing.

Utevo takes Mary's hand and leads her into the bedroom where Arthur is crying and starting to cough in his agitation. When the men are cleaned up, I kneel and pray between the two couches, with a small lamp to keep a check on whether both men still breathe.

How has it come to this? We have made such advances here, such good gains, such love has been shown to us, and yet it has almost been erased in a heartbeat.

My mind is full of anger now, and I do not attempt to stifle these thoughts. I put cooling cloths to John's brow, mindful of the gash on the left side, below the bandage that is already turning the colour of rust. Tears flow down my cheeks.

John's features are sunken and pale. His eyes flick open, now and then, as if he is unable to get into a deep sleep. He rouses at the most faint and distant sounds, whereupon he grumbles and murmurs, shaking his head one side to the other. Marifatu appears to be in a far, far-off place; a deep, dreamless sleep.

As time passes, my anger subsides. I think back to when Dr Munro visited on his final farewell, and so soon before his death in Geelong. He told us how they had called here in 1861 and the Lord's Supper had been taken for the first time with fourteen converts. They had used coconut water for wine and a pudding of arrowroot and coconut for bread. Efaté was then the second island of the whole group to have a Christian church.

"But this church was the fruit of eleven missionary visits and the devoted labours and deaths of more than twenty Polynesian teachers and their families. The seed was sown in weakness … but it has since been raised in power," he said. But then he had gone on to say, "Thus light and shadow have pursued each other, the light brightening for a moment but upon the whole the shadows deepening."

After he had left, John was so sure that he would be the one to bring lasting light to these villages. His faith and hope never wavered. What if it is all taken from him now? I canna help but wonder what it has all been for. I know that John, if he survives, will not feel this way, but it is a bitter taste that fills me.

The next day John is lowest of all. He is white and sweat prickles on his brow as his body fidgets and shakes. He mumbles, then is quiet once more. It is a day of watching and prayer. I keep guard on my knees at the door most often entered, trying to ensure quiet. Lameka instructs everyone to be away from the house and, finally, all I can hear are the birds and the breeze in the trees. I fall asleep too, resting my head on the edge of his couch.

It is not until near dawn that John squeezes my hand, and I raise my head. He manages a weak smile in the dim light. I gasp in relief, before I rush to the bathroom, overcome with nausea.

Marifatu slowly comes around too, and the day that follows is filled with love and kindness by everyone around us. Lameka tidies about the house, and Utevo keeps the children busy, each now and then coming to check on John. Simetone makes enough broth to feed the whole village, not just two sick individuals, and all of us benefit from its restorative effects.

That night, as we are re-dressing both men's wounds, a shot rings out in the darkness. We have heard as loud reports and nearer, when men are killing flying foxes or birds, which cause nothing more than a start and a laugh, but there is something in this shot that makes me spring to my feet.

From his cot, John says, "Someone is shot! Either Taniela or someone by his hand." He has barely uttered the words when the awful death-wail in Basiva's voice comes from outside.

Lameka and Utevo rush in from the bathroom, where they were filling the bath, and Lameka says, "That's Taniela, Pa, for the Imitang people told us not to be alarmed if we heard a shot after dark, as we would know it is Taniela killed."

I gasp. It had all been arranged. Marik Tikaikow must have sanctioned it, I realise, and we knew not a word about it.

"Then I must go and see what I can do for the poor fellow," John says, attempting to rise.

Another loud report makes me implore him to stay, "You're in no condition, we don't know for certain, you might be shot in the dark ..." the words tumble out of me one over the other.

Then Mary comes in from the bathroom and says, in a faint voice, "Pa, will you stay and take care of us?"

John sighs and says, "Aye, I'll not leave."

Samuel rushes into the room, startling us all.

"Taniela has been shot!" He is panting and tries to get his breath back but looks relieved.

"I must go to him," John says, again beginning to rise.

Samuel shakes his head. "You going now would be of no use, Pa," he says matter-of-factly.

I take John's hand and kneel. He recites a prayer and, oh, how our hearts bleed for the fellow. Through all the fear and threats and finally his attack, we did not want to see it end like this. Though, in the end, Taniela had courted death, and I believe it had answered his call.

⤜᷿⤛

The next morning, under the shade of coconut palms, Taniela is laid to rest. John is too weak to attend, though watches on from a verandah chair, with a blanket spread over his knees. Lameka and I decide we must attend. No one shows any animosity toward me, though I canna help but look for it in their eyes.

Lameka, subdued but stoic, lays plaited coconut-palm fronds in the bottom of the grave before her brother's body is lain on top. Tupatai reads some scripture before Kalumtak and Samuel lay more palm leaves. Basiva holds onto her baby, and stands unmoving to one side, staring down at the grave. No emotion disturbs her face, and she will not meet my eyes.

The death-wail is taken up by a group to one side. Some have besmeared their bodies with soot from our pot, though our Christian congregation have not. I hope John can see this, as this change has been a long time coming. This renouncing of *kastom* feels, in a measure, an act of solidarity after what has happened, softening the bitterness I feel over the attack. As I watch the ceremony, I am all at once overcome. This waste of life and those who took it from him. *Am I one of them?* I wonder. I am feeling the hopelessness of what these islanders have had to endure.

My thoughts turn to that day we buried Poma, now lying next to his son. I think, too, to the day when Ma would have been laid to rest in Nova Scotia. I could not be a comfort to anyone then, and really no one could be to me, even John, no matter how much he had tried.

I sigh again, shake off my thoughts and breathe in the heat of late morning, blinking away my tears. This was not Poma, nor dear Ma, but someone who tried to kill us. Yet I only feel sadness. I forgive him. Really, in my heart, there seems nothing to forgive.

Chapter 33

ERAKOR

In the weeks that follow, Marifatu keeps having dizzy spells, putting his hand over his right eye and blinking, as if he canna clear his vision. When I talk to him of it, he shrugs and says his sight is not good. I have nothing that will help him, and I wonder how soon it will be before he visits a *natamole tabu*. Our local one is a hideous-looking old man, dirty in the extreme, who prowls about picking up *garei* – the refuse of what anyone has been eating – to take home to burn. I wonder what Marifatu will offer to appease the spirits. All I can think is that he saved John's life.

John has been subdued since he came around. When I squeeze his hand, his smile is weak, though he never complains of pain. My mind canna help but wonder, *what if?* What if I had lost him? I realise he is my anchor – steady and calm to my anxious fretting, deliberate and measured to my impulsive charge. Were he not, I could not have followed him to the other side of the world and coped without my family comfort. It shakes me to see his vulnerability, something it had not occurred to me he even possessed.

I look more at his face while spooning him broth in the days of his recovery than ever before. His skin is a little less smooth than when I first saw him watching Dr Munro's rousing speech in Nova Scotia, and his beard is wirier in its longer length, though still tightly curled. The lick of hair at the front of his high forehead is tinged with grey, like the spray on the crest of a wave. His cheekbones are more prominent now, emphasising those

215

glacial-blue eyes. But he has always been wiry, and I have never been able to fatten him up. I try to tame his chaotic hair with cooling wet cloths, and I kiss his bruised forehead, while we begin, slowly, to talk of all that has happened. He averts his eyes from mine at the mention of Taniela's name though, and shame is writ across his face.

I decide to restart school, and to try to move forward. But night-time brings restless dreams for me, reliving that day, except in the dreams my legs will not move toward John at all. John keeps to the couch in his study, so that we do not disturb each other at rest, though I surely feel the distance.

My heart flips when the cry of a ship is espied on the horizon a week or two later. It is to my utter joy when I realise it is the new *Dayspring*. Even more wonderfully, Hugh and Christina soon step ashore. Lameka brings tea out to the verandah, and I wrap John in a light blanket before helping him outside. He is losing weight, though I do not believe it is down to any sickness. Hugh and Christina are horrified to hear of the troubles we have endured, though John plays it down as just a trifling matter. But, in truth, it seems little different to many of their own trials on Erromango.

"Well, we have news!" Christina says with delight. "We're going on furlough to Nova Scotia." She squeals a little in excitement. I know my smile is weak as sickening envy fills me, knocking the air from my lungs, but Christina does not notice. Hugh asks John to manage his stations in their absence, and despite the responsibility, I can see he is keen to do this.

"John must recover first," I say.

"Oh yes, of course," replies Hugh. "He'll not be required to visit for some time."

I suppose John will want to have tasks to occupy himself with after the previous tumultuous months I realise, and so I do not object further.

Hugh sighs as we watch the village children playing in the tendrils and dens of a banyan tree; surely no more fantastical hidey hole in all of creation. "We succeeded in placing a chain of schools and teachers around about, but, some months later, when visiting Cook's Bay, we found the school closed and worship stopped. A labour vessel had called in and both the teacher and every young and able-bodied man had gone on board. These so-called labour vessels are an immense curse."

John only nods in response.

"Within just the last four months, three fishers of men have taken away more than a hundred of my promising young men. Thirty labour vessels are now afloat amongst the islands, so I've heard. The people are becoming educated and are realising that beyond their line of vision there are other countries – wonderful countries – which they hear about from the returned kanaka crews, and from the men who come down in ships with bright beads and guns to sell."

"Indeed, the crews come back with reports on wages and the best places to go," John agrees. "They're getting higher wages and more expensive trade gifts now, too, despite the falling sugar prices."

"And did you have influenza here?" Christina asks.

John and I shake our heads. "With everything else that has happened, I am at least thankful we have not," I say.

"Well, we had an epidemic recently, and Hugh took it badly himself. Though it wasn't long until HMS *Espiegle* came to anchor, and when the captain saw Hugh's plight, he sent off at once for their doctor."

This makes me wonder whether I should try to get word to one ourselves, for John and Marifatu to be checked over properly. Though we never know when the ships will appear.

"In the main, visits by HM's ships are pleasant enough, with many officers interested in our work, don't you find?" Hugh says before taking a sip of tea.

"They're usually only here to investigate murders if anything," John replies. His voice sounds cynical and subdued. "Over a dozen traders have been killed around Efaté in recent times, for 'ravishing native women', we've been told, or simply 'murdered for plunder'. Either that or the men-o'-war shell a native settlement in return for the massacre of a boat's crew. The same old story …"

My eyes flit to Hugh and Christina as heat floods my cheeks at John's tone.

"But, of course, only one side of the question is heard, and the chief's answer is invariably, 'We killed them in revenge for our countrymen who have been stolen away, and often killed as well,' and as this is an acknowledgement of guilt, a few villages are shelled as a lesson not to take the law into their own hands. Nothing is ever done to the ruffians who caused all this *misery*," John's voice is rising higher, his anger climbing. "They're most likely carrying on their accursed trade elsewhere and laying the foundation for some other massacre." His voice rings of the hopelessness of it all.

My heart is gripped in a fist for my husband, and I clench my jaw.

"For me," John continues, quieter, "when the natives see the gunboats siding with this anti-Christian traffic, I think the people must come to regard me as not from the same country, or as an outcast from it, perhaps. The traffic appears so important an enterprise that the national gunboats are sent out to protect and foster it. What does this do for our credibility?"

Hugh nods and then, somewhat awkwardly, reaches over and lays a hand on his friend's shoulder, giving it a reassuring squeeze.

Christina turns the conversation back to Nova Scotia and their plans once there. I lightly talk of a time when we, too, might journey back to civilisation and take a breath, but John shakes his head and says, "The time is not right." His tone makes me appear foolish for even suggesting it.

He will not look at me squarely; he has not for days. I wonder, not for the first time, how long he will berate himself for Taniela's death.

"Look, I'm sorry to be the bearer of bad tidings, but there is something else you should know." Hugh sighs then and steals a small smile at Christina before he continues.

"Elizabeth Copeland passed away of consumption back in January. Despite their efforts, she never really did get over the loss of her baby and the consequences to her health from that time. When she learned recovery was hopeless, she decided to stay on Futuna to die amongst the people, despite their apparent lack of success. Her body was lain beside that of her little boy and near the graves of the teachers and their wives."

After a few moments I say, "Poor Betsey. We must pray for Joseph to have strength looking after his two girls by himself." Everyone nods. I think then of Christina's words when we first arrived here, and how Betsey had been determined to carry on, despite her bitterness and her own plight, rather than be the reason for the collapse of their mission by leaving their station.

John's wound heals over, though the resultant scar makes me wince. With his now-greying hair and weather-beaten skin, he looks aged, but somehow that makes me more tender toward him, and I miss his affection more than ever. He is still so closed.

Healing has not been so swift for Marifatu. He finally admits that he has lost the hearing on one side and his vision is diminished too. But his love for and protection of John has never wavered. In fact, as they often compare scars, they seem more attached to each other than ever.

Basiva has remained near the station, and once she is back on her feet, I help her with her baby and offer comfort as she needs it. I ask her if she would like to stay with us, but she seems happy to be independent. After a time, she comes to me with a desire to help the Imitang people and Neheto, the very man who murdered Taniela. She says, "Is there no missionary to go and teach Neheto's people? I weep and pray that they too may come to know and love Jesus."

"Basiva," I say, "if I'd only wept and prayed for you, but stayed at home in Canada, would that have brought you to know and love Jesus as you do?"

She smiles at this. "No, Missi."

John takes her there and says her forgiveness and gentle demeanour encourages them all to listen to what he has to say. Marik remains defiant, but in a little time Neheto rubs off his thick-daubed paint and cuts off his long hair. He comes to the village dressed in a shirt and pants. Then I realise his designs are for more than Christian instruction. Basiva seems shyly to be responsive to his overtures too.

After a little, they come to us and say they wish to be married, in the church. I let them choose what they like from the latest box from Greenhill. Basiva picks a nice green jacket and a white hat, while Neheto chooses a long white nightshirt – nothing else. It evidently belonged to a much taller man as he floats in it, but that is fine with me. At least one good result has come from that whole sorry episode, and if anyone deserves happiness now, it is Basiva.

This seems to reinvigorate John, and his focus slowly turns to his flock once more. He resumes itinerating to a gruelling schedule once back up on his feet, almost as though he is making up for lost time, or there is something coming perhaps that he canna prevent.

PART IV

I cannot hear Thy voice, Lord. Dost Thou still hear my cry?
I cling to Thine assurance that Thou art ever nigh.
I know that Thou art faithful; I trust, but cannot see
That it is still the right way by which Thou leadest me.

— Florence Young, *Pearls of the Pacific*

Within the churchyard, side by side,
are many long low graves;
and some have stones set over them,
on some the green grass waves.

Full many a little Christian child,
woman, and man, lies there;
and we pass near them every time
when we go in to prayer.

They cannot hear our footsteps come,
they do not see us pass;
they cannot feel the warm bright sun
that shines upon the grass.

They do not hear when the great bell
is ringing overhead;
they cannot rise and come to church
with us, for they are dead.

— CF Alexander, *Within the churchyard, side by side*

Chapter 34

ERAKOR

John regularly takes the *Chance* over to Erromango, with a few of his best men, to check on the Frasers' station, though they do not stay long. He always comes back and admires his efforts on Erakor more. Although, as with Hugh, despite already supplying some teachers for other areas, we would have supplied more had not the labour traffic taken many away.

I think often of Christina in Nova Scotia, and how sweet the taste of respite must be. She recently wrote how they had been about to depart Montreal to begin the long journey back when she caught a cold. She thought at first it was island fever but had continued to worsen. The doctor soon told them it was pleurisy, and for nine days she had lain at death's door. She said how by our loving Father's blessing and the skill of their doctors she had rallied. It is no affront of bravery this time that has led them to make the perilous journey and decision to return here. But still, that journey home, I wonder whether I can even bear to make such an arduous crossing again. The months at sea.

Mary and I meet John at the beach on his return from Erromango one afternoon. We walk up together and around my profusion of croton plants, while Mary plays hide and seek with Arthur behind them. "I was longing to get that journey over with," he says as I stoop to run my free hand along some warm-red leaves. John looks particularly tired and thin, I notice.

"Our mission, I'm sorry to say, is dwindling, Ann. The MacDonalds are leaving at the end of the year and perhaps Mr Copeland too. He's in poor health and has had a great deal of work … I mean, such work as draws a *man* down. His two girls had a bad attack of fever and he waited on them himself. It was hard for him to lose Betsey and have no one to speak a word of sympathy to him. He'll go to the colonies to recuperate. Then there are the Archers, who've left too."

"Are you still happy here?" I ask. "After everything we've been through." I wince and my heart beats rapidly at having asked this question, and I do not look to him straightaway. It frustrates me that I should be worried asking this of my own husband. I do not even really know where the question has sprung from, only deep within me I suppose, but waiting, wanting to be asked.

He considers me for a moment before replying. "I feel happy in my work," he says at last, "and I'd be sorry to leave the field. It's discouraging to think they appear a doomed race and are dying out so fast. But whilst there are any remaining, we must do our utmost to bring them to a knowledge of the truth, eh? I'm in better health now, which is a matter of great thankfulness. I think we enjoy very much the tokens of God's love in this far-off field, Ann. I find Him as near and as ready to answer prayer as at home. Nay, I might say nearer than at home, for it's here we can really enjoy his love and sympathy."

This is possibly the most John has spoken to me since Taniela's death, about anything important at least, and for the first time since then I believe his faith in our mission has returned. I wait, then, for him to return the question, to ask if I am happy here, but he does not. *Perhaps he is afraid to*, I wonder, not wanting to think of alternatives. Had he asked, I do not know what I would say. I would have drawn a veil over my feelings most likely. I am not *aching* to leave, but the last year has been filled with such a weight of difficulty. I am tired and I wonder if I have lost the strength I had in the beginning.

I leave Mary following in her father's footsteps while I take Arthur's hand to return inside to write more missives to Tilly and Christina. Arthur settles quickly. He appears tired too. It is late and my hand aches by the time I finish writing, only having taken a break for dinner and to settle Mary. I stretch my fingers out and clench them in again, then rub the two half-moon indents left behind on my palm from my nails digging in as I wrote.

I rise and look down at Arthur in the dim glow of the desk lamp. He has greatly outgrown his bassinet, but it is closer to my bedside. He is still sleeping soundly, and I am relieved. His cough has returned.

I undo the buttons from my dress and slip it off, noticing the fraying hem. I run my fingers over the cotton and wonder at our stores of calico. I will check with Lameka tomorrow whether we need to put in an order with the *Dayspring*. The hem is discoloured too. The rains are late this season, and the tanks are low.

John is stacking books in his study next door as I remove the pins from my hair. One pin has lost its cushioned end and rudely announces its arrival at the tip of my finger. I scowl at it but resist putting it in the waste basket. Who knows when I will receive more. My nightdress is soft from wear and comforts me as it travels down the length of my body. John walks into the room as I am picking up my hairbrush. "I'm saying goodnight, dearest." He sounds weary. "I still have the monthly report to finish."

"Goodnight, dearest." I smile, but he is not actually looking at me and does not do so even as he plants a fleeting kiss on my cheek. I wait until he has left the room before I pull back my blue-and-cream embroidered bedspread. I fold it in half and smooth along the crease before I pull both corners of my pillow out to straighten it. I notice a faint green smear across the lip of the top sheet and remember how the sheets had blown out like sails in the wind before swishing back across the grass.

I climb into bed and the coolness on my feet at the end is delicious. I move my feet side to side to use it up. I sigh deeply, then all at once a flashing knot of tightness fills my chest. I tut. "Not tonight," I whisper. "Not tonight, please," I say as I glance once more at Arthur before I extinguish the lamp.

Even though Utevo is forever at his heels since he started toddling around, I still make them stay close as I worry for the sea. At night it is the last thing I hear as I try to sleep. Sometimes the sound enters my dreams and I wake with a start thinking it is carrying him away from me. I remonstrate with anyone who leaves the gates open. John raises his eyebrows at this. I know he thinks me over-cautious, but he knows little of this night-time habit that has formed of anxiety filling my belly when all I wish for is sleep.

༄

It is arrowroot season, but with another bout of influenza ravaging the islands, harvesting is delayed. None but perfectly healthy people can assist in the arrowroot cleaning, and these must don their cleanest garments. The islanders are keen to get on with it to pay for their gospels being printed in Melbourne, so John is helping out – something he does not ordinarily do. He stays away in the traditional cave in the hills with the people, near where they harvest the crop. But the damp from the cave must have irritated his lungs as he is taken ill upon his return.

The people work on apace without him. The potato-like tubers have the skin scraped off, then the bulbs are reduced to pulp by grating, before being stirred in a tub of clear water. We have introduced tin graters to help them, having received twenty-five pounds from the kirk to be used however we deem best. It has helped put them back on track. When all the poisonous juices have leached away, it is spread out in the sun to dry. Suitable water is always the great drawback and more so this year after the dry season we have had.

I let them draw upon my precious tanks for the last watering, to make it white, and will endeavour to cut back elsewhere to save more. The demands upon me for calico are endless, too, and I sacrifice all my common sheets, and grass-stained ones, plus old tablecloths and whatever else, to make into bags for straining.

But John's sickness develops into influenza, and soon he is lying helpless on the couch. More from the village are stricken, too, and pigs are being killed by the dozen to appease the spirits. At this, John's anger and frustration grows. I know it is not because he is ill. He is short and sharp with everyone, including me, and I quickly tire of being his nursemaid. I administer to the people more instead. Finally, one morning John asks me to summon Samuel and Kalumtak. I am not privy to their conversation in the study, but their faces are subdued on leaving the house.

John is recovering on the couch the next afternoon when Samuel comes rushing in. "Pa, the villagers wish to build a fence around the church. It is to be made from the heathen gods."

I know this to mean the carved and hollowed-out drums from their *malel*. These are regarded with great veneration, so this strikes me as strange that they are abandoning their old practices if they want to use them in this way. I wonder what John requested of Kalumtak and Samuel yesterday, what demonstration of faith he was expecting. I look with anticipation to John at Samuel's news, my eyebrows raised. He nods slowly, then smiles.

"But, Pa,"—Samuel looks a little downcast once more—"I must tell you that sacred stones and bamboo canes filled with sacred earth have been given to me also. They were in the homes of seven people who had the influenza."

John frowns then and says with a sigh, "Some have been taking Christianity with only one hand, Samuel, and with the other clinging on to *kastom*."

His voice rankles with irritation, and a knot of dread twists in my stomach at his words. I put down the seam I am sewing.

"I have been thinking on this," Samuel says, "and perhaps if we burn the sacred banyan, then the root of heathenism will be destroyed?"

"No, you *can't* do that!" I bolt up from my sewing machine, speaking louder than I intended. Pulling myself up I try again. "Samuel, a tree isn't a symbol of heathenism; it's, it's a beautiful creation that means so much to all who live here, even to us, but not as a heathen *idol*." I do not feel I am expressing myself well, but he catches my meaning and nods.

Samuel waits while John thinks, intertwining his hands and tapping his index fingers to his lips.

"The people have been writing down, recording their traditional, heathen ways, have they not? Passing them from one to another?" John asks.

I look at John in question.

"Yes, Pa, they have," Samuel replies.

"Perhaps then we'll take a trip in the *Chance*, when I'm well, with their papers and all of the idols and give them up to the ocean."

I look at John in horror and disbelief, but he has closed his eyes to me, as if deep in thought.

"Yes, Pa, I shall organise it," Samuel says, nodding, not meeting my eyes as he leaves the room.

"John! You *can't!*" I say, clenching my teeth. "We aren't here to teach or *force* them to give up their traditions. Have you forgotten? We're here to open their eyes to God. Remember … remember what Dr Munro said? Don't forbid or denounce their customs, don't ride roughshod over them!" My brain is clouded in my agitation. "It's putting us in danger!"

"But heathenism *is* in the root of their traditions, Annetta. I've always said they won't be forced, and that these things will be given up of their own accord when they're ready ... well, we've waited and waited and now I feel they are ready. Educating them is about giving them the chance to choose."

"But we haven't educated them in how to write only to make them destroy it all once they've done so. Surely, John! This is their *history*." I am pleading, but he remains calm and resolute, angering me all the more.

"Why are we holding on to their language if we're throwing away their customs?" I am shouting now. "We've worked so *hard* with the language, teaching them to write ..."

I breathe and try another tack, "Look, the heathen recognise the Lord's Supper as a *tabu* feast, John, so they've replaced one of their customs for one of ours! Ours are right and theirs are all wrong, is that it?"

John looks at me now as if to say *of course*, and I know I have revealed something more than I had intended. But there we are. I have spoken.

"So, you don't believe ours are right?" he asks, but not unkindly.

I sigh. Seeing what these people endure, people like Taniela, I realise I am not sure what I believe anymore, but part of me does not want to let John down. "We don't *know* everything, that's all. I just mean we shouldna strip away all that they've been before us."

He nods, but not in agreement. "I need to rest," he says simply.

"Don't shut me out this time, John ... You're infuriating!"

He shakes his head and picks up a book.

I sigh and leave the room.

Chapter 35

ERAKOR

It does not matter what arguments or silences I produce over the next few days; John is resolute. He will not discuss it with me any longer. Once recovered from the influenza, the *Chance* is loaded with sacred stones, idols and papers. I stand on the shore that morning, digging my toes into the sand. My arms are folded tightly across my middle, holding in my anger, as I breathe in the heavy heat. The breeze flicks up a scrap of parchment from a stack in the stern and sends it spiralling into the air, dancing, before it sinks toward the clear water. I catch it before the liquid can soak into its pores. Other bits rest silently on the surface around me, while others have curled and slipped under.

I look at the piece in my hand before stooping and picking up as much as I can from the rest of the stack in the boat. I grab a handful of idols that sit next to the papers, put them on my stack and then add some sacred stones too. My back is to the beach, and I do not turn around as such but shuffle my way along the shore with the possessions shielded in my arms. Once I think I am out of sight, I turn and go into the vegetation beyond the beach.

My heart is beating fast as I scan for somewhere, not really knowing what I am doing, but feeling determined nevertheless. I walk on and come to a place I often sit to look out to the ocean. I drop to my knees and start digging at the sand. It is too loose and falls in around my hands, but I persevere until, finally, a hole is big enough for the things. Once they are covered, I find a large, discarded shell and place it over the site. Tears stream from my eyes, but I do not wipe them away, not until I am done.

I sit for a while before walking back to the beach. John and Samuel are at the boat now, looking around them, talking. I go to the house then; I will not witness this. I wonder who else may be looking on at what the missionary is doing. John promised to always discuss these issues with me, but it clearly does not mean he will listen or be swayed from his own judgement in any way. He has become like a man possessed, doing all we agreed not to do.

"The villagers have put up three casks, Ann. What an achievement, what with the good deal of work there is from beginning to end. The arrowroot should realise at least 1s. 6d. per lb … This is their third contribution, did you realise? In a few years, the mission will be self-supporting, of that I'm sure."

I nod. "Yes, impressive, John." I am tight-lipped and I do not care. "I'm going to the shore." He does not look up from his ledger.

I am not much interested in all the bustle that carries on about us. I have given the workers whatever they have needed without a second thought. Despondency engulfs me after John's decision, but that is the least of it – Arthur's pneumonitis has returned with a vengeance.

I thought I had been so careful to avoid him being around those with the influenza, but with John having it too, I have not succeeded. I believed our station to be healthy with the open aspect to the ocean, but now I look around me perplexed, wondering where this thing is, lurking, waiting for my child before rearing its monstrous head and hooking the weakest of us once more. The thought crosses my mind that I am being punished.

I bring Arthur to the shore daily, to let the cooling fresh breezes fill up his lungs, and hopefully clean out the irritants, wishing we were away at sea on the *Dayspring*. My mind is numb, and I become mesmerised by the breeze that plays on the leaves, gusts sweeping over my limbs and over my cheeks, away on its journey to caress the next obstacle in its path.

I transfix my eyes, too, to the white caps of the waves, while Arthur plays on the sand beneath me. Mary sometimes comes but she knows Utevo has more patience for her at the moment. I do not like myself for that either. Even though I can almost smell the water's coolness, cleanness, washing away the miasma, Arthur's cough will not go.

I growl at it one afternoon, like it is its own living thing that racks his sweet body, and Arthur looks at me in surprise.

"Not you, my darling," I say, biting down on my lip and cupping his chin in my hand, "not you. Just the cough, I want the cough to go now."

We spend much time alone there at the shore. I canna speak my fears to John. He is too preoccupied. In any case, I canna say the words out loud. I cry to Him for guidance. But I know Arthur is sinking. No guidance comes. *I believe in Him*, I think, *but I canna find Him*. My unanswered prayers are interrupted by Arthur's sporadic coughing that feels as if a pain in my own chest. He seems in such awful plight.

My stout little snow-haired boy, not yet two years old but already saying Mama and Pa and "Uvo", always "Uvo", toddling after Utevo who spins in cartwheels across the sand and kisses the top of his head, who picks him up and staggers away with him when he has wandered somewhere he should not – usually Kalumtak's hut as he is his favourite.

Arthur shakes hands with everyone, no matter who they are. Not even the most hardened heathen refuses to hold the hand of the little fellow. Kalumtak always has a laugh for him, a tickle and a chase. But Arthur canna toddle anymore; he keeps stopping to catch his breath. He seems forever tired, and his appetite has reduced.

I awake with a start and feel the air knocked from my chest. It is near dawn, and I turn to find John stirring next to me. But it is Arthur I hear, mewling sounds, and I rush to his cradle. Cold dread prickles my skin in the half-light as I feel his hot, clammy skin on my palm. John is awake now too and my voice is hoarse as I say, "He has a fever. Our little boy is sinking." I look to John, who has lit the lamp, and he looks into my eyes, needing no further explanation. He looks up to the heavens with a pained expression.

I scoop Arthur up, but he coughs and whines, arching his back irritably in my arms. John sits and holds his head in his hands while I pace about the room, trying to soothe Arthur. Then John stands and comes to take him from me, to relieve me, I suppose, but I shrug him off. "He needs my comfort," I say through clenched teeth. John nods and stands awkwardly for a time before slipping out of the room, knowing I would rather be alone. I weep then. "Good Lord, *no!*" I beseech. My mouth is dry, and my breathing laboured.

Arthur sinks lower through the day and then seems to lose his will. When he refuses any food, it takes all my strength to keep my breathing calm. I try rubbing his wee mouth with honey, thinking perhaps he is sore, but it makes no difference. His listlessness grows.

I do not move from the room for hours. Time slows though the sounds from outside continue, as though it were a normal day. Occasionally, John enters the room and just looks at me until I look up and shake my head a little, and then he leaves once more. I clutch Arthur to me, putting cooling cloths on his brow, listening to his hoarse, laboured breathing. I will myself to keep breathing too as it has become such a chore, before laying him down again and fanning his hot little body, praying as my tears fall upon him.

When later I hold his little form, he is so light and yielding; no resistance remains. I want to will the life back into him, but his breathing becomes more and more subdued. A little later, still clutching him to me, I press my lips to his now cool, clammy forehead, breathing in his sweet, familiar scent. A surge of bright pain lights in my chest as I already know how much I will miss it.

His eyes are shut but his mouth is open. I put my ear close to his lips, but there is no sound. I feel for his little heart then but only the slightest feeling can be found before all is still. His eyes flicker open, but he is not looking at me anymore, before they close for the last time.

Blood courses along my veins while my heart beats so wildly I think it must surely burst in twain. I cling to his little body, not wishing to believe the truth of it, and realise I am having to make myself breathe, just as he is not. How utterly helpless and alone I am in my despair. But there is nothing neither I nor anybody can do, and Arthur has given up his earthly body. I have to trust he has been taken into the arms of the Lord.

The sounds around me strike me as so unfitting, even in this anguished moment. Utevo is laughing on the verandah, Lameka sings softly in the drawing room. John is away, no doubt attending to someone else's needs.

Blood rushes in my ears as I try to realise, all in one dread moment, that my child has actually gone.

I look up around me thinking I will see his little spirit toddling away into the unknown land. The underside of the thatch photographs itself on my mind with the greatest detail instead – neat reed rows and light-brown battens. *How strange that such little things occupy one's observation when the mind is strung to the highest pitch about something momentous?* I think.

Lameka and Utevo enter the room together, chatting, until they see my face. I give an inward cry for strength before I stand and face them. I tell them as gently as I can that Arthur has gone. Lameka swallows heavily, and I ask her to fetch John. Utevo cries out in pain, sobs burst from her, and she runs from the room. I envy her, as for me no tears will come now.

John appears with Mary in tow and rushes toward me, taking me in an embrace that I canna return. "Where did you go?" I whisper.

"I hoped you were wrong," he says before pulling back. He kisses Arthur's forehead with only a look of confusion on his face. *You still don't believe me,* I think. He takes a seat on the end of the bed and puts his head in his hands. Mary buries her face in my skirts and cries while Lameka brings calico to dress the precious body, but not yet, it is too soon. I stay her arm. She nods and lays the material down before kneeling on the floor to pray.

"Come, Mary, let us leave Mama," John says.

"My knees won't carry me, Pa."

John stoops to pick her up, and she sobs and leans her head on his shoulder, exhausted. I sit with Arthur for some time before I lean into him one last time, inhaling his sweet scent.

I nod to Lameka and can only look on, numbed, while she wraps his body. Utevo has not returned. One of Mary's old toy chests becomes Arthur's coffin and there he lies, all night. I canna eat or wash or move. I simply sit at his side. I know not who comes and who goes. He looks so peaceful, and I have to touch him again, too, to realise he has truly gone.

Chapter 36

A FAR-OFF PLACE

The next morning, we have prayers in the drawing room before Lameka and Kakita clasp an arm on either side of me and lead me outside. Utevo is sitting against the side of the house, and she draws the hem of her dress across her teary cheeks, knowing I can see her. She looks up at last but breaks down again upon looking into my eyes, burying her face in her skirts.

I unhook Lameka and Kakita's arms and walk over to her. I reach my hand down. It is a few moments before she reaches up, and I pull her to her feet before I clasp her to my side to make our way to the grave together. Mary runs over and reaches for Utevo's hand. I am just a body going through these motions – a loud sound reverberates in my head, and I canna give clarity to my thoughts because of it.

The elders have dug a little grave in the mission plot, facing the restless sea. The church members have all come, dressed in their best. John takes the service for his own son, but I do not know what he says. Only the singing of the hymns breaks through the fog in my mind, and my lips move unbidden to, "There is a happy land" and, "Oh, may we stand before the lamb", as Arthur is laid in the earth and, I trust, in the arms of Jesus.

Arthur is now forever looking out on the wide Pacific blue. "Your mama can guide young Arthur into heaven's embrace," John says with a weak smile after the service has finished and the villagers have moved off. *It should be my embrace*, my mind screams. I would choke on my anger to say it out loud. How powerless I am, I realise, as I turn and walk away.

The pain falls on me, smothering me as if in a fog once more, but it remains my own and John's cloud, for I canna bring myself to tell or write to others of it. I hate it and am angry at it, and still do not quite believe it to be true.

As numbness overcomes me, I wonder if I have actually lost a piece of my heart; riven, buried with Arthur in his coffin, the remainder labouring now under an increased load. I do not seem to feel or care for anything now. *Surely*, I think, *I have given enough of myself to this place*, and I wonder then, *What do I have left to give?*

I push everyone away in my retreat. It is a thick and black cloud into which I enter. The Lord has lessons for me to learn here, of that I am sure, lessons that canna be taught in the light. I do not sleep for days, and I slump on my bed, picking indelicately at the calloused skin on my fingers – the horrid habit I have – and I will not allow John to place his hand on mine to quash it this time.

At times I steal away to the peace of the ocean. I know John is worried for me, others probably are too. Sometimes there is a rustle of vegetation or feet on crushed coral nearby, but no one other than Utevo disturbs me. She and Mary are the only ones I will tolerate here in any case. When Mary is elsewhere following Pa, sometimes Utevo shyly approaches and stands a little way off with her head down until I hold out my hand to her. Then she will take my hand, sit down on the coarse sand and rest her head on my shoulder. Sometimes I sing quietly, but most times we are still as we look to the rocks on the shoreline. Sometimes I wonder how it would be to plunge into the water off of them.

Some of the villagers shy away from us. The heathen will probably now condemn us as cursed. Some show kindness though, and Lameka brings messages from one person or another, all to the effect of, "Missi, we are crying about you, and praying all the time." But when Lameka comes into the bedroom one afternoon, she turns right around to me, looks into my eyes and says, "Your baby died, Missi," in wonder that such a thing could happen to us. Such mother-like sorrow is in her voice that I finally burst into a flood of tears. She clasps her arms around me and holds me to her heart. I must collapse with the weight of my exhaustion then as I know nothing more until I awake hours later on my bed.

Battling the physical pain in my chest, I try to turn to the Bible, and indeed all the wise words seem printed for our express circumstances and comfort. But they hold little meaning to me – they do not penetrate my heart as they might have before. I confess to feeling resentment. Resentment at the Lord, for whom I look but do not see, and listen but do not hear.

John, although grieving, seems to have boundless contentment through his faith, and I envy him that but am confused and bitter at it. A seed of bitterness is sown at him, too, I know that. After all, did I not come here for him? It is not a pleasant taste. And where, I ask myself, is my "sweet reward" that Dr Munro spoke of so eloquently?

Everywhere teems with associations of Arthur, renewing my grief at every turn. A few of the shells, shiny and smooth, that he rubbed in his wee hands, now run through mine without end. When I go to church again, the first time for many months, seeing the little empty space where he used to sit with Utevo is too much for me, and I get up to leave again. John catches my hand and beseeches me with his eyes to stay. I sit back at the harmonium and grind my teeth.

It is hard, too, to keep my heart down seeing how the girls and women have sewn bits of black into their hats with white thread. But when a wee fellow, about Arthur's own age, comes into church with a black sash tied around him, the floodgates burst open again, and with a vengeance.

The women still sew on the verandah most mornings, but do not ask me to sew too, though I often sit amongst them just for their company and song. I have taken to administering a dose of castor oil to all the children in the village, who put up a determined opposition to open their mouths for the nauseous dose, so they often run off when they see me coming. I want to keep them well.

The New Year's Day celebrations are our most subdued, and as soon as they are over, we prepare the house for the storm season. Blankets are kept in a box by the door, as well as a lamp and a small supply of biscuits, should we have to run for refuge. Though I have to keep replacing the biscuits as some seem to think them a personal offering. I am gladsome we have prepared as on January 8th, John's birthday, a gale arrives, turns into a terrific storm and rages until morning. I make a mental note to put down a pair of speaking-trumpets in our next colonial order; the wind makes such a deafening roar.

It is not the most violent storm we have had, but owing to the week of incessant rain that follows – rain that tests faith – when we can get nothing dried, it tells more upon me in my grief than many have before. Perhaps I should be getting better at coping with these disruptions to our lives. Instead, I begin to view this season as a long, dark tunnel, which I enter with dread and can only breathe freely from once safely out the other side. Now I just wish to miss this time altogether. I need respite from being on edge, respite from anxiety.

Another great thunderstorm in February throws the sea into majestic grandeur, with great mountain waves going into deep shadow as they arch around, then break into a mass of spindrift. I sit mesmerised by them, sheltered from the rain and wrapped in Tilly's blanket, but lost in my own storms. *Hitherto shalt thou come and no further, and here shall thy proud waves be stayed.*

I finally succumb to fever and ague and my head aches for days. Although John gives me double doses of laudanum, I canna sleep. My dreams are filled with momentous waves that threaten to engulf me with every breath I struggle to take, and they wash away from me anything I hold dear.

As the days roll on, I become more and more frustrated, but I have to admit I am so weakened that I have little choice but to remain in bed. Even raising a glass of water brings a trail of drips to the bedsheets from my shaking hand. *Is this the weight of my years?* I wonder, yet I do not consider myself old. Each day I try to raise myself to tend to tasks, determined, before I find I have forgotten what I was about to do, or Lameka has rushed to my side to tend to it for me. It is as though my mind has been emptied. Pure lassitude engulfs me. I try to keep myself awake when I think John will come in, not wanting him to catch me at rest yet again. I am not successful.

My face is a constant frown when I am alone, and I wring my hands. I secretly hope that I shall bear no more children in my life. John always held a dream of a family of ten, just like his family, though he does not speak of it as readily anymore. He can see what it is taking from me. I canna pretend intimate moments have been seized in any case. The thought of asking Lameka about the plant of *ba aulien*, to become barren, has flashed through my mind more than once, but I do not have the courage to utter it aloud.

When the sun finally shines forth, we turn the house inside out to dry, but some of the matting is ruined. What tremendous washings we have from our filled tanks. The whole island shines verdant, nature rejoicing after the long drought, and I determine to begin the great annual cleaning to save another turn up, though two months earlier than usual. It keeps me occupied. In fact, I am a body working away at my daily activities, but just a body. My soul is in a different, dark place, trapped there by doubts. Doubts about our whole entire life here and whether I can remain.

My smile has become a mask that covers everything. But this mask has a flaw – John can see through it – and I am not strong enough to forever be keeping it in place. He has commenced the annual outside painting ahead of time too. The sun is so strong that in less than a year not a particle of oil is left in the wood and spoils if we do not repaint it with whitewash.

John and Marifatu fashion a ladder of bamboo and there stands John at the top of it, craning his arm up, slopping on the whitewash with a broad brush. Marifatu is receiving sprinkles of white onto his woolly hair as he holds onto the ladder beneath – an unusual baptism, it must be said. On looking down, and the image burns into my mind's eye, John's face breaks into uncontrolled mirth. He bends double with laughter, paint draining off the brush onto the ground. Marifatu is shaking his head, laughing too, while minute, light droplets spin off through the air about him. John brings his head up again and catches my eye.

He stops laughing then. His laughter, each chortle, each guffaw, has pierced me; a pin pricking my skin. My face must express my pain, my anger, my bitterness. He sighs and descends the ladder, throwing the brush into the pot and running his hands down his coveralls as he walks toward me.

"Annetta," he calls. I have already turned back into the house.

He tries to take me into an embrace when he comes through the door, but I push my hands against his chest and crane my head away. "I'm glad you're happy," I say, not even trying to quash my anger.

"I have to go on … that's all … It doesn't mean I don't feel it. Dearest …"
His eyes beseech me, but I stand resolute.

"Look, if you place your trust in God, I am certain He will guide you—"

"It isn't working, John!" I shout.

"He will guide you through any obstacle in your path …" He stops then.

"Obstacle! Obstacle?" I spit the pathetic word out, stepping away from him.

"I just mean ask God for wisdom," he says quickly.

"I'm not sure if I can anymore … I'm not sure I want to ask Him *why* He has done this to me."

John's face belies his irritation. "God's not punishing you, Ann … His omnipotence—"

"John!" I cut through his words, my voice quivering with anger. "I don't … want you … to give me platitudes! I don't … want you … to preach to me, or quote scripture … I am your wife, not a heathen soul to be saved." But even as the words come out of my mouth, the thought, *Am I not?* flashes through my mind.

"We're all souls to be saved!" He smiles.

I clench my teeth together and gasp, my anger spiking as he agrees with my thoughts.

"We'll get through this, Ann … with the Lord's will, with *each other*," he says kindly.

This seems incredulous that he would say this now. "I don't know where our 'each other' is anymore, John," I shout. I canna say more as it would come out in a scream. And I do not know if I can; if I can remain and just get through this anymore. I do not care then if I become just another missionary's wife blamed for the ruination of an overseas mission. My heart is riven. I turn and walk into my bedroom, where I sink into my bed, pull the bedspread over my head and close my eyes.

Chapter 37

ERAKOR

I tell no one of my thoughts; I am consumed in this battle and it is mine alone. I am too afraid of committing my doubts on paper to Christina either. I canna even say them out loud. If God truly is there, He will know of them already, and, somehow, saying or writing them will make them more true. The truth is that my faith has become a weight I am dragging around; it burdens me. I do not want to give it voice because, despite its weight, it suddenly feels to have no substance.

Salvation is only available through faith in Jesus Christ. I am, therefore, no longer assured of my own salvation. My doubts assail me as if a ship in a storm – I am tossed hither and thither. *Will I be reunited with my child?* I wonder daily. Ma said God would not take me where the grace of God could not keep me. But that passage goes on, "Where the arms of God cannot support you," and I do not know that to be true, not anymore. I do not feel supported. And it is not just from God.

When I stare at the flat, glass-like lagoon, I realise it *has* become a lid, keeping everything tightly secret beneath; the people's beliefs drowned. Shame fills me to think of it. But shame fills me to think of the secret hoard I buried too. That I should resort to such measures because my own husband would not listen to me. Why could I not turn John from his course? Why did he not support me? We have never spoken of that day again. Too much has happened since. But he is the missionary here, not I. I am resigned to that now. He makes the decisions and the people do not protest. I do not want to change these people into Europeans. He knows I have not forgiven him, but my angry feelings have drifted in time, weakened after Arthur. I have resigned myself to them too.

When I am finally able to send a letter to Christina – who has heard of our tragedy by other means by this time and has written to me in great concern – I only exchange everyday news and only touch lightly on the subject of Arthur. I have not made a decision about whether I must leave, and I am thoroughly torn in my quandary. I canna tell her of it. I so long to return home now, to feel my family comfort, I think, if only for a short time. But Ma is gone, Tilly is married. There would be no family comfort, and I am fooling myself that it would only be for a short time.

Christina's reply does not berate my lack of candour, but only suggests that our monthly thought be a reflection on the text, "He knoweth what is in the Darkness; for the Light dwelleth with Him." It is not a text I can recall, and I smile as I read it. It resonates with me like no other. That my child could be a ray of light that pierces the darkness and makes it shine becomes the only sustaining flicker of comfort to me. I am so grateful to her then.

I spend more time alone at the little grave, finding the finest, whitest gravel and smoothing it over the top, clearing away the errant leaves. Arthur would have been talking well by now. "An infant snatched from its mother's bosom produces an aching void nothing earthly can fill," someone once said to me, and how my heart aches for him. But I have begun to realise he was not sent in vain. What a little teacher he was. How many frowning faces were reduced to broad grins as they sat the stout little chief on their knees.

I still do not know where Arthur has gone though, and doubts assail me in regard to his salvation. I find myself wringing and rubbing my hands together, picking at my skin, staring into nothingness, consumed in these thoughts. Is Arthur with Jesus, or all alone? I never doubted before being tried myself, and perhaps I took things for granted. It is a question I must settle with my God and my Bible, and I long for relief to my quarrelsome feelings. I try to remember that He loved him, and loves him still, but somehow reassurance does not come.

༄

Toward the end of the year, with the hot season approaching, the dread it brings starts to rise within me once more. The season brings mosquitoes and threat of malarial fever as well as the incessant storms and hurricanes. Even the vegetation grows with a smothering rapidity. Through all that has happened I *need* a trip to the colonies, *at least* to the colonies, if not home, I decide. I wonder if being away will help me find clarity to my doubts.

John has suffered recurrent bouts of fever, and I implore him that it is for the good of his health, as well as mine. He knows how much I need respite. Finally, he relents. *Was it my determination, or simply because it is time for us to place Mary in school?* I wonder. And really, that is long overdue.

The *Dayspring* will be sailing to Sydney in just two weeks hence, so we make haste to be ready, inform the other missionaries of our trip and leave instructions for our absence. John says, "Mr Campbell will be returning, too, having delayed his departure for much longer than is reasonable." I catch his tone but do not pursue the issue. George has been far from my mind.

We write to Hugh about looking after our stations in our absence, and there are the teachers, Tupatai and Kakita, too. The children in our care are received back into their families, and Lameka will look after two orphaned children then with us.

I see in the villagers' eyes that some suspect we may never return. What they know of those who leave for the colonies is that they do not reappear. This is not a question John thinks needs answering at all, but I find it hard to look into their eyes.

I will take Utevo to Sydney to help me, and she is giddy at the prospect, clapping her hands in glee and giggling through her fingers rather than doing anything useful to ready us. It is novel getting her into shoes for the first time. I lend her some of mine so she can practise. I remind her she will have to wear shoes everywhere in the colonies, but she is so unsteady on her feet that I have to hold her outstretched arms to balance her as she goes clamping along, squealing, "Missi, Missi, I'll fall! I'll fall!" to everyone's amusement.

Mary has outgrown most of her shoes too, leaving just one pair of slippers. I lose count of the times over the next two weeks that I point out they are on the wrong feet; both of us too accustomed to not worrying about it. The shoes are strange to me, too, so long has it been since I left the station and had to consider them.

After morning school on the day of our departure, I run my hand down John's sleeve as we leave the schoolhouse. "I'll be back in a little while."

"Where are you going?"

I tilt my head at him. "I think you know where."

He nods and walks on while I take the path around the back of the mission house. I know this path intimately now. I know each crab hole dotted along the edges in the deeper sand, I know each coconut palm's crooked trunk, I know each bend in the crushed-coral path, and I know each purposefully placed shell.

I sit for a little first, enjoying the peace. There is only a slight breeze and already a rivulet of perspiration runs down my neck under my cotton dress. I pant a little and hotness hits the back of my throat with each breath. I run my hand down the edge of the gravestone, as if it were his small, slender shoulder, and the stinging grip rises at the back of my throat.

I crane my head upward again and blink my eyes before closing them, breathing deeply as I relish finding the breeze, which alights on my cheek. I smile, composed now, as I begin to tell Arthur of our last few days, of the service that morning and the lessons at school. I tell him we are preparing to go to Sydney, and, finally, how Mary will be starting school. My lips tremble again before I place a kiss on my fingertips and touch it slowly, lightly, to the gravestone once more. It will be such a trial to leave to others the care of the grave, which I have so often watered with my tears.

Cries ring out that a ship is seen, and anxiety and excitement tighten my stomach. I walk back to the village and crowds are gathering in the *malel*. People have been coming in for days from all parts of the island to farewell us. I make my way over to John and Mary.

"We'll never get them in the church," John says, shaking his head.

"Should we have an open-air meeting, Pa, eh?" Mary asks in excitement.

"No, lass, it'll take too long to get the seats arranged, and the ground is still damp from the late rain."

But everyone is willing to squeeze and when finally everyone is crammed in, we begin. My voice does not hold steady through the music.

John asks them not to come to the shore but to farewell us at the church. When I go to say goodbye to Lameka, neither of us can speak for a full minute. I believe she sees the tumult in my heart.

"Missi, I never knew what you had given up to come to us. I fear … I fear you will never come back to our land again." I hug her and tell her that we will do what we can to return, but I will not pretend that it is a certainty for me. Her mouth twitches as she tries to hold back her tears. I know she understands, and she knows I share her grief.

When it is time to leave there is a general rush to the shore. The people arrange themselves in two long rows and we walk down between them, shaking hands with everyone. The women cling to and cry over me and Mary. Captain Braithwaite awaits us in the small boat, and I call out, "Captain, can you not do anything to show our gratitude?"

"All right, bless yer heart!" he bellows and, at his sign, the little *Dayspring*'s guns boom out a salute.

We have only just seated ourselves in the small boat when Kalumtak wades out and leans in, saying, "You are like a ship, Pa. We get foreign things from you. If you go away, we cannot get them. I need medicine!"

John tells him he cannot get it now, and says, "Anyway, you're not sick."

"Ah, but I may be before you come back!"

The laugh that follows brightens us all up. Kalumtak takes John in his burly arms and says, "Goodbye, my friend."

We assure them we will write from Sydney of our plans, and we ask Kalumtak and Samuel to buoy up the others' hearts. It is almost a relief when the *Dayspring* weighs anchor. "Why! Bless yer heart … I feel like crying myself," Captain Braithwaite says.

I am humbled at their sincere sadness, so often hidden from view, and I realise then how much they have entered my heart. Once we have rounded the point, and I can no longer see the crowd on the beach, I weep into my handkerchief. John puts a consoling arm about my shoulders. It is hard to look each other in the eye; the guilt we feel at leaving will be so reflected there. Neither of us will ever forget the love shown to us this day.

Utevo becomes seasick almost as soon as we weigh anchor. She takes to rolling around in the cabin below, despite my appeals to her to stay in the air on deck. Mary sweetly volunteers to keep her company. Mr Campbell is subdued after he comes on board at Ifira. He sits in the prow, smoking his pipe, but seems barely able to bring himself to look up and meet John's eyes. I look to John in question, but he shakes his head as if to say, *Do not ask me about it*. I sigh and shrug.

I remain at the ship's rail a few more moments, running my hand along the warm wood. Then I make a decision and make my way to where George is squatting down. I steal a glance at John and anger crosses his brow. I do not care.

"Mr Campbell, how have you found the islands this past while? It is so long since I've seen you. I thought you were returning last year. Have you kept well?"

George looks first to John before looking up and addressing me. "The experience has been most interesting and enlightening, Mrs Stewart, thank you. I have found a great deal to occupy my time and further my studies."

"Well, I'm so pleased you have taken so much from your time here," I say.

George clears his throat, subdued again, and nods as John makes his way over to us.

The air is thick with tension. John shifts uneasily next to me. I cast him a glance, but his eyes are to the horizon, though his jaw is set.

"Are you set to return here?" I press on.

"God willing, I shall, yes. Though, I've decided to return only as a fully accredited minister and, hopefully, with a, er, wife!" He looks up at John when he says this.

"I see." I smile, realising he must have felt his solitude sorely.

John smiles too. "That sounds like a wise decision, George."

Chapter 38

SYDNEY, AUSTRALIA

The *Dayspring* is caught in a gale nearing the Australian coast and a boat, hencoop and pigsty – with poor pig still inside – are washed overboard. For hours the little ship rolls side to side, with spars, sails and gear banging terribly. Mary comes up from below and seems to enjoy the adventure, but Utevo is terrified and takes to sobbing in her cot once more. I take a deep breath and force myself to go below. I stroke her smooth cheek and encourage her that it will be okay, hoping it is no false promise, while cleaning her up and appealing to her to come up for air for both our sakes.

She finally agrees. When we enter the Heads at Sydney, having left the loppy water behind, it quite takes her breath away. The hills are covered with gum trees, and magnificent houses are studded here and there, high amongst the trees and far along the shore. Although the town is still unfinished looking, the harbour makes up for it.

When we dock, the casks of arrowroot, brought from the island to sell, are landed and stored. On the deck, Captain gives Utevo a big hug and says, "Bless yer heart, I hope ye find the courage to risk the passage back!" Her smile is weak, and she looks so shaky that I take her hand and hold it as we disembark.

The quay is all bustle and noise about us. It is like a blow to the head, and Mary giggles and nudges my arm to get me to close my mouth and move forward. I am so caught up in it all that I hardly notice Mr Campbell saying his goodbyes before he is striding away from us into the crowds. John looks relieved before he turns to hail a hansom cab.

I have often wondered how I would feel to re-enter civilisation, and I find myself sighing deeply, drinking it in as we make our way through the city. Utevo is wide-eyed but has not said a word; she looks scared. I squeeze her hand, trying to draw out a smile from her.

We give her time when we reach the Port Jackson Hotel to find her feet, rest and acclimatise. I relish the feeling of soft carpet beneath my feet, but I am impatient and after only a little while I rouse Utevo and Mary and we head into the city to shop. John elects to remain, complaining of a headache.

Sydney appears so far advanced from our usual surroundings. I feel buoyed up and confident, finally, after seeing the contrast with my own eyes that schooling here really is the best thing for my little flower. Despite the constant foreboding at the separation, the hand that grips my heart is finally loosening. Maggie Gray's words ring in my ears that it is dangerous to keep children at the mission during their formative years. How Mary will be poorly influenced and coerced into improper ways, and that she is safer in the colonies. I do not share these anxieties, but the opportunities for Mary are certainly here.

It seems children like to make liars of you as soon as you least predict it though, and in the afternoon, while in a store looking for shoes that will fit Utevo slightly better than my own, I suddenly realise Mary is not with me, and neither is Utevo. On rushing out of the store, I first find Utevo, turning in circles and gaping at the bustle of civilisation around her, to the intense amusement of some grocers standing nearby. I shake her arm, more roughly than I had intended, and ask where Mary is, as she is nowhere to be seen.

I walk up and down, then stop short at the sight of her in a store, whirling handkerchiefs from a counter, as fast as a child's mischievous fingers can manage. The shopkeeper is hastening to the rescue as I rush in, and I apologise while gathering the items off the floor. I scold Mary and declare we are going straight back to our hotel. Inside, I am relieved to do so, to take away the staring eyes from the people around us. I canna understand her behaviour, and can draw no explanation from her either, no matter how hard I try.

A few days at the hotel is enough and we remove ourselves to Connie and Douglas MacPhersons' residence, where we all seem to relax over the following weeks. They are long-time supporters of the Presbyterian mission and we simply do not have the funds to stay in a hotel for longer. Some afternoons we visit congregations in the surrounding countryside with John. I find it comforting to be in civilised churches again, listening to sermons not given by us after so many years away. The churches look so arranged and beautiful; often the pulpit of light-grey stone is draped with luxurious burgundy velvet.

On one such Sabbath, when it is mentioned who we are, we are invited to the manse after the sermon. Utevo wears her new shiny shoes and a dress with a bright bow around the middle. I am sure her gentle nature and intelligent face will win all hearts, but almost as soon as we arrive, Reverend Campbell instructs one of his servants to show her to their quarters.

After a while, Mary implores me to go and find her. Utevo is in the kitchen surrounded by a group of young women, who are encouraging her to talk but then laughing at her language when she speaks. I catch her eye and go to take her hand. Her face reveals how deeply this attention affects her as she looks into my eyes. I give her a reassuring smile and bring her back to the main part of the house.

In the drawing room, she is called upon to shake hands with an elderly lady, who then settles her spectacles at the end of her nose to take in a thorough look at her from head to foot. I think the scrutiny will never end. Utevo slips out of the room soon after, and it is a while before I can politely leave again too. I find her sitting on the floor in a bedroom sobbing, knees raised to her chest. I sit and try to console her, but she looks at me quizzically, shaking her head before saying, "Our Father in Heaven made us all, black and white. Why should the white people stare and stare at us black ones, as if we are animals?" I put my arm about her shoulders as she dabs my handkerchief at her eyes. I remind her how the people not only stared at us when we arrived, but even prodded us all over.

"But I do not think you would *feel* it as I do. You were above us, and you knew it, and did not expect anything better from us!"

I keep my arm about her until she has spent her cries. I canna plausibly deny or refute what she has said. I realise Mary is more in tune to Utevo's feelings and has tried, in her own way, to deflect attention from her.

I realise, too, that Utevo had high expectations in coming to "the missionary's land", and that is our fault. She believed she would see only what is pure and good and holy. We have kept her sheltered under our wings, but her perception is sharp. She blushed when she saw the nude statues in the Botanic Gardens, asking if they were put there, "To show how dark-hearted the people were before they took the worship?" Then, one afternoon, she asked if the people had all quarrelled as hardly any of them greeted each other in passing. When told they had to wait for introductions, she said, "Is it not enough they know each other as Christians?" These are hard questions to answer.

Time passes rapidly and we will soon have to make a decision about our next move. John is anxious to hear from the islands as we know a hurricane has passed over, but we have no particulars. We hope our house has not blown over, not that it would take much, as riddled with white ants as it has become. I am relieved to have missed this dread time of year.

The weather in Sydney turns wet and unpleasant too, and even my initial relief at being in civilisation begins to wane, but only a little. John feels it more, declaring one morning, "This is a miserable place! The dust flies in clouds almost enough to blind you." He fiddles with the window latch as he scans the dark skies above. "For the most part it's either mud or dust!" The latch falls, unconquered.

I know he longs to be back in the islands. Somehow being here has been a wake-up call to his own ideas of civilisation, and on some level, he realises he does not quite fit in as he did before. But I am starting to grow attached to Sydney, to carpet beneath my feet and stores with all manner of goods just around the corner.

Mary has started school during the day, but still stays with us at nighttime. I am away from the tumultuous season in the islands, and I have many things to occupy my time. I am probably starting to look *too* comfortable.

John goes to hear the "great guns" of Sydney, as he calls them, but sees neither. Strangers occupy their pulpits, and he returns disillusioned. In St Stephen's, the church's stained glass and the overcast day means the poor Reverend canna see well, and John laments his blundering reading. "It's truly sad to see such small congregations … and how discouraging to the minister after studying hard to get a good sermon and then to have to preach to empty pews." He looks through the window once more, but the view has not changed.

"What must their Christianity be when a little rain keeps people at home? Presbyterianism seems a very lifeless thing here,"—he sighs—"and such prayer meetings they have! At the appointed hour not half-a-dozen persons are present … And I dislike all this instrumental music!" All John's misgivings have come to the fore. "Here they have it in every church I know of except St George's. I went to a congregational church Sabbath before last, Ann, and I heard enough music there to satisfy me for the rest of my life. It was more like a concert. The performers were in the gallery and to that spot all eyes were turned. There was a harmonium, half-a-dozen fiddlers and a sort of trumpet, which made noise enough to scare the rats out of their hiding places." He sits on the bed and clutches at his sides as he coughs, before holding his head in his hands. The hot, damp weather in the dusty city has brought a tightness to his lungs and a scratch to his throat.

I try to buoy up his spirits, and we spend another day out at Botany Bay. We realise it is then ninety years since Captain Cook landed. But, on closer inspection, even I canna help but admit that Sydney appears an awful place for liquor as a rum shop can be found on almost every corner.

We consult a doctor who encourages John to take a trip to the Blue Mountains to revive his strength, clear his lungs and take in the cooler air. I wish to stay and be close to Mary.

We discuss it that evening with the MacPhersons, who suggest we make the long journey home instead, to a cooler climate, and to take some proper respite with family and friends. I wonder if John will consider this idea as it has not come from me. And when he does not dismiss it out of hand, excitement seizes me. He nods and smiles, then says we will decide all after he has been to the Blue Mountains. Butterflies twirl within me that we may actually go home to Nova Scotia. That evening, I canna help writing a letter to Tilly. We might come home!

Over the next few days, I think through what we will need for such a journey. Had I been prepared for this prospect, I would have packed our warmest coats, so long packed away. A new travelling case is one thing – my worn leather bag has holes at the seams. I should purchase gifts too, for my nieces and nephews. We have to arrange to get Utevo back to the islands, of course. I am sure I can arrange everything while John is away. I will ask Mr MacPherson to look into ships for the passage first.

I accompany John to catch his coach. It is a blustery day and I laugh as a gust nearly tears my hat from my grasp.

"When I return from the mountains," he says, leaning in close, "it'll be time for Mary to begin boarding at Mrs Ellis' residence, Ann, and it will be time for us to travel back to Erakor, too."

I pull back and wrap my shawl tighter about me. I sigh, confused. "But—"

"I'm longing to get back to my work again," he cuts me off, looking into my eyes. "I don't think I could settle down to anything else now. It would be a great trial if anything happened to prevent me from labouring in the New Hebrides. I freely admit the field is by no means an encouraging one, but I'm content to labour unknown and unhonoured. All I desire is the favour of God to be smiling on my efforts. It is all I desire. My health was the same in the islands as it is here. Indeed, I believe I felt better there. I only wish I were stronger than at present. I should like, if it is my Heavenly Father's will, to spend the rest of my life on Erakor, Ann." He hesitates before adding, "Can you think on that while I am away?"

I barely nod, unable to speak.

I tremble a little as John's coach travels away from me. Other missionaries take furlough often enough, yet John is so single-minded in his cause. It seems that travelling back to Nova Scotia is not an option at all. *If we do not return now*, I think, *I never will.*

Chapter 39

HOME

I can do nothing but think on John's words while he is away. I decide he has been this way more since Taniela. I know he thinks time is running out for the islanders, but do we have to die trying to help them? Is that it? I find myself thinking, too, of the apple orchards and the farm of home, of Tilly, Thomas and Pa. Even without Ma there, I feel a longing for the deep-seated comfort from being in the place I grew up. I feel it so much now as I think I may never get the chance again.

I know I did not notice the specific green of the grass while at home, but I miss it now I am not there, or the feeling of breathing cold air into my body sitting at the lake, or that I would miss the songs of the birds all around me, despite me being indifferent to them before I left. It is only through leaving that my eyes have been opened to the minutiae of what I have left behind.

I think of the familiarity of the old ways with my brothers and sisters – collecting crunnicks to start a fire, arguing over who would pull the cracker-bone in the roasted fowl. Life was never easy, farming was so much toil, but it was easier than what I now have on Erakor. There was a predictability to my life in Nova Scotia. The farming had a cyclical nature – when the apples would fall, when the crops would ripen, usually when the frost would come.

I realise I want to continue my plan and go home, even if it means going alone. It is a terrifying thought.

One Sabbath when John is still away, I go to church alone. I sit there with my thoughts twirling and tumbling through me until I can bear it no longer. I look around me and think, *These people would think our lives miserable on Erakor.* Then I realise I have found that it is when I am in the South Seas that I feel *most* thankful for any good fortune that befalls us. Life was hard at first on Erakor because I gave up a life I loved, to live a life I did not. People seem to think that all you have to do is get to a heathen island and hold up the Bible amongst a group of people who, with outstretched arms, have been crying in vain, "Come over and help us!" Well, what foolishness.

After the sermon, the last hymn is "O'er these gloomy hills of darkness", and when it comes to the passage on the kingdoms sitting in darkness, I canna sing another word. My thoughts are all on Erakor. How are Lameka, Samuel and Kalumtak coping? How are the boys and girls we care for? Have any labour vessels taken advantage of our absence? What happened in the hurricane? For the first time since we have been away, I feel a longing for home, but now it is for my island home of Erakor. I may still doubt my faith, but I realise I canna doubt our relationship with the people we live amongst, and love.

Sitting in that church, everyone filing out around me, I realise my culture has surely affected my view of what I *need.* As beautiful as all of this is, I wonder, *Do I really need it anymore?* I have let go one thing after another; the strings that bound me to earthly treasures have been loosened. Those people, that little tropical isle – could it be all that I need after all? I realise then what it has truly become to me in my heart, and I find a certain peace falls over me. I have come to realise too that, in truth, my Nova Scotian life does not exist for me anymore.

Now I *am* being pulled back to Erakor after all. But it is not by God, not now. That is not resolved. Is it even by John? No, it is by the people. Maybe I will never reconcile the doubts over my faith, I think, but surely if I try to exclude the possibility of any suffering or tragedy befalling me, then I shall find I have excluded *life* itself.

My life still has a purpose on Erakor. I went there with love in my heart, and that was enough, that was all I ever needed to give them. That walk with Agnes to the heathen village, visiting the dying chief, her affection for the man, it makes perfect sense now. If you're going to share the love of God, people want to see love in you. Agnes is the living embodiment of missionary spirit – love and charity and the example of good lives – which is of greater value than prayers or sermons, I realise. Do you even need God to live this way?

Tears fall down my cheeks and I am glad no one is disturbing me. I think back to when the first of our congregation came out and declared themselves for Christ, our first communicants. It was such a fulfilling of our efforts. I will not forget how they stood to answer the Form of Questions John put to them. I realise I have never felt happier in any society than with our Erakor sisters and brothers. I remember their poignant prayers, their hard-won achievements in school, the pride in their sewing, their laughter.

The biggest hindrance to our task, I decide, must surely be the giving of ourselves. But do not people say that the more you have to give, the more you have to receive? My heart quickens as I stand up and turn to leave. It is time to go home. But almost as soon as I have risen, another thought flashes through my mind. I dart my eyes about me, as if everyone will be able to see the duplicity written on my face.

On the day of John's return, I pace about my room, picking at the skin around my nails, wincing at the sharp pain as it is so pink and raw.

When there is a commotion below, and Connie and Doug's voices mingle with John's, I start toward the door before stopping myself. *Be patient, be patient*, I think, taking some deep breaths. I turn to the clothes I have lined up on the bed and pick them up, lowering them into my travel chest when the door opens.

"Annetta, there you are!"

"John, so good to see you." I turn to him.

"Packing? That's good. I believe the *Dayspring* is sailing in three days."

"We aren't going on the *Dayspring*, John." I turn back to the chest, unable to meet his eye. "Well, I'm not, at any rate."

He waits.

"I have done much thinking on what you said … And I need to go home. Nova Scotia, that is. I should be able to secure passage soon enough."

"I do not feel the time is right, Ann, with the population dwindling as it is. Perhaps in a year or two?"

"No, John. Sorry, but I am going now."

"The people need you … Don't let them down, eh."

I wince, wondering if I can keep this up. "Who's to say I won't come back?"

"Me. I know you." His voice is hoarse.

I straighten and look him in the eye, keeping my voice calm and even as I say, "You don't listen to me, or trust my decisions, John. We're not partners in this. I'm just here to do your bidding."

The carriage clock on the mantle *tick tocks* in the silence.

"I'll change." John's voice catches. "We'll consult and make decisions together."

"Hmm, we've tried that!"

"You have my word. You run the house and the school, I'll run the church, or however you want to do it, but important decisions will be made together."

"I'm not sure how I can believe you. Look what happened with the people's papers and idols."

He looks at me with a steady gaze. "One more chance … please."

The day to farewell Mary arrives. My body goes through the motions, but I canna ready my heart to do so, and I attempt to press my lips closed to hold in my emotion. At once the image of my farewell with my own mama springs brightly into my mind. We both cry but I reassure Mary this is for the best, and that I will be here in a heartbeat if she needs me.

The *Dayspring* is lumbered up with water tanks, wood for houses, boats for missionaries, boxes and stores. We all cramp in, and Utevo is not the only one happy to be heading home at last. At that moment I am reinvigorated by our absence, and I miss the people. I also believe that my lingering doubts about my faith can only be answered in one place – Erakor. I just hope, at least, that my threat to John will not have to be acted on, and I can stay at Erakor too.

We set out upon a heavy sea and the poor tossed *Dayspring* ploughs into the waste of waters. Agnes and William Johnston are on board too, returning from furlough in Britain, and after a hurried but heartfelt reunion we make for our bunks. But for the kindly visit of the captain to see how we are getting on, or to reproach us for being bad sailors, all of us endure the bad weather for the first few days.

Once we have steadied ourselves, Agnes and I catch up while walking the deck. Captain Braithwaite calls out, "I trust ye are feeling better, ladies?"

Agnes remarks, "Captain, the bunks are so narrow below, ye have to make up your mind on which side you're going to sleep before getting in owing to the difficulty of turning over! 'Tis better up here, that is fer sure."

Captain Braithwaite laughs as he tips his hat at us, but the voyage is tedious. The vessel is heavily laden, and we make slow progress. John is sicker than I, and I worry for the consequences.

Agnes tells me the Grays have left the mission. Maggie endured months of sickness and was considered near death, and then their son, Walter, died suddenly after being given medicine at the onset of fever. Agnes saw Maggie in Britain, and Maggie passed her a letter to give to me. I am surprised at this and almost dread what I will find therein, so I put it away to read later.

When Agnes has gone below for a rest, I steal away to the shelter of the deckhouse to read the letter in private. I gasp at the passage she has written about Walter's death, for it so strikes a chord in me and expresses so well what lies in my own heart over Arthur. Then I know why she has written me this letter. Oh, Maggie! Were we really so far apart?

… How our Aniwans walked right into my inmost heart, by their genuine sympathy, at little Walter's death. I have strongly recoiled from the formal visits of condolence in civilisation, and have often wished to smite dumb a certain type of minister who glories in turning a mother's heart round and round in the pulpit, and cutting into it, apparently for no higher purpose than intensifying the pathos of a sermon. It has been my wicked wish that they themselves might have at least as much sorrow as would make them "keep their tongues between their teeth" as our Scotch say. Some of us have been so built by God, that, while grateful for the throb and glance of silent sympathy, and answering to it as the

barometer to the pressure of air, we quiver and suffer when people try to put it into blundering words.

With our natives, somehow, things were not so. Sympathy from them never pained, but always soothed me. They would come before us, sit down on the floor and cry, and bring to mind all the little sayings and doings of the dear one – just like a bairn chattering sweetly about an absent playmate. The night before we left, Hutshi said, almost in a frenzy of exultation, "You yourselves may go, Missi, and leave us; but you cannot rob us of the little ones in the graves. These two are ours; they belong to the people of Aniwa; and they will rise with the Aniwans in the great Resurrection Day ..."

"Now there was a farewell," Captain Braithwaite says from behind me, startling me. "I recognise Maggie's writing there, Mrs Stewart," he says, a little embarrassed, before adding, "Maggie said she'd had no idea how much she loved their islanders until they came to say farewell, bless her heart."

I nod. "I understand completely, Captain."

Soon enough Tanna is in sight. We land the Johnstons and their stores and stop only for tea before impressing upon the captain to make haste for Erakor. My heart races as we hove-to at the head of the lagoon and take the small boat ashore. Little boys wade out to shake hands with us as the boat comes in, saying, "Oh, Pa, Missi, we are glad, glad to have you back." Lameka comes down to meet us. She smiles and stands taller, as if a weight has lifted from her.

In the house, there is originality on everything that only islanders can bestow – sheets spread out for tablecloths and vice-versa, toilet covers for towels and more besides – and it fills my heart.

The villagers seem truly glad to see us back. They have been looking out for us for over a fortnight and were afraid something had happened to the *Dayspring*. Nearly everyone from the Christian villages comes to meet us. They have a present of yams for the vessel and another for us.

John is still weak and gaunt, so he is my first priority. I set Simetone to work on killing a fowl with which to make a broth, and appeal to John to rest before he visits the villagers. While I organise Lameka with the vegetables, I return to see if he is comfortable but, of course, he is not there. Despite my frustration, I had known he would not be.

I steal away then myself. Walking up, I wonder what I will find. Will the grave have been cared for? I smile as I reach it. No stray leaves are on top and fresh red hibiscus sit at the stone. Such a confusion of feelings washes over me then, but I just let them, not trying to fathom how I feel about where my sweet boy has gone or how I feel about my faith.

I sink down and brush at the coral gravel with my fingertips, scooping it up and letting it fall once more. I tell Arthur of leaving his big sister in Sydney, of advances in the colonies, and more, and I feel a certain peace when I am done.

Chapter 40

HOME

The hurricane that passed over has done little damage, and I find John in the *malel* looking much cheered at the work the villagers have undertaken in our absence. They make a show of presenting the new schoolhouse, just completed. This is the third lime house Kalumtak has built. They have done all the work themselves; John only having to put in the desks, the lumber for which we have brought back with us.

They stand with their backs to the trees, drinking cups of tea. As I walk over, Samuel says, "Pa, the labour vessels have been a curse."

The risk of hurricanes has clearly been no deterrent to the vessels as Samuel says the recruiters are impressing upon the people that now is their last chance to, "Go along Queensland to getem plenty kai-kai, takem money, come home, buyem Snider rifle long French trader." Recruiting has become brisk once more. Often, as before, those who choose to go do not tell their families. "They make their signal fires around a point and get off unseen." He turns and points in the direction he is meaning. "A lot of crying is heard next morning. Many who leave now are the young boys, Pa, twelve to sixteen."

John shakes his head. "It is a dark, dark blot on the colony of Queensland, Samuel." He scoffs then and says, "You know, in the beginning we laughed at Robert Towns as he arrogantly said he could do more toward civilising the natives in one year than "you missionaries" can in ten. But you don't civilise someone by teaching them to smoke tobacco, you don't civilise someone by feeding them rice, you don't civilise someone by clothing them in tweeds. Civilisation can only begin *within*." The group around John nod their heads.

At least on this John and I are united. Our whole mission is about the sanctity of life, and yet how easily it is put asunder. The labour traffic is a horrid debasement of human life. I have appealed to the Lord so many times over our years here: *When will the wicked be punished? Why are the wicked not punished?* And I have received no answer, fuelling my doubts still further. It seems we canna do enough. No matter what we do, it will never be enough. John and I both lament our helplessness in this situation for these people.

Although we might not have the same vigour of the early years, our work will go on just the same, and though quiet is, I have to believe, lasting. The steady up-building of our church and the welfare of the people; that is still the duty before us.

Fifty attend the children's school; a number of them belonging to other villages. The third generation are bright and intelligent, and there is scarcely one amongst them who canna read. With the increasing European population, particularly on Efaté, I have decided to start giving a class to the children of European residents too, traders mainly. I hope I can influence them for good. I take my plan to John, but not for his approval, just to keep him informed.

On the first service back, I delight in hearing the people sing. So many hymns they know now, and the children have the sweetest voices. The fervour knocks my heart once more. Sydney simply does not compare.

We are soon back into the routine of things, and as the months pass all I am missing here is Mary's brightness and chatter. We write to her often and she is becoming a good writer in return.

I am thinking of her one afternoon in the kitchen when I absentmindedly say, "Simetone, can you see if there are any more greens in the garden for dinner, please?" All is quiet and I turn to find Simetone's back to me. He is still kneading the bread on the counter.

"Simetone?" I wait, still facing him. After a little he glances over his shoulder before leaving the cookhouse.

I frown and run my hands down my apron. I walk to the cookhouse door and look out. I know he heard me. *Perhaps he has gone to get the greens,*

I think, and turn back to the pudding. Then I realise this is not the first incidence of this, and my mind goes through our other interactions of late.

When there is no sign of him, I go out to pick the greens myself. I rise with my laden basket and Simetone is a little way off, hiding behind a tree. Noai is coming toward him. I am about to call out when Simetone picks up a stone and hurls it at Noai's head.

I gasp, and Simetone turns to me. His eyes widen and he runs off down the path.

"Noai," I call out, "Are you okay?"

Noai rubs at his head and looks at his fingers. He shrugs as there is no blood, which he shows me by turning his fingers toward me and grinning.

I shrug too. Noai moves off, and I think I need to have a chat with John.

We get through dinner without further incident, and as John finishes, I say, "I think you should speak to Simetone. I don't know what has come over him of late, but he acts so strangely. He turns his back to me, and scarcely ever gives me a civil answer, and this afternoon, he threw a stone at Noai and struck him on the head."

John chuckles at the image. "Is he still here?"

"Well, I think so."

"Simetone?" John calls out, rocking back on his chair.

Simetone eventually appears, looking sheepish.

"Mrs Stewart thinks I should talk to you of your conduct, Simetone. Is there something the matter?"

He looks down to his toes and whispers, "Oh, I wanted you to ask me. I want you to know that I am to marry Lameka, and I am anxious to tell you I will still be cook for you."

I laugh. "If that's all then that's wonderful news," I say, "but why did you act like this?"

"Oh, this is our way," he says. "I am a timid man and did not like to speak, but I did these things that you might ask me."

At this, John laughs and this *kastom* finally makes sense to us. "Well, when anyone begins to act in a strange way hereafter, Ann, I will at once take them into my study and ask who or what burdens their heart," he adds.

It is so nice to have good news. Lameka is a bright, clever and fine-looking girl with a most loving heart, though she often bottles up her feelings. Many have sought her hand, but she always replies, "I am queen of my own island, and when I like I will ask a husband in marriage, as your great Queen 'Toria did." Whether she would still say this if her father were alive, we can only speculate. We have just encouraged that her choice be a good Christian man. It seems now she too has chosen; undoubtedly the finest and most handsome man on Erakor, despite his crooked grin, though we may be biased.

Lameka and Simetone have often managed the station together in our absence. We were unaware of their feelings for each other though, and it makes me wonder again how much I just do not see.

I meet Lameka coming from the bathroom that evening. I stop her and take hold of her hands. "Simetone?" I say, looking into her eyes.

She tries to suppress her grin but fails. "I promise it won't change our duties for you, Missi."

"Lameka, I could not be happier."

"He threaten to kill *me* if I don't have him for a husband," she says, her eyes wide.

"What? That's awful—"

"No, no, Missi,"—she laughs—"it is a strong showing of love."

"Oh! Well, I guess the same happens with an enthusiastic admirer in our society too, only they fancy they will kill *themselves* at least." We laugh. It is nice to have a wedding to plan for and a date is set for the new year.

We promise a large bull to be killed as a wedding feast. When the day comes around, Marifatu and Noai attend to that task while Utevo and I string bunting between coconut palms. We have spread the word, so everybody who is able to do so puts in an appearance, including Marik Tikaikow, who arrives with an entourage and much fanfare.

John and I visit Marik often now and, without assistance from us, they have built two grass churches. Basiva and Neheto are happy there and have done a great deal to bring Christianity to them. Many have professed a wish to move closer to us for the gospel's sake, and as the population has decreased everywhere, we do not discourage it. The more central the people; the easier they are reached. I wonder if John has ever discussed Taniela with Marik. I have not, of course.

Marik may not object to his people coming to church, but he is still reluctant. He will laugh with his head thrown back, his belly rolling revolutions in time with each guffaw. "Me no want-im school," he still says, walking off and getting distracted by something if he sees John closing in. In exasperation, one day John told me he attempted to press the issue and kept close at Marik's heels, waiting for his moment.

Marik relented and turned with a sigh. "Suppose me come along school, by and by me no savvy fight. Me no carry-im gun along hand. Me come home, go sleep along bed, some fellow man he come, he hold-im spear, bow and arrow, gun along hand, he kill-im me!"

"Marik!" John had clasped his shoulder. "You no more say, 'me one fellow'. Jesus, He stop now, so you say, 'we two fellow!' Jesus say, 'Lo I am with you always, I will never leave thee or forsake thee'." John wanted to believe it was hope that flickered in Marik's eyes, but he is a hard one to read.

He had nodded, but then said, "You make man give up *kastom* of his father, John." It was not a question anymore, and neither could it be denied.

We are gladsome it has not changed his friendship toward us. He talks loudly as everyone files into the church for the wedding ceremony. By the end it is filled to the rafters and the heat is stifling, so John keeps it quick. After the ceremony, beach games take place – foot races, canoe races, sack races and jumps, and the favourite, tug-o'-war – with prizes awarded to the winners. The grand entertainment, the magic lantern – borrowed from Mr Johnston – is reserved for the evening.

John has all Mr Johnston's slides, as well as his own. He rigs up a screen of dark sheets before asking people to sit around it. Their faces are perplexed, wondering what Pa is up to now, until the images begin, at which they are in perfect ecstasies of delight. Their unabashed faces beam smiles, their eyes wide in wonder.

Marik creeps nearer and nearer before leaping out, attempting to lay hold of a hand in a picture here, or pat a child's head in another, causing great merriment to all. John has a few slides of Poma before he died and the people cry out then, springing up in alarm, looking about them thinking his spirit is with us once more. They yell and holler and declare it must be Supwe who made it, but after some reassurance they calm.

At the end of the evening, Lameka says, "Ah, Missi, I cannot leave you."

"My dear, it is only two minutes' walk from our gate to your home," I reply.

"Yes, Missi, I will see you tomorrow."

"Wait, Lameka. I want you to have this." I give her my pretty looking-glass as her wedding present. It is one Ma gave me with filigree edges. I love it and it seems appropriate that Lameka have it now. She is much delighted, but her face is pained when Simetone comes to carry her box away. I have provided her with everything I can spare to set up house – tin plates, spoons, jugs and saucepans, as well as a tin washing basin.

At the last moment, she slips a letter into my hands before running off. I have never seen her so bashful.

I light a lamp inside on the escritoire, sit down and sigh, gladsome to be off my feet at last. I open the letter and find she has written to thank us for all we have done, saying how sad she is to leave us. She gives her love to each of us in turn, and says her heart remembers Arthur and loves him. I am choked by the time I come to the last lines. I write her a little missive back, giving a little counsel on married life, echoing my mama's words on contented hearts, and end *kaiheung raieung*, "my love to you".

Chapter 41

HOME

Before the hurricane season sets in, we receive our stores from the last trip out of the *Dayspring*. Though it is not the stores that have me standing at the shore wringing my hands in excitement.

I strain my eyes as they cast anchor and set off the small boat. The boat is full, though I only have eyes for my beautiful daughter, coming home to me. Her features look more refined as she nears, and her hair, so long now, is swept up into a neat style that young girls must wear in Sydney at present. It is only a year she has been away at school, but now my mind races. Will she think me terribly plain in my outdated clothes, my hair unruly, always frizzed up with the damp heat, all "mops and brooms" Ma would say, and greying now too? I canna remember the last time I wore shoes. Will she think me terribly old?

Emotions bubble up as she is carried ashore. I chastise myself for being so lachrymose and dig my nails into my palm to pull myself together. Mary is put down on the sand and she stands up straight, then takes a deep breath with a wide smile aimed at me before a look of question comes over her. My heart sinks, believing all my fears realised, but she just peers down at her own feet. Then she swiftly flicks off her petite, black-bowed shoes and curls her toes into the sand with a look of deep satisfaction.

I laugh then, run forward and sweep her up into my arms, swinging her about as if she were still three. Almost collapsing onto the sand together, we giggle and hug. Then I hold her at arm's length to take her all in. She is so grown. Her face is slender, and her golden hair has darkened, except at the temples. She has lost the naturalness of early childhood, I realise, and I want to see her running on the sand here in her bare feet, to shake free her styled hair and bring back the carefree innocence of my child. But I know her appearance is also for my benefit. I hug her and we cry together.

John stands to one side, awaiting his own reunion, wiping at his eyes too. "Sorry, sorry," I say as I relinquish Mary. They embrace then. A little way behind at the edge of the shore, Christina and Hugh stand with their daughter, Mabel, and son, little Gordon.

As Christina and I release our embrace, I sigh deeply. "It's so good to find you in good health," I say then. But she only gives a weak smile in return.

She seems aged, though still fair and elegant. Had I lost my friend in Canada, it would have weakened my resolve still further out here in these islands.

John and Hugh talk quietly behind us as I link my arm through Christina's. Mary and Mabel run off together as we wind our way up to the house.

"What, pray, are you doing aboard the *Dayspring* at this time of year? Are you heading for respite in Sydney once more? Is everyone well?" I say, my mind racing ahead as I speak.

"Everyone is fine, dearest." Christina smiles. "We're simply taking a few weeks to travel the islands and visit the stations with Captain Braithwaite before the season sets in. I'm quietly looking for a new island to settle on … at least, that's the joke between us. Hugh, on the other hand, is simply indulging my need for respite before we return to Erromango!" She looks behind us to see how close the men are as she says this.

"Has something happened?" I stop then and face her, not caring whether the men hear us or not. I look to Hugh in question, too, as they come up to where we stand.

Christina looks to Hugh with a look of expectation that he will speak. "A plot was yet again made to take our lives," he says before looking down at the ground.

I gasp. All of us thought this kind of trouble was over for them.

"We never dreamt of danger," Christina says then, exasperated, as we take a seat on the verandah. "The heathen had seen the rapid advance Christianity was making … the new church, the change in the people. They realised their power was slipping away. They determined to make a last *desperate* effort." She speaks through tight lips, sadness slicing through her words.

"I'd heard nothing of it," says Hugh. "For, knowing how they'd failed in their previous plots, all was kept quiet. The plan was to kill me, the children and Christina, and, as in the former plots, then all of the teachers."

"Oh, let's not … sorry, but I cannot bear to dwell on this again." Christina's voice is laced with bitterness.

As we gaze upon the seascape around us, I am saddened then at the loss to my friend of her merry, light-hearted disposition. So rarely have I seen it in the last few years. Dr Munro's atrabilious nature, too, has become all too understandable the longer we have been here. Christina seems as dejected as we had seen that old soul when we first arrived. I remember wondering if I, too, would feel as he did in the years to come. Now I have my answer. For me, the people are the light amongst the darkness we face. But we have all passed such unquiet times.

After they leave, we have almost lost the *Dayspring* to the eye on the horizon when there is not a breath of wind as the rain pours down. She lies becalmed, our dear friends just out of reach.

I want to show off my beautiful girl to the villagers, to Tilly and everyone at home in Nova Scotia too. Mary is full of chatter of the news at the time, filling all the papers that have arrived with her, of that American man attempting flight in a machine. It sounds truly terrifying, *but just imagine if people can do that one day*, I think. How different a world it would be!

As expected, the villagers love seeing Mary back. They touch and cuddle her and hold her arms and stroke her hair, just as if she were their own child returned to them. They beg her to let her hair down, and when she uncoils it from the neat style, and it falls in waves around her, Kalumtak says, "It is as fine as a pig's tail!" with wide eyes. Mary laughs, knowing it is a compliment. News spreads of her arrival and soon a large group have assembled in the *malel*. Mary sits with them, Utevo squished up at her side, not giving an inch.

John busies himself with organising the storing of new timber from the ship – Marifatu still his right-hand man – while I sit with Mary and the people. Simetone and Lameka bring out rice, roasted fowl, pineapples and rose apples, as much as we can eat and as much tea as everyone can drink. It becomes a feast as the village women bring food too. We sit long into the evening, enjoying the stelliferous sky and Mary telling them of the city and her life in Sydney.

In the days that follow, I take Mary to the grave of her brother, and we sit on the coarse coral paths around it. I remind her how she used to poke sticks into the crab holes here and there and make trails of shells. She talks of her brother and his little ways she remembers, and it does not cause me too much upset.

In the house she notices Arthur's little things still here and there and asks, "Can we put a box together, Mama, of Arthur's things?"

"And do what with them, dearest?"

"Pack them away, Mama." She looks at me squarely.

I swallow and nod. I have resisted this, but I know it is a good idea. Arthur's favourite cone-shaped shells, a rattle Kalumtak fashioned for him from coconut shells filled with seeds, a lock of his silken snowy hair tied in blue ribbon, a shawl. I canna help the tears that water the precious pieces once more. Mary gathers flowers, which we decorate the box with, and I talk to her of his little ways too. I wonder what to do with the box once we are finished, but then I think of another stash of precious things I buried, not far from here. The shame of remembering burns my cheeks once more. I will bide my time until one afternoon I can privately put them together.

Mary starts helping me with the schooling, though I believe she does not realise quite how much she is helping me at all. As she places out slates and chalk, my mind wanders to a time when she might do this with me permanently, but she is too young to talk of such things yet. I know she must decide her own path when the time is right, just as I was given the opportunity to do. At this age I can still encourage her to laugh and question though, and I fuel her imaginative dreams.

When she gets a little frustrated explaining the *Peep of Day* to some younger ones, I remind her of when I had tried explaining it to her, when she was little, and how that sin of our first parent had made us all wicked. She had ended the discussion with a positive protest, "I'm not naughty! I never ate the fruit." This amuses her and gives her a little appreciation of what teaching might entail.

Mary is a comfort to me and a great help in the work of giving *English* lessons too. She can relay much from her own schooling. I have started the lessons for the brighter students. It seems unavoidable and will better prepare the islanders for life in the colonies, which they seem determined to pursue. John has supported my decision in this. The tide will move with or without us.

She is only with us for a few short weeks before the *Dayspring* arrives yet again to head back to Australia. I have never wanted it to *not* arrive, but this time it crushes me to see her at anchor. We canna afford to keep Mary in school for many years, so I impress upon her how wonderful it would be to have her back in the islands with us, though only if it is her wish.

"Do not worry, Mama, I'll think about it. I hope to come out again in a few months, in any case."

"Take care, my precious girl."

Chapter 42

HOME

"The glass is falling," John says as he comes back into the house after morning worship.

"Is everything secure?" I ask. I have been listening to the wind rising higher, feeling my anxiety rising with it. The worst hurricanes always seem to be the March ones. You think you have come through the season unscathed, so you relax a little, the end of the tunnel is in sight, and then it comes and strikes you, *slap*, in the face for your complacency.

The wind increases as the day progresses. Outside, while overseeing preparations, John and I watch as three boats fly past before the wind, their sails blowing out as they rush along in the pitiless sea. The waves pound at the beach. John calls the villagers to bind the church with chains, though the labour will be too great to finish in one day. I put blankets by the front door, take down pictures and place things in boxes and drawers.

We retire about nine but do not get to sleep as the alarming violence of the wind and rain increases until the roar outside is like distant thunder. The glass is falling rapidly now, though time wears on slowly. The roofs of outbuildings begin to yield before sections are torn away. Tremulous shivers run through my body. I am struck with relief at not having my bairns to worry over for once, if we are in for a real night of it.

"If it continues much longer the church will go … it's probably already shaking, despite being so strongly propped," John says in the darkness.

I cling to his hand as the gusts come in waves. I suppose I am waiting for him to decide when we must take our leave. Soon, torrents of incessant rain and squalls of wind sound to be raging outside, and just after eleven the roof of the girls' room is torn away and Utevo brings them to our room. We canna hide any longer and soon all the children and youths then staying with us are crowded into the drawing room.

Trees begin to crash outside, then the doors begin to burst in as the walls buckle and the lamps blow out. We watch the aneroid rise and fall with every gust. To make matters worse, the store behind our house, which is protecting our house, begins to yield too. Piece by piece it flies away, and the heavy timbers that were lain on its roof to keep the iron down are hurled upon our roof, all the while the wind, like a roaring wave, deafens us from all around. Then the wall on the south side crumples and scatters, as if in explosion. It is an awful sound. The men stand with their backs to the other walls, trying to support them, but in vain.

Now it is time to fly. We emerge into the night, and the wind rips the blankets from our backs and sends them spiralling up into the blackness. The lightning is intense and constant, and we seem to be walking or stumbling along in a constant flame. We move in a train, keeping a grip on the person in front while being grabbed from the person behind. As we search around for shelter, the villagers' houses are blown apart all around us. Some people hide behind the bole of the great banyan tree, but the terrific swaying of the branches above is too frightening. I scream at John to make for Samuel's house. That place has withstood us in years past like no other refuge, and if we are not to survive this night, let us be amongst friends and comfort at least.

Sheets of iron fly through the air like a giant's machete, and one comes to within inches of Utevo in front of me – terror grips her face. The little low roof of Samuel's hut at last comes into sight, and I grab Utevo's hand as we make for the door. Others with us make for the surrounding huts. Inside, Samuel sits with Kawiwi, their children, and his best tusked pig. Samuel welcomes us, and we are glad to sit down in the dust or mud beside the old grunter and cling together out of the wind.

Samuel has a circle of large coral stones around his hut, and these protect it somewhat from the violence of the storm. The little thatch covering vibrates with the weight of the wind, and the chief is holding onto it, crying out "Poma!" over and over, hoping the spirit of his father can save us all.

I can make out little in the darkness except black shapes hanging from the roofing above us, which more than once startle me as I think something is falling onto me. We only hope the rest of the village has reached safety and the huts are withstanding the tirade. The hours seem endless.

When at last there comes a lull, I look to John with relief. He shakes his head, his voice quiet, as he says, "It is the stillness that precedes a great storm."

We rush out nevertheless. I steal a glance at the mission house, though canna bear to look further until we have proper light. The path has been lost under fallen trees and ruined huts, so we call out as far as we can for Lameka, Simetone and others, straining our ears for their reply.

A tree has fallen straight across the roof of one hut, crushing the low wall and thatch. I know the inhabitants canna have escaped unscathed, but I know not who they are. Eventually, Lameka and Simetone crawl out from one of the huts, as others do too, all declaring their safety. In an instant the storm bursts upon us once more, with an impossible roar, and from the opposite quarter.

In the blinding rain and stinging sand, I reach out in desperation. I struggle to breathe as the ferocity of the wind whips my breath away, and then John's firm grip closes around my hand. I cling onto him as we dodge falling palms and wonder which direction to turn. Through the vivid lightning we see the outline of Samuel's hut once more and make for it, almost creeping along the ground. We fall back into the hut on our knees, the water pouring off us in rivers. I wince as John subtly rubs his hand from my warm embrace of it, as we sink back down to the floor.

Utevo clings to John too, her lips trembling with fright, her teeth chattering.

Samuel looks around and picks up a coconut. After checking its ripeness with a rap from his knuckles, he cracks it and Utevo drinks before curling up and falling into a restless sleep. The roar of the sea, only a few yards distant, fills me with horror as I have visions of a great wave. It sounds as though the waves are upon us – the thunder so loud – and I imagine it will at once rush in and sweep us all away.

John sees the terror in my eyes as my head is turned to the sea, but he puts his lips right to my ear, sending another shiver down my spine, and says, "The wind is from the north," simply meaning it is the wrong direction to bring in the sea now. I gasp in relief. There is nothing else for us to do but sit and await the morning with sore eyes, stiff limbs and growing chill.

At dawn I look up at the baskets, mats, strings of vertebrae, bones of birds and fish mingled with shells and sharks' fins that hang from the underside of the thatch, just to assuage my curiosity. It is still cold and damp outside, and the wind has not yet spent its fury, but we must inspect the damage.

As we crawl out of the hut and straighten up, the scene around us is both awesome and pitiful: only some four huts look to be still standing. I cry out and gasp as we take in what is left of our lovely house. As we move closer, vases, windows, looking-glasses, pictures … all rise to view, but all are smashed and ruined, as if rubbish in a bin. I do not want to even touch the wee things that were so clean and precious before.

Our boathouse, strongly built, is smashed apart, having taken the fiercest portion of the waves from the shore. Its strong, swinging gate at the sea end, with heavy hinges and padlock, are smashed to pieces, while all around lie fragments of boat-sails, masts, oars and rowlocks. Our little boat, *Chance*, has been tossed like a shell back as far as the chain extends. There she lies, tipped on one edge, her planks all torn away from the stern-post, the boat half-full of mud and sand. A great heap of sand and stones are deposited on the shore, along with dead fish in their hundreds. Old logs filled with slugs are spread over our front premises, while bleached tree roots point to the sky.

We find a group of villagers still crowded in a corner of the church; the only surviving corner, and they have no roof to cover them. We lead them out. The hurricane chains are half-buried in the debris around the church. The whole land lies smitten and blasted, from the seashore to the hilltops. The reed fences have been flattened.

The villagers slowly gather at the *malel* – though that is unrecognisable under the debris. We are just thankful for being unharmed. We do not know yet of loss of life amongst the people, though there are many injuries. We shake hands and commiserate over the scene. We despair of putting all to rights, although many huts and structures farther from shore appear unscathed.

"John, we are going to check the yam crops at the plantations," Samuel says, raising a hand to him.

"Good luck," John calls back.

The pigs are in their glory running riot over everything, no fences standing in their way. A lot of fences were in need of repair as more men went away, so they quickly buckled in the storm. I canna help but worry for our stores.

"There's no time to sit and weep," John says as he puts his arm around me. "It won't put it all back together, and we need shelter."

I look around, wrapping a shawl over my head to keep my hair down in the ceaseless wind. Everyone is at work fixing fences and clearing up debris. "I know. I'll start on the house." In a few days the people will have nothing to eat but dry coconuts, most of which have already been exported as copra. They will be looking for sustenance.

"I'll secure the cookhouse," John says.

"Let me know when you're done, and I'll give out bread from our stores, and tea. Perhaps soup and rice later in the day if we can manage it."

John nods and is gone.

The day turns steamily hot, though still windy, and we get all the mats lifted and washed, mattresses and blankets aired and dried outside. The people's stuff of life – coconuts, breadfruits, oranges – are rescued from where they carpet the ground. The trees that remain standing are just bare poles. The birds are homeless wanderers and add to the sorrow of it all.

Each hour sifting through the rubble brings back letters, papers, photographs and more from the sand, mud and scrub. John squats down next to me and shakes his head at the ruin around me. "The cookhouse is secure, but the flour, rice and biscuits are depleted, not helped by ants making raids of their own. Samuel says the yam crops are ruined."

I sigh. "This is not good, John." Anxiety knots my stomach. *How will we get supplies if other stations are ruined too?* I wonder. "We'll make do somehow," I say at last.

"I've many demands for axes and blankets, so I'll give out what we can spare." John straightens then and looks to the shore.

"Look at that!" he says, pointing out to sea.

I rise and we look as another vessel flies past in the wind, as though she were a mail steamer going full bore, though her masts are crumpling.

Chapter 43

Home

A veering wind strikes the ship on the broadside and she all but capsizes when a tremendous sea pitches her up onto the edge of the reef. We all run to the shore and look on in disbelief. When the mist and spray clears, flags of distress are seen flying and men are seen perched on the rigging. The breakers will surely dash her to pieces, and everyone on board perish, but then a second sea rushes in and lifts her up. She is carried as far onto the reef as the chains will permit, the anchor catching on the coral. People on board clamber into the large and small boats in a rush.

John runs back to the mission house and finds the bell amongst the items that have been recovered, and then runs to the *malel* ringing it furiously. He at once sends out messengers to assemble the villagers of Eratap, Erakor and Pango, as well as the chiefs – Calameta, Samuel and Lauré. Soon a crowd is gathering while the people from the ship are transferred to the shore, boatload after boatload.

John stands on an old cedar box and rings the bell again. Everyone turns to him as he says, "These strangers are cast upon our shores. Will everyone help them, despite the scarcity of our food and shelter? They'll need to be split between the villages and fed until another vessel can come and take them away."

Everyone nods and calls out their assent straightaway. I catch John's eye, and he smiles in relief. A man comes toward him then and John jumps down from the box. I walk over as the man says, "I'm the government agent from the ship. Mr Cecil, sir."

"John Stewart." They shake hands.

"I'm afraid little food can be saved from the wreck; our supplies were already low, and it looks to be too dangerous to board her again. I cannot express how grateful we are for your kindness at such a time."

I look around and notice that some of the people from the ship are clutching at their stomachs and holding on to one another. I can only guess at the fright of their experience. It is clear our work is ahead of us.

"You're welcome to what we can share, Mr Cecil," John says.

Marifatu comes to discuss shelters with John, so he excuses himself. I take my leave too and help sort out which groups are to go where.

Once all the people are landed, and we have given out what food we can, everyone retires in exhaustion to makeshift shelters for the night, though we are invigorated to get back into order the following day.

"What about that, Ann, eh! What will those who speak so slightly of missions to the heathen say to that?" John says later, clapping his hands together, exultant at the immediate offer of help from the villagers.

I can only whisper, "Yes," in reply as exhaustion and sleep overwhelm me.

In the morning, John organises the able-bodied to clear up debris and start building stronger shelters, while I tend to the injured. Some of those from the ship appear to be in quite a sorry state. Utevo asks me about going to her father's village inland for a time to make sure he is well. Although she could be of help, I think it best she leaves the chaos of this place for a time too.

Her father returned an aged and worn man from the colonies some months back, and they were reunited. She is beginning to help him in his dotage. Before she leaves, she slips me a lone tin of peaches she found half-buried in the sand. She laughs at my wide-eyed excitement before she hugs me and is gone.

Many cook up the dead fish that lie strewn about the beaches, though the rest soon spoil in the heat. Some people already look unwell, mainly those stranded from the ship, so I have to caution them to not eat more of the fish.

"Simetone, do we have rice?"

"Very little, Missi."

We stand at the cookhouse door looking about us, hoping for inspiration. "Those people look quite sick," I say, gesturing to a group at one side lying in the shade of a shelter. "Let us find what we can to make a broth for them." I look to him, and he shrugs. I do not know what it will be made from either.

"We'll have to subsist on coconuts or anything else that comes our way," I say.

"There is a turtle, washed up," he says, raising his eyebrows in question.

"How long has it been washed up?"

He shrugs again.

"I know it's a chief's food, Simetone, but I don't think we should risk it."

He nods and we return inside to pick through the stores once more.

Some older people refuse to take more bread when they find our flour is almost done, declaring they can eat roots and leaves like our nannie-nannies – goats – but that we cannot. It is a frustration that they always have plenty of good ground lying bare, and John is always urging them to cultivate more. I share the peaches between the children, before licking the last few drops from the tin.

"I've sent Marifatu to Captain McLeod, Ann. Hopefully he can purchase biscuits and rice," John says that evening. We are sitting on boxes with bare plates in front of us.

Marifatu and his helpers return, but only three or four casks could McLeod spare.

"It's just rice, Simetone, but it's better than nothing," I say as we boil up large pots the next day. Sweat streams from my brow in the sultry heat and with the constant cooking. Lameka is helping us by handing out rice in half-coconut shells. We are quite run off our feet, and the heat and exhaustion are bringing waves of nausea to me. Once we have scraped the pots, I leave the cleaning to the house girls, while I steal off for respite along the shore. It is hard to find peace here right now, but I can still be assured of some at the grave.

I rub my aching feet when I sit down on the gravel, though I am too tired to tell Arthur of these relentless days. I breathe deeply, settling the nausea at least as I cool down. When revived, I rise and am about to walk away when I shake my head at my forgetfulness. I turn and place a kiss to my fingers and then to the gravestone.

As I walk back on the coral paths, chatter greets my ears from a group at the shore. The steamer *Croydon* has arrived. "Oh, thank the Lord," I whisper before a grin spreads over my face and I rush to find John.

Food supplies are already being landed. I have never seen so many smiles and so much relief. It has been the *Croydon's* special business this year to make monthly calls at the various stations, and in that work she has proved most valuable. The *Dayspring* has simply become too small and slow for the increasing wants of the mission.

We set up a procession to bring the supplies to the house so that they can be shared to the widest extent possible. The *Croydon's* Captain, Munroe, shakes hands with John at the edge of the shore, so I go and greet him too. "When I saw the barometer fall, I ran for Tongoa, South Santo, and so escaped the worst of it, but I've been around the islands and, boy, what desolation," he says, shaking his head. "Coconut trees, coffee plantations, banana and yam plantations … all destroyed. On Ambrym, Malekula and Epi not a European house nor a native hut is left standing, nor is there a blade of grass to be seen. All looks perfectly white, would you believe?" He looks at us as if he canna believe what he has seen.

"Two traders have perished," he continues, "also losing ship and crew in the terrible blast that followed the lull. Two or three other boats were lost with their crews, but the particulars aren't known."

Captain Munroe tells us that he cruised between Ambrym and Malekula trying desperately to make the mission at Ambrym. Dr Lamb, the missionary there, had finally set off to the steamer in a boat at great risk but had succeeded in getting to them. He shows us the letter of distress Dr Lamb wrote from Dip Point on the 7th, talking of ruin to them and their people.

"They're appealing for food for the people, not for themselves — rice, hard biscuit, flour, beans, peas, meat — anything that can be found, but I can't give it all to them," he says, despondent.

After bidding us farewell, Captain Munroe sails on for the colonies in the *Croydon* to take the news of the hurricane to the wider world.

"It's probable a vessel will be sent from Noumea to search for other missing vessels," John says as we watch the *Croydon* sail away.

Of the wreck of the *Ika Vuka*, no details appear, but of the *Circe*, of Ambrym, Captain Munroe told us she capsized and all hands but one drowned. More news slowly filters through. Port Sandwich, on the island of Malekula, has literally been swept away and is said to no longer exist. Vessels missing are the *Cook* of Ambrym and the schooner *Sovereign*. At Port Vila and Havannah Harbour, all crops have been destroyed, leaving only the dwellings standing. The *Macgregor* had a narrow escape from being wrecked too.

It is the barque *Empreza*, a labour vessel engaged in the Queensland recruiting trade, that had her three masts snapped off like matchwood off our island. In the calmer weather that follows the hurricane, the captain has managed to get her into Port Vila after the tide lifted her off the reef. Mr Cecil has stayed with us. The vessel's mast will be fixed in Noumea, we are told.

Despite our ruin, the villagers are true to their word. All have set about making shelters and repairing buildings, gathering food and supplies for these extra we are now caring for. The people on the *Empreza* were either trying to get home to their own islands or embarking for labour in the colonies. Despite our misgivings about what the crew are doing in these islands, and the incredible extra burden it brings us, it gives us a new focus to get back into order.

Chapter 44

HOME

Why did no one tell us they were sick? The *Empreza* was still cruising the islands recruiting and yet most on board must already have been ill. The government agent, Mr Cecil, finally admits it to us: dysentery. No mild, sporadic type, but the malignant kind brought from abroad, which, like measles or whooping cough, proves fatal amongst people where such diseases are unknown.

Fear paralyses me when I first find out the truth. The sick are everywhere, and there is nowhere to escape to. My mind thinks of getting word to the *Croydon* to come back for us, but shame overcomes me for even thinking it. We canna leave.

We try to look after them, but it spreads so quickly. Mr Cecil, too, is taken with it.

We distance ourselves as much as we can from the sick, while still tending to them as best we are able. Word is sent that Mr Cecil wishes to speak with me. He lies on a makeshift cot made from fallen trees from the hurricane, which have been cut into supports. Beds have become more necessary than shelters.

I make my way over and look down on him, a shawl about my nose and mouth. He looks into my eyes. "Captain Donaldson wouldn't listen to me, Mrs Stewart," he gasps, clenching his stomach as another spasm grips his gut. "They were sick when we left Brisbane … I tried to keep them apart

… I gave the sick extra food, but they didn't want it … I didn't know who was who."

"Shh, shh," I say, crouching a little, not wanting to take this man's confession, if that is what it is, but he grabs my hand. His grip is weak, and I snatch it away.

This cursed man. The years of hate for this traffic, for what they are doing here overcomes me. Before he can speak again, I look into his eyes, not caring to disguise my anger. "Why were you still recruiting?" I say, my teeth and fists clenched. "You took on board people bound for the colonies who would never reach there alive. Don't you know anything but *money*?"

A tear rolls from his eye as he casts his glance aside. "He wouldn't listen …" he whispers again, his lips trembling.

I rise. I turn my back on him and walk away.

As I reach the house a sob escapes me. Bravado rushes from me, and I put my hand over my eyes, but it does not stem my tears. I am stuck, rooted to the ground, unable to will myself further from him. *What has to replace my anger?* I think.

My anger leaves me, finally, and a tight knot of knowing has formed in my throat, in its place.

I turn and make my way back to the man. I kneel down and take his hand. His frown softens though his eyes do not open. His breathing is thin.

"Do you have a family, Mr Cecil?"

"Yes, yes I do," he whispers, a smile forms on his lips. "Frannie is two now … a little terror!" He chuckles but another spasm rocks him, so he grips his stomach.

He talks a little, of his life, of his messed-up plans. The spasms come more frequently.

"There, there," I soothe. "Shh now."

I stay with him until his life has stilled.

John lays a hand on my shoulder. "Kalumtak needs us," he says. I look up and think John is near tears too. I take his hand as I rise.

With Kalumtak, we sing softly his favourite hymn, but with difficulty get through it.

When we finish, John looks to his old friend and says, "No prayer for us today, Kalumtak?"

Kalumtak shakes his head a little. His breathing is laboured. When John asks him if he loves the Saviour, he nods. I take Kalumtak's hand and press it again and again. We stay in Samuel's hut and, an hour later, peace arrives for Kalumtak too.

So many have died. The dysentery is epidemic around us. All we hear is the ghastly death-wail – a sound I thought I had heard the last of since it gave way to songs of praise and prayers of thanksgiving. But with so many sick and dying it has been taken up anew, and drowns out, in some measure, the awful clanking of the till-irons as people dig the graves.

Some I tend to go into fits of delirium; their voices change, and they become so weak. The ipecacuanha medicine I administer seems to do nothing. Some vomit worms, which lie wriggling in the excrement that lies on the ground. I watch one little boy pick them out of his nostrils with his fingers, clumsily stretching and squashing them. I vomit then, my fear mixed with deep repulsion.

John sends for Dr Gunn on Futuna, but word comes that they have the epidemic too; he canna be spared. The *Empreza* called there first. Their little girl, Connie, who was already supposed to be at school, has just been lain in her grave. Their daughters, Madgie and Ruth, and little boy, Willie, are all now grievously ill. I think of those two older girls, happy, healthy and active, so at home on the rugged paths of Futuna, wasted and dying before their parents' eyes. How glad I am to have Mary safe and away from me now.

Christina has written that forty-eight of their islanders are dead of dysentery. Hugh is undertaking strict quarantining to contain it. They are keeping up and I pray for them, when I can; for her, my friend, for all their troubles and difficulties. I never divulged to her the doubts of my faith but, looking back, I am almost sure she would have had some too. In the end our monthly thoughts became more illustrations of our lives rather than mirrors on the depths of our feelings.

The Lord is my shepherd; I shall not want. He maketh me to lie down in green pastures: he leadeth me beside the still waters.

When my nausea returns, copiously, I know I am smitten. It is perfectly green and is followed by no relief. It shocks me that my body can rebel in such manner. I canna keep up any longer, and so take to my bed.

The schooner *Caroline* removes the ninety-two remaining well return-ees from the *Empreza* to land them at their own islands, and we are left in this plight, but we would not have gone either. The *Empreza* would have been loaded with spare boxes – compensation for the families and friends of those who had died in the colonies. She would not have had enough; so many died on their journey home.

It fills my heart that Utevo and Lameka are well. I would have sent Utevo away had she not already gone after the hurricane. She has a new purpose and has written that she is teaching her father about Jesus. I will not tell her that I am sick; I canna risk her returning.

Lameka will help keep John afloat in the coming weeks, and I need her to do that, so she has to be well. It is a blessing the villagers have been so kind amidst such tragedy unfurling around them. Every morning without fail, a pail is set down inside the door, rousing me from my memories, and a sad smile always escapes me. Noai brings milk in large quantities. But I canna drink it and it seems to aggravate John too. Marifatu now and again lays a breadfruit inside the door, thinking we may be hungry. *Please, Lord, keep them well.*

Some of the villagers pray at my bedside. It is a comfort, but I do not want them to see me so reduced. It has been my position, my pleasure, to care for them, and I canna bear the thought that they may become ill because of me. But the sickness is everywhere; so many have been taken already.

I have seen new insights into their characters since my sickness began, and I have learned that they are the veriest mixture of contradictions in all creation. And I love them as such. One day, you are humbled by their gentle nature; the next you must be at the beginning, middle and end of everything that aggrieves them.

A few weeks back, I talked with a dear old woman whose daughter married one of our village men. They have gone to Efaté as teachers. She cried for her daughter and said she knew what my heart suffered when our daughter went away. She said, "Missi, you did not think we felt like you. You think we are hard and have no feelings, but we have. But the thoughts stay deep *unowamam*, in our hearts, and we cannot say them. We are not

288

like other people. You never told us your troubles. You used to smile when you spoke of your daughter in the far-off land when we knew your heart was crying for her. We knew the language of your heart, Missi, though you tried to hide it from us; and we mothers often cried about you."

The bodies are being thrown into the sea now. Daily between two and five die. We have probably lost a third of the population. Blind David has been taken too – a jewel in the Saviour's crown. I canna bear to think of who else will be lost.

He restoreth my soul: he leadeth me in the paths of righteousness for his name's sake.

So many memories have flooded my mind in the last few days. Memories from our first days here. Sometimes I laugh at recollections and Lameka will come to my side, like this morning. She scowled at me, no doubt wondering if delirium was setting in. She wiped the ever-present perspiration from my brow and her face softened as I caught her focus. "I was just a girl really, Lameka," I whispered. "I felt too closeted I think, in all that I should do, all that I should be. Everything was so new, so exotic, so different; I felt so unsure of myself."

Lameka's brow had furrowed once more. I was making no sense to her, but she took my hand and held it gently in her own. "Keep up, Missi, please keep up," she whispered. I smiled and closed my eyes once more.

I think back, too, to that time at Agnes' when Mary was born. It is so hard to think of my little flower. The pain it causes me that I will not see her again. Dear Agnes too. After we had returned from the heathen village, Agnes had said "… when they die they say their spirits go to another world, called Ipai, which just means very far off. There they live as on Earth, they dig and plant, give and are given in marriage …" This is what they believed. It is only our beliefs that tell them they are wrong, is it not? We all believe something. I knew this from the very start. *Perhaps I shall be going to Ipai now.* The questions around my own faith have never left me.

"As thy days, so shall thy strength be. May He comfort and sustain you in the hour of trial. Cast thy burden on the Lord, and He shall sustain thee." John sits by my bed, reciting this over and over.

At first, he sat at my bedside, his old straw hat on the back of his head and a huge tin basin from the washroom between his knees. He lovingly fed me the sweet thin porridge from Simetone's large iron spoon. He said he had got into the way of making the gruel well now, but that he could not find a clean dish left to put it in. He was so proud of it that I asked for the recipe, and so it is: equal parts of meal, sugar and water (a cupful of each for one dose); boil all together, until there is a smell of singeing, whereby you know it is done.

I couldna pretend for long though; soon just the thought of food, water even, made me retch and I had to turn my head away.

I remember looking down at the mixture and noticing beneath the basin John's dirty, cracked feet. A giggle escaped me, and hurt, but I could not prevent it. On catching my eyes, he shrugged and said, "Who needs shoes anyway?"

As he smiled, I had an urge to touch the scores of lines radiating out from his eyes on his weathered skin, the pink scar snaking down his forehead, the frayed collar of his faded grey jacket, but I could not lift my hands and I was resigned to a small smile in return.

Chapter 45

HOME

The scratching of a rat under the hot iron roof feels as if it is gnawing into my mind. Or is that actually the rat? Am I already buried beneath the hot, sandy ground, my body being picked over by rats and crabs, facing the wide Pacific with my child sleeping peacefully beside me? Or is my soul in the arms of the Lord, in heaven?

My mind swims up to reality, and I try to open my eyes. The effort is harder than raising the sail on the *Chance*. A movement to my right startles me and pain shoots up through my cheek to the top of my head like a lick of lightning. I gasp.

"You want water, Missi?" Lameka is at my side holding out a cup. I relax and nod, whereupon the beaded sweat on my forehead finds its rivers and courses down around my eyes. The air is so thick in the room. I feel like I am breathing fog – thick Nova Scotian fog – yet suffocating in its tropical zeal. Cool water floods in over my cracked lips; it tastes like fresh rain.

"Ssh, ssh, slowly, slowly," Lameka coos as I lapse into coughing while shivers tremble me anew. I look up to her dark face and notice not the usual bunching frown but resignation, and a course of tears in a river on her own cheeks. I have never seen her cry before. Ever.

My eyes widen with sure and sudden clarity; she thinks this is the end. My instinct is to smile, to tell her not to worry, but I canna do either. She wipes cool cloths down my arms; it is a thousand pins pricking my flesh.

My thick hair, slick with sweat, sticks to my neck in greying black tendrils; leeches that will not let go, and the heat – oh this cloying heat – will not leave my skin. I do not want to put my head back down on the hot, wet pillow, but choice is not mine, not anymore. My belly grips like a claw, forcing the expulsion of a gasp yet again, and my head thrusts backward; the roof once more my focus.

The galvanised iron that replaced the thatch, doubly lined for coolness, has been haphazardly rearranged in the wake of the hurricane. *A new project for John*, I think. Life goes on.

"I'll get John," Lameka whispers, as if reading my mind. Her hand smothers a sob as she stands.

With the room settled to stillness, a little bird with a crimson head flies in at the window, still without its pane. Three days in a row this bird has appeared. It hangs in mid-air, twittering, as if it has brought a message. *Kitch kitch kitch* it chirrups, in-between its trilling song. Lameka shoos it away, tutting and shaking her head, mumbling about a bad omen, but it reminds me of Tilly.

When we were children she would chatter on in her beautiful bright way that somehow never tired me. In fact, it disarmed me. Often impulsive, had I launched into an angry outburst she simply giggled and chattered, throwing me off-balance; a fly into honey. I do not want the bird to leave me. *Is the message from Tilly?* I wonder. *Has she come to say goodbye?* Verily the ends of the world are bound by tender human links.

There are so many things I have not told her. She would have worried and cried. All my letters spoke of what they were supposed to – uplifting missives on our good works in heathen lands, accounts of our gains to spur on the congregations at home, stories of success and the light winning out over darkness, or even just the everyday normalcy of our lives.

But lying here, unable to go home to her, and not knowing how long I have left, I find the memories and trials flooding back into my mind. An awful knot of anxiety broils in the pit of my stomach, and rest, my quietus, will not come.

Do I regret coming here, leaving Ma, Pa and them all? I wonder sometimes. I felt my leaving so keenly. It is still hard to think of that day we said goodbye. I did not doubt it was God's will then, but if I were given the grace to choose again, would I still do so with all my heart? If there is a Lord, He does not lead everyone in the same way; that I have learned.

Yesterday morning the steamer came unexpectedly, on its last voyage to Sydney.

"We must leave, Annetta, do you think you can sit? Here, let me help you," John had said in a rush.

I shook my head.

"Come, please, sit up," he said again.

Great sadness washed over me as I looked into his eyes. *I'll not leave, John. This is our home.* My eyes conveyed all they needed to.

Hurriedly, John wrote one or two brief letters to relations and friends, to let them know our plight, not letting the captain into the house for fear of contagion. John wanted to send for Mary, but I shook my head. It is too late.

Last night, John, in despair, sent to tell Samuel I was dying. He was in the room at once, and a score or two of others trooped in behind. Amidst all the din and bustle, clearer than John's frantic appeals, came Samuel's low and earnest voice as he prayed. The words he slowly repeated – *Take care of, take care of Missi Stewart* – flooded my body with quietude and comfort.

A few days past, Samuel asked John to bless Kawiwi. He asked her about her soul, and she said, "I am going to heaven through God's son. He is with me. He is leading me by the narrow way to heaven. Tell Missi that I am trusting in Jesus."

"I will. My love to you, Kawiwi," he had said simply.

As she was buried, the breeze wafted the strains of "Rock of ages" to my ears.

Today I am lucid, but I know what approaches me. My bones are rudely poking through my skin, as if wishing to escape themselves. I have no strength and only few moments free from pain.

Yea, though I walk through the valley of the shadow of death, I will fear no evil: for thou art with me, thy rod and thy staff they comfort me.

Lameka came in for the last time today too. I have made her promise not to come again. She burst into tears and cried – so against her nature it startled me – as she reminded the Lord, with many sobs, of all the wonderful miracles of healing He has performed and beseeched Him to do *all same* for me. When she had finished, she said, "My heart is breaking for you, Missi. I cannot think of you lying here with not your kin to look after you. We cannot turn ourselves into your family, or cook things to make you well, but keep up, Missi, *tete* – mother – you do not know how much we love you, and we are all praying for you. I pray for you often in the day; and I am going home to pray for you now."

"You *are* my family. My love to you, Lameka," I had said, forcing the words out of me, unable even to hug her.

John comes in to mop my brow and change my bed. My faculties are deserting me; I am a light diminishing. But John canna sustain me now even with love, though he would take this from me if he could. He has started to suffer himself and at once we have become a ship foundering at sea, all hands in peril. Visiting the sick has become impossible, even for him, and the people are tending to themselves now.

I dream I am at my place of quietude by the wide ocean, drinking in the beauty one last time, my bairn beside me.

John's voice reaches me through the haze. "You are now getting through the wilderness and soon you'll be at the brink of the river. But all you have to do is lean hard on Jesus, Ann, He will bear you safely across. Are you trusting in Jesus?" John is looking over me, sadder than I have ever yet seen him. He is asking the question I have dreaded these last few years.

Am I trusting in Jesus?

John's eyes are so sunken and dark circles threaten to engulf them. But his hand feels so warm on mine. How can I be cold in this heat? Just a few days ago it was suffocating me. My skin is dry now, tight like weathered paper, no beads of perspiration anymore.

When I am asleep I dream that we are in our church, and you are singing, reading and praying, John, I want to say to him, *and my heart is with you.* But all I can do is smile at his glacial-blue eyes and give his hand a simple, small squeeze. I canna feel bitter toward him anymore. I wanted to be a missionary. I believed everything was right and holy in this cause, though I know now it is not so black and white.

I know the risk he took agreeing to bring me, but it *was* my decision, not Ma and Pa's. I hope I did not disappoint him. A few days ago, I came around to him saying sorry. Sorry for not letting us go back to Nova Scotia. He knew he would have lost me if we had. He did not think I would return. I know that the lessons I needed to learn were here, and I would not have learned them if I had gone.

The rain is coming down again. You could barely hear it on the thatch, just the ripples of water trickling down outside, but the iron amplifies its thrumming. It is comforting. The little bird with the crimson head has come, too, and it hangs in the air, no Lameka to shoo it away, but with no more chatter for me either. I manage to grasp the locket at my throat and run my hands over it. *My love to you, Tilly.*

Although I looked but could not see Him, time and time again, I realise He still sent me here, with light and love in my heart. *God is the strength of your heart*, Thomas had said. I hope it was enough. I trust that I *am* going to a better place, and I am going to be with my sweet boy once more. I trust where he has gone, and it is a place I wish to follow.

Now let me die, for I am happy, I think feebly before whispering to John in reply, "I know that Jesus is mine, and I am His."

Surely goodness and mercy shall follow me all the days of my life: and I will dwell in the house of the Lord forever.

Afterword

*Please note that these notes are intended to be read **after** the reading of the book. They do contain spoilers!*

The Missionary's Wife is a work of fiction, first and foremost, but I took as my inspiration the real lives of John William Mackenzie (of Greenhill, Pictou County, Nova Scotia), and Amanda Bruce (of Middle Musquodoboit, Nova Scotia). They married and set sail from Halifax in 1871 for the South Pacific islands of the New Hebrides (now known as Vanuatu).

I first became aware of the Mackenzies when I visited the tiny island of Erakor, off Efaté, and came across some graves. There lay Amanda Mackenzie. It struck me instantly what this woman had sacrificed in giving up her life and family to sail to the other side of the world to be with a man who had this missionary calling. Even more so because next to her was the shared grave of their sons, Joseph and Arthur. I don't know how Joseph died but we know that Arthur died of pneumonitis, brought on from being drenched in the hurricane of 1878.

The Mackenzies did not publish their missionary lives into a book, as many missionaries of their day did. If they kept journals, they are not known to me, and few personal letters of John's remain. But the events that happen in Annetta and John Stewart's fictional lives do follow many events that occurred in the Mackenzies' lives.

The Mackenzies did indeed start off by travelling to the islands with their friends and fellow new missionaries, Christina and Hugh Robertson (depicted as the Frasers), aboard the *SS Great Britain*. They were stationed at Pango and Erakor. They survived the hurricane that wrecked the first

Dayspring, as well as the subsequent earthquakes, tidal waves and hurricanes in the following years. (Sadly, what remained of the Mackenzies' old house and chapel were cleared away after tropical cyclone Pam in 2015.)

Amanda Mackenzie lost her mother in 1874. Amanda had daughter Jessie first, followed by Joseph and Arthur. Her sons both died and are buried on Erakor. The couple went on to have children Norman, Morrison and Mary Alice too. One more son, Walter Bruce, was born in 1887, but tragically he died, too, aged 13 months, in February 1888. Amanda Mackenzie did indeed contract dysentery, brought to the islands by the labour ship *Empreza* in the way described in this book, and from this she died.

John's mission report of that year states: "On the 30th of April [1893], Mrs Mackenzie was, in the mysterious providence of God, removed by death. Her death has been a sad loss to the work at this station." I couldn't help but wonder if he could have said something just a tad more personal, and perhaps this is where the idea for them not strictly being a "love match" came from before they embarked for the islands.

John Mackenzie did reportedly sail out into the sea and give up papers and books of the people's traditions to the waves, but I'm sure the circumstances would have been very different to how I have depicted them, and Amanda's response is unknown. Annetta's response is fictional, as is her entire character, beliefs, crisis of faith and so on. I am in no way criticising the Mackenzies' mission. From all accounts they were truly devoted to the people they lived amongst. Indeed, one missionary described John as "the ideal missionary".

The characters of the villages of Erakor, Pango and Eratap are entirely fictional, including Simetone, Poma, Lameka, Samuel, Utevo and Taniela, although some of the names are of real people at the time, such as Marik Tikaikow, a formidable inland chief. The chief of Erakor was a man named Kalsakau, and he allowed the Mackenzies to settle.

John Mackenzie did indeed have a scar on his forehead when he was attacked by an islander wielding a club – and a Christian native did step in and take most of the blow – but I do not know the circumstances that led to this.

The devastating story of Taniela is drawn loosely on a man named Mungaw, who lived at Aniwa with the Patons, but it could be the story of any number of returned labourers suffering PTSD. The story of Basiva is based on that of Lutsi, who also lived with the Patons.

After Amanda's death, John Mackenzie went on to marry Alicia Rosa Bertha, née Roberts, from Sydney. William Frederick was their son, born in 1897 at Ambrym. In January 1913, Dr John William Mackenzie retired after forty years of service in the mission field. He retired to Epping, New South Wales, but died a few months later in 1914. Dr Hugh Robertson passed away that same year while on furlough. I am unaware of the circumstances surrounding the death of Christina; certainly, there is no mention of her death when Hugh published an account of their missionary life in 1902.

I relied heavily on other missionary works in putting together this story, particularly of Maggie Paton (a talented writer and a much more loving person than my Maggie Gray) and Agnes Watt (in this novel called Agnes Johnston). I have occasionally used their own words from original letters as dialogue in this book, in fact, and the letter Maggie wrote about leaving Aniwa (fictionally given to Annetta) is in her own words. Agnes Watt, "Misi-Bran", died at Port Resolution, Tanna, on 26th April 1894, one year later than Amanda Mackenzie. Mr Watt placed a memorial window in the church with the text from Proverbs xxxi. 29: "Many daughters have done virtuously, but thou excellest them all." Maggie Paton died in 1905.

The Braithwaites died in 1895. The captain was in command of the *Dayspring* for fourteen years until she was sold in 1890.

Many names of places have changed between now and then (and many places had more than one name at the time). In most instances I have used the place names as they exist today rather than the names the missionaries thought they were. I apologise should any names have been written in error. All errors, in fact, relating to historical events, names, places and times are entirely my own. Sometimes there are intentional "errors" too, such as where elements, usually dates, may have been adjusted to suit my fiction.

The New Hebrides Church received thirty-three European missionaries and their thirty wives up to the year 1880. Five of these died in the islands. Seven more died in the islands or soon after leaving; four men and three wives. There is a record of thirteen missionary children who died and were buried in the islands up to the year 1880.

How Amanda and John Mackenzie really felt about the labour trade and the impact it had on their lives is open to speculation. It no doubt affected all the missionaries deeply and was a real hindrance to their cause. All the facts about the labour trade, as far as I am aware, are accurate, although accounts do differ. Sometimes I had to go with what I felt to be most accurate. The history and tragedy of the case of the *Carl* was put together from court evidence and also other people's perceptions of what really happened, although we will never know whether Dr Murray acted as described. However, the general public, and his own father, believed it to be the case. It was one of the worst tragedies that occurred. As far as I am aware, however, nobody stolen on the *Carl* was from Erakor.

Blackbirding was a general name applied to the whole of the recruiting trade, independent of the style of recruiting. Just over 10,500 South Sea Islanders were said to have been recruited in the initial years of 1863 to 1875, and there is little doubt that recruiting at this time was mostly by illegal methods. Over the following decade, recruiting was done mostly by legal methods, as government regulations were tightened and enforced.

It has been estimated that, between 1863 and 1904, about 62,000 islanders were brought to Queensland and Fiji, mainly from Vanuatu, the Solomon Islands and Papua New Guinea, to provide cheap labour for the booming sugar, cotton and pearling industries. These people were referred to as kanakas. Many of the workers were enslaved, but they were officially called "indentured labourers" or the like.

After Amanda died, we know that the *William Manson* left Brisbane early in 1894, and John Mackenzie lost about a dozen youths out of his school to this ship alone.

The period from 1892 to the cessation of the labour trade was said to be well-regulated, and then importation of Pacific Islanders ceased under legislation passed by the new Commonwealth Parliament in 1901. Governor General John Hope of Australia assented to the *Pacific Island Labourers Act*, barring their entry into Australia and requiring the deportation of those already present within five years. This was one of the first Acts passed by the new Commonwealth Government at a time when the White Australia policy was first being put into effect, and it marked the end of the blackbirding trade.

There were few exemptions allowed under the Act. The old so-called kanaka men and women, some of whom had lived in Australia for more than twenty years by then, were allowed to stay – on the premise that they would soon die out! Occasionally, families with young children being educated in Australian schools could stay on compassionate grounds. Some 2,000 islanders were permitted to remain after the Royal Commission in 1906. By 1907 the majority of Pacific Islanders who had been brought to Australia were repatriated to their own islands.

By 1910 the expansion of the Presbyterian church in the New Hebrides was tapering off. This was caused by a rapidly decreasing population and the feeling that little room existed for further expansion of the work as most areas were then adequately covered. Many second- and third-generation missionaries continued the work at existing stations.

Whatever your views of missionaries, I believe they worked through love and lived as if people really mattered.

Acknowledgements

I am indebted and give my thanks to the many people who helped me bring this novel together over many years. They include my earliest readers – Jean Willows, Amy Bond, Rose King, Fiona Stokes, Peter McGregor, Jennifer McGregor, and Amanda Taylor – as well as others who helped enormously, such as editors Nadine Davidoff and Kellie Nissen, cultural reader Mia Ramon, and previous Vanuatu missionary Tim Zylstra.

SOURCES

My thanks and acknowledgement to the following sources:

Australasian New Hebrides Company, *Australia and the New Hebrides*, 1921.

Barnes, J., "James, John Stanley (184–1896)", *Australian Dictionary of Biography*, 1972, vol. 4, MUP.

Barradale, V.A., *Pearls of the Pacific*, 1907, London Missionary Society, UK.

Bays, D., *The Foreign Missionary Movement in the 19th and early 20th centuries*, History Dept. and Asian Studies Program, Calvin College.

Bixby, S., *Am I Missionary or a Wife?*

Brenchley, J.L., *Jottings During the Cruise of HMS Curacoa Among the South Sea Islands in 1865*, 1873, Longmans, Green & Co., London.

Campbell, F.A., *A Year in the New Hebrides, Loyalty Islands, and New Caledonia*, George Robertson, Melbourne, Australia.

Cochrane, D., *The Story of the New Hebrides Mission*, PCANZ Archives, 2001.

Edmonson, C., *The Diaries of SM Smith, Government Agent: A New Light on the Pacific Islands Labour Trade*.

Falconer, Rev. J., *John Geddie: Hero of the New Hebrides*, 1972.

Flexner, J., "Erromango: Cannibals and Missionaries on the Martyr Isle", *Current World Archaeology*, Vol. 56, pp. 34–39, 2011.

Flexner, J., & Spriggs, M., "Mission Sites as Indigenous Heritage in Southern Vanuatu", *Journal of Social Archaeology*, 2015.

Godden, R., *Notes on Lolowai*.

Gray, W., *The Kanaka*, 1895, ES Wigg & Son, Adelaide, Australia.

Great Britain Diaries, Voyage 37. 24 May 1871 to 28 July 1871, Liverpool to Melbourne.

Gunn, W., *The Gospel in Futuna*, 1914, Hodder & Stoughton.

Hall A.B., *John Inglis – Missionary*.

Herbert, G., & Kingsley, G., *South-Sea Bubbles: By the Earl and the Doctor*, 1872, D. Appleton & Company, New York, US.

Inkersly, A., & Brommage, W.H., *Experiences of a "Blackbirder" Among the Gilbert Islanders*.

Keane, M.D., *Presbyterian Missionaries to the New Hebrides, 1848–1920*, PhD thesis, 1977.

King, Rev. J., *Ten Decades: The Australasian Centenary History of the London Missionary Society*.

Lambert, J.C., *Missionary Heroes in Oceania*, Seeley, 1915, Service & Co., London.

MacDonald, Rev. D., *The Labour Traffic versus Christianity in the South Sea Islands*, ML Hutchinson, Melbourne, Australia.

MacDonald, Rev. D., "Three New Hebrides Languages", *New Hebrides Linguistics*, 1889, Egerton & Moore, Melbourne, Australia.

Macphie, Rev. J.P., *Pictonians at Home and Abroad*, Pinkham Press, US.

Maritime Synod Minutes, 1873–1894.

Markham, A.H., *The Cruise of the "Rosario" Amongst the New Hebrides and Santa Cruz*, 1873, Sampson Low, Marston Low and Searle, London, UK.

Miller, J.G., *A History of Church Planting in the New Hebrides to 1880*, Book one, 2001.

Moore, C., *Kanaka Maratta: a history of Melanesian Mackay*, PhD thesis, James Cook University, 1981.

Mortensen, R., *Slaving in Australian Courts: Blackbirding Cases, 1869–1871*.

Murray, R., "Our New Hebrides Mission", *Foreign Missions of the Presbyterian Church in Canada*, 1899, Nova Scotia Printing Company, Canada.

Palmer, Captain G., *Kidnapping in the South Seas*, 1871, Thomas & Archibald Constable, Edinburgh, UK.

Paton, J., *The Story of John G. Paton*, 1892, AL Burt Company, New York, US.

Patterson, Rev. G., *A History of the County of Pictou Nova Scotia*, 1877, Dawson Brothers, Montreal.

Robertson, H.A., *The Martyr Isle Erromanga*, 1902, AC Armstrong & Son, New York, US.

Squires, N., *The Telegraph*, 10 February 2008 "Vanuatu: Where only the menu has changed": http://www.telegraph.co.uk/travel/748417/Vanuatu-where-only-the-menu-has-changed.html

Stanley, B., *From the "Poor Heathen" to "The Glory and Honour of all Nations"*, 2009, Connecticut, US.

Steel, R., *The New Hebrides and Christian Mission*, 1880, James Nisbet & Co., London, UK.

Stevens, E.V., *Blackbirding*, 1950.

Stewart, D., information on the *Dayspring*, 2001.

The New Hebrides Magazine, No. 24, April 1907.

"The Slave Trade in the New Hebrides", Being papers read at the annual meeting of the New Hebrides Mission, held at Aniwa, July 1871, edited by the Rev. John Kay.

Thieberger, N., & Ballard, C., "Daniel MacDonald and the 'Compromise Literary Dialect' in Efate, Central Vanuatu", *Oceanic Linguistics*, vol. 47 no. 2, December 2008.

Thomas, J., "The Vagabond", *Cannibals and Convicts*, WH Smith and Sons.

Trove for numerous newspaper articles from, amongst others, *The Brisbane Courier*, *Sydney Morning Herald*, *The Queenslander*, *The Argus*, *Launceston Examiner*, *The Telegraph* … https://webarchive.nla.gov.au/collection

Twain, M., *To the Person Sitting in Darkness*, Anti-Imperialist League of New York, 1901.

Vanuatu Online: https://vanuatu.net.vu/

Vanuatu Tourism Office: https://www.vanuatu.travel/au/

Watt, A.C.P., *Twenty-five Years' Mission Life on Tanna, New Hebrides*, 1896, J & R Parlane, Scotland, UK.

Watt, Rev. W., *Cannibalism as practised on Tanna, New Hebrides*.

West, J., *The Role of the Woman Missionary, 1880–1914*, Evangelical History Association of Australia and Southern Cross College, 2005.

Whitecross Paton, M., *Letters and Sketches from The New Hebrides*, 1894, Hodder & Stoughton, London, UK.

Wikipedia: http://en.wikipedia.org/wiki/Blackbirding

Williams, J., *A Narrative of Missionary Enterprises in the South Sea Islands*, 1837, J. Snow, London.

Young, F., *Pearls from the Pacific*, 1925, Marshall Brothers, London.

BOOK CLUB QUESTIONS

- What drew you to pick up this book?

- What are the main themes in this book, and how well do you think they were dealt with?

- Did you know about the blackbirding episode of history in these islands? What did you learn from this book?

- What impressions were you left with of missionaries in these islands?

- Do you sympathise with the plight of missionary wives? How?

- What impressions were you left with of the Indigenous inhabitants of these islands?

- What was your least favourite part of the book?

- What was your favourite part of the book?

- Do you feel the author was writing a story they were not qualified to tell? What could they have done differently or left out?

- What did you feel about Taniela's story?

- Who was your favourite character in the book and why?

- Did you empathise with Annetta in regard to her relationship with John? Did you feel she had a voice?

- What parallels can you draw from John and Annetta's relationship that are still relevant to today?

- What had Annetta learned by the time it came to the dying government agent?

- Were you dismayed at the ending, or did you feel that it was the natural outcome?

Thank you so much for reading this book. If you enjoyed it, please consider leaving a review. Positive reviews help independent authors immensely.

About the Author

Claire McGregor lives with her husband, Peter, and two children, Charlie and Alex, in the rolling hills northeast of Melbourne, Australia. She is an Accredited Editor and book designer who specialises in editing non-fiction, particularly memoir, family history and biography. This is her first work of historical fiction. She helps many independent authors bring their books to life through her business, Kookaburra Hill Publishing Services.

You can find Claire at:
www.kookaburrahillpublishing.com.au
Facebook: https://www.facebook.com/clairemcgregor2015
Instagram: https://www.instagram.com/clairemcgregor37/
LinkedIn: https://www.linkedin.com/in/claire-mcgregor-6b127723a/

The *Dayspring*. Source: State Library of Victoria.

Printed in Great Britain
by Amazon

62915399R00180